Tom Cain is the pseudonym for an award-winning journalist with twenty-five years' experience working for Fleet Street newspapers. He has lived in Moscow, Washington DC and Havana, Cuba. He is the author of *The Accident Man*, *The Survivor*, *Assassin*, *Dictator* and *Carver*.

D0257263

www.**transworldbooks**.co.uk

Also by Tom Cain

THE ACCIDENT MAN
THE SURVIVOR
ASSASSIN
DICTATOR
CARVER

and published by Corgi Books

Revenger

TOM CAIN

CORGI BOOKS

TRANSWORLD PUBLISHERS
61–63 Uxbridge Road, London W5 5SA
A Random House Group Company
www.transworldbooks.co.uk

REVENGER
A CORGI BOOK: 9780552165068

First published in Great Britain
in 2012 by Bantam Press
an imprint of Transworld Publishers
Corgi edition published 2013

Copyright © Tom Cain 2012

Tom Cain has asserted his right under the Copyright, Designs
and Patents Act 1988 to be identified as the author of this work.

This book is a work of fiction and, except in the case of historical fact, any
resemblance to actual persons, living or dead, is purely coincidental.

A CIP catalogue record for this book
is available from the British Library.

This book is sold subject to the condition that it shall not,
by way of trade or otherwise, be lent, resold, hired out,
or otherwise circulated without the publisher's prior
consent in any form of binding or cover other than that
in which it is published and without a similar condition,
including this condition, being imposed on the
subsequent purchaser.

Addresses for Random House Group Ltd companies outside
the UK can be found at: www.randomhouse.co.uk
The Random House Group Ltd Reg. No. 954009

The Random House Group Limited supports The Forest Stewardship
Council (FSC®), the leading international forest-certification organization.
Our books carrying the FSC label are printed on FSC®-certified paper.
FSC is the only forest-certification scheme endorsed by the leading
environmental organizations, including Greenpeace. Our paper-
procurement policy can be found at www.randomhouse.co.uk/environment

Typeset in 11/14pt Caslon 540 by Falcon Oast Graphic Art Ltd.
Printed and bound by CPI Group (UK) Ltd, Croydon, CR0 4YY.

2 4 6 8 10 9 7 5 3 1

MIX
Paper from
responsible sources
FSC® C016897
FSC
www.fsc.org

To Clare

Author's Note

I am greatly indebted to William Hunt for his expert advice on this book and *Carver* before it. Likewise, my thanks go to John Duffy. As with *Carver*, much of the action involves the use of everyday objects in unusual, not to say lethal, situations. Two things should be noted. First: the 'recipes' for explosive devices in both books contain deliberate errors, so there is no point in trying to replicate them. Second: this is fiction. It is intended to entertain, but it is absolutely not, under any circumstances, intended as any kind of do-it-yourself guide. Or to put it another way: don't try this at home.

Prologue

It started with a kiss.

Abou-Ali Bakhtiar had always been a quiet, well-behaved schoolboy, much liked by his teachers and never any trouble in class. As a student at the University of Tehran's faculty of literature and humanities he continued to be a credit to his family, and his grades were consistently excellent. Sex outside marriage is strictly forbidden in Iran, as it is in most Islamic societies, so the fact that Bakhtiar was untroubled by the desperate, frustrated urge for women that plagued his male friends was in many ways a blessing. And then, in his penultimate year at university, that blessing became a curse.

A friendship with another young man called Mehdi deepened over the course of several months and, like a plant that blossoms from a seed into a flower, turned into something new. First came the realization of a love that went beyond mere affection. It was swiftly followed by the exchange of a hesitant kiss that deepened, intensified, set light to Bakhtiar's heart, sent the blood pulsing through his body and filled him with an exultant joy unlike any he had ever known. The two young men spent a night together. They were the most wonderful hours of Bakhtiar's life, only to be followed in the morning by a crashing hangover of shame and fear.

Here he was, a law-abiding model of propriety, engaged in an activity that was both a sin against God and a crime punishable by death. But why was it a sin to love like this? And how could one do wrong when one did not have the choice of doing right? From the moment that Bakhtiar discovered his homosexuality, he saw the whole of his life up to that point from an entirely different perspective. So much that he had not understood before was now explained. He had, he was quite certain, been like this all his life. He could no more become a 'normal' man now than he could suddenly turn his eyes blue. And if he had been made this way, then that must have been God's will. In which case, how could it possibly be criminal?

For both their sakes, Bakhtiar ended the relationship with Mehdi and begged him not to find another lover; the risk was just too great. In public Bakhtiar remained the same friendly, popular, studious figure he had always been. But the endless hours he spent in the university library were not all occupied working on his final dissertation. Instead he pored over the theological debates that had taken place on homosexuality over the centuries, concluding that neither the precise degree of its sinfulness nor the rightful severity of its punishment appeared to have been definitively established. There was, he discovered, a long tradition of homoerotic love poetry in both Arabic and Persian literature, and some of the greatest rulers of the Islamic world had displayed homosexual proclivities. Even Mehmed II, the conqueror of Constantinople, was said to have taken beautiful young men to his bed along with his many wives and concubines.

Bakhtiar entered into these researches as a private exercise, an attempt to reconcile his sexuality with his faith and thus soothe his mind and his soul. It never even occurred to him to participate in any protest against the authorities that had demonized him. But then Mehdi, the lover he had cast aside, was caught in bed with a boy of seventeen. Both were arrested. The boy's father, a senior army officer, insisted that his son had been forced to have sex against his will. The court chose to believe this claim, saving the boy but condemning Mehdi to death.

Two days later, Mehdi was hanged without the knowledge of his lawyer or his family. The first that anyone knew of the execution was when it was announced on the evening news. Bakhtiar sat and watched in anguished despair as pictures were shown on screen of Mehdi blindfold on the gallows, and hanging in mid-air next to thieves and drug-dealers.

It was then that Bakhtiar changed. He saw that it was not enough to hide away. He had to do something to change the society in which he lived. And so the process of radicalization started, as he joined a students' group involved in pro-democracy campaigns and demonstrations. Shortly after his graduation from the university, he graduated as an activist, too, making contact with emissaries from Mujahedin-e Khalq, or the MEK: an exiled dissident group, denounced by some as terrorists, but lionized by others as courageous freedom fighters against the Iranian regime.

For years there had been rumours that the Israelis used members of the MEK as hitmen to carry out their assassinations of Iranian nuclear scientists. Now the group were planning to escalate their anti-government actions to an entirely new level. The search went out for martyrs willing to take part in suicide bombings.

Bakhtiar was a man in despair. He saw no future for himself. The only man he would ever love was dead. His only hope of joining him was to die himself and pray for a meeting in paradise. He put himself forward for martyrdom, and his application was gratefully accepted. On a balmy evening in late April, with the city still fresh and green from the spring rains, Bakhtiar was ordered to make his way to a nondescript workshop on the outskirts of Tehran to meet with a senior MEK officer.

The man introduced himself as Firouz, and showed Bakhtiar a laptop on whose screen was a satellite picture of an apparently unexceptional patch of landscape. A road ran diagonally across the screen from top left to bottom right. In the middle of the picture, next to the road, an area of ground had been outlined.

'This is the highway between Gazran and Khandab,' said Firouz, pointing at the road. His finger tapped on the outline. 'And this is the IR-40 nuclear complex. See, it looks like a pig's head!'

Bakhtiar smiled. He was right. The likeness was uncanny.

'Here is the pig's snout, up against the highway,' Firouz continued. 'And this is the line of its mouth, which is the road from the highway into the heart of the complex. Now . . . there is one barrier here, by the highway, and another at the other end of the road, where all the really important buildings are located. That road is approximately one kilometre long. It is absolutely vital for you to get as far up it as you possibly can before you detonate your bomb. The closer you are, the more damage you will do. It is a very powerful device. But it cannot work miracles.

'So, here are your targets. On the right, in the pig's cheek, you have a heavy-water production plant. That's water enriched in a deuterium isotope, often referred to as deuterium oxide . . .'

Firouz caught Bakhtiar's look of blank incomprehension.

'Not a scientist, huh? OK . . . Heavy water helps them create plutonium-239, the radioactive material at the heart of a nuclear weapon. Now, observe this structure here, above the heavy-water plant. It looks like the eye of the pig, does it not? Well, this is a nuclear reactor. Here is another picture of the reactor, from the side. See how it has a great round dome, and beside it a thin concrete tower?'

'Almost like a mosque and minaret,' Bakhtiar suggested.

'Yes . . . although here it is not God, the most merciful and compassionate, to whom they pray, but the devil. For this reactor is where the heavy water will be used to

13

create the plutonium. That plutonium will go in an atomic bomb, and then the ayatollahs will stay in power for ever, because no one, anywhere, will dare challenge them.'

'You say the heavy water *will* be used. You mean it isn't yet?'

'No, the plant is not operational. There have been many, many delays. Some of these, I am proud to say, were due to us. Let's just say, they had a problem retaining staff.' Firouz smiled at his witticism and Bakhtiar joined him, though it seemed strange to regard death as a laughing matter.

'However, it's finally due to start the process of going operational within weeks – two or three months at the very most,' Firouz went on. 'That's why we have to strike now. But I must ask: are you still with us? Are you willing to sacrifice your life as a martyr for our cause?'

Bakhtiar felt almost physically sick. He thought of his family, whom he loved, and of all the years that still lay before him. And then he thought of the sorrow and deceit that would fill those years and, in little more than a hoarse, dry whisper answered, 'Yes, I am.'

The following morning, well before dawn, Bakhtiar set off on the five-and-a-half-hour drive from Tehran, south-west along the Saveh Freeway to Arak, the capital of Markazi Province, and then north towards the IR-40 complex. He travelled in an old Toyota Hilux truck. The cargo area of the truck was covered with a tarpaulin, beneath which were some sacks of cement, a bundle of wooden joists and an oil barrel. Within that barrel there was a bomb.

For most of the journey Bakhtiar was a passenger. The target was almost four hundred kilometres away, and the leaders of the MEK felt it was too great a risk to expect anyone to drive that far, with nothing but their own thoughts and fears for company, and then have the energy, or the will, to mount a desperate suicide attack against an armed target. So Bakhtiar sat in the passenger seat while an older, more experienced MEK fighter drove, talked to him when he considered it right, or at other times let him alone with his thoughts.

They passed along a river valley where the local farmers' lush green fields clustered together in the flat-lands between two ranges of dusty brown hills. At Gazran they stopped for cups of sweet mint tea. Then they drove a little out of town till they found a turn-off where they could spend a few minutes undisturbed.

Bakhtiar's companion helped him screw a metal plate across the inside of the windscreen, precisely shaped to the dimensions of the glass. It had a narrow slit, allowing him to see out. But unless a lucky shot happened to pass precisely through this gap, the front of the truck was effectively bullet-proof. As an additional precaution Bakhtiar put on a motorcycle helmet. It would not fully protect him against a direct shot, but it would keep out any ricochets or flying fragments of metal or glass.

'I will leave you now,' his companion said. 'Would you like me to pray with you before I go?'

'Yes, I would like that very much,' Bakhtiar replied.

Together, they turned to Mecca, got down upon their knees, prostrated themselves and said the words of Al-Fatiha, the prayer that is to Muslims what the Lord's

Prayer is to Christians: the most basic, fundamental profession of faith.

In the name of God,
The most compassionate, the most merciful,
Praise to God, Lord of all the worlds,
The most compassionate, the most merciful,
Lord of the Day of Judgement,
You alone do we worship, you alone do we ask for help,
Guide us on the right path,
The path of those in your grace, not of those whom you have
   cursed, or who have gone astray,
Amen.

When the prayer had been said and his companion had departed, Bakhtiar got back in the truck, in the driver's seat this time, and turned right on to the road towards the nuclear reactor. He did not have far to go, three kilometres at most, and he was surprised to discover how calm and at peace he felt. It was as though Mehdi was in the passenger seat where he himself had been just a few minutes ago. He was smiling at Bakhtiar, and the thought of his face, his bright eyes and his gentle good humour was like a soothing balm to Bakhtiar's soul.

He drove the truck to the turn-off that led to the IR-40 complex, and when he saw the first barricade he picked up the small, handheld controller that would activate the bomb, depressed the switch and held it down. From now on, there was no going back. The moment Bakhtiar relaxed his grip on the switch the bomb would detonate.

The switch was in his left hand. The wheel of the truck was in his right. Bakhtiar floored the accelerator and the truck leaped forward.

It took the guards a couple of seconds to realize what was happening, and a couple more to bring their weapons to bear. But by the time the first bullets were hammering into the truck, Bakhtiar had smashed through the barrier and was racing down the dead-straight road that led to the heart of the complex. By now he was under heavy fire from the guards at each checkpoint, in front of him and behind.

Bakhtiar had gone two ... three ... four hundred metres down the road.

The glass in the front and rear windows had all been blown out. The metal plate in front of him was clanging like a steel drum to the constant beat of the bullets hitting its surface. His own head was ringing with the deafening noise all around him and the constant patter of debris against his helmet. The engine was smoking like a steam train and screaming in protest at the wounds it was enduring.

Another three hundred metres raced by beneath his wheels, and then the truck slewed wildly as one of the rear tyres blew apart under the relentless fire. Bakhtiar found himself skidding off the road. There were high security fences on either side, and he was heading straight for one of them.

The truck smashed into the fence, which gave way under the impact, collapsing all around the truck and wrapping it in chain-linked wire and concrete posts. Bakhtiar heard more shots clattering around him, then the sound of men shouting as they ran down the road towards him.

He looked to his right.

Mehdi was there. He was telling him not to be afraid. They would be together soon. Their love would last forever.

Bakhtiar let go of the switch.

There was one important detail that Firouz had neglected to tell Bakhtiar.

The device in the oil barrel was an updated version of a fifty-year-old US Army weapon with the designation W54 SADM. It was cylindrical in shape: about 60cm tall, with a diameter of 40cm. It weighed around 70 kilos. The designation SADM stood for 'Special Atomic Demolition Munition', for this was a 10-kiloton nuclear bomb, and it was the culmination of many years of strategic thinking, war-games and military exercises.

For more than three decades, the Israeli government had made it plain that it would not allow any of the hostile states in the region to possess atomic weapons, nor even the capacity to build them. Nuclear installations in Iraq and Syria were bombed, and Iran was given unequivocal notice that it was next in line. An Iran Command was formed within the Israeli Air Force. Its jets flew up and down the full length of the Mediterranean, sometimes even as far as Gibraltar, practising long-range missions.

Everyone knew what the Israelis were doing, not least the Iranians themselves. That's why they buried their uranium-enrichment plants at Natanz and Fordow deep underground; impregnably so, they claimed. To most Western analysts, it was a question of when, not if, Israel would mount airstrikes at the dozen or more key installations on which Iran's nuclear weapons programme depended. But from Israel's point of view, that was the problem: everyone knew.

Surprise would be impossible. Deniability non-existent.

So Israel boxed clever. It used the MEK as its proxies for this strike, as it had for others before. Because of Iran's refusal to halt its nuclear weapons programme, it was under a punitive regime of international sanctions. But where there are sanctions, there will also be smugglers. Mossad agents used those smuggling routes to infiltrate four SADM bombs into Iran.

The 10-kiloton bomb Abou-Ali Bakhtiar detonated beside the IR-40 reactor blew a crater seventy-five metres wide by seventeen metres deep. It created a dazzling fireball from which blew a scorching hurricane. At least half the people within a five-hundred-metre radius were killed instantly, and those that survived received fatal doses of radiation. Human bodies and inanimate objects were transformed into lethal missiles. The blast reduced the heavy-water plant to rubble, and caused sufficient damage to the reactor to render it entirely useless.

Above all, the IR-40 complex was so heavily soused in nuclear fallout as to be unapproachable by anyone unless they were wearing full protective gear. Even then, a stay of more than a few minutes could result in a dangerously high dose of radiation. And that, from the strategists' point of view, was the other great benefit of this form of attack. It was not necessary to destroy Iran's impregnable underground sites. The ground above or around them just had to be turned into toxic wastelands through which no human could pass, and they were effectively useless. The IR-40 nuclear reactor, the two uranium enrichment plants at Natanz and Fordow, and the Nuclear Technology Centre at Isfahan were all rendered inoperable. The Iranian weapons programme was cut off at the knees.

Meanwhile, not a single Israeli Air Force plane had been involved in any hostile action whatsoever. Deniability was ensured. It was a strategic triumph for Israel . . . and an unmitigated disaster for the rest of the world.

As its nuclear sites lay blanketed in radioactive dust and debris the Iranian government looked for a way to strike back, not just against the Israelis, but also their allies in the West. Iranian naval forces immediately launched a series of missile attacks on the Strait of Hormuz – the shipping lane through which one-fifth of the entire global oil trade passed – hitting several vessels and sinking a massive supertanker. Maritime insurance premiums immediately rose to a level that made any passage through the Strait prohibitively costly, even assuming a ship owner or crew was willing to risk the voyage. With that crucial supply-line cut, the resulting spike in the price of oil had a devastating effect on an already battered global economy, ending any slim hopes of recovery. Meanwhile, conflict spread to the streets of

Europe as the Continent's Muslim populations rose up in outrage at the Jewish assault on their Iranian brothers and sisters.

It was difficult, however, to distinguish these Muslim riots from all the other forms of civil disturbance tearing the EU to pieces. Repeated bailouts of the Mediterranean states had drained the Continent's treasuries while failing to address any of the fundamental causes of economic failure. Indeed, they had simply made that failure even more acute. The grinding austerity demanded by Berlin as the price for supporting the failed economies of southern Europe had created economic damage that would take decades to repair. As the second Great Depression took hold, once-flourishing businesses collapsed, governments were unable to meet even their people's most basic needs, and yet more millions of Greeks, Italians, Spaniards and Portuguese were thrown out of work to add to those already on the breadline.

Greeks had long been familiar with the sight of government buildings going up in flames. Now Rome, Madrid and Lisbon were burning too. The French alliance with Germany fractured as the new government in Paris refused to accept the current self-flagellating orthodoxy, and embarked on a policy of spending more government money, not less, risking credit-agency downgrades, rising borrowing costs and even national bankruptcy rather than cutting spending to the bone. And slowly it dawned on the German electorate that by beggaring their neighbours they had destroyed their own most important export markets, harming themselves economically as well as reigniting old anti-German hatreds that the EU had been created to bury for ever.

Little by little the fabric of Europe unravelled. Some of the crises were of minimal significance in any financial or geopolitical sense, but their symbolic weight was crushing. The Champions League, for example, was suspended as the explosive tensions on the streets of Europe's major cities made it impossible for tens of thousands of supporters from different nations to gather together for a competitive event without the near-certainty of violence. Without that revenue source many of the major clubs collapsed under the crushing debts they had amassed in the pursuit of glory.

Meanwhile Britain's relative immunity from the crises of the euro counted for less and less. The EU's implosion acted like an economic black hole, whose gravitational field dragged more and more of its neighbours into the same plunging death-spiral. The first generation of nine-thousand-pounds-a-year students graduated to find that their fees had been wasted: there weren't any jobs for them to take. Their parents were no better off. As their property values plummeted and their painfully accumulated pensions were rendered worthless, so the respectable middle-classes of suburbia became as angry as the underclasses in the sink estates.

The riots that had seemed like a single, exceptional outburst in the summer of 2011 were now a chronic condition, like a bad cold you just can't shake off, or a cut that refuses to heal. No one knew where the next bricks and bottle-bombs would be thrown, or which once-peaceful shopping street or housing estate would find itself under siege. But almost every night, something seemed to kick off somewhere, until the festering anarchy became so commonplace that it took an event of exceptional violence – a policeman killed, or a well-known building razed to the ground – for the media even to acknowledge that anything had happened.

National governments were helpless in the face of such unrelenting disorder, and as conventional politics failed to provide any answer to the chaos, siren voices started making themselves heard. They belonged to populists and demagogues promising simple, under-standable explanations for the incomprehensible collapse of the old world order. They offered bogeymen to blame and hate; pat solutions to put things right. In their desperation, voters listened to these voices. They longed for strong, decisive leaders who could bring order to the anarchy and make everything work again.

Yet even in the worst of times, whether beset by war, natural disaster or economic collapse, people have to get on with their lives. They strive to find work. They do their best to look after their families. They seek what-ever comfort they can in their friends and lovers. And they can always console themselves with the knowledge that the sun still shines, the wind still blows and the world keeps turning, whatever mankind might do . . .

1

As the first rays of the morning sun sparkled on the water, the *Lady Rosalie* made her graceful way between the massive concrete pillars of the Hubert C. Bonner Bridge, left the peace of Currituck Sound and poked her nose out into the dancing whitecaps of the North Atlantic. There was a fresh south-easterly breeze blowing, and as the forty-two-foot sloop left the last shelter of land and felt the full force of the wind, her sails filled, her hull heeled over and she raced away across the water like a racehorse bursting from the starting gate. The four high-powered rigid inflatable boats, crewed by armed men who were keeping watch ahead, behind and on either side of the *Lady Rosalie*, had to accelerate hard to keep up, as did the US Coastguard cutter keeping station a few hundred yards away and the Marines helicopter overhead.

It was a perfect fall morning, with a cloudless sky and

the promise of highs in the mid-seventies, but at eight in the morning there was still a sharp, invigorating chill in the wind that hinted at the colder days of winter to come. The man at the helm was grinning with the sheer joy of being alive on such a day, in such a boat. His name was Lincoln Roberts. He was African–American, well over six feet tall, strongly built, with a hint of silver in the hair beneath his dark-blue baseball cap. He had recently celebrated his sixty-first birthday, yet his vigour was undiminished and his presence and charisma still dominated any room he ever entered.

Roberts gave himself a few minutes to savour the pleasure of playing the yacht that was his most treasured possession against the constantly shifting forces of wind and water. Then he turned to the man standing next to him and shouted over the breeze, 'Damn, this feels good! Worth dragging your ass out of bed for, right? You want a turn at the wheel?'

Samuel Carver grinned back. 'Yes, sir!'

'You don't have to call me "sir", Sam. This is the weekend. And I'm not your president.'

'True . . . but as long as this is your boat, you are my skipper.'

Roberts laughed and gave Carver a friendly pat on the back as they exchanged places. 'I should've said this last night, but it's good to see you again,' he said. 'It's been too long. I feel bad about that.'

'Don't. You've had much more important things to worry about.'

'You saved my life. That's pretty damn important.'

'I was just doing my job. Anyway, you send me those

personally signed and dedicated Christmas cards every year. You should see people's faces when they see one of those babies on the mantelpiece.'

'Yeah, that presidential magic works a treat, doesn't it? I mean, take a look at this jacket . . .' Roberts pointed at the embroidered presidential seal decorating the right chest of his windbreaker. 'Five years I've been in this job, and I still get a thrill putting it on.'

'I heard the presidential jellybeans are pretty special, too,' said Carver.

'You know that's true, they are. I'll get someone to send you a jar.'

The two men stood in companionable silence for a while, feeling the sun and spray on their faces as they savoured the pleasure of being out on the water. Then the President drew a little closer to Carver and, in a lower voice, bereft of humour or bonhomie, said, 'You happen to know what happened to all that money Malachi Zorn stole? It's been more than two years, north of fifty billion's still missing and I've got a whole posse of very angry people – and I'm talking rich, powerful, influential people who could make my life real difficult come election time – wanting to know what happened to their investment.'

'I'll bet they're angry,' said Carver. 'They got taken in by the greatest con-man in history. So did two British prime ministers and at least one member of the royal family, come to that. He promised them the earth if they invested in him, then he took the lot. But I don't know what happened to it all.'

'Really? I heard you had a lot to do with taking

Zorn down. Word is, you were right by him when he died.'

'He was killed at a reception where there were more than five hundred guests. A lot of people were right by him.'

Roberts put an arm round Carver's shoulders. It looked like an amicable gesture, but as Roberts clenched his fingers until they were digging into Carver's skin there was an icy edge to his voice. 'Don't bullshit me, Sam. We both know Malachi Zorn didn't die at that reception.'

Carver looked out towards the horizon, gathering his thoughts for a moment before he replied. 'I didn't kill Zorn, you have my word on that. But I was with him just before he died. I even asked him what he'd done with the money – and forget fifty billion: he said it was over a hundred. Zorn wasn't telling. If you want my opinion, he really didn't care about having the money himself. He just wanted the people he'd taken it from not to have it. He wanted to hurt them and he knew, with rich bastards like that, nothing hurts more than losing money.'

Roberts caught the note of contempt in Carver's voice. 'Sounds like you agree with him.'

'Not enough to do the things Zorn did.'

Roberts relaxed his grip on Carver's shoulder, apparently satisfied that he wasn't holding any information back.

'You know what? I know this sounds nuts but I worry about you, Sam. You must've made a heap of enemies along the way. Sooner or later one of 'em's gonna come back to bite you.'

'Hasn't happened yet.'

'So? You think that'll stop it happening some other time? You've hurt a lot of people and you know things that could hurt a lot more. That's a dangerous combination . . . I guess what I'm saying is, "Watch yourself."'

'I will, Mr President. You can count on it. So . . . you want the wheel back now, or what?'

2

Danny Cropper worked in the hazy no-man's-land between security and crime, where tough men who once served their country, men with shaven heads and pumped-up muscles slowly turning to fat, do dirty work for the rich and powerful who want to keep their own hands clean.

When he wasn't working, Cropper had two main interests: getting wrecked and getting laid. It had been a long Saturday night, and he woke at half two on Sunday afternoon with a sore head, a lurching gut and a mouth that tasted like a fishmonger's dustbin. He heaved himself out of bed, wincing at the backache that always seemed to hit him worst first thing, then sat bleary-eyed on the edge of the mattress with one hand in his well-worn underpants. As he gave his package a ruminative scratch he wondered whether to wake up the girl snoring softly on the other side of the bed. No, why bother? She hadn't been that good a fuck last night, and she looked a lot rougher now than she'd done when he'd had his beer-goggles on.

She farted in her sleep, and that made Cropper's mind up for sure.

There was a packet of fags on the bedside table. The tobacco companies weren't allowed to put their colours or logos on the packs any more, only the health warning and a brand-name in plain black text. Cropper thought it just demonstrated the stupidity of politicians. The economy was in the shitter. The streets were a battleground. The electricity kept cutting out because the Greens wouldn't let anyone build power stations that actually worked, and if the dustmen or the tube drivers weren't on strike then it was the nurses and the cops. The whole world was falling apart, and all the twats in Westminster could worry about was lung cancer.

Cropper pulled on his jeans and a T-shirt and lit his first cig of the day, stuffing the pack into his trouser pocket as he shuffled out of the room. He made a cup of tea – so strong it was darker than coffee, with a shot of condensed milk and three sugars – then took the cup to the kitchen table where his laptop was lying. He logged in and scanned the headlines. A rocket attack on Tel Aviv had killed forty-five Israelis, including a dozen children. Barclays Bank had just been bought by a Brazilian corporation. As net immigration to the UK reached record levels – 'Fuck knows why they want to come here,' Cropper muttered to himself – the government was denying, for the umpteenth time, that it had lost control of Britain's borders. With another half-dozen clubs facing financial oblivion, the football authorities were considering merging the former Premiership and Championship divisions to create a single league, with no promotion or relegation. And some royal tart had stood next to a celebrity tart Cropper had never heard of, but they'd both been wearing the same dress, so that was a big fucking deal, apparently.

He checked his emails. Amidst all the spam, promising cheap drugs and a bigger penis, there was one message that interested him. It purported to come from a girl called Veronika, and the subject line was, 'Baby, I want to meet you.' The message read, 'Hi, Baby, I am looking for new friends. I am cute and I love big men who can make me feel good deep inside. I would really like to meet you, and if you really want to know how much fun we will have together, just open up the video I have sent you and look at my hot, wet pussy. It is waiting here for you.'

Cropper moved the video to a digital editing application, and watched four minutes of tacky Romanian porn until the image faded to black. Three seconds passed with a blank, silent screen, and there was a brief burst of static interference and white noise. Cropper cut and deleted everything apart from this burst, which was less than half a second long. Then he played it again through another app, which mimicked the function of a super high-speed tape recorder, allowing Cropper to replay the message in real time. He heard a voice, itself distorted to the point where it was unrecognizable, saying, 'Got another job if you want it. Wednesday night, starting at eight-fifteen precisely. Three locations: Netherton Street, London SW4; Cleveway Road, Bristol

BS13; Dunstone Lane, Leicester LE3. The aim is maximum devastation of property. Theft and arson would be good. Moderate levels of human collateral damage are acceptable. But we don't want bodies every-where. And arrange for maximum social media coverage at all locations: we want this viral across YouTube, Twitter, Facebook, Instagram – the works. Signal accept-ance by usual means. First payment will be transferred on receipt of acceptance.'

Cropper replied to the email: 'Hi, Veronika . . . I want your hot, wet pussy. Let's meet . . . Big D.'

He jotted down a note to himself, reminding him to sort out the two key personnel at each location: someone local who'd get the scum together to do the actual damage, and one of his own lads to keep a discreet eye on things and make sure everything ran to plan. Then he sat back and finished the rest of his cold, sweet tea. This was the third time he'd got one of these jobs, and the first two had been the most lucrative gigs he'd ever been given. But they'd not been so specific about timing. Usually he was given a two- or three-day window, but this was timed to the minute. What was that about?

Cropper went back online. He looked for anything else that would be happening at the same time as the riots. And then he saw the same name popping up again in countless different news stories, previews and links. And suddenly it all made perfect sense.

3

A little further forward in the boat two women were sitting on padded vinyl banquettes. One was Rosalie Roberts, the President's wife, after whom his boat had been named, and whose willowy figure and beautifully sculptured features made her a suitably regal-looking consort for her man. With her was Alexandra Petrova Vermulen, otherwise known as Alix, the love of Sam Carver's life. She had blonde hair, a wide mouth, full lips and cool blue eyes. One lid was slightly heavier than the other, one pupil fractionally out of line, and that barely perceptible imperfection was the difference between banal prettiness and intriguing, mesmerizing beauty. The two women were sitting close together, their knees almost touching, watching one another with a searching, very feminine intimacy.

They'd been chatting for half an hour or so, swapping titbits of Washington gossip, laughing as they exchanged the stories Rosalie Roberts had heard in the White House for the ones that Alix had picked up in her job as the head of a political lobbying firm. Then Roberts said. 'Do you mind if I ask you a personal question?'

'How can I say no to my First Lady?' Alix replied, with a polite little giggle.

'Trust me, sweetie, people say no to me all the time. They do it real politely and there's always a long explanation, but it's still no.'

'Oh, I know that feeling. Years ago, in Russia, I used to know a very powerful man. Nobody wanted to upset me, in case I told him and got them into trouble. But I was still just his mistress, so I had no real power . . . In the end, I could not stop them saying no to me, too. So, what was your question?'

'It was about Russia, actually. Is it true that . . .' Rosalie paused, trying to find the right way to phrase what she wanted to ask.

'That I was recruited by the KGB?' said Alix, helping her out.

'Yes,' said the First Lady, a little uncertainly, not sure if she might have offended her guest.

'And is there any truth to all those rumours that I used to be a honeytrap spy, trained to seduce Western men and extract their most intimate secrets?'

'Yes . . .'

Alix had known from the start that this was what the question would be about. She'd been debating what to say in reply, but Rosalie Roberts was obviously a good, kind, compassionate woman, and so Alix decided to trust her with a full, honest answer.

'Well,' she said, 'I'm a US citizen, I've sworn the oath of allegiance and I can absolutely promise you that I don't have any relationship whatever with any arm of Russian intelligence. Not any more. But those rumours are true.'

'But how—'

'How could I do it? I was an eighteen-year-old girl, recruited to serve my country – how could I not? All my life I'd been taught that my duty was to serve and obey the Soviet state. And there was a woman called Olga Zhukovskaya. She spotted me and trained me. She was like a second mother to all us girls. She told us that we would be doing work that was vital for the security of the state. And we shouldn't worry if it seemed like we were having to do dirty, wicked things – you know, the things that bad girls did – because we were doing them for the Motherland, and that made everything different.'

'Did that really help?'

'For a time, yes, it did. And in some ways our lives were fantastic. I was wearing Paris fashions, shopping for Western cosmetics at the party stores, dining at the best restaurants. Compared to what I'd known before it was paradise. Then I found out that all the male officers used the videotapes of my assignments as pornography. To them, I was just a whore . . . and when I realized that, it was . . .' Alix broke eye-contact with Rosalie Roberts and lowered her head, peering intently at the wooden deck before she took a deep breath, sighed, and looked up. 'Well, it was hard for me not to think that I was a whore, too.'

'Aw, sweetie, come here,' said Rosalie Roberts,

holding out her arms and grasping Alix in a hug. And just like her husband, it was when she had her friend in her arms that Rosalie Roberts asked the most telling question of all: 'Does Sam know yet?'

'Does he know what?' asked Alix coyly, pulling away from the First Lady's grasp.

'You know exactly what I mean.'

'How could you tell? Don't say I'm looking fat!'

Rosalie Roberts laughed. 'You? Fat? Never! No . . . It was the way you said no to coffee this morning . . . The way you hid the fact that you were feeling sick, even though you were obviously at home on a yacht and we'd hardly even left shore . . . Little things that kind of added together. Don't worry, though, I won't say a word to anyone.'

'Thank you . . . It's just that I only found out last week, and my doctor wants me to take a few tests . . . I just want to be a little more sure that it's going to be OK before I tell Sam.'

'Well, don't wait too long. He may be a guy, but he's not stupid. He'll pick up the signs, and if you haven't told him he'll start wondering why.'

'You're right . . . As soon as I know the test results I'll tell him.'

'Good plan . . .' Rosalie Roberts got to her feet. 'Now, let's see if those men of ours want some coffee. I may be the First Lady everywhere else in the world, but on this boat I'm just the cabin-girl . . .'

Ten minutes later, all four of them were standing by the wheel. Alix was leaning back, her head on Carver's shoulder, his arms wrapped around her. Rosalie Roberts was at the wheel, belying her cabin-girl status, and Alix saw the loving pride in her husband's eyes as he watched the skill and confidence with which she handled the boat. Alix hated to break the mood, but there was something she needed to mention. 'Excuse me, Mr President, but may I talk business for a moment?'

He frowned. 'This is meant to be my day off, but I asked Sam a couple of business questions, so I guess it's only fair. You got two minutes, starting now.'

'Thank you, sir . . . I'll cut straight to the chase. I've been asked to go to London to meet Mark Adams. I don't know if you've heard of him . . .'

'Sure I have. He was a minister in the last Labour administration. Now he's setting up his own party, running as a kind of populist alternative to the establishment.'

'That's the one.'

'Interesting guy. Last time I spoke to the Prime Minister he mentioned Adams. Dismissed him as a racist, neo-fascist rabble-rouser, but I got the sense he was plenty worried about his popular appeal. So what's your connection to this guy, Alix?'

'He wants to establish himself as a credible international statesman, someone the electorate can trust to represent them abroad. And . . .' Alix began, almost wincing as she thought of what was coming next.

'And more than anything else he wants his picture taken with the President.'

'Yes, sir, that's exactly it.'

'You've not told him that we know each other socially, I hope.'

'No, sir, I'd never do that.'

Roberts nodded, accepting her word. 'Good, because I don't want to be within a million miles of some guy who bases his politics on racism. I might just find myself beating the crap out of him, and that wouldn't exactly befit the dignity of my office.'

'We don't know for sure that he is a racist,' Alix pointed out. 'Adams strongly denies it. His people told me that's just propaganda put out by his opponents. They said he's spent years doing voluntary work for a housing association, finding homes for low-income, minority families. It's really hard to get a take on him, to be honest. Depending on who you talk to, he's the saviour of Britain or a Nazi dictator-in-waiting.'

'He could be Winston, or he could be Adolf,' mused Roberts. 'Look, I can't give Adams a one-to-one meeting. But there's no reason why I can't meet a senior British politician at some kind of event, and if there's a photographer present, well, I can't stop them doing their job. But before that happens I have to know that this guy is for real. I don't want that picture coming back to haunt me if he ends up wearing jackboots and sticking people in camps for having the wrong colour skin or worshipping the wrong god.'

'I don't want that either, Mr President. I grew up in one totalitarian system. I have no desire to help someone start another.'

'Good. Then here's what we'll do: I'll get our people doing some due diligence on Adams. We've got to do that anyway if there's even an outside chance of him becoming the British Prime Minister. Meantime, you get close to him. Keep your eyes and ears open. Use your brain, but use your gut, too. Trust your instincts. Then let me know if he's a man that you want to work with and I want to meet.'

'Yes, sir. Thank you, Mr President.'

'You're welcome . . . and now, can I get back to sailing my boat?'

The *Lady Rosalie* was tied up in the dock at Lusterleaf, the Roberts family compound on Knotts Island, North Carolina. Carver and Alix had sat down for a quick brunch with Lincoln and Rosalie Roberts. Now the President needed to get back to work, and Carver and Alix were settled in the back seat of the black Cadillac Escalade that was taking them up to Norfolk for the one-hour flight to Washington. Their hosts were just about to wave them off when Roberts held up a hand and said, 'Wait a second.' He walked across to the limo and tapped on the Escalade's passenger window, on Carver's side of the car.

Carver lowered the window and the President leaned into the car. 'I meant what I said. Keep your eyes open and stay out of trouble. Y'hear?'

'Absolutely.'

'Good . . .' Roberts looked up at Alix, relaxing his face into a smile. 'And you be sure to tell me what you think of Adams.'

'Yes, sir.'

'OK . . . so it was great seeing you both. We'll do it again sometime soon.'

Roberts straightened up, tapped his hand twice against

the body of the car, and it rolled away down the drive.

'What was that about?' Alix asked as they drove towards the compound gates. 'The President looked worried when he was talking to you.'

'He's concerned I've made too many enemies over the years. He thinks they might come after me, or something.'

'God . . . that's a little scary.'

'Well, there was something I couldn't really tell him about my enemies.'

'Which was?'

'They're dead. And if I didn't kill them personally then I damn sure saw the corpse.'

Alix gave an involuntary shudder. 'I'm not sure I wanted to hear that. Tell me that those days are over.'

'Come here,' he said. Alix wriggled across the seat and nestled next to him. 'Yes, I promise,' he murmured, soothing her with the deep, calm tone of his voice. 'Those days are over and I never want to go back.'

4

Samuel Carver had indeed killed a lot of people. His victims had died in cars, planes, helicopters and power-boats. He had dispatched them with bullets, bombs, knives, poisons and nooses. He had even stood and watched in stomach-churning disgust as one had been eaten alive.

But not all of those who had reason to wish Carver harm had paid for their enmity with their lives. And one who had survived against all the odds was at that moment running hard around the lower lake in the Bois de Boulogne – a striking female figure in skintight black training pants and a lightweight turquoise jacket that set off the mane of flaming red hair, gathered into a ponytail, that bounced and swished behind her as she sped through the gathering November dusk.

Her real name was Celina Novak, though she'd called herself Ginger Sternberg when she'd first attracted

Carver's attention at the start of the Malachi Zorn business. Carver had been on holiday at the time, a single man in a beat-up Jeep, taking ferries between the Greek islands with no big plan in mind other than enjoying himself. Ginger had been behind the wheel of a Porsche Boxter in the line for the ferry at Piraeus, the port of Athens. She'd been tanned, carefree, laughing at some private joke when he saw her; mostly she was laughing at how easy it was to catch a man's eye. She wouldn't have laughed so much if she'd known how it would all end.

But that was more than two years ago. Now she was in Paris, running at the very limit of her speed and endurance because her fitness at least was something she could control. Then she slowed as an object caught her eye, lying on the ground amidst the brown and russet of the fallen leaves. She stopped and bent down to find a small stuffed monkey in a bright-red jacket – a much-loved toy, to judge by the way its fur had been rubbed almost bare from all the hugs, sucks and kisses it had received.

Novak looked up and saw the monkey's likely owner a little further up ahead, a girl of five or six walking hand-in-hand with her mother.

'Excuse me, madam!' she called out, holding up the monkey so that the mother could see. She added, 'Your daughter dropped her little monkey!'

The mother smiled and shooed her girl in the direction of Novak, who was crouching down on her haunches, so as to be at the child's level. The girl gave a shriek of delight when she saw the monkey held out towards her, and hurried back to her favourite toy as fast as her little legs would carry her, her face wreathed in undiluted joy. She grabbed the monkey and held it to her heart. Then she looked at Celina Novak and all the happiness drained from her face. For a second the girl's eyes seemed uncertain, as if she did not quite know what she was seeing, and then her expression turned to one of fear and revulsion. She shrieked and ran back to her mother in floods of tears, her pleasure at reclaiming her monkey entirely forgotten.

Novak could hear quite clearly as the mother asked, 'What's the matter, darling?'

The girl sniffed a couple of times, pouted her lips as she thought, wiped her hand across her nose and then said, 'That lady is strange, Mummy. I think she's a wicked witch.'

'Oh, don't be silly. Of course she isn't.'

'She is! She is! Look!'

Novak found that she could not turn away. Something made her keep looking at the mother and daughter as the girl pointed towards her and the woman gently scoffed at her until she herself caught Novak's eye and fell completely silent for a second. An instant later, the mother snapped back into life and almost pulled her daughter off her feet as she dragged her away down the path, calling out over frantic squeals of protest, 'Come on! Come on! We must get back home or we'll be late for your dinner.'

Celina Novak had never been given to crying – not unless she was doing it deliberately as a means of manipulating someone else. But now she found that there were tears forming in her eyes, and she had to dab her face with the sleeve of her jacket to keep them at bay. For she knew exactly what had made that little girl look at her the way she had. She understood precisely why the girl had run to her mother. And as she thought about that, her pain and humiliation gave way to a rage that drove her to run even harder and push herself even closer to the limit. And as she did so she thought of the people who had made her the kind of person whose face scares small children: that vicious bitch Alexandra Petrova and her bastard lover-boy Samuel Carver.

5

Carver and Alix flew into London on Tuesday morning. They queued for three hours to present their passports to untrained temporary personnel in dirty polyester uniforms, brought in to cover the regular Border Agency staff, who were protesting at the undermanning of their posts by simply not manning them at all. Or perhaps they had joined the widespread strikes against the scrapping of all earnings-related pensions for state employees, a move forced on the government by the IMF as a condition of their latest loan. Or maybe they were just bunking off. It was hard to tell these days.

There were no luxury stores to be seen any more in Terminal 5. The number of air passengers was down by more than fifty per cent, and most of those that remained had a hard enough time affording their tickets, let alone a six-hundred-pound purse from Smythson or a spontaneous four-figure jewellery purchase at Tiffany & Co. Carver walked along unswept corridors, past 'Out of Order' signs and shabby staff who were going about their work with a kind of surly, resentful indifference to their customers' wellbeing. Passport control had become a lottery. Some days passengers were held up for hours, others they were waved through without more than a casual glance at their passports. This was one of the slow days, the queues at the immigration desks compounded by the long lines outside the few functioning, but filthy, toilets.

Carver was a man who was always more interested in solutions than problems. But now he could sense himself becoming infected by the negativity he could feel all around him. He'd come to London with Alix because it had seemed like a good opportunity to visit the land where he was born and for which he had gone to war. He still planned to stick it out for the few days it would take Alix to conduct her business. But once that was done, he'd be leaving on the first flight he could find.

'I wouldn't even wait that long, if I were you,' said his old sparring-partner Jack Grantham, when they met up for an early supper on Tuesday evening. 'I'd be off like a shot, if I had the chance.'

'You're the head of MI6,' Alix pointed out. 'If you made a run for it, everyone would think you were defecting.'

'But defecting to where? That's the question,' Grantham replied, with his usual bone-dry, cynical sense of humour. 'Clearly I'm not going to take the Philby road to Moscow, but I don't need to tell you that, do I, dear? You got out as fast as your lovely legs would carry you.'

Alix smiled, knowing that this was as close as

Grantham would ever get to a compliment. 'How about Beijing?' she suggested, playing the game. 'I'm sure the Chinese would welcome you and your secrets with open arms.'

'I'm sure they would, too. But have you ever been to China? There's no way they're going to rule the world. They'll all choke to death on their pollution long before that happens.'

'The Dordogne?' suggested Carver. 'Or a spot of Spanish sunshine, perhaps?'

'You must be joking . . . and don't even suggest Switzerland. I know you've wasted half your life away in some poky little flat in Geneva, but—'

'Don't be rude about Sam's flat,' Alix interrupted. 'I happen to adore it.'

'That can only be for purely sentimental reasons.' Grantham sighed, waving for another bottle of wine. That, at least, was as good as ever. He waited till their glasses were refilled and then said, 'I hate to break the atmosphere of jollity. There's not much of that around, after all, so I'm all for anything that even remotely resembles happiness.'

'Ha!' Carver exclaimed. 'You wouldn't know happiness if it got up on its hind legs and bit you.'

'Possibly not,' Grantham admitted. 'But indulge me, anyway. It's about Mark Adams. I gather you intend to see him, Alix.'

'Yes, I'm a political lobbyist. He's a politician. It's my job to meet people like him.'

'And work for them?'

'That depends on what he expects my company to do

for him, what he is willing to pay, and whether I think he is the kind of client we want to work for.'

'He isn't,' said Grantham. 'Take it from me.' He looked at Carver. 'So are you going to Adams's night rally, too?'

'No, Alix has got work to do. I'd only get in her way. I'm having a drink with an old mate instead.'

'Very sensible. Anyone I know?'

'Snoopy Schultz.'

'Ah yes . . . the one that helped you carry out the hit-that-wasn't.'

'That's him . . . So, what's your problem with Mark Adams?'

'It's not a problem. It's a simple observation of fact. He's an exceptionally nasty, dangerous piece of work. As foolish, incompetent, corrupt and generally useless as ninety-nine per cent of our politicians undoubtedly are, they're still a thousand times better than Mark Adams.'

'You sure about that?' Carver asked. 'Have you seen the state they've reduced this place to? Maybe you haven't noticed, living here. But coming back after a couple of years away, it's a real shock. Those politicians you're talking about did that.'

'Them and the bankers, the regulators, the euro-fanatics, the Iranians, the Israelis and, if we really want to point the finger, all the voters in all the countries who thought they were entitled to health and welfare systems, and pensions, and new cars, and foreign holidays, and bigger houses and God knows what else – all without ever paying the bill,' Grantham countered.

'So maybe that's why you need someone new, with a different attitude, to come in and knock some sense into people,' Carver suggested.

'Someone, maybe . . . just not this one.'

Alix knew that the two men had a complicated, highly combustible relationship: they were two alpha males who couldn't resist butting heads, challenging one another, constantly trying to do the other down. And yet beneath it all they had a fundamental trust in one another that came from working together under extreme pressure, when lives were on the line and the fate of nations was at stake. Neither man had ever broken his word, or disappointed the other, and though they would never even have considered, let alone admitted it, Alix felt certain that neither had a better friend in the world.

'Look,' she said, wanting to resolve the situation. 'I'm sure you have very good reasons for saying all this, Jack. And I know that you have access to information that we certainly don't have. But I've told Mark Adams that I will meet him, and I'm going to keep that appointment. I don't know what will happen after that, but I can absolutely assure you that I have no intention of working with anyone who is, as you say, a nasty piece of work. I have my own reputation to protect. And I certainly don't want to be opening doors in Washington, just so an evil man can walk through them.' She reached across, laid her hand on Grantham's wrist, looked him in the eye and said, 'Can we agree on that?'

Grantham sighed. 'If you insist, yes, we can. But I'm advising you both as the Head of the Secret Intelligence Service and as someone who has known you both a very long time: have as little to do with Mark Adams as humanly possible. Ideally, have nothing to do with him at all.'

6

In Paris another eminent, middle-aged man was having a hard time persuading a determined woman to see his point of view. 'I'm sorry, Madame Novak, but I really cannot have this discussion at the moment.'

Jean-Jacques Levistre rose from his family dinner table, holding his mobile phone in one hand and making exasperated gestures with the other which, along with the exaggerated look of annoyance on his face, were meant to indicate to his wife, sitting opposite him, just how much he did not want to take this call. 'Look, I will go into my office so that we can talk confidentially, but I must insist: no more than five minutes, maximum.'

'I fail to understand why you won't see me,' said Celina Novak. 'I have money, lots of it. Are you seriously telling me you don't want to be paid? I don't believe it. No one turns their back on cash these days. No one!'

'Of course I want to be paid. I have a family to feed.

But I also have professional ethics that I must observe and a conscience that I must live with. What you are asking of me offends both those principles. I'm sorry, but I cannot do it.'

'But you have to! Can't you see that? I insist! You have to do this for me!'

'No, really I don't,' Levistre insisted. He did his best to summon up the soothing, reassuring tones that were one of the major reasons for his success. 'Honestly, Celina, you should be happy with what we have already achieved. You have been remarkable. Your courage, your fortitude, your ability to endure the unendurable – they have inspired me. But we must all know our limits. And we have reached ours. I am very sorry, but there is nothing more to be done.'

Levistre turned off his phone, took a deep, calming breath and then walked back to rejoin his family.

A couple of kilometres away in her hotel room, Celina Novak looked at herself in the full-length wardrobe mirror, running her eyes up legs that possessed not the faintest scrap of cellulite; a waist as slender as a girl's half her age; breasts that had been so perfectly enhanced that most men now had to make a conscious effort to look her in her cool, grey-blue eyes; and hair whose natural length and volume had been boosted by extensions applied by the most expensive stylist in Paris. A great deal had already been done. But Levistre was wrong. There was more she could still do. There had to be.

Two days had passed since the incident with the child in the park. She should have got over it by now. All her life she had lied, cheated, seduced and killed without the slightest backward glance. She possessed a sociopathic indifference to truth, morality, conscience, compassion, empathy or pity. And that included self-pity. As a young child she had learned to fake unhappiness or distress as a means of getting what she wanted from adults. But she did not really feel those emotions. So why was this memory still haunting her?

Even that question itself angered her, since she regarded reflection and introspection as pointless wastes of time. Far better, Novak decided, to work off some of the rage and frustration that was gnawing at her guts. She rode her hired BMW F650GS motorbike out of the heart of Paris to the eastern suburb of Clichy-sous-Bois. The vast majority of its population were North African Muslims, who were now locked in a more or less permanent battle with paramilitary units of the resurgent Front National. The most combative of all the anti-fascists hung out at a mixed martial arts club that stayed open late. Novak turned up there and got in the ring, a head guard her only concession to personal protection. She started taunting the regulars, daring them to fight a white woman. It took a while before her first opponent stepped into the ring. But when the others saw the ferocity with which she fought, and the blows she was willing to take as well as deal out, Novak had no shortage of takers, and she did not leave that ring until the pain and exhaustion were enough to provide some relief, however temporary, from the furies raging inside her.

7

Wednesday evening: Alix watched the blue flashing light of a police car reflecting off the puddles in the rain-slicked street as it came up Knightsbridge towards her, hurtled past the Hyde Park Palace Hotel, and then raced away towards Piccadilly. It was getting dark now, and the streets were starting to clear of cars and pedestrians alike. Even in an area as smart as this, people only went out at night if they had a very good reason to do so. And no one got in anywhere without first proving their right to do so. All new arrivals at this or any other major hotel, for example, had to pass armed security guards, bag- and body-scanners, and even the occasional body search before they could even check-in. Thereafter their room keys acted as pass-cards to get them through the entrance barriers. Once inside, it was like entering a separate dimension of luxury and indulgence, hermetically sealed off from the ever-increasing chaos and shabbiness of the world outside.

Alix found the effect to be more disconcerting than re-assuring. As much as she had never felt a single second of nostalgia for the grim, depressing greyness of her Soviet childhood, there was still a tiny part of her that clung to some of the socialist idealism that had been drummed into her as a girl. The presence of this island of wealth, and others like it, amidst an increasingly rough sea of poverty and lawlessness disturbed her. It reminded her of Moscow in the years immediately after the fall of Communism, when the rule of the state and the secret police was making way for a culture of gangsters and oligarchs. One of those tough, ruthless men had kept her as his mistress, and she had learned first-hand about the way the world worked when the strong took whatever they wanted and the weak went to hell. She didn't want to go back to that, either.

Thinking of the past only served to remind her how far back her memories went. Alix had long since come to terms with the fact that she was no longer the pretty young thing of days gone by. She was more at ease with the face and body she saw reflected in the mirror now than she had ever been in the past. Of course, it didn't hurt her self-confidence to love and be loved by a man who made it perfectly obvious how much he desired her. She heard him now, coming in behind her, and turned to watch him as he walked across the room.

'Ah, there you are,' said Carver, smiling as he caught her eye.

Even now, the sight of him could still make her heart flutter like a teenage girl's. She loved his strong hands and forearms, the taper from his broad shoulders down to his narrow hips, the high, firm curve of his butt. She loved watching his clear green eyes. Their moods were as changeable as the sea: sometimes bright and sunny, sometimes stormy, sometimes as cold as Arctic ice.

She was almost certain Carver had no idea of the effect that his face and body had upon her. It was simply not an issue he even considered; he never for a moment thought of himself as something to be looked at or judged in the way that every woman in the world was constantly obliged to do.

They'd met more years ago than she really cared to remember, one summer's night in Paris on the Left Bank of the Seine. It was a perfect setting for romance, but far from a conventionally perfect introduction. She'd pointed a loaded Uzi in Carver's direction. He'd replied by smashing her face-first against a bus-shelter before she could open fire, knocking her to the ground, rolling her over and cuffing her hands behind her back. Then he'd sat her up against the side of the shelter and interrogated her; someone wanted him dead and he needed to know why. She'd been furious with Carver for the brutal, impersonal efficiency with which he'd rendered her helpless, furious with herself for letting it happen, furious with the whole damn world for the way it treated young women like her. But there'd been an immediate, overwhelming connection between them. No matter how hard she'd tried to deny it, she hadn't been able to. It'd been obvious he'd felt it, too. And all these years later nothing had changed.

He had reached her now and circled her waist with his arms. 'Are you sure you want to do this?' he asked, pulling her close to him.

'Not you as well as Grantham?' she protested.

'We don't need the money.'

'Yes, but the people who work for me need their pay cheques. And that means I have to get new business. Anyway, I promised the President.' She ran her fingers down Carver's face. 'Don't worry. I'm not going to rush into anything. And I'll know if Adams is telling the truth or bullshitting me. I'm not some innocent, naïve little schoolgirl.'

'No, you certainly are not,' Carver said, with a wicked grin, holding her even tighter, letting her feel his hardness. 'So why don't you show me just what a grown-up, experienced woman you are?'

Alix felt herself starting to melt. She had about five more seconds before he kissed her, and then any feeble attempts at resistance would crumble. It took every ounce of will she possessed to deny herself what she very badly wanted and pull herself out of his grasp.

'No,' she said with a certainty she did not feel. 'I've got a car coming to pick me up in twenty minutes, and I've got to shower, change and get myself ready by then. You're just going to have to wait.'

'I don't think I can,' he said, taking a step towards her.

'Well, you'll just have to.'

Alix dashed to the bathroom, slammed the door behind her and locked it before he could charm his way in. At that moment she would happily have cancelled the meeting, let her business go to hell and spent the rest of the night with Carver. But there were people who depended on her, people with mortgages to pay and families to feed. And as much as she might have been tempted, she wasn't going to let them down.

Carver stared at the bathroom door, feeling the throb of his frustrated desire. He wanted to take her so badly: on a bed, on the floor, up against the nearest available wall, he wasn't choosy. It didn't help knowing that she'd felt it too. In fact, it made it worse. How did women do that – say no to sex they obviously wanted? Let the driver wait outside for a few extra minutes, for Christ's sake. It was only just past six o'clock now, and the main event wasn't due to start till eight. There was plenty of time to make everybody happy.

Alix wasn't going to change her mind now, though. He knew her well enough to be sure of that. He wandered off back to the suite's living room and picked up his mobile phone from a side table. He pressed speed-dial and waited for the call to be answered.

'Evening, Snoopy,' he said.

'Oi, show some respect, you cheeky sod,' said the South London voice on the other end of the line.

Carver laughed. 'All right then, I'll start again . . . Good evening, former Company Sergeant Major Schultz. How are you?'

'Getting by. And yourself?'

'Not too bad . . . You still on for that drink?'

'I've got to do some business at a pub tonight, as it happens – the Dutchman's Head, down Clapham way. We can go there, get a couple of pints in first. You getting here by cab?'

'Most likely, yeah.'

'Tell the cabbie it's just behind Clapham North station. What do you reckon, half seven?'

'Sounds good to me.'

'And boss, keep your eyes open, yeah? There's always kids off the estates, playing at being gangbangers. They're just a bunch of chavvy little toerags, but they're all tooled up with knives and that, so watch yourself, yeah?'

'Understood. I'll see you at seven thirty. And if you get there before me, mine's a pint of London Pride.'

8

Between the South London districts of Battersea Park and Vauxhall nine sets of elevated train tracks run side-by-side, like a coronary artery of wood and steel twenty-five feet above the streets. Many of the buildings on either side of the tracks are council blocks, erected after the Second World War to replace the Victorian terraces that had been flattened in the Blitz.

Donny Bakunin lived in a fourth-floor council flat in one of these blocks, though his name was not on any of the rental papers, nor the utility bills that lay unpaid on the mat beneath the front door. Bakunin was fifty-two years old. He had short, grey hair that ringed a bald spot that seemed to get wider by the day. He would never have admitted to being vain enough to have noticed, any more than he would have given any reason for the choice of his plain, metal-framed spectacles other than their extreme cheapness. His face was so lacking in flesh, the skin so tightly wrapped around his nose and cheeks and his surprisingly strong, forceful jaw that the contours of his skull were clearly visible beneath the skin. His body, too, was severely underweight.

Bakunin was no more interested in the pleasure of good food than he was in elegant clothes, comfortable furniture or agreeable surroundings. In his mind all were trivial fripperies. So were intimate relationships of anything more than the most fleeting, functional kind. All he cared about was his own personal faith of anarchic revolution. Much like the Americans who had invaded Iraq without the slightest idea of what they would do once they had conquered it, so Bakunin had spent his entire adult life plotting the downfall of capitalism and no time whatever in planning its replacement. It was destruction that interested him, not the creation of a better world.

Now, after more than thirty years of frustrating, even futile, activism he could finally see his end in sight. It was no longer a matter of insanely optimistic ideology to say that the West was falling apart. It was a simple statement of fact. And that, too, explained why he was not eating. He did not have time. There were so many better, more profoundly nourishing things to do.

A phone rang on the cheap MDF desk at which he was sitting, one of half a dozen prepaid mobiles lined up in front of him.

There were no introductions, and there was no social chit-chat. Just a voice that said, 'You got everything sorted for tonight, yeah? Eight-fifteen, Netherton Street, SW4. Now remember: what we want is maximum damage. They can loot the shops, rip the shit out of the curry house and the Chinky takeaway, take all the money and gold from the cash converters, all that good stuff. But we're not looking for bodies all over the place. GBH yes, murders, no. Capeesh?'

'Yes,' said Bakunin with an oddly clipped, middle-class accent.

'And remember, tell your people that pub's off-limits. No one goes near it.'

'Already done it. How much time have we got before the police arrive?'

'Plenty. They'll all be at that rally down the O2 trying to keep order.'

'How about media coverage?'

'Same thing: all at the O2 as well. Just make your own video. Stick it on YouTube. Have someone tweeting live as you go in. That'll get us all the attention we need.'

'Right, yeah, we need to break the hegemony of state-controlled media and corporate mind-control. This is a much more authentic way of communicating to the masses.'

'For fuck's sake, Bakunin. Save us the political lecture. Just go and fuck some stuff up.'

Well, he was always happy to do that. In that respect, nothing had changed since the boyhood days when he'd still been called Donald Blantyre, and grown up in Tunbridge Wells, acquiring an impressive set of O- and A-Levels at Tunbridge Wells Grammar School for Boys, and a First in English literature at King's College, Cambridge.

It was at that august, yet self-consciously radical seat of

learning that the eighteen-year-old Blantyre first found an ideological voice with which to express the vast, poisonous well of indiscriminate fury that had lived within his apparently perfectly placid exterior for as long as he could remember. To his Tory-voting parents' horrified surprise he'd returned from his first term at university in December 1978 with his hair dyed jet black and sprayed into short, scruffy spikes. He had, he informed them with a defiant snarl that begged for an argument, changed his name to Bakunin and joined the Socialist Workers' Party, the Campaign for Nuclear Disarmament and an anarcho-punk band called The Spartacist League. The Blantyres told one another that this was just a passing phase. They were wrong.

After leaving Cambridge Bakunin went into teaching, but unlike most members of his profession his ambition was not to give his pupils the best and most enriching education; quite the reverse, in fact. He wanted to ensure that they learned as little as possible. His aim – one shared by a small, but influential hard core of extremists – was to create an embittered underclass, whose members would be lacking in skills, motivation or self-discipline. They would be shut out of the labour market and bitterly aware that they had no hope and no future. This would fill them with hatred for anyone better off than themselves, and make them ripe for recruitment as the foot soldiers of the revolution.

In the past few years he had abandoned his teaching career for a life of full-time political agitation, and as the fabric of law and order had begun first to fray, then fall to shreds, Donny Bakunin had become a sort of twenty-first-century Fagin. His gangs of urchins were not chirpy Artful Dodgers and innocent Oliver Twists. They were precisely the kind of young men he had always intended to recruit: functionally illiterate and innumerate, unqualified for any well-paid job but greedy for the gaudiest designer brands, and only too happy to seize by force that which they could never hope to earn by hard work. They came from every one of the myriad ethnic groups of South London, their perennial hostilities temporarily set aside in favour of a joint assault on society. And when the calls went out from Bakunin's flat to others just like it on a dozen nearby estates, the gangs began to gather and an army of the night was formed.

9

The crowds streaming out of the exit to North Greenwich underground station were overwhelmingly white, middle-aged, middle-income, middle-class. They looked on themselves as the law-abiding, hard-working, tax-paying backbone of the country, and they represented both the single biggest demographic group in the British population and the one that felt itself to be the most unjustly ignored and even despised by the political and media elite. As they made their way through the cold, persistent drizzle towards the O2 Arena they were greeted by giant advertising hoardings that screamed out, 'THE ONLY WAY IS UPP!' and 'BRITAIN IS MOVING UPP IN THE WORLD!' and 'IT'S TIME TO GET UPP!'

In smaller letters, below these slogans, ran the words: 'Vote for a new start. Vote United People's Party.'

The only illustration on the posters was a photograph

of a man's face. He looked handsome, but not too handsome. His hair was as grey as George Clooney's and his eyes could grab a camera lens as well as any movie star's, but there was no attempt to hide the lines around his eyes, nor the slight thickening around his jaw and chin. And although he possessed a dazzling smile his mouth was now fixed in a look of grim determination. This was the face of a leader who took action, not an actor who performed. This was Mark Adams.

The route to the huge white dome was lined by policemen holding back protesters who were waving banners and placards that bore very different slogans to those on the posters: 'DOWN WITH UPP!' and 'UNITE AGAINST FASCIST SCUM!' The protesters were shouting the same slogan again and again, 'Mark Adams, Little Hitler! . . . Mark Adams, Little Hitler!'

From time to time people would break away from the steady stream heading from the station to the O2 and start shouting back at the protesters. One group of about thirty shaven-headed men – all in the standard uniform of Doc Martens, jeans, white T-shirts and green nylon flight-jackets that had been associated with the Far Right for the past forty-odd years – had formed up on the other side of the police line, opposite the greatest concentration of their opponents. They started up a chant of 'England for the English', and then another, like a football crowd: 'United!' *Clap-clap-clap*. 'United!' *Clap-clap-clap*.

TV crews were gathering in the area, sensing that there was about to be serious trouble. Passers-by were holding up telephones to take photos and video footage.

A black-suited man wearing a telephone headset was deep in conversation with the most senior police officer on the scene, a uniformed chief inspector. He was pointing at the skinheads and shouting angrily in a Geordie accent, 'You've got to get them out of here.'

'They're your people. You tell them,' the Chief Inspector replied.

The suit was Adams's campaign manager, Robbie Bell, and he was getting nervous. This would all be on Twitter within seconds and on the rolling TV news shows not long afterwards. 'They're not our people,' he insisted. 'They're not the people we want. Move them!'

The Chief Inspector looked around. It was all his men could do simply to maintain the pedestrian corridor. 'How, exactly?' he asked.

Amidst all the noise and the steadily escalating atmosphere of tension and incipient violence one man walked quietly towards the main entrance. His name was Kieron Sproles and he was everything the face on the posters was not: inconspicuous, unimpressive and eminently forgettable. As he passed the group of threatening, shouting men he hunched his shoulders and walked a little faster. He did not like them at all. They reminded him of the boys who had bullied and beaten him at school. He could practically smell the sweat and testosterone they exuded, and the brute physicality of their presence reawakened feelings of helplessness and humiliation that had haunted him all his life.

Sproles was born to be one of nature's victims, the runt of any litter he was in. He stood no more than five feet, five inches tall and was skinny with it. His eyes were a watery grey and their drabness was a match for his clothes – crumpled, charcoal woollen trousers, a maroon crew-neck jumper and a beige winter jacket with elasticated cuffs. He wore shoes like Cornish pasties. He carried no bag of any kind, so bypassed the security bag-check. His ticket was perfectly in order. Detailed examination of the kind he never seemed to attract might have revealed that he was nervous, edgy and perspiring heavily. But what would that have proved? The whole event was charged with an atmosphere of adrenalized over-excitement. Kieron Sproles was by no means alone in that.

Once he was inside, he made his way to the nearest men's room and locked himself in a cubicle. Then he pulled his shirt out of his waistband, ran his right hand up the small of his back, and found the edge of the tape that was fixed right across it, in a broad strip from his lower ribs to his hips. Sproles worked his hand down between the tape and his skin, grimacing as the hairs on his back were tweaked. Almost immediately his fingers came into contact with the edge of the Glock semi-automatic pistol that was wedged against his body.

Sproles gradually loosened the tape until the gun could be pulled free. He looked at it, checked the magazine for the umpteenth time and then placed it in one of the pockets of his jacket.

Sproles pulled the tape off his back and crumpled it into a tight ball. He tucked his shirt back in, left the cubicle and stood at a basin to wash his hands. The reflection that looked back at him from the mirror appeared no different than usual. He did not look like an assassin, whatever an assassin looked like. He put the ball of tape into the bin where the paper towels went. Moments later he was out of the men's room and making his way to his seat. It was located in the front row of the crowd, less than ten metres from the edge of the stage.

10

Maninder Singh Panu had spent an hour that evening in a hospital ward, making his daily visit to his father Lakhbir's hospital bed. Once an energetic, ambitious man, determined to improve his family's place in the world, the older Panu now lay motionless and silent, still trapped in the coma that had held him since the night six months ago when he had been attacked by a gang of teenagers outside the Lion Market, the family's twenty-four-hour store in Netherton Street. A flying brick had caught him on the side of his head. A fifteen-year-old boy called Jaden Crabbe had thrown it. Jaden had been coming to the shop since he was knee-high, buying sweets for himself or running errands for his mum. Now he was at one of the new high-security young offenders' units the government had recently set up, the doctors were threatening to turn off Lakhbir Panu's life support, and Maninder was ready to start fighting back.

He'd got together with some of the other local traders and restaurateurs to form the Netherton Street Self-Help Association. Since the law was no longer willing or able to guarantee their safety, they were going to have to do it themselves. They'd borrowed a motto from *The Three Musketeers*: 'All for one and one for all.' From now on, an attack on any one of their businesses would be treated like an attack on them all, and everyone would respond. The couple that ran the pub had a regular who knew some old-school villains who were no happier with the riots than anyone else. Proper professionals knocking off a posh jeweller's shop or a Securicor van was one thing. Gobby little knobs going round wrecking local people's lives, that was quite another. They'd handed out pump-action shotguns, guaranteed untraceable, to anyone that wanted them.

The idea of firing a gun at someone scared the hell out of Maninder Panu. But ending up a vegetable in a hospital bed scared him even more. He was a Sikh and thus a member of a proud warrior race. He told himself that if he had to fight to preserve the business his family had sweated for years to build, then that was what he was going to do. He was getting married in three months' time. He didn't want his wife-to-be thinking that her fiancé was a coward.

He was manning the Lion Market tonight with his cousin Ajay. Unlike Maninder, who was a short, slightly overweight man in his late thirties, Ajay was a decade younger, well over six feet tall, built like the proverbial brick outhouse and blessed with a magnificent, uncut beard that Long John Silver would have envied. Ajay had placed a baseball bat behind the counter. If anything should ever kick off, he was relying on his fearsome appearance to be sufficiently intimidating to put anyone off attacking him. In truth, he had no more skill or experience as a fighting man than Maninder. But he too was not prepared to take another backward step.

Both men were reassured by the knowledge that if there was any sign of trouble, they could text the other members of the Self-Help Association and know that they would be on their way.

So far, the Panus had never had to ask for that help. Both cousins prayed that tonight would be no exception.

Bakunin's operation began shortly after seven o'clock, with a break-in at a refuse-company depot off the Walworth Road, three miles from the Lion Market where Maninder and Ajay Panu were quietly going about their business. Six armed, masked men approached the security guard in his booth by the main gate, and he was gone before they'd even got within thirty metres of him. He didn't need telling that the guns they were holding weren't just for show, and he wasn't going to get himself killed for a job that only paid six quid an hour. The men entered the abandoned booth and opened the steel gates. One of them worked at the depot, and led them to the office where the keys to the trucks were kept. It was empty at this time of night, like the rest of the place.

The six intruders went straight to the two units to which the keys belonged, started them up and drove out of the depot. Before it turned on to the road, one of the trucks paused for long enough to let a passenger get out, go to the abandoned guard's booth and close the gates behind them. The garbage trucks joined the traffic on the Walworth Road, heading north towards Elephant and Castle, where they turned sharp left, almost doubling back on themselves, down Kennington Lane. They were heading for the industrial estate on Nine Elms, close to the Cringle Dock recycling centre. They planned to park up there for half an hour or so, and keep a low profile till it was time to go to work.

11

Funny how old habits refused to die even when the reason for having them had long gone. As he sat in the cab taking him to his drink with Schultz, Carver was wearing a favourite old jacket, made of heavy, caramel-coloured suede, that was really more like a short coat. He had a zip-up black body warmer under it and a long-sleeved T-shirt that looked like regular cotton but was actually superfine merino wool, a far superior regulator of body temperature.

Carver had no interest whatever in fashion, but he had always paid very great attention to detail when it came to the function and quality of everything in his life. When the slightest malfunction could make the difference between life and death these things mattered. So he'd long been as picky with his clothes as he was with his weapons, and when he found something that worked, he stuck with it. Even so, he was having a hard time understanding why the same old money-belt was still wrapped around his waist. Its pouches contained passports and credit cards in three different identities; a selection of random IDs picked up on various previous jobs; half a dozen anonymous, prepaid SIM cards; and two thick wads of hundred-dollar US bills. He'd worn it every day for the past twenty years and for much of that time it had been an essential insurance policy. Wherever he was, there'd always been the chance that he'd have to get out fast, and the belt gave him the means to do so.

But why now? The secret store in his Geneva apartment where he kept all the gear he'd used to create fatal, unattributable 'accidents' hadn't been opened in more than two years. He'd not even picked up a gun in that time, let alone fired one in anger. But his weapons were all still there; he still spent a fortune every year on the increasingly complicated systems required to keep the location of any phone he was using untraceable; and his belt was still round his waist this evening, even if it did feel a little tighter than it had in the old days. Wasn't it time to let it all go?

They were over the river now, driving south towards Netherton Street. Carver looked at his watch. He was going to get there a few minutes early. On a whim he tapped on the glass that divided the passenger compartment from the driver and said, 'Stop here. I'll walk the rest of the way.'

The cabbie looked up and caught his eye in the driver's mirror. 'You sure you want to do that, guv? Not a good idea round here.'

'I'll manage.'

The driver shrugged. 'Suit yourself. Just hope the next bloke that picks you up isn't driving an ambulance.'

Carver paid him off and started walking. Within a couple of minutes he'd begun to wonder whether he'd made a stupid decision. It had less to do with the run-down drabness of so much of the cityscape around him than the steady drizzle in the air, which seemed to be seeping down past the collar of his jacket and up through the soles of his shoes, chilling him to the bone. Carver looked around. He couldn't be too far from Netherton Street now. There was an old council estate up ahead: the pub should be just the far side of that.

He turned down a road that led through the estate. One entire side of it, at least two hundred metres long, was taken up with a single, gigantic concrete chunk of brutal sixties architecture. It was seven storeys high, and walkways ran the full length of each level, like streets in the sky, one above the other. Carver could hear children's shouts and mocking laughter echoing from somewhere high among the walkways, but when he looked up there hardly seemed to be any lights on anywhere – half a dozen at most across the oppressive, Stalinist bulk of the place. Peering through the drizzle, he realized he'd made a mistake. You couldn't cut straight through the estate. There was a dead end up ahead where another, smaller pile of concrete barred the way, looking even darker, more lifeless and yet more menacing than the one beside him.

The estate's architects must have planned it like this specifically to prevent drivers using the road as a rat run. Instead they had created a rat trap, a dead-end community that had taken the hint and died. But even these architects had to have allowed the inhabitants of their oppressive schemes some way of walking out. A peeling, faded sign beside the pavement showed a map of the estate, and Carver saw that if he made his way to the right of the block at the end of the cul-de-sac there should be a path that would lead past a further set of buildings, arranged around an open central space, towards another road that would take him to Netherton Street.

With every step Carver took it became more obvious that the entire sprawling estate was virtually abandoned. He could imagine the drawings and scale models that had been produced when the place had first been proposed, with their sunny skies, green-leafed trees and happy families living, playing and working in a modernist utopia. Now it looked like a post-apocalyptic wasteland, or the set of a zombie movie. Carver wasn't given to shivers of apprehension, but even he prickled a little walking through the unlit shadows of the alley that led past the dead-end block to the promised open space beyond.

The first thing he saw when he came out the other side was a bonfire of old bits of furniture and building materials in front of yet another unlit building with glass-less, dead-eyed windows. Three men – two black and one white – were sitting on a low brick wall just next to the fire, a scattering of empty beer cans at their feet, having themselves a party with the crack pipe that the white one had in his mouth. He was sucking hard, pulling his pitted, acne-ridden skin between his rotting teeth. His hands were cupped round the bowl of the pipe, making sure that the rain didn't put it out. The other two were watching him hungrily, the way addicts do when they see someone else taking their share – possibly more than their share – of the stash.

It was only when White Boy looked up that he saw Carver coming towards him. He took the pipe out of his mouth and gave a wordless grunt that alerted his mates to the presence of a passer-by.

They turned their feverish, sunken eyes in Carver's direction.

He knew perfectly well how he must look: a little over average height, but with a lean build that was unlikely to intimidate anyone. He wasn't the kind of man who stood out in a crowd or attracted attention by virtue of his size. In his line of work, anonymity had always been a necessity. He'd never wanted people to know just how dangerous he could be.

Of course, this had the drawback that people didn't actually know how dangerous he could be. People like dumb, brain-fried crackheads who were always looking for easy money and who, right now, were pulling out knives, getting down off the wall and closing the few metres between themselves and Carver with scuffling, unsteady steps.

They were drunk and stoned, so their reactions would be treacle-slow and their motor skills shot to pieces. On the other hand, they would also be irrational, incoherent and lacking in any sort of impulse control. Carver really didn't want or need a fight tonight, but negotiation wasn't an option.

'You stay 'ere, don' fuckin' move!' White Boy shouted, stabbing his knife in the air. He still had the crack pipe in his other hand. He wasn't going to let that out of his sight.

The other two spread out to either side of him, blocking Carver's lines of escape. But they didn't make any further move to attack him, so he just stayed where he was, waiting to see how this would all unfold.

To his surprise, White Boy had actually broken into a feeble imitation of a run and was heading across the open space. Carver watched him scramble across the broken, debris-strewn ground and it was only then that he realized that there were more people, maybe as many as a hundred, gathered around another set of fires that had been lit on the far side of the space. And by the looks of them, they weren't there to toast marshmallows.

White Boy disappeared into the crowd, only to re-emerge a few seconds later with another man in a black leather jacket and a beanie hat. This one was a very different specimen. He was squat and barrel-chested with the concentrated raw strength, broken nose and cauliflower ears of a rugby front-row forward. He walked straight up to Carver and asked him, 'What the fuck do you think you're doing here?'

'What does it look like?' Carver replied. 'I'm walking.'

'Well, fuck off and walk somewhere else, then.'

'Get out of my way, and I will. All I want to do is go through this estate and out the other side so that I can have a nice, quiet drink with an old friend.'

'I wouldn't do that if I was you.'

'Thanks for the advice, but I think I will anyway.'

The big man in the beanie hat knew a lot about intimidating people, and he couldn't help but notice that Carver wasn't in the least bit frightened. He was also sober and streetwise enough to have picked up on the calm, methodical way that Carver had been assessing the situation around him as they'd been talking. He could not have known just how precisely Carver had worked out the sequence with which he would disable the big man, take White Boy's knife, place it against the big man's throat and inform him that it was going to get cut to the bone if he didn't tell everyone else to back up and let Carver through. But still, the big man got the clear impression that there was a risk attached to starting a fight with this apparently innocuous new arrival, so he took a step back, swept his arm like a traffic cop letting the traffic through and said, 'Suit yourself.'

'Thanks,' said Carver, 'I will.'

And he walked away towards Netherton Street.

12

Alix had been sent a limousine by the organizers of the rally – one of the armoured BMW 7 Series that had become the transport of choice for those wishing to reach their destinations unscathed, and rich enough to pay the price for such security. As she arrived a woman was waiting to greet her. She was holding a clipboard. She had to shout to make herself heard over the chaos on either side of the police line: 'And you are?'

'Alexandra Vermulen, of Vermulen Associates. I'm expected.'

The greeter gave a warm, professional smile. 'Good evening, Mrs Vermulen. We're so glad you could make it. Mr Adams will see you when he's freshened up after his speech. Follow me, please.'

Alix was given a laminated all-areas pass and led up escalators, across a concourse and past a series of security guards to the VIP suite. There was a bar to one side behind which two hostesses were providing drinks and snacks to the dozen or so people gathered in the room. Most of them were men, hardcore careerists who were barking fiercely into their phones or having the sorts of conversations that are less about sharing any ideas or information and far more about a competitive battle to establish the superior status of one speaker over the other. As she waited to be served a glass of chilled champagne Alix caught snatches of speech: demands to, 'Well, just get it done NOW!'; and insistences that, 'I don't care what's happened in Iran. We have to lead the *Ten O'Clock News*!'

The only person who paid Alix the slightest bit of attention was another woman, standing by the rail that separated the interior of the suite from its dedicated seats in the auditorium itself. She was a few years older than Alix, pretty in a natural, unaffected kind of way, and dressed in smart, high-street clothes. 'Hello,' she said, holding out a hand. 'You must be Mrs Vermulen, I've been so looking forward to meeting you. I'm Nicki Adams, Mark's wife.' She looked at her watch and then back at Alix. 'Uh-oh, it all starts in five minutes. Why don't you sit next to me? I'd much rather have you for company than any of this lot.'

Outside the arena a *Sky News* reporter called Bob Hunter was standing in front of the police line at the point where the skinheads, whose numbers had swelled to well over fifty, were still engaged in a running battle of chants, insults and the occasional thrown bottle with the anti-fascist protesters on the other side. Hunter was holding a hand to one ear, as if to help him hear questions amidst the pandemonium.

He set his voice to 'battlefield reporter' mode. 'The atmosphere here is as bad as ever. In fact, it may be getting worse. I've just heard from police sources that a number of officers have been hit by missiles thrown from both sides. There are now very real fears that the situation is close to spiralling out of control. Meanwhile—'

His words were interrupted by the sound of smashing glass, followed by an explosion and a brief burst of flame just a couple of metres behind him as an amateurish, homemade attempt at a Molotov cocktail went off. 'Whoa!' Hunter exclaimed, throwing up a hand to shield his face. 'We're going to have to move. Things are really heating up. Back to the studio . . .'

'Who do you think put those yobbos there?' asked Cameron Young, the Prime Minister's Chief of Staff. He was watching the broadcast from his office in Downing Street. Young was the sort of man who looked as though he'd been born wearing a suit and tie. His appearance was an exact definition of 'blandness': mousey hair, nondescript eyes hidden behind unexceptional glasses. Yet many Westminster insiders said he was the second most important man in the country. Those that disagreed only did so because they were certain that he was actually the first.

Young frowned pensively. 'It must be good for Adams to have a certain amount of disorder about the place – helps persuade the masses that they need a short, sharp shock. On the other hand, if he really wants to persuade the rest of us that he's basically a decent, reasonable chap, he hardly wants to be associated with louts and skinheads.' He turned back to the rest of the room with raised, inquisitive eyebrows. 'You didn't plant them, did you, Grantham?'

'If I did, would you really want me to tell you?'

Strictly speaking, Jack Grantham had no professional interest in events on UK soil. Those were the preserve of the police and MI5. That was the very reason Young had approached him for, as he put it, 'A special consultative role, reporting solely to me and thus to the Prime Minister.'

Young was determined to use any methods necessary to stamp out Mark Adams and his new party before they became an even more serious threat to the established political order. That task required someone who had no direct ties to domestic law-enforcement; someone who understood that there were times when a problem was so serious that unconventional methods were required – the kind of methods that could never and would never be discussed in public. Grantham fitted the bill perfectly.

For his part, Grantham's unrelenting ambition would be satisfied by even closer access to Number 10 and the promise of an accelerated knighthood. His greed, a relatively minor vice in his case, was covered by the assurance of a significant performance bonus on completion of his task. Meanwhile – and this was an essential consideration for a man who loved intrigue, but was very easily bored – his interest and curiosity were piqued by the lengths to which the government was prepared to go to discredit and destroy a political opponent.

With Grantham already in the bag, Young just had his traditional enemies to worry about.

'Anything you'd like to add, Brian?' Young asked.

Brian Smallbone, Young's opposite number as political advisor to the Leader of the Opposition, shook his head. 'Not at the moment, no. It all seems to be going well enough. Let's just enjoy the show.'

13

There were times when Paula Miklosko wondered why she'd ever bothered getting married or working for a living. It wasn't that she regretted committing herself to her husband Marek. True, they couldn't have come from much more different backgrounds: she was a half-Ghanaian, half-Welsh Baptist, he was a Czech Catholic. But they loved each other as much now as the day they'd met six years ago, and that was all Paula cared about. She wanted him, and was longing for the day when they could afford to start a family together.

In the meantime, she had something she'd always dreamed of: a little hairdressing salon of her own. She'd saved up since she left college to put down the deposit. Marek and his pals had done a great job gutting the old interior and giving it a whole new look. If she was given even half a chance, she knew she had the talent, the energy and the determination to make a real go of it.

So far, trade was holding up all right. Even in times of hardship, women still wanted their hair to look nice. But they couldn't pay as much for it as they'd done a few years ago, and the tips were pitiful. Meanwhile, prices and taxes just kept rising all the time, and even when Marek and his crew charged rock-bottom rates they still found it hard getting building or decorating work.

After years of apparent immunity from the general decline of the British property market, London prices had collapsed in recent months. All the wealthy foreigners were leaving town, and banks had finally stopped paying bonuses. Without all that silly money the price-bubble had burst. Nobody was moving house. Nobody could afford to tart up the houses they'd got. Even if they could, what was the point? Areas that had once been promoted as up-and-coming were now little better than warzones. Even the respectable, desirable parts of the city were overrun with muggers, beggars and crazies. Any middle-class families that had country houses had fled. The rest were trying to find a way out. And those who had no choice but to stay, who were trying to live the right way, were being spat on by the system as much as those who sought to destroy it.

'I don't understand this crazy country!' Marek liked to say. 'If you work, they pay you less and less. If you just sit on your ass, then every year the benefits go up and up. No wonder the English are so lazy. Is a waste of time to work here. And having family is impossible! Maybe I should give you baby then leave. You get more money that way.'

Paula tried to explain that people on benefits weren't living in luxury, whatever people said. She had enough friends trying to raise two or three kids by themselves in a council flat to know it wasn't easy. But she also knew that none of those friends even tried to get jobs because they'd never earn enough to make it worthwhile. Plenty of them came from families where no one had worked for years and years. No one stayed married; no one even tried to get a decent education. Paula was desperate to avoid becoming another welfare statistic – and even if she hadn't been, her mother would never have let her. She'd always taken the same view as Marek: lazy white folk could waste their lives away if they liked, but her children were going to make something of themselves.

That was what Paula planned to do. All she asked for was just a little help, a little recognition that she and Marek should be rewarded for at least trying to lead a productive life that would actually contribute to society.

As she cleaned up the salon after the last customer had left, Paula had the radio on. They were talking about that big rally Mark Adams was having at the O2. Paula didn't quite know what to make of Adams. Marek often said, 'Every other politician in this country full of bullshit – but this Adams I like.'

Paula had told him, 'You wouldn't think that if you were black.' But she didn't make a big issue of it. There were a lot of good reasons to have a fight with her husband, but politics wasn't one of them.

She turned the radio off, closed up the salon, pulled down the security shutters and walked off to her car. It was only a little Suzuki Swift, eight years old with over a hundred thousand miles on the clock. But it was Paula Miklosko's little luxury. She'd paid for it. And she loved it.

14

Standing behind his shop counter, Maninder Panu watched Ajay put fresh produce into the clear plastic bowls of fruit and vegetables arrayed on a table outside. Each bowl cost one pound. Ajay had to lift up the clear plastic sheet that kept the rain off the bowls in order to refill them.

A man had stopped to watch the whole procedure as though this was something new to him. He was a white man, somewhat shorter than Ajay and less heavily built, but there was something about the way he stood that gave Panu the impression that he knew how to look after himself. He had none of the fearful nervousness that afflicted so many people these days. Nor was there any of the bullying aggression of the criminals and gang-members who wallowed in their ability to intimidate. Instead he seemed relaxed, self-confident, as though he felt certain he could handle whatever the streets might throw at him. He might, Panu thought, be an off-duty soldier or policeman. The man asked Ajay a question, nodded with interest at the answer, looked at his watch, then came into the store.

Sam Carver walked up to the counter, scuffing a hand through his short, dark-brown hair – that now had a few faint streaks of grey – to get rid of some of the rainwater. He'd never seen groceries sold by the bowl before. It made him feel like a stranger in his own country to admit that, but he liked the idea anyway. Inside, the Lion Market looked a cut above your average urban corner shop. It was air-conditioned and the goods on the shelves were an odd mix of bargain-basement offers and surprisingly upmarket brands. But then, this was a corner of London where great swathes of council flats mixed with terraces where four-bed family houses went for a million quid – or had done until a few years ago, at any rate. The families that lived in places like that wanted to eat sun-dried tomatoes, ciabatta bread and organic avocados. The Lion Market was obviously happy to supply them.

Sweets and chocolate bars were on display by the checkout, presumably to tempt shoppers into last-second impulse purchases. Carver scanned the racks until he found what he was looking for: two bars of Cadbury's Fruit and Nut. Geneva was filled with fancy confectioners selling the finest Swiss chocolate, but he missed the taste of home. As he paid for the bars he noticed that the man behind the counter looked a little jumpy. There were signs by the door as he came in warning that the shop had full CCTV coverage, never kept more than fifty pounds in the till and was protected by (this handwritten in large black capital letters) 'FAST-RESPONSE ARMED SECURITY'.

Carver didn't blame the owners for being nervous. A place like this was a magnet for crime, from spotty little shoplifters to armed burglars. Still, the average urban lowlife was as cowardly as he was stupid. The lad out front looked big and mean enough to make most would-be perpetrators think twice. Carver thanked the shopkeeper for his change and walked out. Spotting the sign for the Dutchman's Head fifty metres down the road he licked his lips. Snoopy Schultz should be getting the drinks in any second now, and he could practically taste that first pint.

15

In Row A of Block A2 – the front, centre section of the arena's ground-floor seating – Kieron Sproles was sitting by himself, surrounded by an expectant buzz of chatter. His hands were in his jacket pocket. His right hand was gripped around the handle of the Glock. Not long now, and all his years of obscurity – that solitary insignificance that had marked his existence since his first day at primary school – would be over. By the end of the evening, everyone would know who he was, and what he had done.

And then, without warning, the lights began to dim.

As intense, doom-laden music boomed out from the speakers suspended above the stage a video screen came to life. A helicopter camera panned across a desolate waste-land of derelict buildings, boarded-up shops, abandoned tower blocks and open spaces – once intended for cheerful recreation, now given over to bare earth, weeds and dogshit. A single man was walking down a street of semi-detached houses, now all abandoned. Each had once had front and back gardens, though these were now overgrown. The camera zoomed in to reveal Mark Adams, and a huge cheer went up around the arena as he began to speak.

'This used to be my street. These were all council houses . . . And this was the house where I grew up: 37 Cambrai Road.'

Adams stopped by a wooden gate, hanging half off its hinges. Beyond it, a path could just about be seen under a carpet of dandelions and bindweed. It led to a house with scorch marks round the windows, and bare patches on the walls where all the rendering had fallen off.

He began walking down the road again, speaking to the camera with the practised fluency of a man who had first become known to the public as the presenter of documentaries on military history; a war-hero-turned-TV-star. With a sweep of his arm, Adams encompassed all the houses around him: 'The people who lived here were working-class, but they were proud of who they were and where they came from. Proud of Leeds, proud of Yorkshire, proud of England, proud to be British.

'No one had much money to spare. Yet all the front gardens were immaculate: no weeds in the flower beds, paths and front doorsteps swept clean.'

Now Adams was walking down a row of empty shops.

'I was brought up to behave myself properly – and expect a clip round the ear if I didn't. Just because we weren't posh didn't mean we couldn't have manners, or treat each other with respect. Then, when I was eleven, my whole life was transformed.'

The image on the screen cut from the devastation of the old estate to an image of a very different world. Now Adams was walking across a school campus of clean, modern buildings grouped around a lawn on which pupils sat and talked in the shade of leafy, well-tended trees.

'Without Leeds Grammar I'd be nothing. My parents were so proud. No one in my family had ever been any-where near a place like this before – not unless they were a cleaner or a tea-lady . . . But you've heard enough from me. Time for the people who know me to say their piece.'

A grandfatherly, silver-haired man appeared on screen. A caption read, 'Edward Trower: former housemaster.'

'Mark was always a bright boy,' Trower began. He gave a fond, indulgent chuckle. 'I wouldn't say he was an intellectual, but he had plenty of brains in his head when he felt like using them. Of course, he loved his rugby and played for the school at every age-level. It was no surprise at all to me when he said he wanted to apply to become an army officer. After all, he was the head boy of Lupton House. He was a natural leader.'

16

Donny Bakunin was almost exactly the same age as Mark Adams. He had also attended a grammar school, albeit at the other end of the country. But no one had ever described him as a natural leader back then. He had countless intellectual justifications for his anarchism, but the simple truth was that he loved the idea of a political creed dedicated to smashing the kind of people who naturally ascended to positions of power. Only in middle age had he discovered that he had quite a taste for power himself.

As he made his way down Stewart's Road towards the Wandsworth Road, past the low-rise estate on one side and the close-packed light-industrial units on the other, Bakunin could have been any drab, insignificant Londoner. He was walking fast, as people tended to do in this damp, depressing weather, his duffel-coat hood was turned up to keep the rain off his head, and there was an increasingly soggy roll-up in the corner of his mouth. There was no one else on the pavement, but if anyone had been there to hear the words he was muttering they probably would have taken him for just another nutter – there were a lot of them around these days.

Only if they had paid particular attention would they have realized that the hood of his coat concealed Bakunin's Bluetooth earpiece, through which he was giving a series of orders to the forces now massing in the abandoned council estate. Even then, it would have taken a highly unusual, specialized level of awareness to have deduced that the commands related to a violent act of criminality that was due to begin in a little over twelve minutes. Bakunin was running a minute or two late. He upped his pace still further, almost breaking into a run. It made the rain hit him harder, so that his glasses became so covered in water that he could barely see where he was going. But that did not matter. Bakunin could not afford to be late.

He wasn't the only one on the move. In a deserted side street off Nine Elms Lane one of the men in the parked-up garbage trucks checked his watch. Then he turned to the driver next to him and said, 'Time to go.'

The truck's engine fired up, the lights came on and it rumbled off towards the main road. The second truck was close behind. The man in its passenger seat was checking his reflection in the driver's mirror. His name was Jordan Hayes, but his mates called him 'Random' because they never knew what he'd do next. He had an armoured motorcycle jacket with black plastic plates protecting his chest, back, shoulders, elbows and fore-arms. The plates were outlined in red and made him look well sick, he reckoned, like some evil motherfucker out of *Tron*. Random had a black balaclava over his head with goggles covering his eyes. A tiny ContourROAM HD helmet cam was clipped to the band that held the goggles to his face. Random pressed the record button. From now on, anything he saw, the camera would see too. And he planned to see it all.

17

At the Lion Market, Maninder Panu caught his cousin Ajay's eye and nodded his head to one side, towards the main window of the store. Ajay picked up the hint and looked in that direction. Half a dozen teenage lads, all African by the looks of them, were standing outside on the pavement. One of them was fingering a bowl of apples. He picked an apple up, stood holding it until he was certain that he had attracted the attention of the men inside the shop, then took a large bite out of it and started chewing the fruit, exaggerating every stage of the process, smacking his lips so much he almost seemed to be blowing kisses. He was trying to wind them up, that much was blatantly obvious. He wanted a reaction. So now what?

Maninder turned his attention to Ajay. It wasn't so many years since Ajay had been living the thug life, wearing his trousers halfway down his backside and calling everybody 'rude boi'. He'd grown up a lot since then, but he still wasn't the sort of man to back down from the offer of a fight. Maninder could see the temper rising in him. Any second now he'd be reaching for the baseball bat and walking out the front door, waving it in the African kids' faces. Something told Maninder that that was exactly what they wanted him to do. This was a trap, a set-up, he was sure of it.

'Don't,' he said, before Ajay had even made a move.

'Come on, man, we can't let them disrespect us like that. If they get away with it once, they'll never stop.'

'And if you start a fight you could end up in jail. They're winding us up. They want us to react. Don't give them that satisfaction.' Maninder frowned. Out of the corner of his eye he'd seen something on the CCTV screen that hung beside the till. He lowered his voice and gestured with his index figure: 'Come here, Ajay. Quick!'

The big man scurried over on surprisingly light, nimble feet and looked up at the screen. It showed the views from each of four cameras in rotation. 'There!' whispered Maninder as the picture shifted to the liquor cabinets. 'Look at her!'

There was a young woman on the screen, young enough that she would need an ID to buy any booze. For a moment Ajay thought that Maninder was simply trying to distract him from the goings-on outside, because this chick was stunning, blonde hair falling over the shoulders of a short, furry jacket. Beneath it her breasts were spilling out of a corset a couple of sizes too small to contain them, her crotch was barely covered by a tiny, skintight black microskirt, and she was wearing black tights and heavy red boots. She had a black nylon knapsack in one hand.

Then he noticed what the woman was doing.

She was taking a bottle of vodka off the shelf and sticking it in her bag.

'That's the second one,' hissed Maninder.

The woman wasn't alone. She had a man with her; a boyfriend or a pimp by the looks of things. He looked a lot older than her and a lot bigger: Ajay-sized, in fact.

And it seemed to Maninder that these two, like the kids outside, were putting on a show. They wanted to be seen.

Something was going on here. But what the hell was it?

The next man on screen at the O2 was a sharp contrast to the previous one. For one thing, he was standing outdoors, on a balcony several floors up in a tower block. For another, he was black. His name was Curtley Mackenzie. 'Thirty years ago, it wasn't easy being black in the British Army,' he said. 'There were racists who'd call you a darkie, say you had no place in a white man's regiment. But Mark Adams treated me like a man, like a Para; nothing more and nothing less. If he gave you an order, you jumped to it. But if you were in trouble, you could go to him and he would always listen, always say something to make you feel better.'

The atmosphere in the arena changed. The schoolmaster had been posh, talking about a world that was foreign to most of the crowd. But irrespective of his skin colour, Curtley Mackenzie was talking a language they could understand, and even those who'd never been anywhere near the forces felt as though this was a world that they knew.

'When we went to the Falklands, well, everyone knows about Lieutenant Adams charging an Argentine machine gun single-handed. But what they don't know is what he was like with the lads. He kept us going when we were cold, hungry, frightened, and so tired we felt like we couldn't take another step. He never asked any man to do anything he wouldn't do. I've been to war with Mark Adams. I've trusted him with my life. I'd do it again, and all.'

18

'Typical fucking glory boy,' Schultz muttered into his beer-glass. 'Like Paras are the only bastards who ever took out a GPMG . . . I'm going to need a Scotch after that.'

He and Carver were sitting at the bar of the Dutchman's Head. There was a large-screen TV on the wall, left over from the days when Champions League nights were a virtual guarantee of a packed pub, filled with thirsty punters. There weren't too many people willing to go to a pub just to watch a politician give a speech. But of the half-dozen regulars, most were keeping at least an eye on proceedings at the O2.

Carver caught the barmaid's attention. 'Get him a double whisky or he'll be moaning all night.'

'What's his problem with Paras?' she asked, pushing the whisky glass up to the optic.

Carver leaned forward, 'Can you keep a secret?' he asked.

The barmaid giggled. 'Depends how good it is.'

She put the filled glass on the bar, tantalizingly out of Schultz's reach, and leaned forward towards Carver. 'Well, it's a sad story,' he said. 'See, he always wanted to be a Para but he couldn't get in. Scared of heights. I mean, really, really scared. Forget jumping, he couldn't even get in the plane.'

Carver started laughing as he heard Schultz's voice off to one side going, 'I'll get you for that, you bastard!'

But he had laughed too soon. A look of profound sympathy crossed the barmaid's face. She stood up, picked up the glass and carried it over to Schultz, who downed the contents in one.

'I know just how you feel,' she said. 'I'm the same. I get terrified even thinking about having to fly. Has it always been a problem for you?'

Schultz nodded sorrowfully. He'd been given an opening and he was going to exploit it. 'No, it came over me quite recently,' he confided, lying through his teeth. 'I always used to be able to fly. And maybe I could do it again, you know, if I had the right company.' He looked her right in the eye. 'Someone to comfort me, know what I mean?'

'Do you think that would help?' the barmaid said. 'Maybe we could comfort each other . . .'

'It would help if I knew your name.'

'Chrystal. What's yours?'

'Snoopy . . . to me friends.'

'Aw, that's sweet!'

Schultz looked across at Carver, a smug look of triumph on his face. 'You can leave now, mate,' he said.

A few miles away across the river, in his Downing Street office, Cameron Young pressed the 'pause' button on his Sky Plus controller. 'What next, do you think?' he asked, to no one in particular.

Jack Grantham was the first to answer. 'After two men? It's got to be a woman.'

'Or an Asian,' Brian Smallbone pointed out. 'Muslims are the new Jews. If he's fascist and stupid, he'll attack them. But if he's smart he'll make a point of playing nicey-nicey.'

'So there we have it,' said Young. 'We think it'll be an Asian woman. Let's see if we're right.'

They were. Samira Ahmed looked young, elegantly dressed, glossy haired, impeccably professional – like an Asian Kate Middleton. She'd been filmed in a coffee-bar with a cup of cappuccino in front of her. 'Little Miss Starbucks – very normal, aspirational, nice touch,' Cameron Young murmured.

'When I was a little girl, I was the only person in the family who could speak English, and I often had to be the interpreter for everyone else,' Ahmed started. 'So when they applied for accommodation from the local housing association, I went along with them, and there was Mark Adams, this famous bloke off the telly, doing volunteer work for the association, and he was the one who took care of everything. I remember him being really kind to me. And he made sure we had somewhere to live. As far as my mum and dad are concerned, he's a saint.'

'Shit, that's not bad,' said Smallbone. 'I mean, it might just work.'

Young grimaced in agreement.

'Don't panic just yet,' said Jack Grantham. 'Adams hasn't even got onstage yet. There's still plenty of time left for him to cock it up.'

'You think he will?' Young asked.

'Why not? He's a politician, isn't he?'

19

Alix suddenly felt a hand grip hers and squeeze it tight. It was Nicki Adams.

'I'm sorry,' she said with a nervous smile. 'Mark's on any second now. I'm just a bit tense.'

Then the screen went blank. The stage was shrouded in darkness and the crowd roared as if they were about to see a rock star, not an MP.

'The time has come,' boomed a voice familiar from countless Saturday-night TV shows. 'So please put your hands together for a man who has served his country and its people . . . A man who dreams of a better future for all of us . . . A man who knows that the only way is UPP . . . Ladies and gentleman, this . . . is . . . Mark . . . ADAMS!!'

Suddenly the lights came back up again, blindingly bright, and there in the middle of the stage stood Adams himself. He had no podium in front of him. He was pacing up and down, from one side of the stage to the other, soaking up the adulation and stoking it even higher as he returned the crowd's applause.

'Isn't he wonderful?' cried Nicki Adams, ecstatically.

Alix was taking in the frenzy of noise and excitement all around them. She had to admit that this man was blessed with genuine charisma, the kind of star quality that can be neither taught nor faked. She wasn't sure how well he'd go down with the sophisticated opinion-formers of Washington DC, but the Fox News demographic – white, ageing, conservative and fearful – would lap him up. It helped that he had the same quality as Lincoln Roberts: he absolutely looked like a leader and exuded an alpha-male aura of power that she was certain was making every female heart in the arena beat a little faster. No wonder Nicki Adams was excited if she was the one he was coming home to.

'Good evening. My name is Mark Adams.' He could not have said the words in a more casual, understated way, but they were enough to start the cheering all over again. He waited for the noise to die down and went on, 'I just want to say thank you ... Thanks to all of you for coming here tonight ... Thank you for giving me the chance to share my vision of a better, happier, fairer Britain with you tonight ... And ...' He gave a wry, self-deprecating smile. 'Thanks for the money. It means a lot. You see, in this party we don't have a bunch of multi-millionaire bankers and property developers keeping the coffers filled. We don't have trade unions using their members' money to pay our bills. All we have is what you, the people, are willing to give us. And that's a good thing. In fact, it's a great thing.'

Adams paused. He looked out at the hall, scanning the stands so that thousands of people out there would be convinced that he had made eye contact with them personally, and then continued with a steadily rising intensity as he declared, 'We are the United People's Party. We don't answer to anyone but the people. And if we do any favours, we do them for the people!'

Once again, Adams had to wait to let the cheers and clapping die down.

'Now, some of my opponents don't like the way I'm taking power back to the people. They moan that I'm some kind of fascist . . . a neo-Nazi . . . a right little Hitler. Mostly it just makes me laugh. I know the only reason that the major parties and their toadies in the media keep slandering me and this party is because they're scared. They know they've been found out. They've got us all into this mess. They haven't got the first idea how to get us out of it. And they're terrified that someone else has.'

Now Adams started pacing again, as though there was something eating away at him, making it impossible to stay still. 'But sometimes . . . sometimes . . . I can't help but get angry at the lies they tell. I've gone to war for this country. I've risked my life to defend freedom . . . to stand up for the values of tolerance, decency and fairness that make Britain great. So when I am accused of betraying those very same values by the cowardly . . . corrupt . . . incompetent . . . dishonest . . . money-grubbing pack of stinking sewer-rats currently occupying the Palace of

Westminster, well, that just makes me want to take their lies and their slanders and their accusations and stuff them straight . . . back . . . down . . . their throats!'

Listening to the roar that greeted those words, looking at the rapt, ecstatic expressions on the faces all around her, Alix began to worry. Adams might deny that he was a little Hitler, but the fever he was stirring up reminded her of the images she'd seen in countless documentaries of the Führer working his followers into a frenzy at his night-rallies in the Berlin Sportpalast; the Soviet officials greeting Stalin with rapture at this or that party congress; the massed ranks of uniformed followers roaring their allegiance to China's Chairman Mao, or any one of North Korea's endless succession of Kims. Adams had an astonishing ability to arouse and manipulate emotion, and if he could somehow use that ability for good he might actually be the saviour his followers were praying for. But if that power was used for ends that were evil, well, then he might just be the demon that his enemies insisted he was.

20

The longer Mark Adams spoke, the angrier Kieron Sproles became. He could feel his guts tying themselves in knots as Adams kept blathering his mindless, meaningless slogans. 'You, me, all the people who are sick of seeing our country falling apart around our ears . . . We're going to get UPP on our feet, roll UPP our sleeves, and get this great nation moving on UPP in the world again!'

They were cheering, the idiots. Couldn't they see he was lying? Couldn't they recognize bullshit when they smelled it? Well, he'd had enough. Adams had come right to the front of the stage. He was standing almost close enough for Sproles to reach out and touch. Except that he wasn't going to touch him, he had something else in mind.

Kieron Sproles reached into his jacket.

He pulled out the Glock.

He pointed it.

And at the very moment that the woman next to him noticed what was in his hand and screamed out, 'Gun!'

He fired.

'Jesus Christ!' Carver shouted as he heard the shot and saw Adams fall to the floor.

Nicki Adams screamed – a wail of animal pain as she saw her man go down.

'Bloody hell,' said Cameron Young, almost casually, as if he were far too sophisticated a player to be shocked by anything.

Kieron Sproles kept firing.

All around him there was total panic as people tried to get away from the gun.

The security men in their fluorescent yellow waistcoats were all cowering behind the barrier that separated the crowd from the stage. No way were they going to charge an armed man.

And then Mark Adams got to his feet. Even as Sproles was blasting the last two shots in his magazine, Adams was standing, stock still, in front of him. And then, when the trigger clicked on an empty magazine, Adams walked very calmly to the edge of the stage. He stepped over to the barrier until he was right opposite the gunman, who was standing motionless, looking dazed, as though his brain had been emptied like his gun.

Adams held out his right hand. 'Give me the gun,' he

said, very calmly, and because he was wearing a radio mike, the whole arena heard him.

All the people who had been rushing for the exits stopped and turned, staring back at the stage or up at the images on the video screens as Adams repeated, 'I said, "Give me the gun."'

There was a hypnotic certainty about the way he spoke. He had not raised his voice at all, but somehow he conveyed the message that his command was essentially a statement of fact. The gun would be handed over. No alternative possibility existed.

Kieron Sproles felt exhausted. The nervous energy that had sustained him through the past few days and sleepless nights had fled from his body, and the gun seemed to weigh so much that he couldn't even hold it up any more. His right arm just hung limply at his side. It was almost a relief to do what Adams asked and hand over the Glock. Once he did the last shred of strength left him, and by the time the security men came to carry him away he was slumped, barely conscious, in his seat, and had no desire at all to resist.

Nicki Adams was in Alix's arms, sobbing helplessly, unable to comprehend the evidence of her own eyes. Her husband had been shot dead. Then he had risen up without a scratch on him. It was all too much to take in.

'It's got to be a set-up,' said Cameron Young, and not only did the two men in that Downing Street office agree with him, so did a host of bloggers and tweeters. Soon the arguments were raging back and forth between Adams's supporters – for whom this was one more example of their idol's heroism – and cynical critics who saw anything between a cheap stunt and a full-blown fascist conspiracy.

Donny Bakunin hadn't been aware of anything that had happened at the O2. He'd been picked up by one of the garbage trucks on the Wandsworth Road as it made its way towards Netherton Street. They were only a couple of hundred metres away now. He spoke into his earpiece. 'Five minutes. Get ready.'

At the bar of the Dutchman's Head, Schultz had broken off negotiations with the barmaid and was frowning at the screen, trying to work out what the hell was going on. Carver laughed to himself as he lifted his glass in an ironic toast. 'Nice one, you jammy bastard,' he said to himself. He'd just worked out how Adams had done it.

21

Mark Adams got back onstage and faced the crowd. Many of the seats were empty now, and the gangways were packed with people uncertain what to do next. His head of personal security was screaming at him, 'You've got to get out of here – now! There's a car waiting. Come on. Get out. Go!'

Adams ignored him. He knew he had a few seconds in which to find the right words to get everyone back in their places. If he could do that, if he could somehow get the show back on the rails, this might still be remembered for all the right reasons. 'No!' he snapped, and physically shoved the other man away from him. 'I came here to give a speech, and I'm bloody well going to give it.'

A murmur went through the crowd. There were a few isolated cheers and shouts of encouragement, but nothing like the mass excitement that had been there just a minute or two beforehand.

Adams took a deep breath. He closed his eyes and ran a hand through his hair, aware that all his gestures were still being captured by the cameras and shown on the video screens. Then he opened his eyes again, nodded to himself and looked back out at the arena. He had to keep this very simple: direct words that would make sense to scrambled minds and senses.

'Don't worry. It's all right.' A rueful smile. 'I've been shot at often enough. I'm used to it. And I'm not going anywhere.'

He could feel the atmosphere change a fraction. They were a little calmer. Another smile and a polite enquiry: 'So . . . is everyone all right out there?'

There was a feeble, ragged response – no more than a smattering of assent.

Now Adams smiled like an indulgent father faced with a recalcitrant child. 'Oh, come on, you can do better than that. Is everyone all right?'

This time the 'Yes!' that came back at him was just a little louder.

'Do you want to hear what I have to say?'

'Yes!'

'Do you want me to carry on?'

The energy was coming back to them now: there were cheers and whistles as well as shouts of, 'Yes!'

Adams was grinning now and there was a touch of pantomime knowingness as he asked, 'Are you sure about that?' And then, 'I can't hear you . . . I said: "Are you sure about that?"'

Now the noise was back and the arena was rocking again.

'All right . . . that's better,' Adams said. Like all great performers he had made his audience feel that they were part of the show, so that they were cheering themselves now as much as him. For the next couple of minutes he coaxed them all back to their seats, picking out individual members of the audience, stopping for a joke or a quick chat, sealing the bond between him and them. Finally, when everyone was settled, he said, 'Right then, we've got a job to do – all of us – so let me tell you just what it is.'

22

Netherton Street was nothing special: typical inner-London. It was terraced on either side in a random mix of red- and grey-brick buildings, bay-fronted and flat. Some of them were painted in faded pastel colours or dirty white, others were rendered. For a block and a half the ground floors on either side of the road were occupied by commercial premises – at least a third of them empty – with flats on the first and second floors. The Dutchman's Head stood on the corner of a block and was painted dark green.

Paula Miklosko used the street as a short cut, the kind of rat run every Londoner knows through his or her own neighbourhood. As she first turned into it in her Suzuki Swift she wasn't aware of anything unusual. She was too distracted by the pandemonium on the radio, the shooting at the O2 and Mark Adams's amazing response, to pay much attention to what was going on around her. But then the first flaming bottle went arcing through the air and crashed on to the tarmac in front of her, and suddenly there was nothing else in her mind but the fire on the road – a fire that blazed despite the falling rain – and the prowling, hooded figures that had suddenly appeared out of the darkness all around her. As she slammed on the brakes, Paula caught the glint of streetlights falling on the blade of a machete. She saw a man with a length of iron piping walking towards the stationary car and realized that the teeth behind his wolfish grin were gold. She suddenly felt horribly vulnerable, knowing that the locked door of her car offered no protection, no sanctuary at all.

She had to get out of here right away.

She put the accelerator to the floor and rocketed up the road, not slowing for anyone, feeling a couple of glancing impacts as bodies bounced off the racing machine, ignoring the explosions going off on either side of the street and the brick that smashed against the windscreen and sent a spider's web of cracks through the safety glass.

She had almost reached the far end of Netherton Street. She was so close to safety. And then a huge black shadow crossed her field of vision, blurred and indistinct through the shattered, wet windscreen. It took her a second that seemed to last an age to work out that she was looking at a massive garbage truck. And this was no insubstantial shadow, but a solid mass of metal. She was heading straight towards it. And when she braked as hard as she could her tyres just skidded against the rain-slicked tarmac and she found herself sliding helplessly towards that huge, unyielding, deadly cliff of steel.

23

It happened so fast. One second the couple inside the shop were just another couple of lowlife shoplifters and the lads outside were simply cocky, piss-taking teenagers, and the next the man Maninder Panu had taken for a pimp had a bottle in his hand. It hadn't come from the Lion Market shelves. It had a rag stuffed into its neck.

The pimp was putting a match to the rag and now Ajay was grabbing the baseball bat, vaulting over the counter and charging at the man, bellowing in rage. The girl started screaming, but the pimp stayed quite calm and waited until Ajay was within two or three metres of him before he gently lobbed the bottle in his direction.

Ajay hurled himself to one side and his life was saved by a stroke of pure chance. There was a gap in the line of shelves at that point, and he didn't hit anything more substantial than a free-standing promotional display for

Haribo sweets, which gave way under the impact of his seventeen-stone bulk. He hit the ground, rolling away from the impact of the bottle as it exploded in a shower of jagged glass shrapnel and sent a mist of flame rolling across the supermarket floor.

Ignoring the fire licking at the shelves, Ajay picked himself up and chased after the couple, waving the baseball bat in their direction. They were heading for the exit, the pimp in the lead, leaving the girl to fend for herself. Ajay couldn't bring himself to hit her with the bat, but he used the end of it to give her a sharp shove between the shoulder blades which sent her stumbling forward into the pimp.

They were right by the door. A brick smashed through the window from outside, landing between him and the girl. Just before she followed the pimp outside, she turned round, looked straight at him, her face twisted and ugly with poisonous fury, and shrieked a high-pitched blast of furious invective, and he caught the words, 'Muslim scumbags!'

Now Ajay was shouting, but not at her, at Maninder: 'Close the shutters ... and hit the fucking fire alarm!'

Maninder's warrior spirit had deserted him, if it had ever existed at all. He had been paralysed by what he'd seen happening in front of his eyes. Not just the couple inside the shop: the African kids outside had somehow got hold of bricks and small, rough lumps of concrete and were throwing them at the front window. The glass was supposed to be specially strengthened but some of the missiles were getting through, others cracking the surface, and any second now the whole thing was going to give way.

Maninder heard Ajay scream at him again, 'Fuck's sake, Maninder man . . . Shutters! Alarm!'

But there wasn't any need to break the glass on the alarm because there was smoke rising from one of the shelves, a detector picked it up and suddenly a siren was howling and a blue light was flashing on the outside wall, casting an eerie light on the gaggle of young rioters on the pavement.

Maninder could see them gathering round the table that had held the one-pound fruit and veg bowls. They were sweeping the bowls on to the ground, and for a second he couldn't help himself thinking about the cost of all that ruined produce. As if that mattered now. Out on the street he could see a crowd of people running to and fro, attacking other businesses just like his. The whole world was falling apart. There was nowhere to run to. He was panicking, his mind was scrambled, and he could not remember what Ajay had told him to do – Ajay, who was taking control now, even though he was the younger cousin.

Ajay appeared out of the smoke and glared at Maninder. Without saying a word, he leaned across the counter and pushed the button that controlled the shopfront security shutters.

'Pass me the fire extinguisher,' Ajay said. 'If you think you can manage that.'

The shutters began rattling down over the cracked and broken glass. But then Maninder, whose eyes were still fixed on the people outside, realized what they were doing. They'd lifted the table, turned it round and were smashing it against the window like a battering ram: once . . . twice . . .

Ajay aimed the fire extinguisher at the flickering flames on the supermarket floor. The shutters were coming down but they seemed to be taking an age.

Three times . . . four . . .

Maninder cursed himself for his foolhardy optimism. Most mini-supermarkets like his had shelves running along their outside wall – even if it was windowed. Their owners wanted to use every square millimetre of space to sell more goods. But Maninder had said no, it was better to let customers walking down the road look in and see all the wonderful things they had on offer. He had won the argument, but now he wished that he hadn't. He felt horribly exposed by the huge pane of glass that covered almost the entire frontage of the store, and he longed for a long, tall, heavy line of shelves to act as a wall against the evil of the outside world.

Five . . . six . . .

The flames were out. The shutters were almost down to the level of the table. If they could cover the window before the table broke through it . . .

But that wasn't going to happen. The table broke through, the entire window shattered and the table was left half in and half out of the shop just as the shutters reached it, hit the table top and came to a grinding halt.

Seconds later there were rioters scrambling under the stranded shutters and Ajay was lashing out at them and shouting at him to get the gun.

Maninder knew what he had to do. That gun was their

only hope. But somehow he couldn't reach for it. He was paralysed. And meanwhile more and more rioters were coming through the window. Ajay was being driven back.

Only then did it occur to Maninder that there was one obvious thing he should have done the minute he saw the two shoplifters acting suspiciously: call the police. He dialled 999 . . . and all he got was a pre-recorded message saying that the line was experiencing an exceptionally heavy volume of calls. He was offered a menu of options for leaving messages. Or he could dial 0 and wait for an operator. But the phone seemed to ring for ever without a response.

No one was going to answer.

The police weren't going to come.

All the other members of the Netherton Street Self-Help Association were too busy dealing with their own problems to worry about his.

And the Lion Market would soon be overrun.

24

Random was well pleased with the scenes he was getting on his head cam. It was more like a party than anything. Everyone was loaded. They went charging into shops and takeaways shouting at the top of their voices, waving knives and crowbars above their heads, some of them pulling faces for the camera. They'd grab whatever they wanted and scare the shit out of everyone in the place. Nothing heavy – just aim a kick or a punch at people as they ran away, maybe cop a feel of the girls' arses and tits. A few of the lads had guns, but they were just firing them in the air, mostly, blowing holes in ceilings and smashing plate-glass windows. It was all a big laugh, really. Even when they were setting places on fire it seemed like a bit of a lark.

Then they got to this curry house called the Khyber Star. In they went, kicking over tables, sending plates of chicken tikka and pints of beer flying. There were only half a dozen punters in here, and they were bricking it. The women were screaming. The men were dragging them to the door, trying to make them shut up. One of the men slipped on the curry sauce lying on the floor, fell over and got a good kicking before he managed to crawl away. All the waiters had gone behind the bar, trying to get out of the way. But then Random saw one of them, this skinny little Bangladeshi geezer, reach down below the bar and pull something out. It took Random a second to work out what it was because it was the last thing he expected to see. A sawn-off shotgun – what the fuck was that all about?

The Bangladeshi didn't even know how to use the gun. He just waved it in the general direction of the mob piling into his restaurant, pulled the trigger, and was almost knocked off his feet by the unexpected power of the recoil. The deafening noise of the gun going off was still echoing round the cramped dining-room as a shriek cut through the ringing in everyone's ears. Random turned his head and saw one of the rioters, a teenage girl, screaming incoherently and pointing to something on the floor. He pushed through the crowd, knocking tables and chairs out of the way to get a better view, and then wished he hadn't because the thing the girl was pointing at was the mashed-up bloody remains of a lad's face. The full force of the blast had hit him and blown his eyes, his nose, his mouth – every single recognizable feature – to pulp. They just weren't there any more.

And suddenly it was like a switch had been flicked. All the positive, high-spirited energy turned nasty in the blink of an eye. Forget the orders to keep violence to a minimum. The people wanted revenge. They wanted blood.

The crowd surged towards the bar. The Bangladeshi threw the gun away, as if he was trying to pretend it had nothing to do with him. But it was too late. People were grabbing the Khyber Star staff and hacking at them with their knives, butchering them where they stood. A couple of the cooks made a run for it. They got to the door and were a few paces out on to the street by the time they were caught and chopped to pieces.

People who'd not been in the Khyber Star saw that, and somehow it infected them with the same bloodlust. Some of them started running towards the pub, the Dutchman's Head, and there was a new air of menace about their charge. The old man they'd picked up in the truck, Bakunin, was trying to stop them but they were ignoring him. Another, smaller posse was heading in another direction, towards a small car that had crashed broadsides into one of the garbage trucks. A woman was trying to get out of the car.

Random decided to follow the lads who were making for the car. He had the feeling he'd get some more great pictures there.

25

Carver heard the first bottle-bomb detonating as it hit the road, followed immediately after by several more explosions, then shouting, the squeal of a skidding, desperately braking car and the smash of metal on metal. Then the front door of the pub burst open and there were people streaming in. They were male and female, black and white, aged anywhere from early teens to middle age. They carried knives, pipes, clubs of every kind. One of them was even waving a handgun above his head. All they had in common were the hoods, hats and masks covering their faces and the hostility and aggression blazing in their eyes.

Schultz was staring at the mob, but he didn't seem scared. The look on his face and the expression in his voice was more one of outrage as he shouted, 'What the fuck are you doing here?' like they were disobeying an order.

The intruders ignored him. The gun went off, blasting a hole in the ceiling. But it didn't have the effect they might have expected. Instead of yelling in terror and running for their lives, the regulars in the pub seemed to be galvanized by the sound of the shot. Two or three of them were even pulling out weapons of their own. Carver saw one of them wielding a fearsome-looking machete with a long, curved blade – like a cross between a scythe and a scimitar – that could slice through a human limb as easily as if it was jungle undergrowth.

A battle was breaking out, and Carver wanted no part of it. He looked across at Schultz: 'Time we got out.'

Schultz snapped right back into the role he had played almost two decades earlier: the tough NCO taking orders from a Special Boat Service officer who'd earned his respect the only way that really counted with him – on the battlefield.

'Got you, boss.'

'And bring her.'

Schultz grabbed Chrystal by the upper arm. 'Where's the back way out of here?'

'Through there,' she said, pointing to a door behind the bar, and trying to make sense of the transformation that had suddenly come over Snoopy, the man who was scared of flying. He didn't look scared of anything now.

'Right, love,' Schultz said. 'Lead the way. Fast as you can go.'

She lifted up the flap at one end of the bar to let them through, and they followed her into a small kitchen. Schultz stepped across to a rack of knives and got out the longest one he could find. Carver moved past him to a broom that was leaning against the wall. The handle was wooden. He leaned it against a counter, stamped down hard and snapped it in two. Now he had a baton, roughly 75cm long, with a jagged end. Stick that in someone's throat or face and they'd know all about it; jab the round end hard under their diaphragm or into their kidneys and, again, they'd be nicely softened up.

The back door at the far end of the kitchen led to a small, cobbled yard, no more than four metres across. Plastic crates and empty metal beer kegs were piled against the back wall of the pub. On the far side of the yard were two large, wheeled metal rubbish bins, about one and a half metres high, with hinged metal lids. To the left the yard ended in a double gate made of high, spiked metal bars. The gate was secured by a thick chain. Carver cursed to himself. The girl had led them into a dead end. No! There was a way out. If they rolled one of the bins up to the fence it should give them enough of a leg-up to get over without too much trouble, the girl included.

It was still raining, if anything a little harder than before. No, make that a lot harder.

Carver went up to the nearest bin and positioned himself behind it. He called across to Schultz. 'Give me a hand.'

Schultz didn't need to be told what Carver was thinking. One look at the bins and the gate was all it took. He stood next to Carver, stuck his knife in his belt and they started pushing. The swivel wheels rattled against the wet cobbles and swung from side to side as skittishly as a supermarket trolley, but they were making steady progress when Schultz said, 'What the fuck's occurring now?'

Carver had been pushing with his arms out and his head down. He looked up to see a group of rioters crossing the road towards the gate, coming in their direction. If the pub hadn't been overrun by now it would be very soon. There was no way out apart from the gate.

The three of them were trapped.

26

A much older man was leading the rioters coming towards the gate. The hood of his duffle coat was down, enabling Carver to see his painfully thin, sunken face, topped by a few unbrushed tufts of grey hair, the eyes hidden behind rain-spattered, metal-framed glasses. Physically, he was less imposing than any of the people around him, and yet he was unquestionably their leader. 'Hey, you!' he shouted out, looking at Carver and the others. 'What happened in the pub?'

'Fuckin' 'ell,' Schultz hissed. 'He thinks we're on his side.'

'Better not disappoint him.'

'No worries.' Schultz raised his voice and called out: 'Just moppin' up the bastards now.'

To Carver's surprise the older man seemed bothered by the news. 'That wasn't meant to happen,' he snapped crossly. He turned his head towards one of the other rioters next to him, a Rasta with his locks piled up inside a knitted tam cap. 'Open the gates.'

The Rasta stepped forward. He was carrying a heavy-duty, 760mm bolt-cutter. It snapped through the chain like scissors through ribbon. Bakunin called out. 'We need that rubbish bin. Bring it here. Now!'

'Posh fucker, isn't he?' Schultz said to Carver as they started pushing again.

'Maybe, but he's getting us out of here.'

Schultz turned his head towards the barmaid. 'Oi, Chrystal, give us a hand!'

As she joined them, Schultz told her, 'Don't say nothing, yeah? Just do whatever we do and we'll get you out of here. All right?'

She nodded, her expression wide-eyed and fearful.

As they pushed the bin out into the side street, the grey-haired man directed them to turn right. A barricade was being erected about twenty metres away, blocking off the road and preventing any access to Netherton Street. The bin was taken from them and shoved between an overturned Transit van and the side of a parked BMW 5 Series. Carver saw Schultz wincing as the bin scraped along the BMW's glossy flanks, leaving a trail of dents and scratches in its wake until it was finally jammed solid. More rioters followed, bringing the second bin and a trolley piled with beer kegs.

The massive shadowy figure of a man was perched halfway up the barricade. His back was turned, but something about him sent an apprehensive chill through Carver. A woman who'd been walking beside the trolley called out, 'Curtis!' The man stopped what he was doing, turned around and looked at her. 'What do you want us to do with these?' she asked.

Carver took in the leather jacket, beanie hat and rugby-player's face. Curtis was the big man he'd encountered less than half an hour earlier in the abandoned council estate. He hadn't spotted Carver yet. He was too busy dealing with the woman's question. He walked over to the trolley, picked up an eleven-gallon keg as easily as if it were a pint of milk and threw it on to the barricade.

Now he spotted Carver, walked right up close and growled, 'Thought I told you not to come here.'

Carver said nothing.

Curtis looked at him and very quietly said, 'And now I'm telling you to get the fuck out. All right?'

Carver nodded and started walking away.

'What was all that about?' Schultz asked as they headed back up the road.

'He thought he knew me. Right . . . Time to get back up to Netherton Street. We need to be out of here before this place really kicks off.'

'Bit late for that,' said Chrystal, pointedly.

'So we need to get out even faster, then, don't we?'

27

They had reached the junction with Netherton Street. The Dutchman's Head was right beside them. Someone had torn down the pub sign, which was lying on the pavement being stamped on by a rioter in construction boots. A wisp of smoke seemed to be seeping out through one of the upstairs windows. On the ground floor the windows facing the street had been broken and they heard the sound of someone inside, a man, begging for mercy.

The pitiful sound of his pleading caught Carver off-guard and he felt a stabbing pain in his guts at the unwanted memories it brought back: all the times when he had been battered and helpless, down on his knees, or bound and gagged waiting for the end to come.

'I'm not listening to that,' said Schultz, pulling his knife out of his belt and stepping towards the broken windows.

Schultz was as impetuous as he was courageous. He never stopped to consider the odds against him when he went into battle. Carver had always been more calculating. He was only willing to risk his neck when he knew what he was up against, had worked out his plan of attack, and possessed the equipment needed to do the job. None of those conditions applied now. He came up behind Schultz, swung his right arm and wrapped it tight around Schultz's neck, gripping him in a chokehold. 'Forget it,' he said. 'There's nothing we can do.'

Carver could feel the energy coursing through Schultz's body. He was fired-up, breathing heavily, the knuckles of his right hand white with tension around the handle of his knife. Carver readied himself. Schultz might just be so angry he'd try to fight his way out of the hold. He wouldn't take kindly to being shown up in front of Chrystal, who was watching the two men anxiously. She'd trusted her safety to these two. The last thing she needed was them starting on each other.

'Stop it!' she cried out. 'Stop fighting!'

For a second or two they stayed locked together, then Carver felt the tension ease a fraction from Schultz's body and heard a grunt of grudging assent. He let his arm drop from the other man's neck. They stepped apart. Neither man said a word, but when Carver turned round and walked out into Netherton Street itself Schultz and Chrystal both followed him.

And walked right into a vision of total, unrestrained anarchy.

Fires had broken out everywhere: parked cars were ablaze, and searing orange and yellow flames billowed from the scorched windows of looted shops. The rioters had trapped several cars in Netherton Street, cutting off their attempts at escape. One was slewed across the road. Its driver's door was open and a man's body was hanging half out of it, suspended from his safety belt. A group of kids who barely even looked in their teens were clustered around another car. An elderly woman was lying motionless on the ground beside it, but they were ignoring her completely as they squabbled amongst themselves, fighting for the right to get in and drive. Small groups of rioters were running to and fro aimlessly, looking for something to do, some new target to attack.

Carver looked up the street and saw a blue alarm light flashing outside the Lion Market. The shutters were half-down, evidently blocked by some obstruction, though he could not see what it was: the dozen or so people gathered outside, shouting and throwing things, were in the way. One of them made a dart for the shopfront and dived under the shutter. A few seconds later he rolled out again, clutching his head. Blood was streaming through his fingers. Carver thought of the big lad he'd seen putting out the fruit and veg. It looked like he was holding the fort. The other one, behind the counter, had been no one's idea of a fighter.

He looked around for a means of escape and his spirits fell even further. Both ends of the road were completely blocked by garbage trucks, and both trucks had people by them. It would be next to impossible to sneak past undetected.

A car had skidded to a halt by one of the trucks. Another scrum of people was gathered round it. They'd pulled open the door and were dragging out a woman. She was long-limbed and slender as a gazelle, and about as defenceless, too, as she writhed frantically, trying to wriggle out of her attackers' grasp and evade the punches they were raining down on her, and making futile attempts to hit or scratch them back. Some of the men around her had hunting knives or machetes in their hands, their blades glinting in the firelight.

This time Schultz didn't give Carver the chance to stop him. He just started running towards the car.

'Shit!' muttered Carver. He looked at his old sergeant. It was one thing being calculating enough to stop him doing something stupid. It was quite another standing by and watching him go to his death. 'Stay here,' he said to Chrystal. 'Do nothing. I'll be back.'

And then he sprinted after Schultz, his baton in his hand, straight towards the mob and the screaming, desperate woman.

28

Paula Miklosko wasn't thinking any more. She was barely conscious of fear or pain. Hers were the raw, instinctive, unconscious reactions of a trapped animal, operating on nothing but survival instinct. The snarling, shouting faces around her were as much animal as human, too; as untamed and unfeeling as a pack of wolves.

Through the crowd she could see another two men rushing towards her like more scavengers running to feed on a bloodied corpse. But then they got to the pack and suddenly everything changed. She saw a knife flash and blood spurt from a severed throat, and another one of her attackers double over as a blade sliced into his gut. One of the new arrivals had what looked like a stick in his hand. It didn't seem like much of a weapon but he was jabbing it at his targets and following up with a blur of kicks and jabbed elbows that left them doubled over in pain – and defenceless against further brutally effective slaps to their lower faces that made their heads twist round on their necks and sent them spinning to the ground.

Most of the men around her took one look at the clinical brutality being meted out and ran for it. But one stood his ground. His face was hidden behind a black balaclava and a pair of goggles with a black metal cylinder that looked like a small torch attached to them. He looked like some kind of futuristic warrior in a suit of black armour plating as he reached round to the small of his back and pulled a gun out of his waistband. He raised his arm, bringing the gun to bear on the two onrushing men. But before his arm had even straightened in front of him the knife was flashing through the air and burying itself up to its hilt in his throat. He dropped the gun and fell to the ground, dead by the time he hit the pavement.

One of the newcomers came up and took Paula in his arms. 'You OK?' he asked, looking into her eyes as though they might give him the answer he needed.

Paula mumbled some kind of incoherent reply. The man who was holding her said, 'It's all right, it's all right,' and it was the tone of his voice more than the words themselves that calmed her a little.

The other man, the taller and burlier of the two, was standing over the corpse. He picked up the gun that was lying nearby. He took the magazine out, checked it, replaced it and racked the slide. Then he said, 'Piece of Chinese shit, but it might just come in handy.'

* * *

Carver heard Schultz's voice, but in the deafening cacophony of the riot could not make out what he'd just said. He turned his head in Schultz's direction and was about to ask, 'What?' when something caught his eye: something black on the side of the dead man's head. He pointed at it and shouted, 'What's that?'

Schultz bent down again to take a look. 'Video cam!'

'Take it!'

Schultz got down on his haunches to detach the camera from the goggles. At close range he could see there was a cheap gold-plate chain round the man's neck, just below where the knife had hit. In the middle of the chain, underneath the knife itself, was a name: Random.

'Well, you got that right,' Schultz said to himself.

He removed the camera and held it up so Carver could see it. 'You want this?'

'Yeah, thanks.'

Schultz threw the camera over to Carver, who caught it one-handed and stuffed it in a jacket pocket.

'Now what?' Schultz asked, stepping back to Carver and the woman, who was still visibly shaking with fear and shock.

'We've got to get out of here before anyone decides to get their own back on us,' Carver replied. He paused as a thought struck him: 'Shit!'

'What's the matter?' Schultz asked.

'We could leave right now, just crawl under the truck and vanish . . . But Chrystal's back up the road and we're not going without her.'

'Too bloody right we're not . . . Look, she's my bird, so

I'll go get her. You take this one, get the fuck out now and I'll catch up with you.'

Carver shook his head. 'No, I'm not leaving you in the middle of this. Get Chrystal. Bring her back. I'll wait.'

Schultz didn't argue. He sprinted back down the road. Carver looked past Schultz towards the undiminished mayhem and confusion of the riot. He heaved a sigh of relief when he spotted Chrystal. She'd done as she was told and stayed put, just moving a few metres to make herself as inconspicuous as possible in the shadow of a building. He saw her wave as she realized Schultz was coming back to her, excitedly letting him know where she was.

Carver turned back to the woman they'd rescued. 'Don't worry,' he said to her. 'We'll have you out of here in no time.'

He was about to ask her name when he saw it would be pointless. She was glassy eyed and entirely non-responsive. Through the open door of her car he could see her handbag, sitting on the passenger seat. He pulled it out. There was a wallet inside and a driving licence in the name of Paula Miklosko.

'There you go, Paula,' Carver said, though in her present state it made no more sense than talking to a cat. Her body was as slack and lifeless as a puppet with no strings. Carver passed the bag over her limp hand and up her arm so that it was hanging from her shoulder. He looked for Schultz and Chrystal. They were walking back down the road. Schultz had his arm round Chrystal's shoulder. She was gazing up at him. They were both concentrating on each other.

They had no idea of the crowd bearing down on them from behind. The mob was no more than thirty metres away from Schultz and Chrystal, and those at the front of it were just breaking into a run.

29

The men who'd fled when they rescued Paula Miklosko must have gone for reinforcements. Carver could see a couple of them among the runners bearing down on his friends. The presence of so many people around them had restored their fighting spirit and now they were bent on revenge.

There were more scurrying figures dashing down the side of the road. Carver understood at once that they were trying to outflank him, get behind the garbage truck and cut off his line of escape. Another figure caught his eye, if only because he was standing quite still at the centre of the storm: the skinny, grey-haired man who'd given them their orders in the yard at the back of the Dutchman's Head. He was very coolly directing his forces and, Carver had to admit, doing it pretty well.

Carver shouted at Schultz, 'Behind you!' He sounded like a kid at a pantomime and had about as much effect.

Now the runners were twenty metres behind Schultz and Chrystal.

Carver had to move fast, but Paula Miklosko wasn't going anywhere, so he hoisted her over his shoulder in a fireman's lift, thanking his lucky stars that she was so lightly built. Then he started running towards Schultz as fast as his burden would allow, waving his free arm and shouting as he went.

Finally Schultz noticed Carver's wild gesticulations and looked around. The first rioters were barely ten metres behind him as he shoved Chrystal away in Carver's direction, screamed, 'Move!' and turned to face the mob.

The pistol appeared in Schultz's hand. He fired three times in quick succession. The first round hit its target right in the middle of the chest, smashed through his ribcage and ploughed into his heart, dropping him immediately. The second struck another man just below the collarbone. Cranked on a chemical cocktail of speed, alcohol and adrenalin, and brandishing an axe, he barely broke stride, and Schultz had to resort to a head shot at point-blank range to finish the job. As the two shot men dropped to the ground, several of the people nearby flung themselves down, too, in fear of another shot. The rest stopped, recoiling as if hitting an invisible force field, and in the fractional pause that followed Schultz was able to sprint like hell and buy himself a bit more space and time.

He caught up with Carver and Chrystal, who were making their way across to the far side of the road, heading away from the garbage truck to a point about midway up Netherton Street.

'Now what?' Schultz asked.

'Over there!' Carver said, pointing down the road.

Carver was about to say more when he heard the whipcrack sound of a bullet passing by him, going faster than the speed of sound, followed a fraction of a second later by the blast of the gunfire itself.

'Suppressing fire!' he shouted at Schultz, who stopped and fired two more quick shots at the pursuing horde – aiming to scare rather than kill this time – before chasing Carver again.

'I need another couple there,' said Carver, pointing at another, smaller group of rioters ahead of them. 'Above their heads!'

'You sure?' Schultz asked.

'They're just kids,' Carver replied.

Like that makes any fucking difference, Schultz thought to himself, bringing his gun to bear as another fusillade of bullets crackled behind them, ricocheting off paving stones and lamp posts, blasting holes in the brick-work of nearby houses, and smashing a couple of windows – but somehow missing their fleeing figures.

Schultz fired and saw the people ahead of them scatter: job done.

Then he felt a sickening shock of pain in his left arm and heard a sharp crack of gunfire, and that was when he shouted, 'I'm hit!'

30

As battle raged on Netherton Street, Mark Adams was outlining his own vision of a country slipping out of control.

The bizarre assassination attempt had left the crowd edgy and ill at ease. It had taken Adams a while to calm them down, talking almost conversationally, and avoiding controversy or even passion. Now, though, he felt that they were ready to get back to the tough, no-nonsense speech that they'd all come to hear.

'I am not a racist,' he began. In the press boxes and TV studios the media people, many of whom had only just finished filing their copy on the shooting, sensed the start of the real political story of the night. In the box where Adams's inner circle were sitting, Alix saw the men in suits lean forward as if sniffing the air for the mysterious aura of public approval or rejection. She felt fierce pressure on her hand as Nicki Adams squeezed it again, quite unconsciously, unaware of this physical expression of her tension and excitement.

Adams waited, letting the words sink in before he continued, 'More than fifty years ago the great equal-rights campaigner Dr Martin Luther King said, "I have a dream that my four little children will one day live in a nation where they will not be judged by the color of their skin, but by the content of their character." That'll do me . . .'

In the press box a *Guardian* blogger and columnist called Dan Brix muttered loud enough for those around him to hear, 'He's got a nerve. A right-wing racist quoting Dr King . . . it's like Hitler quoting Rabbi Blue.'

'But I cannot escape the simple truth that the population of this country is undergoing a massive demographic shift,' Adams continued. 'This is the result of an entirely deliberate strategy, planned by your political leaders without your consent or even your knowledge. For years they have told you lies about trying to control immigration. They never had any intention of doing that.

'So now I'm going to tell you the facts, based on the government's own figures, and I'll leave you to decide what you think when you've heard them.'

Dan Brix tweeted: 'Adams moving on to immigration. About to scare us with "official" numbers #justlikethenationalfront.'

Up on the screens, the shots of Adams's face had given way to an outline map of the United Kingdom as he said, 'In February 2012, the government published its official National Population Projections, showing the potential effect of immigration on the population of Great Britain over a twenty-five-year period between 2010 and 2035.'

Adams was talking with calmness and clarity, reassuring his audience that even if the facts and numbers seemed complicated, he'd make them all easy enough to understand.

'They wanted to know how much difference it would make if there was a lot of immigration, a bit of immigration, or none at all. They started out with the population in 2010, which was a little over sixty-two million. At this point, England was already the sixth most crowded country in the world.'

The map suddenly filled with little graphic figures, most of them concentrated in England, packed so tightly that there was hardly any room between them, while the wide open spaces of Scotland, Wales and Northern Ireland remained almost empty. Then, superimposed on the map, appeared the number: 62 MILLION.

Adams let the image sink in, then said: 'Now, imagine there is no net immigration at all – that the number of people coming into the country is no greater than the number leaving – well, in that case the population rises from 62.3 million to very nearly 66 million by 2035. That's an increase of 3.7 million.'

More figures filled the English section of the UK. Now they were packed even more tightly. Then the graphic image changed to a close-up of the West Midlands, with the outline of Birmingham like a great black ink-spot in the middle, as Adams said, 'Now to give you some idea of what that means, the second biggest city in England is Birmingham, and it has a population of almost exactly one million. So that's the equivalent of more than three new cities, each the size of Birmingham, we've got to find room for . . . in one of the most crowded nations in the entire world.'

Splat! Splat! Splat! Three more Birmingham-sized black ink-spots splashed on to the screen, obliterating the rest of the West Midlands.

'But actually, we're not going to need three Birminghams. We're going to need much, much more than that,' said Adams.

The screens switched back to the map of the UK, and great arrows started moving towards England, and the numbers of little people began multiplying out of control, so that they merged into one great seething mass.

'You see, the idea of no net immigration is a total fantasy,' said Adams while all this was going on. 'By the government's own admission, the actual net migration figure is closer to a quarter of a million extra newcomers to this country every year . . . And if we carry on at that rate, the population in twenty years' time will be more than seventy-six million people, and living in this country will be like living on the platform at Piccadilly tube station in the middle of the rush hour . . . everywhere . . . all the time.'

The figure '76 MILLION' up on the screen was bigger and more menacing than any other had been. But Adams was still in documentary-presenter mode: 'So let's just sum this all up. If there is no additional immigration, this country's population goes up by 3.7 million . . . But in fact there are two hundred and fifty thousand extra immigrants every year and the population is going to rise by 13 million . . . So that's almost 10 million extra people who are all immigrants or the children of immigrants.

'Meanwhile, the people who are already here . . . particularly the average, white, middle-income men and women who think of themselves as the backbone of this country . . . well, they're not having very many children at all.'

Adams's forehead creased with a frown that looked almost apologetic. 'In fact, you could say that if they're not careful . . . if we're not careful . . . those average Englishmen and women are going to become extinct.

'So forget the polar bear . . . forget the panda . . . forget the whales and the creatures of the Brazilian rainforest . . . if you want to see an endangered species, just go and look in the mirror, Middle England . . . because it's you.'

31

The Lion Market's security shutters were made of powder-coated perforated steel. The tiny holes punched in their surface allowed a certain amount of visibility. Not long after the first attacks had begun, Ajay Panu had yelled at Maninder to turn out the lights in the store. Now the interior of the shop was darker than the street outside, making it easier for the Panus to see out and harder for anyone on the street to see in. For the past few minutes Maninder Panu had watched in terrified fascination as Ajay had initiated a bizarre form of gopher-bashing, hitting out at the young rioters as they'd come in under the barrier. Initially they'd crawled in one at a time, but after a while they'd taken to attacking in twos and threes, so that Ajay had to race from one side of the shop to the other while the kids shouted and laughed as though this was just some kind of game.

Maninder could tell that they knew Ajay was too

decent a man to do them any serious damage. If he'd ever used his full strength he could easily have killed someone. Instead he held back a fraction, hurting them, often quite badly, but never seriously. But now Ajay was getting tired. His chest was heaving as he struggled for breath, and he no longer had the strength even to shout at Maninder for help. Both cousins knew it was a waste of oxygen.

Maninder also knew that for all the paralysing fear that had overwhelmed him, things could have been a lot worse, and might yet become so. The rioters had descended like locusts on the electronics store, which stood directly opposite the supermarket, and looted it so thoroughly that it was now an empty shell. He'd seen the way the Dutchman's Head had been overwhelmed. It was now completely ablaze, as was the Khyber Star, the Indian restaurant across the way. Two of the Bangladeshi waiters had been dragged out on to the street and hacked to pieces. Maninder could not bring himself even to think about what must have happened to the cooks and managers. The local businessmen's attempts to defend themselves had been totally overwhelmed, and what had really kept Maninder so rooted to his spot behind the counter was not the attacks that had already taken place upon his shop, but an awful premonition of what would happen when the full force of the criminal storm descended upon him.

He was wondering what on earth he or Ajay could do to escape, or maybe bargain their way out of trouble – exchange every single item in the store for their safe passage, perhaps? – when he heard the sound of gunshots: three quick, distinct rounds, followed not long afterwards by apparently random outbreaks of firing. And then there were more shots, much closer at hand, and the kids in front of the Lion Market scattered and ran.

Maninder's spirits soared. Help had arrived!

Then he looked through the mesh shutters and saw what was really happening. Two men and a woman were dashing towards the store. A second woman was draped, apparently unconscious, over one of the men's shoulders. Maninder frowned. He knew the man's face, he was sure of it, but he couldn't place him. And then it came to him. This was the customer from earlier in the evening, not long before the violence began, who'd watched Ajay resupplying the bowls outside the shop. He'd come in and bought some chocolate, Maninder remembered. And then he recalled what he'd thought about him: that he'd looked like a man who could handle himself.

The other man held a gun in his right hand. His left was hanging limply at his side, flapping uselessly. Blood was pouring from a hole just above the elbow. He'd been shot.

'Help us, please!' the first man gasped. He eased the woman off his shoulder and held her just above the ground. It was obvious he wanted to pass her under the shutters, through the empty space where the window had been. Ajay went over and grabbed the woman's motionless body under the arms and started pulling her head first into the store. The other woman was already clambering in under her own steam.

Then Maninder saw what the four of them were running from. There was a huge crowd of rioters coming after them. Maninder watched one of the rioters lift a gun and fire on the run, and then he shrieked in fear at the clang of the bullet hitting the steel shutters.

'No!' he screamed. 'You can't come in here! Ajay, don't let them in! We'll all be killed!'

Ajay said nothing. He had dragged Paula Miklosko over towards the counter and propped her up so that she was sitting with her back against it. She started shaking and making incoherent, whimpering noises. Behind him, Carver was helping Schultz to get into the shop. Maninder watched as the wounded man gasped in agony with every movement of his broken arm. Carver was the last in. Ajay ignored what was happening by the window. He simply looked Maninder in the eye with an expression of pity and contempt that filled his older cousin with a shame so deep that he knew it would never leave him. And then Ajay slapped his face, a single fierce blow with the flat of his hand.

'You are supposed to be a Sikh,' he said. 'A man of honour. A warrior. A lion. But you are nothing but a pathetic, screaming old woman.'

Ajay Panu turned back to the four new arrivals. 'Can you fight?'

'I've got two rounds left,' said Schultz. 'After that . . .' He nodded at his wounded arm, grimacing as another jolt of pain stabbed through him.

'Do you have any more weapons?' asked Carver. 'Another bat would do.'

'Do you know how to use a gun?' asked Ajay.

'Yes.'

The simple, direct certainty of the answer told Ajay all

he needed to know. He called out, 'Maninder, give us the gun!' but there was no need. His cousin was already reaching under the counter and unclipping a weapon. He held it out, and in the flickering light from the street Carver saw the matt black silhouette of a Mossberg 590 pump-action shotgun. This was the armed forces derivative of the standard Mossberg 500 hunter's shotgun, chosen by criminals the world over for the same reasons as soldiers and police officers: it was tough, dependable and perfectly engineered to deliver lethal doses of twelve-bore buckshot. God only knew how these shopkeepers had come by it, but Carver was extremely glad that they had.

Chrystal screamed in alarm. The mob was massing outside the store. Bricks started hammering against the steel shutters, immediately followed by a bottle-bomb that bounced off and ignited on the pavement outside, right in front of the rioters. The front ranks of the crowd pushed backwards to get away from the flame.

Carver took charge. 'We need to get the shutters back down. I'm going to buy us some time. You two,' he said, pointing at the Panus, 'get ready. I need you to get that table out of the way. Chrystal, get Paula behind the counter, under cover. Then see if you can find something to bandage Schultz's arm.'

The fire from the bottle-bomb had died down. Now the mob was advancing again. A couple of shots rang out, and one of them punched a hole in the shutters. A bottle of wine at the back of the shop shattered as the bullet hit it.

There was a low line of brickwork, about 50cm high,

beneath the window. Carver got down on his belly and, wriggling on his elbows and knees, used this as the cover he needed to get to the far side of the window. There he took up a shooting position, kneeling by the window frame, his body partly sheltered by the narrow vertical strip of solid wall at the very edge of the shopfront. He smashed away a few shards of glass that were still attached to the lower line of bricks, and then used that as a solid base on which to rest his left elbow. Then he looked along the barrel and slowly traversed the crowd, searching for his first target.

Another rain of bricks and bottles clanged against the shutters. One of the bottles hit right at the bottom of the perforated metal. The rioters had started thinking. They were aiming for the gap. It was time Carver made them think about something else. A Mossberg's magazine held nine cartridges. Carver had to make every one of them count.

Then he heard a voice in the crowd shouting, 'That's right – aim low! Aim low!' and recognized it at once as belonging to the skinny, grey-haired figure who seemed to be masterminding the riot. If Carver could take him out there was every chance that the attack would soon peter out. These weren't professional soldiers he was up against. They were civilians without training or discipline, still less a proper command structure. He swivelled the gun in the direction of the voice. And then, for a fraction of a second, the crowd parted, Carver saw that familiar bespectacled skull of a face and pulled the trigger. But at the precise moment he did so, another rioter ran across the line of his shot, waving a gun in the air, only to have his head almost blown from his shoulders as it was hit by a fist-sized load of buckshot.

Carver's gun-barrel kept sweeping round the crowd. He saw the big man, Curtis, running towards them, and fired again, hitting him in the right shoulder, aiming to wound, rather than kill. Curtis had twice tried to keep him out of this nightmare and Carver owed him that much at least in return. He traversed again until his sights came to rest on a rioter in a black leather jacket and with a Mohawk haircut. He had his right arm cocked behind his shoulder, ready to throw a bottle-bomb. The rag in the neck of the bottle was alight. Before the Mohawk could move a muscle, Carver put another shell smack into the centre of his chest. The force of the impact knocked him off his feet and flung him at least a metre back through the air. As his body hit the ground, so did the bottle-bomb, igniting right in the midst of the crowd, which broke and ran for cover, dispersing as fast as a startled flock of pigeons. Curtis staggered away after them, screaming in agony, with his one good arm wrapped around a mate's shoulder. Within a few seconds the road in front of the Lion Market was deserted, just the two dead bodies lying amidst the debris of the riot.

'Now!' shouted Carver. 'Get that table sorted.'

Maninder Panu pressed the control of the shutter, raising it up off the table. Ajay dashed across to the centre of the shattered window, lifted up the near end of the table and heaved it out of the way. Maninder hit another button and the shutters came clattering down until the whole window was covered in a sheet of metal from ceiling to floor.

'We did it!' shouted Maninder. 'Oh, praise God, we survived!'

'We've survived for now,' Carver corrected him. 'But they'll be coming back. And when they do, we'd better be ready for anything they throw at us.'

32

Donny Bakunin was covered in blood. Carver's first shot had showered him with another man's blood and brain matter, and peppered the exposed skin of his hands and face with needle-sharp skull-fragments that stung like an assault by a swarm of bees. None of this had bothered him in the slightest. On the contrary, the more bloody the fight had become, the more he had exulted in it. He was a veteran of civil disobedience, from the Brixton riots of 1981, through all the campaigns against American cruise missiles, Rupert Murdoch's Wapping print plant, Thatcher's poll tax, G20 summits, globalization, GM crops and wars in the Middle East. He had charged countless police shield-walls and faced their batons, tear gas and water cannons. But absolutely nothing had excited him like the sheer murderous frenzy that had been unleashed in Netherton Street that night.

His rational mind had been aware that he had been

given specific orders to avoid unnecessary bloodshed, and he had obeyed those orders for as long as he could. But then all calm calculation had ended, overwhelmed by the primal berserker battle fever that had infected him as powerfully as everyone else.

Now, though, some of Bakunin's troops were having second thoughts. Five of them had been killed so far, and of those, four had gone down in the last few minutes, three felled with single shots. Another had been very seriously wounded. For the first time they had encountered resistance from people who were not only armed, but obviously willing to use their weapons to deadly effect. Bakunin wondered who they were. Had the traders managed to hire mercenaries to defend them, or were these a new, armed cadre of the Adams fascist movement whose political wing was meeting at the O2? If so, that had to be taken into account when planning any future riots. The presence of armed opponents could prove troublesome. Then again, any escalation of violence would serve to amplify the destabilizing effect of any acts of subversion, only adding to its political efficacy.

That was a matter for consideration at a later date. For now Bakunin had a more pressing task on his hands. He could sense the energy on the street dissipating fast. He needed to impose his will on the core elements of the riot, the gang-leaders and community activists who could rally their followers, like shepherds herding sheep, leading them on to the next phase of the action. Bakunin wanted to take the Lion Market. Nothing and no one could be allowed to exhibit such defiance without crushing retribution. It was plain that a straightforward charge against armed defenders would not prevail – not, at least, without an unacceptably high level of casualties.

It was not that Bakunin gave a damn about the lives of those who died. The sacrificial deaths of a small number of martyrs to the cause could always be used very effectively to inspire new members, as insurgent groups from the Nazis to the IRA and al-Qaida could testify. A massacre by government forces was also a fine recruiting tool. But a straightforward defeat by another group of citizens was altogether less encouraging. People would not come looting if they thought they were likely to be blown away by shopkeepers. It was therefore too late to worry about squeamish scruples. Circumstances had changed. Now that war had broken out, it had to be won, and a very public, very bloody example had to be made of the occupants of the Lion Market.

Bakunin summoned his lieutenants. They were given their orders and the second phase of the attack began.

33

Carver, too, was using the lull in the fighting to make his preparations. He knew exactly what he would do if he was in the rioters' shoes, and he had little doubt that they would soon come to the same conclusion that he had done.

He reckoned it would take several minutes for the rioters' grey-haired leader to restore control, work out his strategy and put it in motion. So it was down to Carver to use that time better than his opponent. First he had to secure command and control of his own little band of defenders. Without waiting to be asked or allowing any doubt to creep in he said, 'Right, I'm going to need the lights on. But let's make it quick – I don't want them on for long.'

As Maninder Panu reached for the switch, Carver was already asking Ajay: 'Is there any other way out of here?'

The big man shook his head. 'Not really. We've got a

yard behind the shop we use for storage, but it backs on to someone's garden and they've got a trellis above their side of the fence, with roses growing up it. They've got to be seven or eight feet high: big thick bushes. I don't see the four of you getting over that in a hurry.'

'What about to the sides?' Carver asked.

'More yards like ours for all the other shops and restaurants. And there's only two ways you get out of them. One: climb into the next yard. Two: go out through the premises—'

Carver finished the thought, 'And that takes you right back out on to the street.'

'That's why we didn't do it already,' said Ajay with a grim, humourless smile.

Behind the counter, Chrystal, acting on Schultz's instructions, had poured vodka over both his entry and his exit wounds and improvised a bandage out of a roll of kitchen towel and some Sellotape. Schultz was reaching for the packets of ibuprofen and paracetamol racked next to the cigarettes behind the counter. 'Do us a favour, love,' he said. 'Go and get us some cling film. A whole packet.'

As she walked off he caught Carver's eye and gave a sideways jerk of the head, as if to say, 'Come over here.'

Carver did as he was asked. 'What's up?' he asked.

Schultz leaned close and spoke below his breath: 'Get out, boss. You can get over a few bloody rose bushes, no worries. We're fucked here, you know we are. But there's no sense you copping it if you don't have to.'

'Nice try,' Carver replied, in an equally low voice. 'But

I'm not walking out on you, or the rest of them. Anyway, we can still make it.'

Carver went back to Ajay Panu. 'Do you have a basement?'

'Yeah. You get to it through the storeroom. That's our only hope, I reckon. Just hide down there and pray no one finds us.'

'It might be our last hope, but it's not our only hope,' said Carver. He turned to Maninder. The older of the two cousins was close to tears. Carver felt no anger or contempt towards the shopkeeper's helplessness. He'd seen trained soldiers fall apart amidst the chaos, the danger and the sheer, all-consuming terror of battle. He didn't hold it against a civilian.

'Do you have any more ammo for this shotgun?' Carver asked.

'No,' said Maninder. 'I was praying I would never even have to use it once.'

That was pretty much what Carver had expected to hear. 'Then we'll make do with what we've got,' he said. 'How you doing, Snoop?' he asked, nice and loud, so everyone could hear.

Schultz took the hint: this one was for public consumption. He was standing with his right arm lifted up while Chrystal wound cling film round and round his torso, binding his wounded left arm tight to the side of his body. Now he forced a devil-may-care smile to his face and called out, 'Just a through-and-through, boss. Hurts like a fucker, but don't you worry about me.'

'Right, you watch the rear of the property. We have to have control of that storeroom, so we can't have anyone coming over those side fences into the yard and getting in the back door.'

Schultz nodded. 'Yeah, boss.'

'Call me on the mobile, use your earpiece and keep the line open. Then keep me posted if anything looks like kicking off.'

'Got it.' Schultz looked down at his shiny, shrink-wrapped body. 'Christ.' He sighed. 'I look like a fuckin' packed lunch.'

'Is that all the thanks I get?' asked Chrystal in mock-indignation.

Schultz laughed, winced at the pain that caused and said, 'Nah, love, you did brilliant. Job done.'

'Well, give us a kiss, then, before you go.'

Schultz leaned towards her, she tilted her face up to meet his and they kissed with fierce intensity, both knowing it might be the last, as well as the first, time it happened.

Carver cleared his throat and Schultz pulled away from Chrystal with a sheepish grin. 'Right then, I'll be off.'

Before the girl had time to miss him, Carver was handing out her instructions: 'Can you keep an eye out the front? I want to know exactly what's happening out there. OK?'

She nodded.

'Good girl.' As she took up her position, peering through the perforated shutters, Carver turned back to Ajay: 'This place is air-conditioned, right?'

'Yeah – Maninder insisted on it. He really wanted this place to be special.'

'So where's the vent?'

'The unit just behind you, on the wall there.'

'Good. Do you have a microwave?'

'Of course, on a shelf behind the counter. We heat up food for customers to take away.'

'Then get ready for a supermarket sweep because I need the following items, fast, starting with flour, 00-grade if you've got it.'

Ajay frowned. 'You mean pizza flour? Yes, I know where that is.' He hurried off towards one of the shelves.

'And a spray can of deodorant,' Carver continued. 'Roll-on's no good to me.'

'I'll get that for you,' said Maninder, like a child wanting to make himself useful.

Carver watched the Panus dash to and fro across the store as he continued reciting his shopping list. 'Good, and grab me some soap flakes – got to be flakes, not powder . . . And lighter fluid, while you're at it – one of those plastic litre bottles people use for barbecues would be ideal . . . And an open bowl – like a mixing-bowl or something.'

Maninder came to a sudden halt and looked at Carver plaintively. 'We haven't any. Home goods you have to get from the hardware store, two doors down.'

Carver thought fast: 'OK, then I need anything that comes in a tub, like an open plastic tub. I don't know – ice cream maybe?'

'Ariel Liquitabs!' called out Chrystal, from her post by the shutters.

Carver hadn't a clue what she was talking about, but Maninder's face brightened at once. 'Oh yes, yes, we have those, certainly.'

'Then get them, whatever they are.'

He rushed off to get the last item Carver had requested. The rest had now been piled on the counter. Carver told Ajay, 'I need a ladder and a screwdriver.'

'In the storeroom. I'll get them straightaway.'

'Good man.'

As one Panu went off to the storeroom, the other arrived with a plastic tub filled with little purple pillows of liquid detergent. Carver took the tub from Maninder, opened it and emptied the contents on to the floor. Then he handed it back.

'Listen carefully,' he said. 'Take that tub and fill it with the soap flakes till you're about an inch from the top. Got that?'

Maninder nodded eagerly.

'Good,' said Carver. 'Now pour the lighter fluid on top and stick it in the microwave, full power, for two minutes.'

As Maninder got to work, Carver called out, 'How are we doing at the front, Chrystal?'

'Nothing yet. It's like everyone's vanished or something. Maybe they've all gone.'

'Don't count on it.'

Ajay arrived with the ladder. Carver took it from him, along with the screwdriver. He placed the ladder beneath the air-conditioning vent, climbed up and unscrewed the grille. Then he called down to Ajay, 'Hand me that flour. Thanks.'

Carver opened the flour and poured it all into the front of the air-con unit. The fan began wafting it towards him and Carver coughed as the fine flour got into his nostrils and throat. He quickly screwed the grille back on and came down the ladder as a dusty miasma of flour began seeping from the grille into the air all around it. Ajay looked on with the look of a man who was desperate to know what the hell was going on but hardly dared to ask. Before he could say anything, Carver had another question: 'Is the fan on this thing adjustable?'

'Yeah. Those buttons on the front, at the bottom. Low power to the left. Full power on the right. You should be able to reach them all right.'

The unit was on low power. Carver pressed the medium button and the flow of flour into the atmosphere became a little stronger.

The microwave pinged. The two minutes were up.

'Take the tub out,' said Carver to Maninder Panu. 'What does it look like?'

'Like a sort of jelly,' Panu replied.

'Perfect. Give it a stir, then put it back in the microwave and stick the can of deodorant into the tub.'

'I am sorry, but could you please explain the point of all this?' Maninder asked.

'There isn't time. Just trust me. And when you've done it, close the microwave, but do not, repeat, do not turn it on.'

Maninder got to work. He was just closing the door of the microwave when there was a stifled cry of alarm from the window. 'Hey, tough guy...' Chrystal said nervously. 'I think you'd better come here.'

'Turn out the lights,' Carver said to Panu. Then he made his way to the window. It only took one look to see that his worst fears had been confirmed. The other side knew exactly what they were doing. They were massing for their attack, and as he saw them take up their positions Carver had to admit that he couldn't have done it any better himself.

He turned to face the others, not letting any of his worries cross his face. In a firm, confident tone of voice he told Ajay Panu, 'Why don't you take your baseball bat and go and give Schultz a hand at the back of the building?'

'Understood.'

Carver gave him a quick, appreciative nod. Panu and Schultz were going to take some beating, even allowing for Schultz's wrecked left arm. And he didn't need them to hold out for long – even a minute might be enough. Now he focused on Chrystal and Maninder. 'You two, take Paula and get down to the basement, quick.'

They propped the shocked, semi-conscious woman between them and carried her off towards the storeroom, Maninder lighting the way with a black rubber torch he'd retrieved from beneath the counter. These days, with power cuts a regular occurrence, everyone kept camping lanterns handy for when the electricity went off. The Panus were no exception, and Maninder gave Chrystal one to carry in her spare hand, too. As soon as they were gone, Carver set the air-conditioning to full blast and turned on the microwave. Through the window he could see the bizarre combination of a plastic tub filled with grey jelly, with a can of spray deodorant sticking out of it, turning round and round. In his earpiece he heard Schultz giving Ajay Panu some instructions and then a crash as something heavy and metallic was heaved over in an attempt to block the door into the yard outside.

Then Carver heard Schultz, very calm, very professional, saying, 'They're coming over the fences into the yard, boss. Fuck me, there's a lot of the bastards, an' all.'

'Same this side,' said Carver. 'Good luck, mate.' Then he took up a position behind a shelf, close to the storeroom door, and waited for all hell to break loose.

34

The people milling around Netherton Street were like any other lawless crowd: a very small quantity of hardcore agitators and organizers at the top; a larger number of committed followers; and then an overwhelming majority of incidental hangers-on. Donny Bakunin's first task was therefore to get the leaders onside. If he could only do that, the rest of the herd would follow like iron filings after magnets.

It wasn't easy. The dozen or so gang-members and career criminals who formed the hard core of the rioters had no interest whatever in the political implications of their actions. They simply wanted to loot as much as they could, as quickly and efficiently as possible. Their status with their underlings came from their ability, in the most literal possible sense, to deliver the goods. They had no objection whatever to violence, provided that they were dishing it out – beating and knifing restaurant waiters and pub customers was fine. But being shot and even killed by armed men who knew what they were doing was another matter altogether.

Bakunin listened to the sociopathic thugs and self-professed hard men make their excuses for accepting defeat. And then he said, 'I understand. I get it. You're all a bunch of gutless cunts and you don't mind who knows it.'

While the shock was in their eyes and before any of them could retaliate, he stepped up his attack. 'Because if you walk away from here, with your tails between your legs, people are going to know you didn't have the balls to beat a bunch of fucking shopkeepers. And they're going to start thinking they don't have to worry about you, because you're just a bunch of bitches. You'll be a fucking laughing stock. You might as well cut your own balls off right now.'

Bakunin looked around the assembled gaggle of shaved heads, thick necks, mad eyes and tattooed skin that surrounded him and asked, 'Is that what you want?'

He was met with a sort of sulky, wordless grumble of dissatisfaction.

'I said, is that what you want?' Bakunin repeated, blithely unaware that he was echoing the way that Mark Adams, the politician he hated above all others, had wound up a hesitant crowd at the O2 Arena.

''Course it fuckin' ain't,' a voice replied.

'Then do what I say and we'll overrun these shopkeepers like a steamroller crushing ants. We'll smash into their precious little shop, and we'll fuck it up and fuck them up, and by the time we've finished and they're all dead and ripped to pieces then everyone will know that that is what you get for trying to defy us. And then they won't laugh at you. They'll be on their knees, sucking your cocks and begging for your mercy.'

At any other time, a man like Donny Bakunin might not have got away with talking like that. But the blood and matter drying on his skin, leaving drip marks all over his hair, his skull-like face and his scrawny neck, had given him the look of an ancient witch doctor, painted in gore. The sight of him struck some primitive chord in the men surrounding him, and they came over to his way of thinking. They then took the message back to their people. The word spread through the bigger groups milling listlessly around the fringes of Netherton Road or picking their way through looted shops, searching for one last overlooked item to steal. And then they were all back, his battalions of the ignorant, the unemployed and the dispossessed. Bakunin felt almost paternal towards them, as though he were a political Dr Frankenstein and these the monsters he – and others like him – had created in the educational laboratories of a thousand failed schools.

Aptly enough, they were going into battle behind a garbage truck. By ordering one end of the street to be blocked with cars, trash cans and anything else that came to hand, Bakunin had been able to move the lumbering machine from its original post. Its presence had encouraged his people to come out of the shadows and start massing on the streets. That was what Chrystal had seen. That was when Carver had turned on the microwave. Another half minute or so had passed as final preparations were made. Now the truck was rumbling slowly down the street, offering cover to the hundred-plus rioters trotting along in its wake like infantrymen behind a tank.

The truck stopped opposite the Lion Market, executed a slow, ponderous three-point turn and then accelerated towards the metal shutters. A roar went up from the people behind it. There was a crackle of gunfire as shots were blasted into the night sky, and then they began their charge towards the perforated metal shutters of the helpless supermarket – a sociopathic tsunami about to crash down upon the little store and wash it and its occupants clean away.

35

The maps and numbers had vanished from the screens beside the O2 stage and Mark Adams's face had taken their place again: 'For fourteen straight years from 1996 to 2009 the most popular boy's name in this country was Jack,' he said. 'Then in 2010 a new name hit the top, and it's stayed there ever since. It wasn't William or Harry or Charlie or Jim . . . It certainly wasn't Mark . . . no, the most common new boy's name in Britain for the past five years has been . . . Mohammed.'

There was a wordless murmur in the crowd, a sense of bodies shifting, a palpable unease.

'If you want to know how Britain has changed, and will continue to change unless something is done, then Jack giving way to Mohammed is all you need to be told,' said Adams.

'The change began about twenty-five years ago. In the 1990s the British population rose by about 2.2 million.

According to official National Census figures, some six hundred thousand of those 2.2 million new Britons were white. And 1.6 million – almost three-quarters of the entire new growth – belonged to ethnic minorities.'

He paused for a while to let the facts sink in. Assuming that they were facts, which many in the media covering the event seriously doubted.

'That can't be right . . . can it?' asked one.

'No, it's Far Right,' another replied. 'Just listen to him. He might as well be reading an editorial from *Der Stürmer* . . .'

Yet if Adams really was the Hitler he was accused of being, he wasn't screaming at his audience, or shaking his fist as the original version had done. He was sticking to his tone of reasonable, factual, logical analysis.

'Over the first decade of the new century the population kept growing, and the growth was overwhelmingly among the ethnic population. In London, for example, roughly three out of ten people are immigrants. But six out of ten children have at least one parent who was born outside this country. So thirty per cent of the people are having sixty per cent of the children . . . and the people who were born here aren't having many children at all.

'You can see the same pattern all over the country. For several years, the majority of schoolkids in cities including Leicester, Birmingham and great swathes of London have been from ethnic communities. Now that applies to grown-ups as well. Leicester recently became the first city in Britain in which whites are officially the minority of the population. Others will follow very soon.

'Now, let's not forget that these islands have always

been a destination for immigrants. We've always had a mixture of Celtic, Viking, Roman and Saxon blood. But even allowing for that, there is such a thing as the British people. And until very recently it was possible to say who they were and what they were like.

'They were white. They were overwhelmingly Christian. They were united by the world's most magnificent language, by the kings and queens who ruled over them and the parliament that gave them their voice. They were courageous in battle, extraordinarily inventive in industry and science, and creative in the arts. They had a profound belief in fairness, free speech and the rule of law. They fought for what they believed in, even when the cause seemed lost.

'But what's happening to the British now?' Adams asked. 'Just by seeing the massive change in school populations, it's clear that they are reproducing much less quickly than the rest of the population. In fact, one hundred average native British produce just eighty babies between them.'

New graphics appeared on the screen: a cluster of white figures like the male and female symbols on toilet doors, set against a dark-grey background, with the number 100 next to it. Beneath that cluster was a vertical white line down to a second, slightly smaller group of figures and another number: 80.

'Now that next generation reproduces at the same rate, and they produce sixty-four babies,' Adams said.

Now there was a third cluster, somewhat smaller than the one directly above it, but appreciably diminished from the very first.

Adams picked up on that difference. 'So you started with one hundred adults, and now you've got just sixty-four grandchildren. That's down by more than a third. And if they keep reproducing just like their parents and grandparents, well, they'll produce just fifty-one great-grandchildren. So the native British population has halved in three generations.'

Up on the screen, a fourth, much smaller cluster of little white figures made the point impossible to miss or ignore. And more clusters, each smaller than the last appeared as Adams intoned, 'And forty-one great-great-grandchildren ... And thirty-three great-great-great-grandchildren: just a third as many native English people as we started out with ... And there's just a quarter left by the next generation: twenty-six descendants of the one hundred British we started out with. That is what is going to happen to the British race unless something is done to reverse the trend before it's too late.

'Now there will be people watching this who will say that I am being racist, just by mentioning this fact. But how on earth is it racist to be concerned about the future of one's own people? No other nation feels this shame. Russians, Japanese, Jews, Italians – they all talk about the crisis in their own populations, and what can be done to reverse it. But not the British.

'So I ask you: do we really hate ourselves so much that we won't do anything to ensure our self-preservation? Is it racist now to care about oneself, one's children and one's grandchildren? I do not deny anyone else the right to maintain their nation, their race and their culture. All I ask is the right to maintain my own.

'Once again: I have no hostility whatsoever towards anyone, of any colour or religion, who wants to commit himself or herself to this country, work hard, make a contribution and share in our culture. All I'm saying is that if we don't wake up and start dealing with our self-preservation now, then it's going to be too late.'

36

As Mark Adams would happily have pointed out, given the opportunity, British soldiers spent hundreds of years standing and waiting for their enemy – from the thin lines of archers charged by French knights in armour at Crécy and Agincourt, to the small band of men confronting thousands of Zulu warriors at Rorke's Drift. They stood and waited ... and waited some more ... waited until the absolutely final possible second before unleashing their arrows and bullets. Now Carver stood in a corner of the Lion Market, close by the storeroom door, with one of the shelves for shelter. And he waited.

From where he stood, he had no view through the shutters, but he did not need it. He could hear the garbage truck's engine revving, and the shouts of the crowd. He sensed the noise coming closer and the vibrations of the truck's tyres and engine through the floor. Louder and louder the noise became as he told himself to stay calm, breathe steadily and maintain control of his pounding heart and the rush of blood and adrenalin through his body.

Closer . . . louder . . . his guts and throat tightening . . .

And then the truck hit the shutters with a crashing, clanging scream of metal, and smashed through the flimsy perforated steel like a charging rhino through a mud hut. Carver screwed up his eyes as the truck's headlights cut through the darkness of the shop, and the first rioters appeared on either side of the great steel beast, silhouetted against the blinding white glare as they picked their way through the debris.

There were angry shouts as the charging mass behind barged into the backs of the more slowly moving people at the front, and a couple of cries of pain as rioters cut themselves against the jagged edges of the smashed shutters.

A few more seconds passed. The red digital readout of the microwave timer kept counting down towards zero. More light, fine flour pumped out into the air around the air-conditioner.

Then the wave of people broke upon the shore of the supermarket and suddenly the rioters were coming in by the handful, then tens of them, filling up the aisles, pressing towards the corner where Carver stood concealed behind his shelf.

They thought the shop was empty. They thought it was theirs for the taking. Now they were whooping and cheering, and the only thoughts they had of fighting came from the desire to barge one another out of the way as they raced for the shelves where the alcohol was kept.

Someone fired another gun, glass shattered and an angry voice shouted, 'Not now! Kill the shopkeepers first!'

The skirmishing around the booze racks broke up as the mood in the shop changed once more. 'Kill them!' the voice shouted again.

In his ears Carver could hear the sound of Schultz, breathing heavily, swearing in pain and fighting fury as he and Ajay Panu fought to hold back the human tide by the back door.

Still Carver waited.

Finally, when the rioters were almost close enough to touch, when he could not only see and hear them but smell them, too ... finally Carver stepped out from behind the shelf and fired three more times. Each explosive impact of hammer on cartridge was followed by the sound of another round being pumped into the breech in a smooth, relentless sequence. His targets were all male, none more than ten feet from where he stood, and this time he shot to maim, rather than kill instantly.

A twelve-bore cartridge, fired at a distance of less than five metres, can rip an arm right off. And when that happens, the sight of a man with blood spurting from his raw, tattered stump doesn't look half as funny as it might do on a video game, or in a scene from Monty Python's *Holy Grail*. Nor does even the most hardened, psychologically damaged street kid react well to being hit in the face by a severed limb.

The screams of a man whose stomach has just been blown away and whose entrails are unravelling in slimy coils across a linoleum floor strike fear into any heart.

And when there are two of them lying howling in front of their mates, and a third is running around, screaming, like the human answer to a headless chicken, and people are shouting out in alarm because there's blood all over their face, or they're slipping on the intestines underfoot, then even the biggest, angriest crowd can be seized by confusion, chaos and panic.

And in that chaos Samuel Carver slipped through the door behind him and into the second battle that was going on inside the storeroom.

37

Schultz and Ajay Panu were desperately pushing against the metal shelving they'd leaned against the back door. The top half of the door itself had long since been obliterated by a combination of gunfire, iron pipes and even an axe that one giant, Viking-like rioter had smashed against the wood until Schultz had stood up, aimed through the hole the man had made and blown him away with one of his two precious bullets. He and Panu were both powerful, heavily built men, but they were tiring badly, and even a man of Schultz's fighting pedigree – a Marine commando who had spent most of his career in the SBS – could not for ever overcome the handicap of a shattered arm, nor ignore the pain and blood-loss that came with it.

Panu was leaning his left shoulder against the shelf to prevent the invaders from pushing it over, and using his right arm to swing his baseball bat at anyone who clambered up over the top. But he, too, was now wounded. The full force of the shotgun blasts from the other side of the door had missed him, deflected by the shelves and the boxes filled with packets of rice and sugar that had been piled on them. But still he was peppered with bits of shot and splinters of wood, and the dark pinpricks on his shirt were slowly seeping together until more and more of his upper body was slick with seeping blood.

Now another attacker was clambering over the shelves. Ignoring Panu's attempts to bat him away, he crouched at the top and then sprung down, straight on to Panu. The attacker's momentum caught Panu by surprise and knocked him off his feet. The big Sikh hit the concrete floor with an impact that drove the air from his lungs and as he lay helplessly pinned to the ground, the attacker lifted a carving knife into the air, held in both his hands, pointing directly down at Panu's throat. He arched his back, brought his arms up to the top of the killing stroke, and then launched all his strength through his shoulders and arms to bring the blade plunging down.

Schultz fired his final bullet, a shot to the attacker's temple from point-blank range that killed him instantly.

But the action of turning to shoot took Schultz's attention away from the men climbing up the shelves and exposed his shattered left arm at the precise moment that another man jumped down from the top of the metal and hit him almost precisely at the point of the wound. The pain was more excruciating than any Schultz had ever experienced. It left him sickened and paralysed with agony. He was barely even conscious of the machete swinging down towards his throat. With Panu still struggling to free himself from the weight of the corpse now lying on top of him there was no one to save Schultz as the blade sliced deep into his abdomen, just below the ribcage.

At that precise moment Carver came through the door from the supermarket. He blew away the man standing over Schultz, then pumped the gun and hit another shadowy figure looming over the shelving. Carver raced across to Schultz, who was lying in the middle of a rapidly expanding pool of blood. It was obvious that there was no saving him, but he seemed to be trying to say something. Carver bent down and caught the words, '. . . It wasn't meant to be like this', before the flickering life in his old comrade died.

Carver wasted no time in mourning: leave that for the funeral. He switched his attention to Panu, pulled the body off him, lashed out with the butt of his gun, cracking it into a grimacing, tattooed face that had suddenly appeared out of the darkness, and shouted, 'Run for the basement. Go! Go!'

Panu scrambled away on all fours until he found his feet for the last few paces that took him to the door to the basement steps. Carver followed him, stepping backwards, keeping his gun still pointed towards the shelves.

He had two cartridges left.

A hand clutching a gun appeared over the top of the metalwork and fired blindly downwards.

Carver ignored it. His attention had suddenly swung one hundred and eighty degrees to the sudden sound of hammering on another door – the one into the supermarket. With an explosion of dust and wood, the lock was blown away and the door swung open.

Carver fired another round straight into the exposed doorway, hitting at least one, possibly two targets. Then, as the bodies were thrown out of the way and the first rioters from the supermarket ran in, just as the invaders from the back yard began to climb en masse over Schultz and Panu's abandoned barricade, Carver ran for the basement door, yanked it open, dashed through, pulled it close behind him and turned the key in the lock.

He threw himself down the steps as the first bullets ripped into the door.

The door crashed open. A rioter burst through and stood at the top of the stairs. He was a wiry little hoodie with a hunting knife in his hand. Carver had one round of ammunition left. He could use it to take out a rioter, or he could give one of the women an instant, painless death instead of the gang-raped mutilation to which the rioters would subject her.

He was just about to make his choice.

And then the timer in the microwave went, 'Ping!'

38

A combination of soap flakes and lighting fluid makes a substance that is both highly combustible and very sticky. It is, in effect, a domestic form of napalm.

An aerosol can of deodorant contains chemicals that react under intense heat to create a violent explosion.

Fine-grade flour is, like icing sugar, a surprisingly explosive substance when suspended in air, which is why history is littered with examples of fatal explosions in flour mills. The principle is very simple. Explosions are intense chemical reactions that require an energy source and a supply of oxygen. Flour and sugar are both powerful fuels, which is why we eat them, and air, of course, contains oxygen. A full packet of tightly packed flour has relatively little contact with the air around it and is thus quite safe. But when every single particle in that bag is individually suspended in air, then the proportions of fuel and oxygen are potentially far more dangerous.

But there is still one more element to add to the mix before anything goes bang: a detonator. And that was provided by the contents of the microwave.

The heating of the aerosol deodorant in the Lion Market microwave set off one explosion that blew open the oven and projected a blazing hot spatter of napalm into the air inside the Lion Market. This in turn detonated a secondary, even more powerful explosion of the flour suspended in the atmosphere.

A deafening blast of white-hot flame ripped through the packed shop. It set light to any flammable materials. Much of the napalm was vaporized immediately by the blast, but the rest stuck to people's clothes, skin and hair, turning them into human torches. The shock wave from the explosion, travelling at supersonic speeds, tore through the rioters' bodies, inflicting catastrophic soft-tissue damage. Most critically it induced severe pulmonary contusions, bursting blood vessels and causing a condition known as blast lung, in which victims drown in their own blood as fluids build up in their shattered lungs until breathing becomes impossible. As ways of dying go, it is almost as horrible as being burnt alive.

The blast ripped through the open door into the storeroom, and though its effects were far less devastating than they had been in the shop itself, the deafening sound of the explosion, the flames, the screams and the terrible sight of people tearing at their clothes and their own flesh, desperately trying to pull away the napalm, which stuck to them like burning coal superglued to their bodies, were enough to end any further thoughts of combat or robbery. All that anyone who was lucky enough to be alive and more or less in one piece – temporarily deafened, perhaps, but flame-free and still able to breathe – wanted to do was to get the hell out as quickly as they possibly could.

They scrambled back over the shelves, out into the yard, and retraced the steps that had got them into this earthly hell in the first place. And meanwhile, in the shop, all that could be heard were crackles of flame from a few small fires, moans of pain from those burn-victims who were still able to breathe, and the gurgles, wheezes and desperate, futile gasps of dying looters being killed by their own blood.

39

Down in the cellar Carver heard the explosion, the screams, the shouts of panic and the scurrying feet desperately rushing to get away. In the cold light of the camping lantern he could see Chrystal sitting weeping with Ajay Panu's bear-like arm around her shoulder. Paula Miklosko was looking a little more conscious of what was going on around her, though she was still a long way from being fully alert. Maninder Panu was sitting alone, staring into the darkness of the basement, as if his circuits had simply overloaded under the strain of what had happened since the riot first began. Barely fifteen minutes had gone by, but it might as well have been a lifetime.

Carver crouched on his haunches beside him. 'Where's the control-box for the CCTV?' he asked.

Maninder said nothing. Carver repeated the question. Still no response.

'In the back office,' said Ajay. 'Across the storeroom

there's a door with a glass panel. Through that's the office. The box is in there. It's connected to the computer. Why do you need it?'

Carver didn't answer the question. He just asked, 'What's the password?'

Maninder paused.

'It's all right,' said Carver. 'I don't want your money . . . or your porn.'

Ajay gave a tired smile. 'It's "prosperity",' he said. 'Ironic, innit?'

'At least it wasn't "peace".' Carver saw the black torch lying on the floor in front of Ajay and Chrystal, picked it up and said, 'Right, I'm going now. I can't be certain it's completely safe up top, so don't move from here till the police find you.' He nodded at Paula Miklosko. 'Make sure she gets seen by a doctor as soon as possible. I made a mess of your shop. Sorry about that. About tonight . . . I wasn't here. If anyone asks, you defended yourselves with a bit of help from a bloke called Snoopy. You were heroes. He was a hero. The people who attacked you were murderous filth. You'll probably get medals. You deserve to. But I wasn't here. Is that understood?'

They nodded at him wordlessly and Carver turned to go.

'Excuse me,' called out Maninder, 'but you never even told us your name.'

'I know,' said Carver.

Maninder nodded. 'Well, thank you, anyway. We owe you our lives.'

'You're welcome.'

He went back up the stairs, the torch in one hand, the

shotgun in the other, and slipped through the damaged door to the storeroom. Inside it was deserted apart from a small group of the dead and dying strewn by the scorched hole where the door to the shop had once been. As the torch-beam swept the room, Carver heard a rustling sound and shone the light in its direction, catching a shadowy figure staggering, doubled-over in pain, as it fled through the back door. One of the blast-victims made a feeble attempt to lift a hand in supplication and gasped, 'Help me.' Carver knew there was absolutely nothing he could do. He turned the torch off, then stopped for a moment and listened for any other signs of movement or hostile action, but the only sounds to be heard were coughs, wheezes and gurgles coming from the supermarket, making it sound like a hospital ward filled with consumptives and lung-cancer patients. Carver would check it out in due course, but first there was work to be done.

Even without the torchlight he could see the outline of the office entrance. He slipped through it, closed the door behind him, and turned the torch back on to find little trace of the carnage elsewhere, just the usual paperwork of a small business. There were box-files on shelves; plastic trays filled with invoices and correspondence; more papers strewn chaotically across a desk; a mug containing half a dozen pens and pencils; and a Dell PC next to a black box whose facia was covered with buttons like a domestic satellite receiver. Carver pressed the 'on' button on the computer and was not entirely surprised to see that it worked. It struck him that the air-blast had worked a bit like a neutron bomb: killing human beings but leaving property largely intact.

Two minutes later the entire CCTV feed for the past twelve hours had been deleted. He sprayed the computer keyboard with screen-cleaner fluid from a pump-spray bottle standing next to the Dell, then wiped it down with his handkerchief. Carver looked up to establish the position of the door so that he could find it again in the dark. Then he turned off the torch and repeated the cleaning process.

He had one more use for the cleaner fluid, so he put it in his jacket pocket, and it was then that he realized the head cam was already there. Carver took the camera out. The 'record' light was on, a glaring red dot in the darkness. It must have been running all the while, capturing the sounds, if not the images, of the supermarket battle. What was more, the head cam's owner had been wearing and presumably using it when Carver and Schultz had gone to rescue Paula Miklosko. So their faces would be on it, too. Carver's immediate instinct was to go straight back to the computer and delete all the head cam's video files, just as he'd done with the CCTV. Then he stopped. There was evidence against him on here, true, but there might also be evidence against other people, evidence he could use. He turned the camera off. For now, at any rate, its contents were staying put.

Carver, however, had to get going. And that meant doing something he'd been putting off for the few minutes he'd been in the office. He had to go back into the shop and see for himself the havoc that his home-made bomb had wreaked.

40

Carver had been in bus-stations attacked by suicide bombers. He'd seen hospitals hit by air-raids, and the burned-out remnants of an Iraqi tank regiment, blown to smithereens on the road from Baghdad to Kuwait. But there was something uniquely hellish about this. The corpses lay thick on the supermarket floor, a gruesomely vile and pointless slaughter that resembled a circle of hell as the blue-grey gloom and deep-black shadows were pierced by the flickering light of the flames and the sulphurous orange glow of the street lamps outside.

It disgusted Carver that he had been reduced to doing this. It shamed him that he had had the perverted skill to wreak such havoc. It angered him, too, for what choice had he had? He and the others would have died otherwise, of that there was no doubt. And for what?

Carver had known men who had killed for vast profits, or out of political or religious conviction. There were no excuses or moral justifications for their acts, but he could at least follow the calculations of those who thought their ends were important enough to justify such violent means. He could understand how suicide bombers believed that their self-destruction was in a great and worthy cause, even if he disagreed with them. But what had these people died for? Free fucking groceries.

Something caught Carver's eye – a movement by the window. He stepped back into the shadow and stood motionless and silent as the slight figure of a girl appeared at the far side of the crashed garbage truck, peered in and then hesitated, not daring to come any further. From the size of her Carver guessed she must be around eleven or twelve. There was no sound in the room beyond the hacking and burbling of the rioters' breaths, the occasional pathetic attempt at a call for help, and the fearful weeping of the dying. Some of the bodies were moving. Others were holding out hands in desperate supplication. Carver hoped to God that the girl would not understand what she was looking at; that the meaning of it would somehow pass her by.

She said something, but her voice was very faint, and Carver could not make out what it was. She straightened herself up and tried again, more loudly this time. 'Ricky?' and then again, 'Ricky! Are you there? Mum says you gotta come home. You got school tomorrow.'

There was no reply. The girl stood there uncertainly, not sure what to do next. Then a barely audible whimper came from somewhere at the back of the room, an expression of pain unrelated to anything she had said.

The girl must have recognized the voice as her brother's, for she cried out, 'Ricky!' Carver could hear the relief, but also the mounting terror. She had still not taken a single step further into the shop. 'Come on, Ricky, come home . . . please! Mum'll kill ya if you don't.'

There was another moan: the same voice as before, from the same place. Then the girl sniffed and cried out, 'I don't understand . . . I don't know what to do!'

Every professional instinct told Carver to ignore the child. What mattered now was to avoid detection. The last thing he should do was to make himself identifiable. But as a human being, as a man, he simply could not stand by and ignore the girl's distress. He'd brought the shotgun with him, just in case that last cartridge was needed for self-defence. Now he switched the gun to his left hand, held it casually down by his side and stepped out of the gloom. The girl gave a little squeal of alarm as she saw him loom up in front of her.

'Don't worry,' Carver said. 'I won't hurt you.'

She looked at him. 'Who are you?' she asked.

'Go home and tell your mum she needs to call an ambulance. Your brother Ricky needs an ambulance. Soon as possible.'

'Where is he? I want to see him!'

'I don't think that's a good idea,' Carver said. 'Just go and get an ambulance. That's what Ricky needs.'

She didn't move.

'Please, just go,' Carver insisted. 'I'll look after your brother.'

'Why? Are you a doctor?'

Carver said nothing. The girl was trying to decide what

to do. There was nothing more he could say now to help her make up her mind. He got a feeling she was about to turn and go but then there was another cry from the same direction as the previous ones.

'Ricky! I'm coming!' the girl shouted. She took a pace or two into the shop but then stopped. The bodies carpeted the floor of the shop so thickly that it was impossible to pick a clear path through them. At least half were still alive, though the number of survivors was diminishing with every minute that passed. Carver sighed to himself and gave a shake of the head; he could not believe what he was about to do.

'Here, I'll help you,' he said and held out his right hand to her. The girl took it and let him guide her through the carnage.

'Watch out,' he said, seeing her about to tread on a twitching, outstretched hand.

The girl said, 'Sorry,' as she kicked into another body, cutting the end of the word short as she realized the body was dead. He was close enough to see her eyes now, and the bows on the ribbons that held her braids in place, close enough to see the look on her face as she suddenly gasped, 'Ricky . . .'

There in front of them, slumped on the floor with his back up against a shelf, was a teenage boy, no more than fourteen, wearing an Adidas tracksuit over a Chelsea shirt. His eyes were still open, filled with fear and incomprehension, and there were small bubbles of foaming blood at the corners of his mouth as his lungs fought against the liquid filling them from within. The girl sat down next to her brother, taking his hand in hers and leaning her head against his shoulder. 'I'm here, Ricky,' she said. 'I'm here . . .'

The boy was going to die for sure. But as Carver stepped away from the two kids and began spraying screen-cleaner all over the Mossberg he realized that there was something he could do to put right some of the wrong that he had been forced to do here. This riot had not been a spontaneous event. Someone had planned it. They'd brought a man in to act as the commander on the ground – that scrawny, grey-haired guy with the un-expectedly upmarket accent – and Carver was forced to admit that his old friend Schultz must have played some kind of a role in it too. Schultz had known things were going to kick off in Netherton Street, but he'd thought they'd be safe in the pub. That was why he'd been so astonished to see the mob come streaming in through the door, and that was surely the meaning of his final words: 'It wasn't meant to be like this.'

Outside, Carver could hear the sound of people com-ing to investigate. A woman started screaming. He put the gun down on the floor, in among the bodies. If any of his prints were still recoverable, which he doubted, they'd take days or even weeks to process, and he'd be long gone. There was a baseball cap, lying on the floor, blown from a rioter's head. Carver picked it up and jammed it on, pulling the peak down over his eyes. He grabbed a scarf that had got wedged into one of the dis-play units, and wrapped it round his face.

As he straightened up, his mind turned back to the implications of what Schultz had said. The riot was meant to be controlled and contained. It was intended to remind the public of the lawlessness of modern Britain.

Carver knew exactly who would want to give them a reminder like that.

The question was: how could he prove it?

Then he looked out of the window and got his answer.

41

Donny Bakunin had given the order to the truck driver to smash into the supermarket and then stood in the middle of Netherton Street urging on his foot soldiers as they had run towards their target. Only when most of them had been past him had he joined the surging mass, and he had only just run by the side of the truck and up to the mangled remains of the security shutters when the bomb had gone off.

The force of the explosion had punched into him and flung him several feet back the way he'd come. He had landed on the road and skidded across the tarmac like a human skimming stone until he'd hit the front wheel of an abandoned car. He had been winded so badly that several terrifying airless seconds had passed before he'd been able to take his first rasping breath and drag some air down into his bruised and battered lungs.

His face was scorched. His glasses had been thrown

from his face and his eyes were in any case so dazzled by the explosion that he was virtually blind. He could hear nothing beyond a tinnitus shriek because his eardrums had been shredded by the pressure-wave passing through him. His clothes were torn almost to shreds and his body was covered in small, deep incisions that were all now bleeding profusely. His spine, ribs, elbows, thighs and even the back of his head were scraped and bruised from his impacts with the ground and the car.

All in all, Donny Bakunin was a sorry, fucked-up mess of a man, but he was still alive, and though every breath was agony his lungs were just about functioning. He screwed up his eyes, trying to see through the bright white glare imprinted on his light-blasted retinas, and gradually, over a period of minutes, he was able to get a blurred, short-sighted picture of the devastation that had been wrought on the supermarket and the people in it. Looking around, he could just make out the shadowy outlines of local people, venturing out on to the street now that the riot appeared to have ended. He saw two men by the garbage truck trying to hold back a screaming woman, preventing her from entering the supermarket as she kicked and fought against them. Another man came up to him and leaned down with a worried expression on his face. Bakunin could just about make out his lips moving, but he had no idea what they were saying. He pointed at his ears and shook his head. The man nodded his understanding then reached down a hand to help Bakunin up.

Bakunin got unsteadily to his feet. Everything hurt. Nothing was working properly. The man was trying to guide him away. Somewhere in the periphery of his vision Bakunin caught the blue glimmer of an approaching emergency vehicle. He didn't want to be around when the police appeared, so he impatiently waved his helper's arm away and set off as best he could in the direction that seemed to lead to his flat.

Bakunin didn't hear the man who'd been trying to look after him say, 'Suit yourself.' Let alone mutter, 'Ungrateful old bastard,' a few seconds later.

Nor did Bakunin see the man in the jeans and the long suede jacket, his face hidden by a baseball cap and a scarf, come out of the supermarket and, using the bulk of the garbage truck to hide himself, slip on to Netherton Street.

Carver could see that the riot leader was badly injured, disorientated and suffering severe sensory damage. Good, he was glad to see him suffer. And if those wounds made his target far, far easier to tail without any risk of being detected, then so much the better.

42

'We all want to feel proud again,' Mark Adams said. 'And we will. I promise you. We will feel proud again.'

He was heading towards his conclusion now, and he knew it had to be good. He'd given his people plenty to think about; plenty to worry about, too. But that wasn't enough. He had to show them that he had the answers and was willing and able to deliver them, given the chance. He had to give them hope, a positive vision of the future and – above all – a lot of good reasons to vote for the United People's Party.

'This is the good bit,' Nicki Adams whispered to Alix. 'This is what makes him different – just watch.'

'I want you to help me – all of us, working together – to create an independent Britain that can forge its own future, determine its own destiny,' Adams said, still sounding very much like any other politician. 'I want a Britain that's prosperous, with a vibrant, growing economy, peaceful and secure from external threats; where people of all races share common values, a common understanding of our way of life ... and an appreciation for the culture that makes our country unique.

'Together we can create an England fit for decent people to live in. All we need is a crackdown of common sense to sweep away all the daft ideas that have brought this country to its knees. And here, in four steps, is how we can do it ...

'One! We will declare unilateral independence from the European Union within twenty-four hours of taking power.'

There was a cheer as big as an England goal at Wembley. Adams nodded as the cheering and applause continued, smiling more broadly than at any other time since he'd come onstage. This was the promise no major politician had ever dared make, but it was one that more and more of the electorate had been longing to hear. And Adams knew it. 'I thought you'd like that,' he said, provoking another smaller cheer. 'We won't hang around. We'll leave the EU and the European Court of Human Rights immediately. And we'll stop all foreign aid, too. So we won't be sending twenty billion pounds a year to Brussels, and another ten billion pounds to corrupt dictators in Africa, or countries like Brazil and India that have bigger economies than ours and don't want to be treated like impoverished beggars any more, thank you very much. That's thirty billion pounds to be spent on British people as a properly elected British government sees fit.

'It also means no more EU regulations. No more British jobs being taken by foreign workers. No more European judges telling us that we have to let immigrant terrorists, rapists and murderers walk the streets because it's against their human rights to pack them off back to wherever they came from . . .The United People's Party is giving Britain back to the British!'

There were more cheers, but Adams didn't wait for them to die down as he continued, 'Two! We will re-introduce the death penalty for murderers and terrorists. It's time a British government finally got tough on crime. That means no more softly-softly sentences. No more letting rapists, murderers and paedophiles back on the streets, and no more worrying about the human rights of criminals. A man who steals, or rapes or kills does not give a damn about the human rights of his victims. Why should he expect anyone to give a damn about his? Three! We will radically reform the benefits system. Decent working people are disgusted by the idleness, fecklessness and shamelessness of the scroungers they see all around them. Men and women who work hard to buy modest homes and can only dream of affording families of their own have to pay taxes to fund the work-shy scroungers who fake disabilities, find endless reasons why they cannot work, and fill four, five or even six-bed-room houses with kids they never have to pay for. Well, we'll be putting an end to that. You won't be paying for scroungers any more. I promise you that.

'Of course if you take people off benefits you have to put them into work, and that is precisely what we will do.

There are millions of jobs being filled by European immigrants. Well, we'll give the British people those jobs back. And if the work-shy unemployed and the disability fakers don't take the work they are offered, they will lose their benefits. Every single last penny of benefits.'

All Adams's proposals were being met with rapturous approval. The people of Middle England were finally being offered things they'd wanted for years, but been told were bad for them. And they were loving it.

'The scary thing is,' one of the reporters in the press box said, 'this is only one step on from what respectable politicians are already saying.'

'No,' Dan Brix replied, 'the scary thing is what he's not saying. He's just shown us the icing. But there's a great big cake of shit underneath.' Brix paused for a second, listening to the words now coming from the stage, and then added, 'And now here it comes . . .'

Adams held up a hand with all his fingers splayed: 'And . . . four! We will finally keep another promise that has always been broken by other governments in the past. We will spend whatever it takes to secure Britain's borders. We will ensure that there is no immigration-driven increase in this country's population. And we will eject all illegal immigrants from this country. This will take a lot of time and a lot of effort. So to make the process easier and to provide proper interim accommodation for those in transit back to their places of origin we will replace the current system of detention centres with a network of resettlement areas: designated zones, created on surplus Ministry of Defence land, where outgoing families can be housed, with their loved ones and fellow-members of their communities, until a new home for them can be found.

'For those who remain, we will follow a policy of "active integration". For decades, British people have been ordered to adapt our ways to those of newcomers to this country, not the other way round. Surely that cannot be right. We in the United People's Party want a tolerant, inclusive England. All we ask is that you respect our culture, too. In this country we don't hide our women behind veils and masks. We don't use schools and places of worship to preach hatred. And if you want to go abroad to fight for terrorist groups, fine. But you're not coming back.'

The crowd were on their feet now, and they weren't bothering to sit down.

'Anyone who wants to contribute, who wants to join in, who wants to be proud of being English, has my full and total support, irrespective of race, religion, sexual preference or anything else,' Adams said. 'But if you don't like it here, and you don't want to integrate into our way of doing things, well, there are two hundred other countries in the world, and I'm sure that one of them can offer something that might suit you better.'

The line went down a storm, but Adams barely paused before adding: 'In the meantime, I'm going to save my efforts for people who want to earn their own money, pay their own bills and bring their children up to be decent citizens . . .'

Now he started pacing the stage as he had done right at the very start of the speech, pausing to punch out his words, jabbing the air with his index finger as he talked about, 'The decent, law-abiding majority . . . The ones who've been taken for granted for years and years . . . Who've never been consulted as their country has been taken from them . . . Who've seen standards of public life slide into the gutter . . . Who've watched criminals literally getting away with murder; bankers getting away with theft and fraud; MPs getting away with blatant corruption . . . Who've had to pay through their noses so that others can be feckless and bone-idle . . . Who've been taxed and regulated and held in contempt by the political class . . .'

He'd come to rest in the middle of the stage. And now he stared hard at the audience and asked them, 'Do you know who I'm talking about?'

There was a roar of pent-up emotion: of anger, frustration and righteous indignation.

'I'm talking about people like . . . you!' Adams exclaimed, with another jab of the finger, receiving another shout of acclamation in return.

'You know something has to be done. We all know it. We all long for a better, prouder, harder-working, happier, more decent country . . . And we can get it, together, that better country.'

One last pause, one last deep breath and then one final line: 'We can get it because we are united . . . we are the people . . . and the only way is UPP!'

Mark Adams left the stage to a standing ovation, and while the crowd went crazy the professionals who were watching – the media commentators, political rivals or professional consultants like Alexandra Vermulen – were all forced to accept the same conclusion. They might not like Mark Adams. In fact, they might actively dislike Mark Adams and everything he stood for. But he was about to dominate the political agenda, and they had no alternative but to take him very seriously indeed.

43

'So ... how do you think we should deal with him?' asked Cameron Young, turning away from the TV screens filled with pundits digesting Adams's rally at the O2, and pressing the 'mute' button on his remote control.

'Well, we could start by telling the world that this is the racist, Islamophobic, xenophobic extreme right-wing agenda of a man who wants to reintroduce fascism to Britain,' suggested his Opposition equivalent, Brian Smallbone. 'Mark Adams is just a twenty-first-century Oswald Mosley.'

'Well, Mosley was fanatically pro-European union, not against it,' Grantham observed. 'Although he and Adams certainly have one thing in common: they were both ministers in a Labour government.'

'Do I have to listen to this?' Smallbone snapped back.

'Really, Jack, was that strictly necessary?' Young asked, doing his best to disguise his amusement at Smallbone's anger. Grantham's uncanny ability to get under people's skins had certainly not diminished over the years.

'Well, I'm always a believer that you can't defeat your enemy without knowing him. It also helps to understand his strengths and weaknesses, even if it's uncomfortable, or even embarrassing, to admit them,' Grantham said.

Smallbone looked disgusted. 'Strengths? The man's a turncoat who's betrayed every worthwhile principle he ever stood for. What fucking strengths can a slime-coated shitbag like that possibly have?'

'He filled the O2, how's that?'

'So did the kids from *Glee*, and I'm not taking them seriously as political thinkers either.'

'My point is, twenty thousand people just did take him seriously. And so should you. So my advice is: forget ideology or moral objections, and consider the logic of the situation. If the electorate looks at Adams's ideas and thinks they're as vile as you say they are, then you've got nothing to worry about. But if people start thinking that he might have a point, then you should at least consider what that point might be.'

'The point is that if the electorate go for Mark Adams then they're fucking morons.'

'Even morons have votes. But what if they're not morons? What if they have genuine concerns and they think Adams is answering them? Shouldn't you have answers too? And shouldn't you make sure they're better than his?'

Cameron Young had said nothing, but he'd not missed a syllable of the argument being played out in front of him. This, he was thinking, was the next election in miniature and Adams's best way of winning it: let the two parties on either side of him beat themselves to a pulp, then step in and take the prize. Then Cameron Young's phone buzzed, alerting him to the arrival of a text. He looked at it and frowned as the other two continued.

'What kind of answers can you have for a man who thinks the white race is dying out?' Smallbone asked.

'Depends on whether he's got his facts right,' said Grantham, 'and whether anyone actually cares. If he's talking bollocks and you can prove it, no problem. But if he isn't, and the voters do care, then you can't just tell people, "You're not allowed to care about that." Not as long as this is a democracy, anyway.'

'Which it won't be, if Adams has his way.'

'Well, then,' said Young, finally entering the fray, 'let's make sure he doesn't, eh? Thank you so much for coming over, Brian.' He got up and held out his hand, making it clear that the meeting was over. 'I think we're all going to need a little time to digest what Adams said, get a feel for the media and public response and then make our plans accordingly.'

Grantham had risen from his seat and was preparing to leave, too, but Young stopped him: 'Jack, if I could ask you to stay for a moment . . .'

Young let Smallbone leave the room and then, as Grantham settled in his seat again, said, 'There's been a significant development, and I'd like to have your input on it.'

'What kind of development?'

'There's been another riot.'

'There's always another riot.'

'Not like this one. Mark Adams is about to find he's been knocked off tomorrow's front pages. Someone's just turned South London into a warzone. We're talking fifty deaths, maybe more . . .'

'Fifty? Bloody hell, what happened?'

'That's what we're going to find out. Make yourself comfortable. I'm going to order us some coffee and sandwiches. This is going to be a long night.'

44

Robbie Bell was in the VIP bar, backstage at the O2, watching his boss fawn all over Alexandra Vermulen, the lobbyist who was supposed to make him a star in the good ol' US of A. Bell had introduced them and had watched the look of delight spread across Adams's face, like a fat kid in a sweet shop, as he took in the blonde hair, the impressively well-preserved face and the dress that clung in all the right places. Bell wondered if Adams realized what an idiot he was making of himself gawping at Vermulen like that. She was smiling politely at his terrible jokes, but she obviously had no interest in anything other than his business, and meanwhile Nicki Adams was starting to get seriously pissed off with her old lech of a husband.

They were all the same, these political couples, Bell decided. The men were egotistical middle-aged bastards. The wives smiled bravely, then went home to stew in white wine, bitterness and tears. However much Adams might try to trumpet his uniqueness, he was no different from the rest.

Bell felt the phone buzzing in his jacket pocket. It was his press secretary, Carla Shepherd, calling, presumably updating him on the post-speech briefings she was giving the media, or asking for an official answer to a tricky question.

'How's it going?' he asked.

'It isn't,' she replied. 'They've all gone.'

'What do you mean, they've all gone? You've only been there five minutes.'

'I mean, Robbie . . . darling . . . that I was just talking them through the scintillating issue of the White Death when they all started looking at their phones and just getting up and walking away.'

'What was it? Some kind of pathetic, overgrown student protest against our disgusting racist policies?'

'No . . . that hadn't gone down too appallingly. Once I'd persuaded them that the numbers were kosher, some of them were actually quite interested.'

'So what was the problem?'

'Apparently there's been a riot in South London.'

'Good. That's just what we wanted.'

'I don't think so . . . not like this. Apparently some obscure little street in South London now looks like downtown Tehran. Fifty people dead.'

A chill feeling of dread started seeping through Bell's system, like icy rain down the back of his neck. Casualties like that made for a major, major story; much too major for his liking.

'How the fuck did fifty people die?' he asked, thinking there had to be some kind of a mistake. He could just about believe fifteen people dying in a riot. Maybe. But fifty?

'Someone started fighting back,' Shepherd said. 'There was an explosion, a bomb or something. It's all still very confused.'

'Shit!'

'Look, you really need to see what's happening. Get your laptop. It's all over the news . . . and Twitter's going mad.'

Bell picked up his briefcase and slipped from the room. The backstage area at the O2 is a warren of passages, offices and dressing rooms. Bell found an empty room, pulled up a plastic chair and logged on. Minutes later he was on the phone again.

Though Mark Adams didn't know it, there was rather more to his campaign that met the eye. Such as, for example, the secret campaign fund that had been established, supported by wealthy donors who had been promised repayment in the form of preferential treatment as and when Adams took office. That fund had helped pay for the rally at the O2 and funded some of the supporting activity around it. It was the brainchild of Hartley Crewson, the founder of a public relations company that specialized in Westminster politics and City finance. He had been Bell's boss before Adams had hired him. In many ways, he still was.

In fact, the entire Adams campaign had been Crewson's idea.

He had spotted the gap in the market caused by the

spectacular unpopularity of all the mainstream party leaders, and realized that the time was right for an outsider to take them on. He'd spotted Adams as the perfect candidate, mentioned the idea in passing on two or three occasions when the two men had met, and then watched with great satisfaction as Adams, like any other politician, had effortlessly persuaded himself that the idea of forming his own party was entirely his own stroke of genius.

Crewson had wanted to be the silent, invisible power behind the throne – one whose existence was unknown even to the man who thought himself king. So far the plan had been working perfectly, but now the Adams train was suddenly in danger of leaving the rails.

'Yes, I know. I just saw it on the news,' Crewson said when Bell told him about the riot. 'This isn't what we needed at all. It's going to dominate every news-cycle for the next week at least, just when we wanted to be driving the agenda. I thought we were all on the same page about what was required.'

'We were,' Bell replied. 'And it worked perfectly at the O2. We had a perfect battle between our supporters and the usual rent-a-mob, with the police stuck uselessly in the middle. The choreography was perfect.'

'So what happened at the other place?'

'I have no idea.'

'Well, you'd better find out, asap. I'll keep an eye on things from my end.' Crewson sighed. 'We may have to be ready to take decisive action to contain the fallout.'

'I understand. What do you want me to do about Adams?'

'As little as possible. Keep him out of sight of the media. I don't want him saying anything or doing anything until we've decided on the correct response.'

'He's meant to be talking to that American, Alexandra Vermulen.'

'Perfect. I hear she's a little cracker. She can keep the candidate entertained for the next couple of hours. If she wants our money, she might as well start earning it.'

When Bell got back to the VIP bar, Adams was looking flushed with success. Evidently no one had dared to tell him that he'd been wasting his time.

'Ah, Robbie, there you are!' He beamed. 'We were wondering what had happened to you.'

'Just a few loose ends to tie up.'

'Excellent . . .' Adams turned to Vermulen and said, 'I would, quite literally, be at a loose end without Robbie.'

She gave him another politely enthusiastic smile.

Adams looked back at Bell. 'I was just telling Alexandra about our plans for dinner. I thought she might care to join us. She was married to a general, you know? And her current beau is an old soldier, too . . .' Now he glanced at his wife. 'Nothing like a girl who loves a man in uniform, eh, darling? Anyway, I was thinking that the two of them ought to join us. What do you say? Can we call the restaurant and get a bigger table?'

'Of course,' said Bell. He was, by nature, opposed to any ideas he had not had himself. But there was something to be said for getting this old soldier along for the ride. He and Adams could tell old war stories, get pissed

and pretend to be heroes . . . and with any luck it would
be morning before Adams found out about the riot. 'I'll
get on to it right away.'

45

Carver was just walking past a boarded-up pub on Stewart's Road, keeping fifty metres between himself and the riot leader, when Alix called. He had his phone on vibrate and his earphones plugged in.

'I hope I'm not interrupting,' she said.

'No . . . it's all right,' he murmured into the scarf, keeping his voice too low for the man ahead of him to detect it.

A slight note of anxiety entered her voice. 'Are you all right? You sound a little down.'

'No,' Carver lied. 'Just can't speak very loud. How about you? How was Adams?'

'Very, ah . . . interesting. He's why I called you, actually. He was wondering if you'd like to join us for dinner. I didn't know if you and Snoopy had already made plans . . . you've probably eaten already. Well, maybe you could join us for coffee.'

Carver really didn't feel like going off to dinner with some puffed-up politician. He didn't feel like doing anything. He was empty, washed-out and badly shaken up by what had happened in Netherton Street. The safest place for him right now was anywhere but here, and if he had any sense he'd be getting the hell out of London and taking Alix with him. But if he did that, he'd have to spend the rest of his life weighed down by the knowledge that he'd done nothing, if not to put things right – it was far too late for that now – then at least to find an explanation for what had happened and to make sure that those responsible were punished. Every instinct he had told him that it was all in some way connected to Mark Adams and his political campaign. If that was the case, then he needed to see the man for himself, hear what he had to say, look him in the eye and get a sense of just how far he was prepared to go and how many people he was prepared to sacrifice in the pursuit of power.

'In the end, we didn't eat,' Carver said. 'Snoopy had ... well, he had something else to do. He found a girl. She seemed to like him ...'

Alix laughed. 'So he left you high and dry? Poor baby! Does that mean you're coming to dinner?'

'Why not? I've got an errand to run so I may be a little late. Where are you going to be?'

'It's called Roast,' she said.

An image flashed across Carver's mind: the scorched flesh of the bomb-victims. He swallowed hard and said, 'Sounds great.'

46

Detective Inspector Mara Keane was over six feet tall, broad-shouldered and big- footed. But then, as she liked to point out, you could say the same about Maria Sharapova. She had long since conquered the crippling self-consciousness of her youth and now saw her size as an advantage. It was much harder for a male colleague to patronize her if he had to look up to her while he did it. But even DI Keane wasn't mentally strong enough to be able to walk unaffected through the carnage of Netherton Street.

Ambulances had been going to and fro in a constant stream for the best part of an hour. There hadn't been many wounded rioters or local people for the doctors at the A & E department at St Thomas' Hospital to deal with. Many of those who had still been alive when the first emergency service personnel had arrived had been beyond treatment: the best that could be done had been to make their passing slightly less terrible than it might otherwise have been.

Meanwhile, the sheer number of corpses that had to be photographed in situ and given a preliminary forensic examination was so great that even though police officers and forensic pathologists had been drafted in from the entire Metropolitan Police area, the fatalities were all still lying where they had fallen. The figures quietly going about their business amongst the dead looked like ghosts themselves in their hooded white scene-of-crime suits, which glowed in the spotlights set up to illuminate a crime-scene encompassing an entire street. The rain had stopped, but the pavements were still slick with water and there were puddles by the side of the road.

Keane heard a polite cough beside her and turned to see a balding man in his late fifties, with his remaining hair cropped as close as his beard. His name was Dr Karl Lewisohn. He had a wise, gentle face with liquid black-brown eyes, and they looked at Keane over the top of the glasses he required for the close-range examination of dead bodies. He stood half a head shorter than her.

'Hello, Mara,' he said. 'I would have said "good evening" but it hardly seems appropriate . . .'

She gave a little smile. 'Hello, Karl . . . Ghastly, isn't it?'

'Well, let me put it to you this way. In a typical three-month period, roughly sixty-five post-mortems are carried out in the whole of Greater London, and less than thirty of them are determined to be homicide. We've got over fifty dead bodies here, in a single night, and every one of them was killed by another human being.'

'So when are you going to be able to give me the post-mortems?' she asked, getting down to business.

'Oh, it'll be several days, maybe weeks, before you get them all. But I can give you the basic summary right now.'

Together, Keane and Lewisohn ran through the deaths at the Khyber Star restaurant and the Dutchman's Head pub. They were all the results of frenzied, uncontrolled acts of violence. Then Lewisohn pointed towards Paula Miklosko's car, still wedged against the garbage truck, and said, 'Now this is where it gets interesting.

'There are two clusters of bodies on the street itself. One, by that abandoned car over there, shows more examples of knife deaths, but whoever carried out the killings wasn't just another rioter. He knew exactly what he was doing. He even killed one victim with a knife thrown to the base of the throat – a very rare skill indeed. Now, moving on, there are two men in the middle of the road who have both been killed by firearms – almost certainly the same firearm in the hands of a single shooter, and I'm betting it was a pistol.

'Again, you're looking for an expert. Both victims were shot at extremely close range, which of course makes the job easier in some ways, but both were carrying weapons of their own: a machete and an axe, respectively. It takes very considerable courage to maintain a steady hand and a clear eye under those circumstances, but this man was remarkably self-controlled. He hit one of the rioters in the shoulder, but the man just kept coming at him. Our shooter didn't flinch. He stood his ground and fired a second, fatal round.'

'That sounds like someone with military training,' Keane observed.

'Absolutely,' Lewisohn agreed, 'and not just training. I'm certain we're dealing with more than one serving or recently retired soldier with considerable combat experience. I haven't even got to their real pièce de résistance yet.'

'You mean the Lion Market?'

'Quite.' Lewisohn began walking towards the wrecked supermarket. He paused to let an ambulance drive past them, taking bodies away to the morgue. Then he went on a few more paces and stopped on the edge of the scene, where it was still calm enough for them to talk in peace.

'Again there are several shootings,' he continued. 'Two victims were killed outside the shop, this time with a shotgun, and the blood evidence suggests that a third may have been wounded. I presume this was a straightforward defensive action against some sort of a charge. But then the rioters managed to get into the shop, and that's where at least two more of them were hit at point-blank range – in the guts – again with a shotgun. Once more we see the same pattern of a shooter remaining calm enough to fire with deadly effect when almost overrun by assailants.'

'So we have either one man who's very heavily armed or two equally well-trained shooters.'

'I'm sure it's the latter. At the back of the building

there's a storeroom. We found another four shotgun-victims there, and two more killed with what I suspect will turn out to be the same pistol that accounted for the ones in the middle of the street. Now all the threads of our story come together. You see, a pistol was found in the grasp of a dead male. His abdomen had been cut open by a large blade. One of your people found a bloodstained machete by a rioter whose body was lying less than a metre away, and that rioter . . .' Lewisohn paused for effect, like a comedian tantalizing an audience before delivering his punchline, '. . . had been killed by a close-range blast from a shotgun.'

'So Shooter One is killed. Shooter Two gets the man who did it . . . and then mysteriously disappears,' Keane summarized.

'Precisely . . . and I'll tell you another interesting thing about Shooter One. He couldn't have fired the shotgun. It's almost impossible to use without both hands, and he had a bullet wound in his left arm, to which someone had applied a crude, improvised dressing. He had cling film wrapped around his torso to immobilize the arm.'

'And then he'd gone back to the fight . . .'

'Exactly.'

Keane nodded to herself, silently taking in everything Lewisohn had said and getting it clear in her mind. He said nothing, knowing her well enough to wait until she spoke again.

'So what about the bomb-victims?' Keane asked.

Lewisohn shrugged. 'I wouldn't be so confident that this explosion was caused by a bomb, if I were you.'

'How do you mean?'

'Well, it's the nature of the wounds,' Lewisohn explained. 'When a conventional bomb goes off, there's a tremendous amount of shrapnel flying through the air. Arms and legs are torn off, and heads are ripped from torsos, but there's relatively little of that kind of damage here. The overwhelming mass of fatalities were due to internal damage as the shock wave from the explosion passed through the victims' bodies. I took a quick look inside a few sets of ears, too. The eardrums were all shredded. These poor people were dazzled, burned and deafened before they drowned in their own blood.'

Keane swallowed hard, then said, 'I still don't quite understand, though – what caused the explosion in the first place? What exactly went bang?'

'You'll have to ask the army chaps about that. They're all in there, looking at scorch-marks and whatnot. But I can tell you crudely what went bang: the air did. These people were actually inside the explosion. It was all around them, everywhere at once.'

'My God, who could do such a thing?'

'Well, whoever had the expertise to create that explosion certainly knew the effect that it would have. He knew how these people would die. And if you'll excuse me for departing from my proper professional objectivity, I think that makes him a monster.'

'A cold-blooded, calculating monster, by the sounds of it,' Keane agreed. 'But think about what he was up against – an armed mob that had already looted and killed. What kind of people were they?'

'Savages,' said Lewisohn mournfully. His eyes were filled with sadness as he added, 'Terrible, isn't it? A nation of monsters and savages ... Is that really what we've become? How utterly bloody depressing.'

47

Donny Bakunin climbed the stairs to his fourth-floor flat like a mountaineer trying to scale Everest without the benefit of oxygen. Every step required its own individual effort and act of concentration. He was seeing a bit better now through the slowly diminishing glare and had recovered a little of his hearing, though everything still sounded as though it was coming to him from the far end of a very long tunnel: even his own footsteps seemed a million miles away. Most of the bleeding seemed to have stopped, but the pain of each individual cut pierced him even more sharply than before, and every single part of his body appeared to have been individually battered, making its own particular contribution to his overall world of pain.

He fumbled for the first of his two front-door keys, a Banham, and then jabbed it helplessly at the hole until it somehow slipped in and turned. The Yale was even harder to master, and Bakunin was almost weeping with frustration before he finally made it work and was able to open the door.

His attention was entirely focused on himself and his personal suffering. He was unaware of the figure observing him from the stairs, and shuffled into his drab, barren living space without the first idea that he was in any immediate danger. He was just relieved to have got away from Netherton Street in one piece, unmolested by the police. Then he turned to close the door behind him, and suddenly it didn't seem to want to shut. In fact it was pushing against him, and he was being forced backwards. His jumbled senses were unable to make sense of what was happening until the weight on the far side of the door shifted and manifested itself in front of him as the figure of a man.

His eyes were shaded by the peak of his cap, and his nose and mouth were hidden behind the blue scarf knotted around his face. Something about him seemed familiar, though Bakunin was in no state to remember where he had seen him before. Bakunin didn't even see the two hands that slapped him hard on either side of the face, one after the other, hurting and disorientating him still further. He was unable to offer any resistance as he was bundled across the room and sat on a plain wooden chair. He was hit again, the same way as before, and then, from far, far away, he heard a muffled voice say, 'Don't move.'

Bakunin wasn't capable of movement. He was physically shattered, mentally drained and close to tears. He felt as helpless as a small boy at the mercy of a playground bully, and he just wanted to curl up in a small, foetal ball and cover his head with his hands until all the monsters went away.

He was hardly aware of the telephone cable, ripped from the wall, that was being tied around his shins, binding them to the chair legs. Nor did he make the slightest protest as his arms and chest were secured to the back of the chair. He was almost grateful for the immobility. He felt supported, and just sat there limply, with his head hanging down, lacking the energy even to be curious about what was going to happen next.

Carver had absolutely no concern whatever for the riot leader's well-being. He never wanted to kill another human being again if he could possibly help it. But hurting one was another matter. Carver needed information, and he wasn't going to be bound by any rules or regulations while he got it. He was filming the interrogation, too. He wanted the whole world to know the truth of what had happened.

He started with the basics: 'What's your name?'

The man raised his head. There was a frantic look on his face. 'What? What? Can't hear,' he whined, turning his head to one side and leaning forward so that his ear was tilted towards Carver.

Carver bent down and put his mouth close to it. He repeated, 'What's your name?'

'Oh,' said the man, as if surprised that it was such a simple question. And then: 'Not telling you.'

Carver gestured with his finger, bringing the man's ear closer to him again. 'Yes, you are,' he said. 'What's your name?'

The man sat back, his mouth clamped shut.

'Suit yourself,' said Carver and kicked the man in the chest with the flat of his sole, knocking over the chair. The man cried out as the back of his head hit the floor, but that was all he could do as he lay there like a dead beetle, immobile and helpless.

Carver left him there and went into the flat's grubby kitchen, which was lined with decrepit old units, fronted in chipped and scratched white melamine. The sink was filled with dirty crockery, making a mockery of the yellow washing-up gloves draped over its edge. Carver put them on. He took the towel and stuck it under the cold tap until it was wet through, then wrung it out just enough to stop it dripping. Next he filled a teacup with more cold water before taking both the towel and the cup back into the living room.

Carver got down on one knee by the man's head. 'You've heard of waterboarding, right?' he said.

The man's eyes widened in alarm and he jerked his head from side to side as he whimpered, 'No, no . . . please . . .'

Carver pressed the towel down over the man's face, drawing it tight across his nose so that he couldn't breathe without inhaling the water still left in the fabric. He held the gathered ends of the towel bunched beneath the man's chin in one hand. With the other, Carver raised the cup and then delicately poured a thin stream of water down on to the towel, pulling hard on the fabric to prevent the desperate man from moving his nose and mouth away from the dripping water.

It would, Carver knew, feel exactly like drowning –

mostly because it actually *was* a form of drowning. Waterboarding could be fatal, even to a fit interrogation subject. This man was in very bad shape and his lungs had certainly been damaged to some extent by the blast, so his tolerance would be much lower than the average. Carver gave it fifteen seconds, knowing that it would have seemed far, far longer to the man being tortured, and then released his grip on the towel.

The man fought for breath, and the sounds he made as he struggled to get air down into his lungs were so like those of the dying bomb-victims in the Lion Market that Carver just wanted to press the towel back down on his face and keep it there till he couldn't breathe any more, simply to shut him up.

He fought against temptation and made himself stick to his mission.

'One more time: what's your name?'

No response.

'What's your name? Or do you want another helping?'

The man shook his head. 'No . . . no . . . I'll tell you my name. I'll tell you anything. Just, please stop hurting me.'

'All right then. We're going to talk. And I'm going to film it.'

Carver fished the head cam out of his pocket, turned it back on and pointed it at the man. 'So, let's start again,' he said. 'What's your name?'

'Bakunin. My name is Donny Bakunin.'

'And you organized the riot at Netherton Street tonight?'

'Yes . . . well, no . . .'

'Which: yes or no?'

'Yes, I got everyone together on the street. I gave them their orders . . . and I told them not to hurt anyone . . . I made that very clear! I want everyone to know that!'

'I'm sure people will really appreciate your efforts. Now, who told you to start the riot?'

Bakunin's eyes widened. 'How did you know?'

'Who was it? Who told you not to hit the pub?'

Bakunin's eyes darted from side to side. 'Have you been listening? What are you? MI5? GCHQ?'

'I'm a man who wants to know where you get your orders.'

'I don't know! I never got a name. We never met. I tell you, I don't know!'

'Did it have anything to do with Mark Adams?'

'Adams! I'd never work for a fascist like Adams!'

'Yes, you would. You'll work for anyone. We've already established that. So, was this the first time?'

Bakunin shook his head.

'So what was the procedure?'

'I got a call, telling me where it had to happen and when.'

'When was the last call?'

'Today, about six o'clock.'

'Did you get paid?'

Bakunin's silence was almost as good as a confession. Almost.

Carver held the towel up so Bakunin could see it. Then he lowered his hand again and repeated the question: 'Did you get paid?'

'Yes.'

'Cash? Bank transfer?'

'Transfer.'

'What bank?'

'First Global.'

'Based where?'

'Grand Cayman.'

Carver burst out laughing. 'An anarchist with an off-shore account. That's just perfect. Where's your phone, you hypocritical sack of shit?'

'In my coat.'

Carver searched the pockets of the duffel coat until he found the phone. 'Security code?'

'One-one-five-nine.'

Carver punched it in. The washing-up gloves made it hard to press the numbers, but the inconvenience was worth it: he'd leave no fingerprints on the phone. As the home screen appeared he said, 'Let me guess: first of January, 1959 . . . the date of the Cuban revolution. What does that make you, the Fidel Castro of Clapham?'

He opened up the phone's call history. There was an incoming one at 18.03 all right, and it looked like the correct one because the number was blocked.

'What did you do when you wanted to call him?'

'There was a number, but it only led to a voicemail. It's in the address book under Hegel.'

'Of course it is.'

Bakunin had been the last stop on a series of cut-outs between the original planners of the riot and the foot soldiers who had actually put it in motion. The whole purpose of the system was to ensure that no one could betray anyone else's identity. For now it was enough for Carver that he knew for sure that someone, somewhere, had planned everything. And speaking of that someone, he was late for dinner with Adams.

Carver used the towel to wipe down the cable tying Bakunin to the chair. He kept the gloves on as he left the flat, and disposed of them in a waste-disposal bin several blocks away. The cap and scarf each went into separate bins. Then he grabbed a cab and set off for the restaurant.

48

It was as if the events at the O2 had never happened. The demonstrations, the apparent assassination attempt, Mark Adams's speech – in an instant, they'd all been put to the back of the media queue; footnotes at best to the headline story of the riot in Netherton Street. There were almost as many outside broadcast vans as emergency vehicles parked in the area, clustering as close as they could get to the scene-of-crime tape that cordoned off more than a hundred metres of the street itself, and a couple of residential side roads, too.

The police had set aside a small area for TV crews. It allowed reporters to stand in front of their cameras with a suitably dramatic scene of urban devastation behind them, without allowing them to get close enough to impede the work of the myriad people investigating the riot and dealing with its victims. The individual stars that viewers saw on their screens were lined up almost shoulder to shoulder, each delivering an apparently unique perspective on events, while standing within easy touching distance of someone else saying almost exactly the same thing.

'The scenes here are by far the worst that London has seen since the seven-seven bombings in July 2005,' pronounced a grim-faced brunette with an Irish accent, representing the BBC. 'Fifty-two people as well as the four bombers died that night, and the final death toll here may be even higher. We know that the staff of an Indian restaurant, the Khyber Star, were massacred, as were several customers at a pub, the Dutchman's Head. But the worst carnage was reserved for the mini-supermarket behind me, the Lion Market.'

'It is still not clear precisely what happened here,' said the man from *Sky News*, his eyes narrowed like a hunter surveying the horizon, his voice clipped and authoritative. 'But I have been able to piece together some key elements in the story. The rioters made a concerted attack against a small group of people who were taking shelter in the Lion Market. A garbage truck stolen earlier in the evening was rammed into the shop's security shutters, smashing them. Rioters flooded into the store, and very soon afterwards there was some kind of explosion. At this stage, no one knows precisely what caused it.'

'Just a few minutes ago, I spoke to one of the policemen at the scene,' revealed a rosy-cheeked young man from ITN. 'He told me that when he arrived at the store it was filled with people coughing and vomiting up blood. They were struggling for breath and were clearly in great distress. Some of them, he said, were little more than children. The first ambulances arrived no more than five minutes later. And by then, the policeman said, every single one of those people in the supermarket was dead.'

The BBC woman said, 'Senior police commanders are genuinely shocked by what has happened here. We have been suffering riots and disorder for so long that we have, perhaps, become numbed by them. But the horror of the Netherton Street killings is so extreme that it is taking us into a whole new realm of violence. And now, back to the studio . . .'

49

Chrystal Prentice was sitting in an interview room at Kennington police station, with a female police officer and a cup of hot, sweet tea for company, waiting to be interviewed. She was trying to decide what to say. They were going to expect honest answers, but Snoopy's mate had helped save their lives. So if he wanted to keep out of all this, she owed it to him to do what he'd asked. And it felt like what Snoopy would have wanted, too. That was the deciding thing, really: what Snoopy would have wanted.

Poor Snoopy. It was all Chrystal could do to stop herself crying at the memory of him lying on that storeroom floor, and equally hard to drive that memory from her mind.

The door opened and as the female PC excused herself and left two other people came in. The first one introduced himself as Detective Sergeant Brian Walcott.

He was black, about thirty-five, Chrystal reckoned, dressed in a basic suit and tie and quite fit, really, for a policeman. The second one was a woman. She introduced herself as Detective Inspector Mara Keane, which made her Walcott's boss, and in her heels she towered over him, though he wasn't exactly short. When Keane spoke her voice was soft and quite low, like a newsreader on the TV: the kind of voice that made you believe whatever it was saying.

'So, you were working at the Dutchman's Head . . . what happened?' Keane said, giving Chrystal a look that was not in any way aggressive, but which still made it plain to the younger woman that she was being sized up, too.

'Well, I got talking to one of the customers,' Chrystal began, trying to keep those terrible images away from her mind. 'He was sitting at the bar, and he said something about being scared of flying, and I said that was, like, well funny, 'cos I am too, terrified.'

'And this man, was he the one who ended up in the Lion Market with you?' Keane asked.

Chrystal nodded, trying to hold back the tears.

'Did he give you his name?'

'He just said his name was . . .' Chrystal could feel herself welling up. 'I'm sorry,' she said. Then she covered her mouth to hide her trembling lips.

'Take your time,' said Keane.

Chrystal took a deep breath and said, 'Snoopy. He said his name was Snoopy.'

'And this Snoopy, was he drinking alone?'

Chrystal couldn't quite manage a direct lie. 'Yeah, well,

he must've been, mustn't he? Otherwise he wouldn't have been talking to me.'

'I don't know, you tell me. Was he alone?'

'Yeah . . . yeah, he was alone.'

Both women knew that wasn't the truth. Walcott did, too. He wanted to press Chrystal harder, but before he could, Keane changed the subject.

'So tell me how you got from the pub to the Lion Market.'

Chrystal sighed heavily, as though she'd been holding her breath: maybe she had been, she wasn't sure. The relief was evident in her voice as she explained how they had left the pub, bumped into the rioters and rescued another woman. She described Snoopy firing at the rioters and being hit by one of their bullets before they reached the Lion Market.

Walcott had been asking a lot of the questions: 'So when you got to the shop, who was there?'

'Er . . . me, Snoopy, the woman he'd rescued from the car and Maninder and Ajay, obviously, 'cos it's their shop.'

Now Keane came back into the interview. 'The woman from the car, that was . . .' She consulted her notes: 'Paula Miklosko?'

'Yeah, Paula, that was her.'

'And how would you say she was – her physical and mental condition, I mean?'

'She was well out of it. She'd been punched and that and she was, like, all shaking and in shock.'

'So how did she get from the car to the Lion Market?' Keane did not raise her voice at all when she asked the question. She didn't have to.

Chrystal scrambled for time. 'I'm sorry?'

'If she was out of it and in shock, how did she manage to get from the car, where she was rescued, to the shop?'

'She come with us, didn't she?'

Keane frowned. 'So she ran, is that it? She managed to run fast enough not to be caught by this mob ... even though she was in shock?'

'Well, we helped her.'

'You and Snoopy?'

'Yeah.'

'At the same time that he was turning round to shoot at people?'

Chrystal hated this. She was trying to do the right thing, but every question just made her dig herself deeper and deeper into trouble. 'I don't know! It was mental out there. How am I supposed to remember everything?'

Keane nodded. Again she backed off, like an angler who lets the line run out when the fish has already been hooked. 'All right, let's get back to the market. You were there and you were tending to Snoopy's wounded arm, and there was a big mob outside. So then what happened? Did the mob attack?'

'Yeah.'

'Were any shots fired at them ... from inside the shop?'

'They might have been, I don't know.'

Now Walcott intervened again, sounding impatient: 'Come off it, Chrystal. If a gun goes off in the same room you're in, you know all about it. Were any shots fired from the shop at the mob outside?'

'Yeah . . . maybe . . . two or three.'

Keane again: 'So who fired them?'

'I don't know. I wasn't looking. I was doing Snoopy's arm.'

'So he definitely didn't fire the shots?'

'Well, no, how could he?'

'Which means it had to be one of the two Panus.'

'Well, yeah, maybe . . . Like I said, I didn't see.'

'Then what?'

'Me and Maninder went down to the cellar with Paula.'

'What happened to the other two: Ajay Panu and Snoopy?' Keane asked.

'Snoopy went out the back, in case anyone came in that way.' Chrystal bit her lip as she felt it start to tremble again.

'So . . . what about Ajay Panu, where did he go?'

Chrystal gave a helpless shrug of her shoulders. 'I don't know. Like I said, I was in the cellar.'

'Did you at any time see him shoot at anyone?'

'Ajay?' Chrystal asked her voice rising in surprise. 'No! He never!'

'But he joined you in the cellar – Ajay, I mean . . .'

'Yeah, he did, right at the end. Just before the explosion.'

'Tell me about the explosion. Do you know what it was that exploded?'

'No, it just, like, happened – know what I mean?'

'Then what did you do?'

'We just waited, you know, down in the cellar. We were too scared to go upstairs, to be honest.'

'I understand,' said DI Keane. 'So let's leave it there, shall we? It's getting late and you've had a very shocking, traumatic experience. So what I want you to do, Chrystal, is to think about all the things that you and I have discussed. And when you're feeling better we can talk again. We'll start with Snoopy's friend . . . the one who was drinking with him at the pub . . . the one you've been trying so hard not to talk about just now.'

50

Carver kept thinking about the girl. The sound of her calling out, 'Ricky!' clung to him like a song he couldn't get out of his head. He'd spent most of his professional life bringing death to other people and risking it himself. He'd become adept at distancing himself from uncomfortable, unnecessary emotions. But tonight, when all he'd wanted was a quiet drink with an old mate, he'd ended up doing things which had taken him to a dark and bitter place. And now he was having a hard time getting out of that place. He was stuck in a bad dream, and he couldn't seem to wake up.

'Get a fucking grip,' he muttered to himself as he made his way to the restaurant entrance. There were armed guards outside it, just as there had been at the hotel. Carver had to wait before his name was confirmed as one of Mr Adams's guests, and even then he didn't get in without passing through a scanner. These days, everywhere was an airport. He got in the lift that would take him up to the dining room and felt an unexpected sense of confinement, of claustrophobia.

At the top there was a reception desk where he gave his name and a waiter was summoned to direct him to Mark Adams's table. The room was laid out beneath the soaring roof of the old market hall, with glazed walls and a huge fan window – whose panes of glass were held within an intricate iron tracery. It was a typically Victorian cathedral of commerce, and the men and women who were tucking into the menu of hearty British foods – from Dorset crabs and Skye scallops to Hereford beef and Hampshire pheasant – had a Dickensian air about them, too: the rich filling their faces and calling for more claret and ale while the poor descended into squalor all around them.

The sight of Alix raised his spirits. He kissed her on the cheek as he was taking his place, then managed polite, confident smiles as she said, 'This is my partner, Sam,' and introduced him in turn to Adams, his wife, whose name went in one ear and out the other, and some guy who worked for Adams: black suit, shaven head – looked like the creepy butler in *The Rocky Horror Show*. Carver didn't even hear his name, still less remember it. Not a good sign.

'I ordered for you,' Alix said. 'Baked crab to start with, and then the steak. I hope that's all right.'

'Thanks, that sounds fine.'

'So, did you see the speech?' Alix asked, knowing that was what Adams would most want to know.

'Not all of it. But I did catch the assassination attempt.

Very impressive . . .' Carver laughed. To his surprise something genuinely funny had occurred to him.

'What's the joke?' Adams asked.

'I was just thinking of a mate of mine. We were having a pint while the speech was on and he, ah . . .' Carver stopped himself before he said 'was'. 'He's a big fan of yours but the exact words he used were, "Typical fucking glory boy."'

The women looked startled by Carver's rudeness. The shaven-headed guy gave a sly, private smile. Adams just laughed.

'Was this mate of yours another bootneck, by any chance?'

'We were proud to serve together in the Royal Marines, if that's what you mean,' said Carver, with exaggerated formality. He was beginning to feel a bit more like himself again. Schultz would've had a good laugh if he'd known that Adams had been told exactly what he'd thought of his military record.

'And he somehow failed to hold the Paratroop Regiment in the respect which it certainly deserves . . . how odd,' Adams replied, knowing full well that the Marines and Paras despised one another, and enjoying the old soldiers' banter. 'Bloody hell,' he said, catching sight of Carver's glass. 'You've not been given a drink. Here, have a drop of this: not a bad claret, if you like that sort of thing.'

It was a Château Daugay 2000, a Grand Cru St Émilion, and it hit Carver's palate with an earthy, almost excremental funkiness that gave way to warm, rich, dark fruits that belonged to a different, better world than the one he'd been dragged into that night. 'God, that's good.' He sighed. 'Thanks. I really needed that.'

'Bad day?' Adams asked.

'Something like that. Not as bad as yours might have been, though ... if that shooter at the O2 had been armed with an actual gun.'

'Ah ...' Adams took a drink of his own, keeping his eyes on Carver all the while, sizing him up. 'All right then, how did I know?'

'Well, my first guess was that you didn't hear the bullet in the air ...'

'That could have been a possibility.' Adams turned towards Alix, the polite host, not wanting the women to be excluded from the conversation. 'You see, the thing is, Alix, that a bullet travels faster than sound, so you actually hear the bullet going by before you hear the shot itself ...'

'Really? How fascinating,' she said sweetly, thinking that it was probably best not to mention the two men she had shot dead on the night she first met Carver, or the third she'd killed less than a week after that.

The men, meanwhile, were continuing with their conversational game, each enjoying the attempt to get one up on the other.

'But you were standing too close to the gun to be able to notice that,' Carver continued. 'The time difference would have been milliseconds.'

Adams smiled. He swirled his wine round the bottom of his glass. 'So what was it?'

'Well, I'm guessing that the gun looked, felt and sounded exactly like a normal one, except for one thing.'

Another, broader smile. 'Which was . . . ?'

'The colour . . . orange, perhaps. That's bright enough that you couldn't miss it . . .'

'And it's also the colour that current gun regulations specify for replica weapons that are capable of firing blanks. Well done.' Adams raised his glass in salute, then continued, 'The gun was a replica Glock and it was, as you say, perfect in every respect except for resembling a tangerine. But that's actually not the main reason I was certain I was safe. You see, I knew the man holding it.'

'What?' asked Alix. 'You mean this was all a set-up?'

'Good lord, no . . . His name's Kieron Sproles. He's a constituent of mine, and I knew he wasn't trying to kill me. This was the proverbial cry for help – my help, to be precise. See, the daft bugger thinks I'm somehow responsible for the fact that the council aren't giving his mum proper care. She's got Alzheimer's, poor old dear. I keep telling him, if the council aren't looking after her, then he should leave me alone and go and complain to them . . .'

Adams was a politician with a taste for speechmaking, a natural raconteur and a middle-aged man with a lot of red wine inside him. The combination made him loquacious. 'I've written to the council and the local paper highlighting the issue. I've done the whole number about why are they cutting back on care for vulnerable old folk when they're still advertising in the bloody *Guardian* for strategy implementation officers, tasked with coordinating effective monitoring of equal-opportunity policy delivery, or some such politically correct bollocks . . . Excuse my language, love, but this kind of nonsense really gets on my tits.'

Carver wasn't in a mood to listen to a politician doing his man-of-the-people routine, this one in particular. Luckily the first course arrived and the conversation switched to inconsequential chit-chat as the five diners concentrated on their food. More wine was ordered, the main courses were consumed, and still nothing at all was said about the riot. Surely they must have heard about it? The cabbie who'd brought Carver to the restaurant had had his radio tuned to a phone-in. The original subject of the show had been Mark Adams, but Netherton Street was the only thing on any of the callers' minds. So why had no one even mentioned it here?

Carver waited until everyone had ordered their coffees and desserts and then asked, 'So what do you think about this riot in South London tonight?'

Adams looked blank. 'What riot?' he asked.

Either the guy was an Oscar-worthy actor, or he genuinely didn't know.

'Haven't you heard? They were talking about it on the radio on the cab-ride over here. Apparently it was total mayhem. Shops and restaurants looted. Buildings set on fire.'

'Isn't that typical?' Nicki Adams snapped. 'Don't tell me – the police did nothing to stop it.'

'Of course not, darling,' said Adams.

Carver went on: 'They couldn't get there in time. And I haven't come to the worst bit. Several people were shot dead . . .'

'That's terrible!' Alix exclaimed.

'And there was some kind of explosion. Thirty, maybe even forty people were killed in it. It's the only thing anybody's talking about.'

With every word that Carver said the shaven-headed guy's face had grown more tense, his jaw more clenched, his complexion paler. He was obviously furious, and it was clear to Carver that he had known all about the riot but had chosen not to inform his boss. Why? Was he trying to avoid, or at least postpone, the bollocking he'd get when Adams realized that the whole thing had spiralled out of control and made an irrelevance of the O2 event? Or was the riot his baby, something he'd planned behind Adams's back?

'This is appalling, simply appalling,' Adams said, and once again his reaction seemed entirely genuine. He turned to the shaven-headed guy. 'So, Robbie, how do you think we should respond?'

'The first priority has to be to put your speech back on the news-lists,' Robbie said. 'Then—'

'Don't be so bloody ridiculous,' Adams interrupted him. 'If this is true, if all these people have lost their lives, then they are the first priority. And that means catching the people who did this.'

'Well, let's not rush to any hasty judgements. We need to be in possession of the full facts before we decide on our strategy.'

'Well, we'd better get in possession bloody fast then, hadn't we?' Adams gave an apologetic look at his guests. 'I'm sorry, Alexandra, Sam . . . I'm sure you'll understand that we have to cut dinner short. Another time, perhaps . . .'

As Carver escorted Alix out of the restaurant he couldn't help thinking that he'd met his fair share of megalomaniacs, murderers, fanatics and psychopaths in his time. And whatever else he might be, Mark Adams did not seem anything at all like any of them.

51

Robbie Bell made his living by watching, assessing and calculating. He'd long ago perfected the art of feigning interest; faking the smile that seems like a response, watching and waiting while other people dug themselves into deeper and deeper holes. And while one part of his mind was occupied with the problem of how to keep Adams from doing anything too stupid before Crewson and his people had come up with a containment plan for the Netherton Street disaster, the other was thinking about Alix Vermulen's boyfriend, Sam. Something about him wasn't right.

No, make that lots of things.

For a start, the Vermulen woman had only introduced him as 'Sam', no surname. Bell hadn't thought anything of it at the time, assuming she was just being informal. But on reflection it seemed bizarre for a grown man to sit down to dinner with a senior politician and not give his full name. Most people would want to be remembered by a powerful man who might be the next prime minister. But Sam did not, and that was odd.

Then there was the whole way he'd raised the subject of the riot. He'd had that ridiculous macho-bullshit conversation with Adams about fake guns and waited until two entire courses had been cleared away – long after it was obvious no one on the table knew about the riot – to mention the minor fact that there were dead bodies littering the streets of South London. By Sam's own account, he'd heard about it in the cab on the way over. So why wasn't that the first thing he had mentioned? Why hadn't his first words been, 'Have you heard about the riot?'

Next, there was the whole business about his friend – the one who'd called Adams a typical fucking glory boy. (A perfect description, Bell thought. He'd use it too, one day.) Sam had said that he was another Marine, and there'd been the strong hint that they'd both been more than that, which meant special forces. But there was just something about the way Sam had spoken about this man, something, well ... elegiac, like he was remembering a lost friend. But how could that be? Sam had said that they'd been having a drink together earlier in the evening, watching the beginning of the speech.

And then the penny began to drop and something else struck Robbie Bell. Sam had been wearing a suede jacket – a good one. A man as well-off as he seemed to be would take the trouble to have a jacket like that cleaned on a regular basis. But there had been marks on it, like brown sprinkles . . . or spatters . . .

Bell realized that Nicki Adams was saying something to him. She was asking him when the taxi would arrive to take her home. He looked her, nodded and said, 'I'll go and check right away.' But all he could think was: Crewson needs to know about this.

52

Cameron Young was a very modern Chief of Staff. He didn't just have flat-screen TVs tuned to the BBC, *Sky News*, CNN and Al Jazeera, he followed Twitter and a slew of blogs and news-feeds, too. Social media, after all, were frequently faster and more accurate than any other source of information. And they had already begun speculating on who had caused the explosion at the Lion Market, and asking whether one of the people responsible had got away from the scene of the crime. In fact, #whowasthesecondman was the top trending topic among London Twitter users. Young's latest piece of information, however, had come to him the official old-fashioned way: from the Metropolitan Police Gold Command that had been set up to deal with the disaster under Commander Mary Stamford, a Scotland Yard high-flyer tipped as a future commissioner of the Met.

'Intriguing information from Netherton Street . . .' he said to Jack Grantham, whose mouth was full of bacon sandwich. 'The police found a body they think belongs to one of the men who were helping the occupants of the Lion Market defend themselves against the mob. There was no wallet on his body and no other form of identification except for a Royal Marines crest tattooed on to his left shoulder. Apparently he began the night in a local pub. The barmaid says he called himself "Snoopy" when he was chatting her up.'

Grantham's full mouth made it hard for him to say anything in reply, and he was extremely grateful for that, because that name was one with which he was very familiar. His tongue played around his teeth, extracting bits of sandwich, while he waited to see whether Young would make the connection.

Evidently he hadn't, because he continued, 'It's good news in the short-term, of course. Kills that Adams speech stone-dead. But he's bound to want to use this going forward. I mean, it's perfect for his whole law-and order agenda. We need to have answers when people start asking why the police weren't able to prevent it. Should we be alarmed, do you think, that an ex-Marine was involved?'

'Why?' Grantham replied. 'From what you say, it sounds as though he died a hero's death.'

'I suppose so, though it also makes it sound, somehow, as though military personnel were involved. You know . . . deliberately.'

'I don't see that,' Grantham reassured him. 'And Adams is hardly likely to pursue that line of attack. He's ex-military himself. He's never going to say anything that criticizes our brave boys and girls in uniform.'

'I suppose not. But I think we'll have to get a COBRA committee together, first thing in the morning. We need to be seen to be taking this very seriously. Do you want to sit on it?'

'No, I don't think so . . . It's a purely domestic affair. If I turn up, people are going to ask why. And I don't think either of us wants too many questions at the moment.'

'Mmm . . . good point. The less said the better, you're quite right,' Young agreed. 'So . . . would you like a drop more coffee? I'll be mother.'

Grantham nodded and stuck out his mug for Young to pour into. As he did so he thought about Carver telling him he was planning to have a drink with Schultz while Alix was at the O2. There was no reason for him not to have kept the appointment, in which case it was all but certain that Carver was the Second Man. So now things were about to become a lot more complicated. No one wanted Carver ending up in a police interrogation room. And that meant that Grantham would have to deal with the situation – fast.

53

They sat in near-silence on the way back in the cab, with just a few fitful bursts of meaningless conversation. When they got to their room Alix rounded on Carver and said, 'What haven't you been telling me?'

He put a finger to his lips and made a silent, 'Shh . . .' Then he turned on the TV, switched to a music channel, and turned it up loud. Finally he stood close to Alix and, with the absolute minimum volume required to make himself heard to her said, 'Can't be too careful.'

'So . . . ?' she asked.

Carver grimaced. On the ride from the restaurant he'd been thinking about two things in particular: how to tell Alix, and what to do next. He'd made a lot more progress on the second than the first. But now that it couldn't be avoided he gave it to her straight. 'I was at the riot. Snoopy was tied up in it somehow – not sure exactly how.

But I think he was there as some kind of spotter for whoever organized the whole thing.'

'What do you mean? It was a riot. How do you organize that?'

'Very carefully, professionally, with cut-outs at every level. The question is: who's behind it? And there's one obvious candidate . . . literally.'

It took a second for the penny to drop. 'You mean Adams?' Alix said.

'Well, who else stands to gain more from a lawless, violent society? He needs that so he can be the strong man who comes in and cleans it all up . . . which is pretty easy to do if you created it in the first place.'

'I can see that . . . But he was surprised and shocked when you told him about it. I don't think he was faking. I don't think he had any idea.'

'I know. I got that feeling too. But what if it wasn't him doing the planning? What if it's that shaven-headed guy, Robbie, doing all the dirty work, so that his master keeps his hands clean?'

'Robbie Bell? That makes sense, I suppose. He didn't look happy when you started talking about the riot . . .' She paused, associating ideas, realizing she'd been ignoring the obvious issue. 'The riot . . . what happened?' She saw something in his face, and there was real worry in her voice as she said, 'Sam . . . please . . . tell me . . . what happened?'

'It got out of control. We were in the pub, and I think that was meant to be off-limits. When the rioters piled into the place, Schultz couldn't believe it. He'd obviously been told he'd be safe there. He wouldn't have

264

asked me along if he'd thought it would turn nasty. I honestly think he was expecting to have a couple of pints, watch some yobs kicking off, and then go home. Anyway . . .' He shook his head and sighed. 'Then it all went crazy. We ended up under siege in this supermarket place. There was an army of them out in the street and they attacked . . . and . . .'

Carver was having a hard time keeping it together.

Alix squeezed his arm and tilted her head so that she was looking directly up into his eyes. 'It's all right,' she murmured. 'I'm here and I love you.'

He managed a sad smile and then said, 'Schultz got killed, took a knife to the guts, and I . . . well . . . It was the only choice, the only way I could save us all . . .'

'What was?'

'The explosion . . . I set off the explosion that killed all those people. The whole supermarket was full of them, and . . .' Suddenly the girl was back in his head. He could hear her crying, 'Ricky-y-y-y-y!'

'They all died,' he said. 'Men, women . . . kids, too . . . But I swear to God, there wasn't anything else I could have done.'

She took him in her arms and held him, stroking his back to calm him. She didn't say, 'It's all right,' because it so obviously wasn't. But she knew the way Carver's mind worked, so after a while she asked him, 'What are you going to do about it?'

'The only thing I can: find out who did this and deal with it—'

'For God's sake, Sam, not more killing . . . not now.'

'No, not now . . . I can't do that. I'm done with killing.

But I can get to the truth, and then . . . then the police, or the politicians, or whoever's supposed to be in charge . . . they can decide what to do.'

'Then what about us? The police must know Schultz wasn't alone. They'll be looking for another man, and it won't take long to discover that it was you.'

'I don't need long. I just need enough time to work this out, and then I'm gone.'

'Gone? What do you mean?'

'I mean I'm leaving . . . and I'm going to make it look like I'm gone for good. I've arranged enough accidents for other people. Time I did one for myself . . .'

'I'm sorry, I don't understand.'

'You said it yourself: the police are going to come after me, and they're not going to stop; not with the number of people that died tonight. So the further away from me you are, the safer you'll be. First thing in the morning, you're getting out of here. Check the news. If it doesn't look like they know who I am, then get on the first plane back to the States. If they've got my face, or my name, then find somewhere you can lie low – an old friend, the US Embassy, anything. You can prove that you had nothing to do with the riot, so the only reason anyone will want you is to get to me. Just stay hidden until that's not an issue. And it won't be long: twenty-four hours at the absolute outside, probably a lot less.'

'So what are you going to do?'

'It's best that you don't know. That way you can't tell anyone. But don't be alarmed if you hear that I'm dead, all right? I have to make it look like I'm gone for good, no threat to anyone, no need for the cops to keep looking for me. But you have to believe that I'll come back ... I promise you, it may take a while, months probably ... but I will come back to you.'

Alix was about to say something, but she stopped herself.

'What is it?' Carver asked.

'Nothing ... it's not important.'

He knew she was lying. There was something on her mind. But if she didn't want to tell him there had to be a reason for it, and he trusted her judgement enough not to force the issue. 'OK ... well, I'd better be going. There's a lead I need to follow up. One of the rioters was wounded, and if he made it then he'll be in a hospital bed. Tommy's, most likely. So that's where I'm going.'

She nodded silently and let go of him. Carver had his iPad in the small canvas bag he'd used as carry-on baggage. He picked it up and they stood there for a moment, several feet apart, feeling awkward, until he broke the silence and the distance between them. Now it was Carver who took Alix in his arms and held her tight to him as he lowered his mouth to hers. They kissed with a fierce intensity, consuming one another, feeding themselves with the sensations that would have to sustain them when they were apart. Finally she pulled away from him, the two of them both breathing heavily, and said, 'Must you go now? Can't you stay with me ... just for a little while?'

Carver told himself that he was being rational. He'd blown a hole in Curtis's shoulder. If Curtis had got to hospital at all he'd need an immediate operation, then the recovery time. He wouldn't even be awake yet. If

Carver arrived at the hospital too soon and had to hang around there he was liable to get noticed. People would ask questions. It was a stupid risk.

That was what he told himself. The truth, though, wasn't rational at all. He wanted one last time with Alix. He needed very badly to feel her skin against his, to be kissing, licking, stroking and fucking until they melted so deep into one another that he could no longer tell where he ended and she began.

And so he said, 'Yes, just for a little while, I can stay . . .'

54

The files that told the truth about the last few hours of the Malachi Zorn affair were classified under the seventy-year rule: not to be opened until all the people mentioned in them were either dead or standing at the very edge of the grave. But there is no point in possessing money, status or influence unless one can use it to obtain those things that are denied to everyone else, which was why a powerful man in a hurry, who needed to find someone with the motivation to drop everything and do a dirty, dangerous job right this second, with no time to plan or prepare, was skimming through them now.

He wanted to confirm his recollection of one apparently insignificant detail of the events inside the Goldsmiths' Hall in the City of London on the night it was used to host the launch of Zorn's fraudulent investment fund. The great bulk of the document the man was reading related to the grenade attack on the men and women attending the launch. He, however, was only interested in something that had happened less than five minutes before the first grenade struck.

One of the witnesses interviewed by the Metropolitan Police was Alexandra Petrova Vermulen. She described how she had just arrived through the main entrance of the Goldsmiths' Hall when she'd spotted Celina Novak, a freelance female assassin suspected of an involvement in the Zorn plot, coming down the stairs from the reception on the first floor. The two women had immediately recognized one another because they had known each other in Moscow, many years earlier. Vermulen did not specify the precise nature of their relationship beyond remarking that, 'We were both the same age, going to the same parties, and a pretty girl is always aware of her competition.'

Having spotted one another, Vermulen and Novak did not immediately exchange any conversation. Vermulen had been caught in the traffic en route to the reception and obliged to run some distance to the Goldsmiths' Hall, leaving her hot and dishevelled. So she went down to the ladies' room in the basement of the building to repair her hair and make-up and was joined there by Novak. At this point they did have a conversation; not a particularly friendly one as it transpired, though Vermulen chose not to go into the details of their argument, beyond saying, 'It involved a man whom we had both known.'

Vermulen's statement continued: 'I have been asked if I saw a considerable quantity of blood on the floor of the ladies' room or on the counter top surrounding the handbasins. To the best of my recollection there was no such blood visible at that time. At the conclusion of my brief conversation with Celina Novak, I checked my appearance and went upstairs to the reception. Ms Novak was still in the ladies' room when I left.'

The man reading the file leaned back in his chair and closed his eyes as he replayed the events Vermulen had described. He imagined the ornate marble entrance hall and stairs of the Goldsmiths' Hall . . .

Vermulen dashes in, feeling distinctly hot and bothered. She spots Celina Novak on the stairs – an old rival with whom she's shared a male friend, doubtless a lover. Presumably, Novak is leaving the reception because she knows it is about to be attacked. But Vermulen doesn't know that. She just sees a beautiful woman with whom she has always competed, looking down on her, both literally and metaphorically.

Vermulen goes to the ladies' room. Meanwhile Novak should be getting as far away as possible. Yet she chooses instead to follow Vermulen down to the ladies' room. It isn't enough to feel her victory over Vermulen. She needs to see Vermulen's defeat.

But then what?

The man flicked through the file till he came to the section on forensic evidence. A significant amount of blood, along with small fragments of skin, strands of female hair and even bone splinters had been found beside and beneath the ladies' room basins.

The spatter pattern of the blood indicated that it had come from the sharp impact of a human head or face against the hard plastic counter top.

It was extremely unlikely to have been caused by someone falling over due to the explosions upstairs, which would not have caused more than a slight tremor in the basement-level bathroom.

It certainly did not come from a wounded blast-victim who had somehow descended to the ladies' room to examine or tend to her wounds. The blood patterns simply did not match that scenario.

The only possible conclusion was that a woman had been very badly wounded by someone grabbing her head or hair and smashing her face hard into the counter. The man winced at the thought of it.

The victim certainly wasn't Vermulen. She had gone back upstairs to the reception without a mark on her. Her only injuries had been inflicted by flying debris after the grenade had exploded. Her blood did not match that found on the counter.

No one else had gone down to the ladies' room in the short time before the explosions.

So the victim could only have been Novak. She had come down to gloat at Vermulen and been taken unawares. A very deadly woman had met her match.

And now, it was reasonable to assume, she would be very keen indeed to get her revenge. All he had to do now was find her. And the man knew precisely how to do that.

It was midnight in Puerto Banus – early in the evening by Spanish standards – and Olga Zhukovskaya was just finishing her dinner, alone in her penthouse. Her short-cropped hair was snowy white. Her face was lined, and her stick-thin body was developing a stoop. But her mind was still as sharp and her memory as comprehensive as ever. She had just poured herself a glass of Russian tea when her mobile rang.

'Hello, old friend,' she said when she heard the Englishman's familiar tones. 'How nice to hear your voice. But why call me now, of all times, after so many years? I've been retired for almost a decade.'

'From what I hear you're still keeping your hand in with freelance consultancies.'

'I have made introductions, that's true. I know a lot of people, and it is always good to bring people together.'

That was one way of putting it. Another would be that Zhukovskaya acted as an unofficial agent for a number of Russian ex-special forces and intelligence agency personnel who were now working as hitmen and women.

'Could you bring me together with Celina Novak?'

'Celina? I hadn't expected you to ask for her. You do know that she was very badly wounded two years ago?'

'At Goldsmiths' Hall?'

'Exactly. Her face suffered third-degree burns across a wide area. Several bones in her nose, cheeks and sinuses were broken. It was remarkable, really, that she was able to escape the scene.'

'So how is she now?'

'Very fit indeed. Her combat skills are unimpaired in any way. Of course, she looks – how can I put this? – somewhat different. But it does not affect her operational ability.'

'So where is she?'

'Paris. Where and when do you need her?'

'London. Now.'

The man was trying to sound decisive. But Zhukovskaya could sense the desperation in his voice, and it intrigued her: why the frantic urgency? And how could she exploit it?

'I am sure she can get to you within the next forty-eight hours,' she said.

'No. I mean right now. I need her at Le Bourget within an hour, at the outside. I'll have a plane waiting for her.'

'It's a little late, surely. Aren't there night-flying regulations over southern England?'

'Yes. But exceptions can always be made, for example, for an air ambulance carrying a desperately ill patient.'

'Of course . . . I assume that such an urgent mission, commissioned at extreme short notice, will carry a very generous fee.'

'Absolutely . . . and you can tell Miss Novak that there will be a generous bonus attached to the job, too.'

'How generous?'

'Oh, this is a gift beyond money. You see, I can make her dearest wish come true.'

55

Celina Novak could still get a man into her bed. It was just a matter of quality. She had once had her pick of suitors begging for her favours, men willing to maintain her in a style to which she had very rapidly become accustomed. She had never had any qualms at all about accepting accommodation, clothing, jewellery and whatever other gifts might have come her way from men for whom she had felt precisely nothing. To her, all life was essentially a series of transactions. Now, though, she had much less value as a marketable commodity, and so she had to look for the kind of man who was drunk enough, or indifferent enough, not to care about a face, or the woman behind it, if the tits were big enough, the ass tight enough and the legs wide enough. The drunken Austrian businessman she had picked up in the hotel bar was proving to be so tediously unexciting that when the phone rang it came as a relief, rather than a distraction.

'Stop,' she commanded him. And then, 'Get off me,' as she rolled over to take the call.

'Zhukovskaya gave me your number, Ms Novak. I have an assignment for you. The fee that we have agreed is more than double your usual rate. But I require your immediate presence. Are you available?'

'Absolutely,' Novak replied, silently shooing the Austrian out of her bed.

'I'm so glad to hear that. An associate of mine is not well. I fear he may not last the night. I was also hoping you might be able to look after two friends of mine. Sadly, they are also very poorly.'

'I'm so sorry. Can you give me the names of these individuals?'

'Yes. They're a charming couple: the Carvers – Samuel and Alexandra. I believe you may know them.'

'We have met, yes,' said Novak, giving no trace whatever of the exultant thrill those names had given her. 'How do you wish to proceed?'

Fifteen minutes later a private ambulance had pulled into a side street half a dozen blocks from Novak's hotel. She climbed aboard. As the ambulance drove away she undressed and sat on the edge of the gurney while a male nurse, working with deft efficiency, wrapped her head in bandages. Novak had to fight back the nauseating rush of alarm that came with the sensation of disappearing behind the gauze. It was too familiar to her, too closely associated with all the agonized, mummified months she had already spent having plastic and metal prostheses inserted where healthy bones had once been; new skin to replace burnt tissue; chemical fillers substituting living tissues. Her nostrils seemed to fill with the smell of her own roasting flesh, and her ears could hear the crunch of her face hitting the counter top. But then Novak remembered why she was doing this, and the momentary anxiety disappeared. More bandages were wrapped around her torso and along her left arm and hand. Then she lay down quite calmly on the gurney and held her bare arm out for the saline drip to be inserted.

The ambulance raced away, its light flashing and siren blaring, towards Le Bourget airport in the north-west suburbs of Paris. En route to the waiting jet her attendants presented the passport control official with documentation that gave her name as Mrs Anja Morrison, a UK citizen seriously injured in a road crash, who was being flown home to be close to her husband and three children. Minutes later, the plane's wheels left the runway tarmac.

Soon after that, Novak sat up. She was handed a tablet computer. On it was a file containing details of her first target and the location where the hit would take place: a building in the West End of London. She examined the plans of the building and the description of its likely occupants and then, since she could not talk through the bandages, typed one-handed on to the pad, specifying what she would need in order to do the job.

Then she lay back down. Her drip was swapped for another that provided a high concentration of glucose, proteins, C and B-complex vitamins, minerals and antioxidants, giving her the energy and endurance she would need for the night ahead. As the liquid seeped into her system, Novak dozed. There were still twenty minutes left of the flight, and she wanted to be as well rested as possible before she went into action.

56

The two Panu cousins were questioned simultaneously. Walcott took Ajay. The purpose of the interview was pretty straightforward. There had to have been two hard-core fighting men in the Lion Market. One of them was dead, killed in the fight in the storeroom. The other had been at the front, firing the shotgun and, it seemed certain, making the bomb go bang. The problem was proving it. And they weren't going to get anywhere unless someone who'd been in the shop came out, stopped covering it all up and told the whole story. Ajay Panu would be a good start.

Walcott took him through the first incidents in the supermarket: the man and woman who'd let off the incendiary device and the African kids who'd thrown bricks and concrete and then been coming in and out through the shattered window. But, he pointed out, the most serious threat to the supermarket and the people in it only occurred after the arrival of the man known as Snoopy, the two women, and the second male who was alleged to be with them.

'These people turn up,' Walcott said, 'and suddenly, after that's happened, there's a huge angry crowd outside your shop. Next thing you know there's bottle-bombs and even a few shots being aimed at you.'

'Yes.'

'And you shot back.'

Walcott said it so casually that he could almost see Ajay thinking, Did he mean me?

The big man said, 'I'm sorry . . . ?'

'I said, "You shot back." See, there's people lying dead on the street outside the shop. Someone blasted them with a shotgun. Where did the shotgun come from?'

'I don't know.'

'And who fired it?'

'I don't know.'

'Come off it, Mr Panu. It had to be you.'

'No, it didn't . . .'

'Well, who else was it? The shooter can't have been Snoopy, because he was wounded and Miss Prentice was bandaging him up.'

'Yeah, that's right.'

'So that leaves just you and your cousin, Maninder Panu. But, no offence, your cousin wasn't exactly Action Man last night, was he? So it had to be you that fired the gun.'

Ajay shrugged like a sulky teen. 'If you say so.'

'What's that supposed to mean? Did you fire the gun, or didn't you?'

'I suppose I must have done.'

'So how many times did you fire it?'

'I don't know . . . a few.'

'And how many people did you hit?'

'I don't know, I can't remember exactly. It was very confusing. I was just, you know, blasting at them, trying to make them go away.'

Walcott leaned forward into Ajay Panu's personal space. 'Bollocks you were blasting,' he said. 'We've spoken to other witnesses. Three shots were fired from the supermarket. Every single one of them hit an individual target. Two of the victims died. The third is currently in intensive care at St Thomas' Hospital.'

'I don't know anything about that.'

'No, you don't. But let's talk about something we can all agree on. You went to the back of the property, to the storeroom, to defend that with this Snoopy individual.'

'Yes.'

'So when the attack got going you weren't in the main shop area. You were at the back.'

'Yes.'

'So, Mr Panu, how do you account for the fact that three more of the rioters were killed inside the shop by the same shotgun that killed the ones outside it?'

'I don't understand.'

'I'm saying, if you were in the storeroom, who was doing the shooting in the shop?'

'I don't know anything about any shots at the front.'

'Is that so? Well, then, for your information, there were another three victims. One had his arm blown off. The other two were shot in the guts. Whoever did it waited until they were just a few feet from him and then shot them in such a way that they did not die immediately. He wanted to make them suffer. Think about the kind of man who can do a thing like that.'

Ajay said nothing. Walcott's description of those last three shootings had obviously got to him in a way nothing else in the interview had done.

'Yeah, I know, cold-blooded bastard, wasn't he?' Walcott said.

'I don't know who you're talking about,' Ajay replied, but his heart wasn't in it any more.

Walcott was so close to landing him. 'For God's sake, give it up,' he said. 'Whatever he told you, he's not worth this.'

'If there was this person in the shop, then he saved our lives,' Ajay replied. 'That's worth a lot.'

So he wasn't ready to crack just yet. Walcott took a deep breath and tried to get his prey by another route.

'So let's talk about the storeroom. We found a pistol. Two bodies at the rear of the premises were killed by bullets from that gun. Do you know anything about that?'

'Yes. We were under attack from the yard.' Ajay started talking more confidently now that he wasn't having to hide anything. 'The lad I was with – I think his name was Snoopy – he shot one of them coming over the top, but then another jumped on to me and he was about to kill me when, er, Snoopy shot him and he fell on top of me. He was dead and there was blood everywhere. But then there was another one. He came up behind Snoopy and stabbed him in the guts.'

'And this man, who stabbed Snoopy, what happened to him?'

'I don't know. I didn't see.' Suddenly all the honesty, all the openness had gone again.

'Oh, come on, Mr Panu,' Walcott insisted, pressing again. 'You're lying there, trapped under a dead body and your mate is being cut to pieces. My guess is you remember that very well. And the obvious question is, how come you didn't die, too?'

'I don't know. It was dark in there. I couldn't see what was going on.'

'Well, here's a clue. We found two bodies of rioters in the immediate vicinity of your dead friend. One had been shot with a bullet from a Chinese-made pistol, so that must have been the one who'd been attacking you.'

'Sounds like it, yeah.'

'And the other one had a large hole in his chest caused by the impact of a twelve-bore shotgun cartridge fired at point-blank range. There was another shotgun victim the other side of the shelving, and one by the door into the storeroom, just for good measure. Who shot all those people?'

Panu said nothing. Walcott watched him trying to think through his options and work out what he should do. Finally Ajay asked, 'Am I allowed a lawyer?'

'Of course,' Walcott answered. 'If you think you need one.'

'Good. 'Cos I'm not saying fuck all till he arrives.'

57

DI Keane had been leading Maninder Panu through the events of the evening, and was becoming progressively more frustrated by his obvious evasions, when Brian Walcott appeared at the interview-room door and indicated to her to join him. She followed him out into the corridor and there he told her, first, that Ajay Panu had claimed to be the second shooter and, second, that he had called for a lawyer. 'The brief'll be here any minute,' Walcott said.

'I'd better get a move on, then.'

'I reckon so, ma'am.'

Keane was perfectly capable of acting like a bloody-minded copper when the need arose: like now, for instance. She sat down opposite Maninder, looked at him without a shred of human kindness in her face and said, 'You're in a lot of trouble.'

His liquid brown eyes widened in alarm. This was the

last thing he'd been expecting. 'Me? What have I done wrong? I'm the victim! My shop was attacked. People tried to kill me. Why am I the one in trouble?'

'Let's start with the shotgun that was found on your premises – the one used to kill a number of individuals in and around your shop. Would you care to account for that?'

'I don't know how it got there!'

'Did you buy that gun?'

'I don't remember.'

'Buying a gun is hardly something you're likely to forget,' Keane said. And then, for the first time, she softened a fraction and offered Maninder Panu a tiny crumb of comfort, saying, 'I don't blame you if you did,' before snatching it away with her next breath. 'Of course, it was highly illegal. You could get ten years in jail for owning that gun, did you know that?'

The look of horror on Maninder's face indicated very clearly that he did not.

'But you were afraid,' Keane went on. 'The riots keep getting worse. I can understand how a man in your position might feel vulnerable – in need of a little protection.'

Maninder nodded in vigorous agreement, 'Yes, that is true. I did feel vulnerable.'

'So you acquired a fully-loaded Mossberg 590 shotgun . . .'

'I wasn't the only one! Lots of people had them.'

'Maybe, but yours killed at least eight people. Can you tell me who was firing that gun, Mr Panu?'

'I don't know.'

'That's odd. You see, someone's actually admitted firing the shotgun.'

Once again, Maninder was caught off guard: 'Really? Who?'

'Your cousin, Ajay Paninder.'

'No, I don't believe you! He would never say that!'

Keane remained entirely impassive. 'Your cousin is in very real danger of being tried for the murder of those eight people, Mr Panu. He freely confessed to my colleague DS Walcott that he had shot two people dead. Six others were killed with the same gun, and unless you can tell me who else might have committed those murders there's every chance that he'll be convicted of those killings too, and spend the rest of his life in jail.'

'But he didn't do it!'

'I repeat, that's not what he says.'

'No! No!' Maninder exclaimed, his voice becoming high-pitched in his distress. 'He has never shot a gun. He is a good man. He would never kill another human being.'

'Well, if he didn't shoot those people, who did?'

'I don't know.'

'That's not much good to your cousin, I'm afraid,' said Keane. 'But I'll tell you what. I'll make it easier. We know there was another man in the shop. We know this despite the attempts made by you, your cousin and Miss Prentice to deny the existence of this individual.'

'What man? How do you know?'

'Because we've been very busy, Mr Panu. We now know the identity of the man who introduced himself to Miss Prentice as "Snoopy". We believe he served in the special forces. The man who accompanied him probably had a similar background. He is an exceptionally dangerous individual. We have to find him before he kills again.'

'But he saved us! We would have died – all of us! He may be a dangerous killer to you, Inspector. But I owe my life to him.'

'So you agree that he exists?'

Maninder nodded disconsolately. 'Excellent,' said Keane. 'So now why don't you do yourself and your cousin Ajay a favour and tell me what you know?'

'If I tell you what I know, will you drop the charges against Ajay?'

'Well, I can't either bring or drop charges. But clearly, your cousin can hardly be a suspect if we can establish that the shootings were committed by another individual.'

For all his weaknesses, Maninder Panu was a natural trader. Now that he knew he was in a position to negotiate, he immediately felt more confident. 'And what about me?' he asked. 'What will you do for me?'

'We will be very grateful for any help you can give us that leads to the arrest of our prime suspect,' said Keane. 'Once again, I can't make any promises. But I'm sure we'll have much more important things to worry about than how a gun did or did not happen to come into your possession.'

Maninder looked at her shrewdly, trying to work out whether he could sweeten the deal any further. He concluded that it wouldn't be possible; not right now, at any rate. For the first time he seemed to relax into his chair. 'Then, in that case, I will tell you—'

'Absolutely nothing.'

The voice came from the door to the interview room. A smartly suited Asian man – in his late twenties or early thirties, Keane guessed. She muttered, 'Shit!' under her breath as the man came into the room, extending his hand.

Keane got up. 'And you are …?' she asked, though she already knew at least half the answer.

'Dipak Sharma,' the young man said. 'I am Mr Panu's lawyer, and you won't need me to tell you that my client is not saying a single additional word until I have had a chance to confer with him . . . in private.'

Walcott was waiting in the corridor outside. 'Sorry, ma'am,' he said. 'I tried to slow him down, give you as much time as possible, but he wasn't having it.'

'That's all right. Nothing you could do. It's just frustrating, that's all. I was this close to getting Maninder Panu to talk.'

'You still will,' Walcott reassured her. 'Meantime, I've got some good news. We just got a call from St Thomas' Hospital. Paula Miklosko's back in the land of the living: conscious, aware of her surroundings . . .'

'Is she talking?'

'Just about.'

'Then the Panus can wait. Get the car. We're off to Tommy's.'

58

Carver and Alix had spent a little more than an hour together before he finally rose from the bed, showered and got dressed: clean underwear and T-shirt, but the same jeans, body warmer and suede jacket. He picked up his iPad and put it in a small leather satchel he'd used for carry-on baggage on the flight from DC. He was wearing his money-belt, too; this time he had no doubt that he would need it.

Alix was still in bed, watching him go about his business. Carver kissed her, walked across the room and then stopped at the door.

'Wait for me,' he said. 'I will come back for you. I swear I will.'

He took the lift down to the ground floor. In the foyer two cleaners were deep in conversation with one another, talking in a foreign language Carver didn't recognize. The girl behind the reception desk was reading a book and didn't look up as he went past her and exited through the security barriers. He came out on to Knightsbridge and spent another five minutes standing in a cold, biting wind until a taxi came along.

'St Thomas' Hospital,' he said.

'It's mental round there tonight,' the cabbie said.

'Well, get me as close as you can.'

Carver got in and took out his iPad. Looking ahead, he'd foreseen a number of occasions when the screen on his smartphone wouldn't be good enough for what he had in mind, and this was one of them. The floor plans of St Thomas' were all online, and there were also photographs of all the corridors and doorways for the benefit of wheelchair-users. From this Carver discovered that the intensive care unit was on the first floor and was accessed via powered, inward-opening double-doors precisely 1,470mm wide. 'There is a buzzer to press to the left of the doors which when pressed will open automatically.' Well, the syntax was pretty clumsy, but the meaning was clear enough. And there was more: 'The automatic doors remain open long enough for a slow-moving person to walk through.' Carver planned to be moving fast, but if he didn't keep his wits about him, someone else would have time to get in after he did.

The taxi crossed Westminster Bridge and turned right at the roundabout on the far side. Carver put the iPad away as they pulled up opposite the drive that led to the hospital's main entrance. 'Sorry, mate, can't get you any closer,' said the cabbie. 'Like I said, it's mental down there.'

The whole area was jammed with police cars, emergency vehicles and media vans. Carver paid and walked through the chaos. Reporters, paramedics and nurses jostled against armed policemen. The normal A & E entrance was almost two hundred metres away on the far side of the complex, but there were so many victims needing admission that every possible way in was being called into action. And since most of those victims were already dead, A & E was hardly relevant anyway.

There were police guards at the door. Carver flashed an MOD identity card from his money-belt and was asked his business. 'A bomb went off. A former Marine was killed. That makes it Ministry of Defence business.'

'What part of the Ministry of Defence?' the policeman asked.

'A part I'm not prepared to discuss. Just let me through.'

The policeman looked uncertain. But before he could think of what to say or do next there was a shout of, 'Get out the way!' behind them, and a crash team appeared, racing towards the door with a patient who was still alive. The policeman stepped back to let them through and was then distracted by the arrival of two other people: a tall, broad-shouldered woman and a younger, black man. The policeman suddenly stood tall, and said, 'Evening, ma'am,' as the woman went by.

In the confusion Carver slipped into the entrance lobby, turned right and walked through what had been a mini shopping-mall, though the WH Smith, Marks & Spencer Simply Food and assorted coffee shop signs now stood above empty units. The corridor was filthy. The whole place felt like a third-world hospital in the midst of a civil war. He walked through a glazed lobby where a bitter draught blew between the holes in smashed panes, and into another one of the hospital's towers. Two long corridors took him past a bank of lifts, surrounded by people waiting for the next ride up, to a door that opened on to a stairwell.

The walls were covered in graffiti, and the staircase was entirely deserted. The only sign of life was a small puddle of urine beside the landing wall. Half of it had evaporated, because the mark of the puddle's original edge was clearly visible, and it had evidently been left to dry out undisturbed. Obviously the stairs were hardly ever used. That was useful to know.

Carver went up to the first floor and there, right in front of him, were the double-doors to the ICU.

Another police officer was standing in front of the doors. He was fully dressed in the combat gear of an armed surveillance unit: a Heckler and Koch G36 assault rifle in his hands; a Glock pistol holstered on his right thigh; Kevlar body armour; a balaclava covering his face; and a headset that held a headphone over his left ear and a mic by the side of his mouth. It was wired to an encrypted digital radio attached to the webbing by his left shoulder.

The cop was a big lad and he was armed to the teeth, but he was also carrying at least ten pounds of excess weight, so he wasn't in prime condition. And judging by the way he reacted with a start as Carver came through the door from the stairs, he'd not exactly been on a heightened state of alert. It was a tendency Carver had noticed in the police at the airport, too. They assumed that if they showed everyone their guns nothing could possibly happen to them, and that made them careless. He'd walked within two or three feet of men with their backs turned to him. It had struck him that if he'd meant them harm, they'd have been dead before they'd even known they'd been attacked.

Carver showed this one the MOD pass and said, 'I'm looking for a patient. A big man, bigger than you. He was brought in here earlier this evening suffering from serious gunshot wounds to his right shoulder. He must have had emergency surgery. The only name we have is Curtis. Is he in there?'

'Who's asking?'

'Oh, I'm sorry. I didn't realize you couldn't read. My name's Jenkins.'

'Don't get smart with me . . . sir,' the policeman said. 'Wait . . .'

The police officer put his left hand up to the radio unit and tilted his head to speak into his mic. Carver hit him very hard with the palm of his hand on the exposed side of his chin and then stepped forward, inside the barrel of the gun. He grabbed the balaclava and smashed the policeman's head against the metal frame of the double-doors: three quick, brutal impacts. He felt the body go limp and let it fall to the ground. Carver picked up the G36 rifle and slung it over his shoulder. A metal carrying handle was attached to the policeman's webbing to make it easier to drag his body to safety, should he be wounded. Carver grabbed it and pulled the unconscious body back through the door into the empty stairwell. He extracted the Glock from its holster and stuck it in the waistband of his trousers.

Carver had no intention of getting into a serious fire-fight, particularly not in the middle of a hospital, and so had no need of a semi-automatic assault rifle. But since he didn't want anyone else using it either, he unslung the G36, removed the two small locking pins from the receiver unit, unclipped the grip and trigger mechanism, and threw the locking pins down the stairwell. The G36 was now useless. Time to make sure the cop was, too.

Carver took the man's laces from his boots and used them to secure his hands behind his back. He removed the headset, twisted the balaclava so that it was back to front, completely covering his face, then replaced the headset to keep the balaclava in place. He took the belt from the cop's trousers and draped it round his masked head, forcing his jaw open and placing the thick leather between his teeth. Then he pulled the belt as tight as it would go so that it acted as a gag. Finally he pulled off the cop's boots and trousers and tied the trousers tight around his ankles, rendering him completely immobile.

Now he dragged the unconscious body to the edge of the downward stairs, pulled it out a little further and draped the policeman's torso face down over the first few steps. His chin rested on a step, forcing his lower jaw to press hard against the leather gag. He was blind and dumb, his hands were tied behind him, and his feet couldn't move. It was safe to say that he was no longer a threat.

Carver went back upstairs, pressed the buzzer by the

doors and walked into the ICU. The first part of his mission had been accomplished. Now he just had to find Curtis.

59

Keane and Walcott went straight to the room where Miklosko was being treated. A doctor was just emerging.

'How is she?' Keane asked.

'Still very shaken,' the doctor replied. 'She's suffered from an extremely acute stress reaction.'

'Can she answer questions?'

'If you mean, "Is she coherent?" Yes. But her memory is still very patchy, and I must ask you not to push her to recall things that her mind has chosen to keep buried. There's a reason why we forget. Sometimes remembering can be more than we can bear.'

'I'll go easy, I promise. She's an innocent victim in all this. I have no desire to victimize her any more.'

'Good. And please, make it quick, all right? Five minutes. Tops. And only one of you, I'm afraid.'

'I'll do it,' said Keane. She looked across at Walcott. 'Sergeant, why don't you call forensics, the bomb people and the incident room? Get me a summary of where we are on all this.'

'Yes, ma'am.'

Keane went into the room. Miklosko's face was heavily bruised, and the swellings looked all the more brutal because the bones of her face were so elegant and fine. She was a slender, bird-like woman, and for a second Keane found herself envying her delicate proportions and then being cross with herself for allowing such selfish, inappropriate thoughts to cross her mind. Telling herself to get back to business, she sat down beside the bed – still feeling enormous – and began: 'Do you mind if I ask you a few questions?'

Miklosko gave a wan half-smile. 'No . . . no, that's all right.'

'I just want to ask you about the riot.'

Miklosko flinched.

'Can you remember anything about what happened to you?'

A shake of the head. 'Not really, not much . . .'

'All right, well, let's start at the beginning, anyway. Why had you gone to Netherton Street?'

Miklosko seemed relieved by such a simple, harmless question. 'I was driving home from work.'

'So what do you remember about the drive?'

'I was listening to the radio. That politician was on, making his speech . . .'

'Mark Adams?'

'Yes, that's right. Well, I was listening to that, and then suddenly, out of nowhere, there was an explosion on the road in front of me, and I was really frightened, so I started driving as fast as I could to get out. But there was a huge truck in front of me, right across the road, blocking the way.'

Miklosko had been perfectly calm up to now, but Keane saw that her hands had started grabbing at her hospital blanket, her fingers gathering up the fabric and then clenching until her knuckles showed pale beneath her skin.

'It's all right,' said Keane, trying to sound as soothing as possible. 'Just take it nice and slowly. If it gets too hard, we'll stop. You said you saw a truck . . .'

Miklosko nodded. 'Yes, so I braked as hard as I could and turned the wheel to try to miss it, but the car started skidding and I ended up right next to it, kind of side to side. And that was when . . . these men all crowded round the car, and there were so many of them. And I tried to lock the doors, but they just smashed their way in – through the windows, I suppose . . . I was so scared . . .'

Keane could sense what an effort it took for Miklosko to bring back these memories. She wondered whether it was fair to continue the interview. But Miklosko seemed determined to complete her story.

'I could feel their hands all over me,' she went on, 'grabbing me and pulling me out of the car. They started hitting me all over. I thought I was going to die. I mean, there was no way I could fight back or get away, and then suddenly I saw these men coming towards me.'

'Men,' Keane noted, trying not to show any reaction as Miklosko kept telling her story.

'At first I thought it was more people coming to attack me, but then one of them got out a knife and started slashing at the people all around me . . . And the other one was hitting them with a stick and punching and kicking them . . .' Miklosko's voice died away.

'Are you all right?' Keane asked.

'Yes . . . it's just that it's all gone a bit blurry, if you know what I mean. I don't remember exactly what happened, but it felt like all the people round me ran away . . . all except one, and I think he had a gun.'

'Are you sure about that?'

'I think so. I mean, it all seems like a nightmare now, like it wasn't real at all, but, yes, I am sure, because I remember one of the men picking it up later.'

There it was again: 'one of the men'. Keane was very close now to getting the first details about the Second Man, but she had to resist the temptation to charge right in.

'So what happened to the man with the gun? The one by the car?'

'He killed him . . . with the knife,' said Miklosko.

'Let me get this straight,' said Keane. She knew what Miklosko meant, but she needed it in unambiguous form. 'There were two men who came to rescue you?'

'Yes.'

'And one of them had a knife?'

'Yes.'

'And he killed the man with the gun?'

'I think so, yes.'

'And then what happened?'

'I don't know. I remember the other man holding me and telling me it was going to be all right . . .'

'This is the second rescuer?'

'That's right . . .'

'Can you describe him?'

Miklosko made a visible effort to conjure up a picture in her mind of the man who had held her, but then sighed and shook her head. 'I'm sorry. He was bigger than me, obviously, and I think he had dark hair. But apart from that it all goes blank, really, and there are just a few images, as I say, like trying to remember a dream the next morning. The next thing I really knew was waking up here, in hospital.'

'But there were two men who came to rescue you?'

'Yes, definitely. There were two.'

Keane smiled with entirely unfeigned gratitude. 'Thank you, Mrs Miklosko,' she said. 'Thank you very much indeed.'

Outside in the corridor, Walcott was studying his smartphone with a look of boyish glee on his face. He saw Keane and his grin became even wider. 'I know who Snoopy was,' he said, triumphantly.

'That's great, how did you find out?'

'Well, the pathologist said he had a Royal Marines crest tattooed on his left shoulder, and Chrystal Prentice told us his nickname was Snoopy. So I tried calling the Ministry of Defence and the Marines and no one there was going to be able to check out the records till to-morrow. So then I thought, Sod it, and Googled "Snoopy" and "Marines", and there he was, from a local newspaper story a couple of years ago, running an assault-course day for underprivileged kids.'

'So who is he?'

'Norman Derek Schultz. He was a company sergeant

major in the Royal Marines. Only left about a year ago. And I'll tell you something else. That event he was doing for the kiddies, it was in Poole, Dorset. And that's where the SBS are based. What if he and the other bloke, his mate, were both in the special forces? That would explain why they were able to take on a whole bloody riot, just the two of them.'

'Yes, it would,' Keane agreed. She yawned and then closed her eyes for a few seconds. 'Sorry,' she said, coming back to life. 'I'm very tired. Must be getting old. Still, there soon won't be any need for people like you and me to stay up all night trying to solve murder cases.'

'Why not?' Walcott asked.

'Because they'll be able to work the whole thing out on Google.'

60

The ward sister had objected strongly to letting Carver anywhere near her patient. Mr Curtis, she pointed out, had lost a great deal of blood and then suffered respiratory failure during his operation. But Carver had waved his official papers, said the magic words 'national security', then pointed out that tens of people had already died, and more might still be in danger if the perpetrators weren't caught. Finally, without voicing any overt threat, he made it clear that he was armed, and she had very grudgingly relented. Now he was sitting beside the bed of an extremely sick man – a man whose injuries he had inflicted – wondering whether he could afford to trust his own instincts.

Carver had been thinking about the way Curtis had acted – the warnings to stay away from Netherton Street or get the hell out; the fact that he had been unarmed when he had been charging towards the supermarket; the general sense of competence he exuded – and come to a conclusion. So the first thing Carver said was, 'Who are you working for?'

Curtis looked at him blearily and mumbled, 'Don't know what you're talking about.'

'Yes, you do. You weren't there by accident tonight. You were undercover. I could tell. That's why I didn't kill you. Sorry for shooting you, by the way.'

Curtis was in no state to feel like being grateful.

'But look on the bright side, I also saved your life. If you'd made it to the supermarket, you'd be dead.'

Still Curtis saw no reason to say thank you.

'OK, I don't blame you for feeling that way. So, I'm guessing you're either an undercover cop or security service. Either way, you won't want to tell me anything. Not some bastard who comes from another ministry and blew the shit out of your shoulder. So I'll keep it short. I've already got to Bakunin . . .'

Carver saw Curtis's eyes widen in recognition, and for the first time thought he might be getting somewhere. 'He told me he got his orders from someone, he didn't know who, he only had a voicemail to call if he needed to get in touch. But maybe you know more than he did. So here's my question: who was calling Bakunin?'

Curtis didn't look at all bemused or surprised by what Carver had said. But he said nothing.

'You know what I'm talking about,' Carver said. 'That's obvious. You don't want to tell me. That's understandable. But here's my problem: I need to know who that man was. So either you tell me . . . or I make you tell me. And I don't want to do that. So please, tell me.'

'Can't do that. Only talk to my cover officer . . .'

'He's not here and I've not got time to call him. Tell me: who was Bakunin talking to?'

Carver held up the Glock. 'See this? It's got a very hard barrel. If I push that barrel right into your wound it's going to hurt you more than you can even imagine. And the fact that you're hooked up to painkillers won't help. This'll cut right through the drugs.'

Curtis stared back at him, defiantly silent.

'I've already tortured one person this evening, I really don't . . . Oh fuck it . . .' Carver clamped his right hand over Curtis's mouth. With the left he drove the barrel of the Glock hard into the centre of the bandaged area around the shotgun wound. Carver knew where he had hit Curtis and he was going right for the heart of the impact.

Curtis's body writhed. The veins on his forehead popped. His eyes were so wide open Carver half-expected the eyeballs to pop out. He gave a muffled cry of agony.

Carver pulled back the gun, but kept the hand where it was. 'Tell me, calmly, no shouting or screaming, or I do it again . . . For fuck's sake, we're on the same side! I'm trying to catch the man who ordered the riot. I just need one fucking name!'

'Cropper,' Curtis said. 'We never confirmed it for sure. But we think he's called Danny Cropper. Ex-Para . . .'

Now there's a surprise, Carver thought.

'Operates out of a strip joint he owns in Brewer Street, name of Soho Gold.'

'Thank you,' said Carver. 'See, that wasn't so difficult. And I'm sorry I hurt you. Tell you what, I'll make the pain go away.'

He reached across to the bag from which an opiate analgesic was dripping into Curtis's arm and dramatically upped the dose. Curtis looked at him blearily then closed his eyes.

'Thanks,' said Carver, when he saw the ward sister on the way out. 'We only talked for a couple of minutes, but he was very helpful. He's fast asleep now, though. Probably the best thing for him, eh?'

Walking through the lobby towards the main exit Carver was passed by the two plain-clothes police, the tall woman and the black guy who had come in at the same time as him. The woman bumped into him on the way by.

She said, 'I'm so sorry.'

Carver said, 'Quite all right.'

And then they were gone.

61

Celina Novak was wearing a short, black, fringed wig and an enormous pair of dark glasses when she arrived at Soho Gold. Between them they hid both her natural hair and almost all her face, so that the only thing visible was her mouth, which was painted a rich, glossy scarlet. Everything else was black: the fur-trimmed jacket, open to reveal a miniskirted dress; the stockings; the knee-length, high-heeled boots; and the evening bag. She had been flown into Biggin Hill and driven away in another ambulance. Ten minutes later, the ambulance had driven into an empty office car park and Novak, now freed from all the bandages, had been transferred to the London taxi that had taken her to a discreet hotel in St James's, just off Piccadilly. The equipment she had requested had been waiting for her in her room. She'd collected it and gone straight back out again. Now she was picking her way along the litter- and dogshit-strewn pavement, straight past the short line of damp, shivering punters waiting for the security check. She went up to one of the two thick-necked bouncers standing by the door with identical black suits and Bluetooth earpieces.

'You on the list, hey?' he asked her in a guttural South African accent.

'No.'

'Then fuck off to the back of the queue.'

'I am here to see Mr Cropper,' Novak said with a blank, almost robotic assurance that surprised the bouncer. 'He is not expecting me. Tell him I have a message. It relates to the event he organized earlier this evening. He will know what I mean.'

The bouncer gave her a hard, intimidating stare but she stood her ground, saying nothing, showing no fear or unease whatever. So he put a finger to his earpiece, waited for his call to be picked up and then said, 'Got some fuckin' fresh here wants to speak to Cropper. Says she's got a message for him ... some shit to do with an event this evening, something he organized ... Ja, all right, I'll send her through.' He jerked his head towards the door of the club and said, 'Mr Cropper's by the bar. He's expecting you.'

Novak walked through, her expression still as fixed as an Easter Island statue's. Inside, the club was decorated to match its name. Around the sides of the room, gold swag curtains were draped around booths whose furniture consisted of gold-upholstered banquettes wrapped around circular tables, each with its own set of golden steps. In the middle, facing the stage, there were more tables, partly surrounded by black and gold chairs arranged so that there was always a clear view of the stage. One dancer was doing her routine around the pole that rose from the middle of the stage and others, in various shades of undress, were entertaining the men gathered around the tables. These were the Golden Girls, the club's principal attraction, and the garters they all wore on their right thighs were stuffed with ten-, twenty- and fifty-pound notes. Even in the midst of a depression sex, at least, was still selling.

Without slowing her pace, Novak discreetly opened her little evening bag and removed a small, clear, plastic phial, no more than 4cm long and roughly the thickness of a pencil. It was filled with a colourless, virtually taste-less dose of digoxin, the poison derived from the digitalis, or foxglove. At this extreme concentration it would induce an acute, and almost certainly fatal, bout of cardiac arrhythmia. Novak slipped the phial under her watch strap and cast a cold, dispassionate eye over the men all around her. She wondered if they knew how pathetic, how desperate, how impotent they looked as they were ripped-off and prick-teased by strippers who so obviously despised them. Some were sweaty, red-faced and over-eager. Others tried to sit back with a seen-it-all-before sophistication. Not one had managed to establish any degree of command over the woman who was supposedly performing for their gratification.

Cropper wasn't hard to spot: a big man in a tightly but-toned suit sitting on his gold leather stool with his back to the bar and his arms round two topless bottle-blondes. He was running his hands around the insides of their lacy knickers while they stood there passively, letting themselves be fondled. Novak had met men like him in clubs like this all the way from Boston to Bangkok, and though she held him in as little regard as any of the other men there, she did at least admire the fact that he alone made it plain that these women were his possessions, to do with as he pleased. All relationships, in Novak's view, were fundamentally about power. And she was always on the side of the person who wielded it, particularly if that person was her.

The moment Cropper noticed her presence she saw his attitude change. There was a nervous, uncertain falseness in the smile that he beamed in her direction, a desperation in the way he dragged his groping fingers away from the girls' underpants, got to his feet and held out his right hand for her to shake. She ignored it, and as he withdrew it he started blathering, 'So, yeah, yeah . . . great to see you, er . . .'

'Magda.'

'Magda . . . yeah, right . . . well, run along, girls . . .' He gave the two blondes a pat on each rump. 'Me and Magda are going to talk a little business. Can I get you a drink, Magda? Vintage champagne, a cocktail, anything you like . . . on the house.'

'Iced water is all I require,' she said, sounding as though that was what ran in her veins, too. She took the stool next to Cropper. His half-empty glass of vodka was sitting on the bar between them.

'Water, right . . . with ice, lemon, all the trimmings, eh?' he said.

He waited for a second, expecting her to manage a please or thank-you at that point, and even some sort of fractional smile. Most women would do that just to be polite, no matter what they thought of the man in front of them, but Novak's face remained frozen and she said nothing.

Cropper was getting a little angry now. She could tell. As terrified as he might be by the prospect of the message she was bringing from his anonymous masters, he still didn't like anyone taking the piss quite so blatantly. He turned around, not giving a damn that he was turning his back on her, and called out to the girl behind the bar, 'Oi, Shelley, get us a mineral water, flat, lots of ice.'

'Nice and cold, yeah?' Shelley called back.

'Frigid,' said Cropper, tersely. 'And another double Goose with a twist. I'm gonna need it.'

As he stood watching Shelley prepare the drinks, Cropper reached for his old drink and downed it in one. Novak had her bag open on the bar. She was fiddling around inside it, the way women do when they're trying to find something. Cropper didn't pay her any attention. He didn't see that she was actually putting a thing back, rather than taking it out: the little plastic phial. It was empty.

Cropper collected the two drinks and Shelley took away the drained glass. Novak sipped at her water as she watched Cropper down half the fresh vodka. Now that his arrogance had gone, now that he was so obviously trying to summon up his courage, she had no respect for him at all.

He ran a finger round the inside of his shirt-collar, loosening it from his neck, and said, 'So, right, what's your message then?'

'I was asked to tell you not to be concerned.'

Cropper visibly deflated in front of her as the tension that had held him taut and pumped-up poured from his body. 'Fuck me . . . that's a relief.' He gave her a grateful smile. 'I thought . . . well, I'll be honest with you, love, I thought I was in the shit.'

'The rest of the message is that they understand that it is not always possible to control events, and that sometimes things happen that were not planned for.'

'Exactly! Exactly! Fuck, anyone who's been in the army knows that. Anything that can go wrong will go wrong, and that —'

'You are instructed to do nothing and say nothing to anyone . . .'

'Fuck no! I'm staying proper schtum, don't you worry about that!'

'The mess will all be cleaned up.'

Novak sipped a bit more of the water and then got to her feet. 'That is the end of my message. Thank you for the drink,' she said and then walked away without bothering to acknowledge Cropper further in any way at all.

He leaned back against the bar and finished his drink as he watched her make her imperious way between the tables. 'Fuck me.' He sighed to himself. 'That is one cold fucking bitch.' Then he pulled himself together and waved at the two blondes who were still standing a few paces away, talking to one another with bored, exhausted looks on their faces.

'Oi, you two little sluts!' Cropper shouted. 'Get your dirty arses over here!'

The girls trotted towards him, giggling at his brilliant wit. That was better, Cropper thought. They knew what was good for them.

A few minutes later, with Novak already on her way back to her hotel, Cropper started feeling unwell. Sweat was pouring off him. His heart was pounding like a madman's drum kit. He clutched his hands to his chest. His legs gave way beneath him. And the last thing he heard was one of the blondes desperately screaming for a doctor.

62

As Carver turned into Brewer Street he saw the light of an ambulance up the road. It was parked beneath a neon sign saying 'Soho Gold – Home of the Golden Girls', and the rear doors were opened in readiness for a patient. A knot of people were clustered on the pavement, some in anoraks and overcoats, others in their clubbing outfits. Heavyset men in black suits were running in and out of the club, talking into headsets, their composure shattered, panic setting in.

A couple were taking advantage of the chaos to sneak a crafty cigarette: a man in a suit and a young brunette wearing no more than lingerie, with the man's overcoat draped across her shoulders. She had to be one of the famous Golden Girls. When Carver went up to them he realized that she had been crying.

'What's happening?' he asked.

'It's the geezer that runs the place . . .' said the man.

'Danny,' the girl added, with a sniff.

'Yeah, Danny . . . well, he's gone and had a heart attack. That's what I heard, anyway. Someone told me he was dead.'

'Don't say that!' cried the girl, feebly batting him with the back of her hand.

'I'm sorry, love, but he's gone all right . . . Look.'

Bodyguards were forcing a way through the crowd as two paramedics brought a stretcher on a gurney out of the door of the club. Underneath a blanket, the outline of a human body could be made out. The blanket covered its head.

The girl put a hand to her mouth, her eyes wide, then she sucked hard on her cigarette, shaking from shock as much as the cold night air. 'I don't believe it,' she said, starting to cry again. 'Poor Danny . . .'

'I don't believe it,' Carver said to himself, feeling sick to his stomach as he saw his great scheme for uncovering the brains behind the riot falling apart before his eyes.

The girl misunderstood his disbelief. 'I know,' she sniffed. 'He was so full of life. I can't believe it, neither.'

The man put an arm round her shoulder and said, 'Don't worry . . . Look, why don't I get you a nice cup of tea, eh? That'll make you feel better.' He turned to look at Carver and winked, as if to say, 'I'm in here.'

Carver thought about the kind of man that Danny Cropper must have been. He'd run a strip joint, selling female flesh. He'd been an equal-opportunity exploiter, of course, because he'd traded male muscle, too. But he hadn't made the men who worked for him sell their naked bodies the way the women had to do. And though he might have screwed the men over metaphorically, he hadn't done it literally, as he surely had with any girl who'd wanted to be golden. Then again, a half-decent stripper in Soho Gold probably earned more than ninety-five per cent of the British population did, so that might explain why one of them would cry at Cropper's demise.

It had to be a hit, Carver thought. Adams, or someone around him, was cleaning up, breaking all the connections between themselves and the riot. So what had the killer used? Ideally, it would be something whose effects weren't immediately obvious. That way there was time to get away before anyone knew that anything was wrong. And using something that hit the heart was a smart move, too. Cropper was ex-forces, so the chances were he smoked. It was a certainty that he liked a drink or two. And he wouldn't be the kind of man who ate a lot of salad, either. Carver imagined a burly Para, going to seed, maybe in his early forties, making his legitimate money running a strip joint. He was a heart attack waiting to happen. On this night, of all nights, with every morgue in central London filled with bomb- and gunshot-victims, no one was going to have the time or the inclination to do a post-mortem on Danny Cropper. So no one would even think of looking for a killer.

But there had been a killer, and a good one too. Whoever did this wasn't your common-or-garden hitman, walking through a crowded nightclub with a gun in his hand. This was someone who could pass the guards on the door, get close enough to Cropper to slip him the poison and then get out unobserved. And that meant a serious, high-end professional.

At which point two further thoughts occurred to Carver. The first was that anyone who wanted rid of Danny Cropper would soon work out they had to get rid of him, too. And the second was that poison was often considered a woman's weapon.

63

Dipak Sharma was a smart guy. He knew that Ajay Panu's confession was rubbish, and he knew that the police knew that too. But there it was, in black and white, given without any improper pressure from the officer doing the interview, and so it had to be dealt with. Then there was the matter of the illegal shotgun that had been in Maninder Panu's possession. It had been used to kill eight people, and he had to deal with that, too. So when Keane told him that she could make all that trouble go away, if only his clients would tell him everything they knew about the man who had actually carried out the shootings, and fabricated the explosive device that had killed all the victims in the Lion Market, well, he didn't need a second invitation. His clients were advised to give the police their full cooperation.

Half an hour later a police technician was seated at a computer screen, putting together an image of the man suspected of being both the second Lion Market shooter and the person responsible for the fatal explosion. Both Panus and Chrystal Prentice had helped compile the image.

'Get it out to the media, right away. I want it on every website, every TV channel, every front page – now!' Keane said when the image was done.

And then she looked again at the face and realized that she had seen it herself, less than an hour earlier. She called Walcott over, pointed at the screen and said, 'Does he look familiar to you?'

Walcott shrugged. 'Should he?'

'Look again. Think about Tommy's . . .'

'Oh shit.' Walcott gasped. 'He was right there, in front of us. I mean you . . .'

'Yes . . . I bumped into the Second Man. He was right there and . . .' she shook her head in disbelief, '. . . I actually apologized to him.'

'You want me to get the car again?'

'Yes . . . we're going back to Tommy's. If our man was there, then we need to know why.'

64

Carver had hit a brick wall. Now he needed a Plan B. He also needed a coffee to keep him awake and alert. There didn't look to be anything open on the street except clubs and sex joints, but he found a Turkish café a few hundred metres away near the Berwick Street market. As he walked in he realized that the only other customers were the couple he'd met outside Soho Gold. Christ, he thought, giving them an embarrassed nod of acknowledgement, they must think I'm stalking them. He went up to the bar and ordered a double espresso and a glass of still water, no ice. The waiter behind the counter looked at him strangely and seemed nervous as he served him. No sooner had Carver paid him than he vanished into a back room, hurrying away as though to an unmissable appointment, like the White Rabbit in a grubby, neon-lit wonderland.

Carver took his coffee and water to a scuffed, dirty

table and sat down on a rickety chair. He drank some coffee and sat for a minute or two, considering where to start. There were a number of issues to sort out. Was he going to keep trying to get to the bottom of the riot? Maybe he should go public with the stuff on the head cam: stick it on YouTube, or just give it to the cops. There was enough on that to make anyone realize that there had been some kind of conspiracy. Once that ball got rolling, with all the media chasing after it just as hard as the authorities, it wouldn't stop until the whole truth came out. But his face was on that tape, too. He had to edit it . . . but where?

He needed somewhere to spend the night. It wasn't just the camera footage. He'd already got an idea about how he was getting out of the country, but it would take time to put together. But first, before anything else, he needed information. He had to know how far the police had got, how close they were on his trail. Carver got out the iPad and waited for it to come to life. Then he opened Safari and went to the BBC website to check out the news.

And now he knew why the man behind the counter couldn't wait to get away from him.

His picture was on the homepage of bbc.co.uk, beneath the headline: 'Lion Market "Second Man" – Police Issue Picture of Suspect'. It was a photofit, but there was no mistaking the resemblance. And when Carver opened up the story the copy spoke of the suspect, 'wearing dark-blue jeans and a long brown suede jacket, over a black waistcoat'.

A police spokesman was quoted: 'This man is very

dangerous. Members of the public should on no account approach him, but should call the Metropolitan Police at the first opportunity.'

It didn't take a genius to work out that that was exactly what the waiter had just done. Carver tried to work out how long he'd spent sitting at his table before he'd logged on to the site. Five minutes? Could be ten, even? He thought about where the nearest twenty-four-hour police station was: somewhere off the Strand, if he remembered correctly. It wouldn't take them long to get to Berwick Street, not in the early hours of the morning. Carver got up and walked towards the door. The Golden Girl glanced at him.

'Just nipping out for a quick smoke,' he said.

As soon as he was out of sight of the café Carver looked for the first large rubbish bin he could find. It was full to the brim and surrounded by discarded boxes and bulging garbage bags, but it would have to do. He emptied the pockets of his jacket and then dumped it in the bin, pushing it down as far as it would go before walking on up the road. At the corner he turned left, towards Carnaby Street, and started running hard. He could hear sirens in the distance, getting closer. He couldn't afford to slow down.

Keane and Walcott were at the hospital, and none of the news was good. The armed officer who had been assigned to guard the intensive care unit had been found halfway up a staircase, trussed up like a dirty judge in an S & M dungeon. His G36 rifle was lying in pieces on the landing. His pistol was missing. And though the officer had tried his best not to admit it, the man who had done this to him had been unarmed. 'Had' was the operative word. Keane had to assume that the Second Man was now armed with a fully loaded Glock.

Both the officer and the ward sister confirmed that the man, who conformed exactly to the descriptions given by the Panus, had identified himself as a Ministry of Defence official called Andy Jenkins. Keane assumed that in this context 'Ministry of Defence' had the same relationship to the man's real job – if he was genuine – as the Home Office IDs carried by MI5 agents, and the Foreign Office status of MI6. So now she had a dead ex-Marine and someone who either was or was posing as some kind of military intelligence operative. That was, at least, consistent with the genuinely terrifying skill set he had demonstrated over the past few hours, and it raised the even scarier prospect that there was government involvement in the evening's events.

Keane prayed for anything but that. She'd seen enough in her job to rid her of most of her illusions, but she'd never thought that someone in power would be crazy enough to start riots in which tens of people were killed. Worse still, she could see no way in which she could follow that line of investigation without causing serious, even terminal, damage to her career.

The one person who might be able to shed some light on all this was the patient known as 'Curtis'. Keane had recently received a call informing her that he was in fact an undercover police officer: real name and rank Detective Sergeant Kevin Mallinson. The ward sister revealed that he had been rendered unconscious by an extremely strong dose of a painkiller called fentanyl. Luckily, however, doctors had been able to revive him easily enough.

'Good. Then I need to speak to him. Now.'

'That won't be possible,' the sister replied. 'And don't give me a speech about dead children, or national security. I've already fallen for it once tonight, and it won't make any difference. You still can't talk to the patient.'

'Why not?' asked Keane, with barely suppressed irritation.

'Because one of the side-effects of fentanyl is aphasia. Or to put it another way, you can ask your man all the questions you like. But he won't reply. You see, he's lost the power of speech.'

Jesus wept: was nothing going to go right tonight?

Keane's phone rang. She ignored the glare of disapproval in the ward sister's eyes and answered. It was Walcott. 'The suspect's been spotted.'

'When, where?' Keane asked, feeling her spirits rise. Maybe it wasn't all lost, after all.

'An all-night caff in Brewer Street. The owner called the helpline saying that he'd just had a customer come in who looked exactly like the photofit. Two units from Agar Street nick were immediately dispatched there, but the suspect had legged it. He must have been spooked because he went outside, saying he was going for a quick fag, and never came back.'

Keane's spirits sank as fast as they'd surged. 'Did we get anything – anything at all?'

'Yeah, a little. A suede jacket was found in a dumpster just down the road. It resembled the one described by the Panus, and the people in the caff confirmed that the man they'd seen had been wearing it. It's been sent to forensics for immediate examination. I told them to drop everything else and get straight on it. Hope that was the right call.'

'Completely – a live suspect has to be a greater priority than dead victims.'

'And there was one more thing,' Walcott went on. 'There were two other customers in the caff: a dancer from that strip joint Soho Gold and one of her customers. They said that they'd seen the man outside the club just a few minutes before he turned up in the caff. Seems like the bloke who runs the club, name of Danny Cropper, died about an hour ago. He had a sudden, fatal heart attack, right out of the blue. Then our man turns up and looks disturbed when he hears the news of Cropper's death. The stripper thought they must have been friends or something.'

'So he comes here waving an MOD pass under people's noses. He incapacitates one of our men. He interrogates another officer before incapacitating him, too. Then he goes straight to the club, presumably looking for Cropper, and discovers that he's just had a fatal heart attack. What the hell is going on?'

'I don't know, ma'am, but there's something else. I've started looking into Cropper, and guess what he used to do for a living . . .'

'Please don't tell me that he was in the Royal Marines.'

'Close. He was a warrant officer in the Parachute Regiment.'

65

A tramp was sitting by a street corner, wide awake, watching Carver run down the street. The tramp held out his hand for money and called out, 'Spare us a quid, guv.'

Carver had no intention of stopping until he saw the green military jungle hat the tramp was wearing. It had a floppy brim that cast a shadow over his face.

'I'll give you twenty for the hat,' he said.

The tramp looked at him. Anyone willing to make an offer like that was clearly either mad or desperate enough to go higher. 'Fifty,' he said.

Carver got out his wallet and held out two twenty-pound notes. 'Forty, or I take it for free.'

The tramp grabbed the notes from Carver's hand and gave him the hat in exchange. It was filthy, greasy and it stank, but Carver didn't care. His most easily identifiable item of clothing had gone and his face was half-hidden by the hat. It wasn't much, but it was a start.

He walked down Carnaby Street, past all the closed-down boutiques that had once catered to the tourists who weren't coming to Britain – or anywhere else – any more. So now what? The police had his face, but they hadn't put a name to it yet, and he didn't think they'd find it too easy to do that. There weren't too many people who knew Carver's full identity – not unless Grantham gave him up, but that wasn't going to happen any time soon. Grantham didn't want him sitting in a police cell any more than he did: they both had too much to lose. If anything, Grantham'd want to help him get out.

There was that little shit from Number 10, Cameron Young. He wouldn't do anything public: he had almost as much to lose as Grantham if Carver started spilling the dirt. But they'd never exactly been best buddies, and Young was just the kind of creep who'd enjoy getting his own back by grassing Carver up anonymously. And what about Adams and Bell? They didn't know his surname, and they'd have to think very carefully before they did anything. Adams would be admitting that he'd had dinner with the Second Man . . . Shit! The restaurant staff – they could put him at Adams's table. That would lead the police to Adams, who would have to cooperate, and even if he didn't have Carver's name, he had Alix's and the address of the hotel where she was staying.

Carver had to call her, warn her, tell her to get out right away.

Alix was anything but weak. She didn't cry easily, or give in to despair, or let herself be overcome by regrets. But there were exceptions to every rule, and tonight was one of them.

She wept because she hated seeing Carver go and she couldn't rid herself of the feeling that she would never see him again. She couldn't bear the thought of this 'accident' he was going to arrange. The whole point of his accidents was that people died. How was he planning to get out alive? And she bitterly regretted that she hadn't told Carver about the baby. She hadn't wanted to burden him, not when he had so many other things, including his own survival, to think about. But if he'd known, surely he'd have abandoned his attempt to find out what had happened tonight and stayed with her instead. He'd have found a way to get them out: him, her and their child. Or maybe she'd just have been a burden to him. Perhaps the best thing to do was concentrate on herself and the child. Hadn't he said that the further she was from him the safer she'd be?

Alix was just going round in circles, getting nowhere, and she had to get some rest. So she turned off her phone and told the hotel switchboard that she didn't want to be disturbed under any circumstances. Then she curled herself up, her posture as foetal as the baby inside her, and waited for sleep to take her.

No matter how many times he called Alix's number, or how hard he argued with the hotel operator, Carver couldn't get through. In the end he left a simple message. 'Switch to Plan B. Text me your location. Just make sure I'm the only one who can understand it. And, yeah . . . I love you.'

Carver kept hitting brick walls. He could feel the presence of the mind behind the riot: simultaneously invisible and yet so close he could almost touch it. Cropper was dead and the links in the chain were broken, but there had to be another way of finding the answer. So now, as he walked through the filthy heart of London, his head down to keep his face away from the cameras, Carver was working out his next move.

66

Carver headed south, towards the river, moving fast to keep himself warm. Along the way he called Grantham. The phone was answered with a tired, irritable, 'Yes?'

'It's Carver.'

Suddenly Grantham was wide awake. 'Where are you?'

'London. I had that drink tonight. The one I told you about.'

'Yes.'

'So now you know what happened.'

'Yes. What do you plan to do about it?'

'I'd hoped to find out who set everything up. But they're cleaning up the trail. There was a man called Cropper, ran a strip joint, Soho Gold. He was definitely involved in it, but I don't know how exactly, owing to the fact he just happened to die of a sudden heart attack minutes before I could get to him. He needs a seriously thorough post-mortem, to see what actually killed him.'

'I'll look into it. Meanwhile, you realize the entire Metropolitan Police force is after you?'

'Yeah, I'd gathered.'

'So what's the plan?'

'I've got an idea, but I need a place to hang out, just for a few hours . . . just long enough to work a few things out and get a couple of hours' rest. I was wondering about that flat you had in Lambeth. The one I used before. Is anyone in it?'

'Not at the moment. But it's locked. You'll never get in.'

'Yes I will. I never gave you back the keys.'

Grantham managed a dry, exhausted chuckle. 'Come to think of it, you didn't.'

'Don't worry, I'll be gone in the morning; eight or nine at the latest.'

'When you say gone . . .'

'I mean really gone. For good . . . I don't have much of a choice.'

'With a supermarket full of dead bodies, no, you don't.'

'So, anyway . . . it's been, ah . . .'

'Yes, it has. Goodbye, Carver.'

The line went dead. There was no point in long-drawn-out farewells. Carver understood that Grantham was a practical man. He was helping him get away because it suited him to do so. After that he was cutting him loose. That was fair enough. They were both in the same business. They both understood that you couldn't have real friends. You just had some contacts that you disliked less than the rest of them. So there were no hard feelings. Feelings didn't come into it.

Carver kept walking. He stopped at a number of cash machines along the way, using a series of different cards to draw more than one thousand five hundred pounds in total. On every occasion he kept his head tilted away from the CCTV camera monitoring the machine. At one point he came within one hundred metres of the Agar Street police station, several of whose officers were still combing the area near the café in Berwick Street, looking for him. On the corner of Trafalgar Square and Northumberland Avenue he went into a Tesco twenty-four-hour store and bought coffee, porridge oats, milk, nuts and raisins. Along with the chocolate he'd bought in the Lion Market earlier, that was enough basic nutrition to keep him going all day. To this he added a razor, shaving foam and a packet of dark-blonde hair-colouring mousse.

Something had been bothering Carver: an element of his appearance he'd forgotten to deal with. At the check-out he asked for an extra plastic bag, and when he got out on the pavement, he stuck his satchel in it. A delivery van pulled up right by him. The driver had a bundle of early-edition morning papers next to him on the front seat. As he carried them into the store, Carver caught a fleeting glimpse of a single front page, but he saw enough to know he was on it. Thank God for short winter days, the darkness that still afforded him some protection, and the deep shadows cast by the tramp's floppy hat.

When he reached the Embankment he walked across the Thames on the Hungerford footbridge. Even in these bad times the view past the South Bank complex and the Tate Modern gallery, across the bend in the river towards the City and St Paul's on the far side, was still magnificent. The cathedral's dome was a comforting reminder that some things remained as symbols of solidity and permanence long after all the people who tried to tear civilization down had departed.

He walked past the rundown, half-empty terrace of restaurants and shops that ran alongside the Festival Hall and past Waterloo Station, heading for the flat he and Grantham had discussed: a grubby, decrepit apartment that was used as an occasional safe house in a development halfway between the station and the Imperial War Museum. It was about as welcoming as a prison cell, and rather less tastefully decorated, but Carver had a few good memories of the place.

Once inside, Carver went into the bathroom, covered his head with mousse and – thanking God that the flat was not equipped with any surveillance cameras – put a plastic bath cap on his head to keep the colourant in place. He fixed himself a cup of instant coffee – a poor substitute for the espresso he'd had to leave behind at the café. Then he cooked up the milk and porridge oats, pouring a large helping of raisins and nuts into the mix and stirring it all together. He ate it all straight from the pan, finished the coffee and then went back to the bathroom and rinsed the gunk out of his hair. There was a single thin, dirty towel hanging on a rail by the bath. Carver rubbed it over his head a few times and then waited for his own body-heat to finish the job, scuffing his fingers through his short-cropped hair a few times, just to hurry everything along.

He looked in the bathroom mirror. His hair was several shades lighter; not blond exactly, so much as a pale, non-descript, mousey brown. The kind of colour a witness would find difficult to describe.

Next he shaved his temples and forehead, giving himself a receding hairline, which he emphasized by shaving a large bald spot on the crown of his head and then chopping at the remaining hair around it to make it look thin and uneven. He looked in the mirror, slumping his shoulders, letting his stomach muscles relax into a little pot belly, slackening his facial expression and drooping his lips. He practised a weedy, nasal London accent, channelling the sound of David Beckham in one of his early interviews. The man who now greeted him in the mirror was no one's idea of a trained killer, capable of taking on a mob single-handed. He was a loser, an invisible man, of no interest whatever to males or females alike.

So that was one job done. Now to get on with the rest.

The flat where Carver was doing his best to make himself untraceable was less than half a mile from the Kennington nick where the police were still working to trace him. Keane had gone home to get some rest, leaving Walcott in charge. So he was the one who got the call from forensics regarding the brown suede jacket, found in Berwick Street.

'There was gunshot residue on both sleeves, and blood spatter, too. We're just collecting DNA to see if it matches any we get from the bodies out on Netherton Street or in the supermarket.'

'So this was the shooter, then?'

'Most probably. It's like Cinderella's slipper. Find the man who fits this jacket and you've got your killer.'

67

Carver spent a couple of hours online, planning his escape strategy. He looked at a specific category of 'For Sale' ads, and watched YouTube for more than thirty minutes, taking notes on his phone as he did so. He downloaded and used an iPad app. He made a separate shopping list of items on his phone. As he worked, he ate his chocolate, laying down energy reserves for the day ahead.

Celina Novak had returned to her hotel. In due course she would be given the information she needed to carry out the hit on Carver. He was the prime target: so far as her employer was concerned, Alexandra Petrova Vermulen was a secondary consideration. That was not how Novak saw it, but for now she was willing to bide her time. And so, feeling a relaxed, luxuriant sense of anticipation about the day to come, she enjoyed one of her shortest, but best night's sleep in a very long while.

At five o'clock in the morning, London time, it was six in Puerto Banus and eight in Moscow. Olga Zhukovskaya had decided that it was prudent to put in a call to the FSB, the security service of the Russian Federation that was, to all intents and purposes, the KGB under another, post-Soviet name. A situation had arisen in which one former agent might be killing another. She doubted that would cause any great concern in the FSB headquarters on Lubyanka Square, but it never hurt to make sure. In her time, Zhukovskaya had risen to the position of Deputy Director of the FSB. One of her immediate staff had been an ambitious young officer called Slava Gusev. Recognizing both his talent and his sharp elbows she had given him a series of speedy promotions. Today Gusev was the agency's Director. He had not forgotten his former mentor, so when Zhukovskaya put in a call to his office he took it. And when she told him what Novak had been commissioned to do, named the targets, and revealed who had ordered the hit, she had his full attention.

'I must admit that I had underestimated the ferocity of this power-struggle in London,' Gusev said. 'Clearly we must commit more resources to monitoring and if possible influencing the situation. For now, though, my only concern lies in the fact that Petrova is now an American citizen, and a very well-connected one at that. She and Carver are personal friends of President Roberts. Do we really want Roberts to think that we were responsible, even at one remove, for their deaths?'

'I would look at it in another way, Slava,' Zhukovskaya replied. 'If they die in London, and their deaths were commissioned by a prominent Englishman, that will anger Roberts even more, driving a wedge between the British and Americans. And how many years have we spent trying to do that?'

'An excellent point. Very well, then, how do you think we should proceed?'

'As always, information is power. The more we know, the better we will be able to manipulate events to our advantage. And so, this is what I would propose . . .'

Zhukovskaya laid out a plan that avoided the need for an immediate commitment to any particular course, thereby retaining the FSB's flexibility to respond to changing events and maximize opportunities as they arose. Gusev made a few small adjustments of his own and then declared himself satisfied. Within a matter of minutes the appropriate orders were on their way to the FSB's London station.

Walcott only realized that he had fallen asleep when his telephone extension rang and he awoke to find that he was slumped on his desk with his head in his arms. He looked at his watch. It was ten to six. He picked up the handset. 'Uh-huh . . .'

'Is that Inspector Keane?'

'Do I sound like a woman to you?'

'Oh, sorry, well who am I speaking to, then?'

'Walcott. I'm her DS. How can I help?'

'Well, I'm calling from the incident line. I was just checking the messages and there's a guy who says he saw that Second Man bloke yesterday evening. He's a waiter, and one of his customers exactly matched the description.'

'Give me his details then, and I'll get someone to speak to him.'

'I will . . . but before I do, there's something else you need to know. The reason the waiter remembered this bloke is because he was sat with someone famous, having dinner.'

'Famous? What, like a celebrity?'

'Sort of . . . It was Mark Adams. You know, the politician. The Second Man was his guest at dinner.'

Walcott groaned. That was all he needed – the most controversial politician getting messed up in the investigation. Then a happy thought occurred to him. There was no way he could go charging off after Adams. This was way above his pay-grade. Even Keane wasn't in any position to haul Adams in for questioning. It would have to go to Commander Stamford at the very least, almost certainly to the Commissioner of the Met, possibly to the Home Secretary himself. And from Stamford on up, none of them would appreciate being woken up just so they could be dumped in the middle of a political shit storm.

He'd wait till Keane got in, tell her and let her deal with it. And having come to that decision, Walcott laid his head back down on his arms. He told himself it was just for a minute or two . . .

68

It was just past six in London. Carver was clear in his mind now about what he had to do to get out, but he needed a little help. There was one man he knew he could count on, an ex-SBS lance-corporal called Kevin Cripps who'd served with Schultz and been tight with him afterwards. It took a while for the call to be answered, and Carver was starting to think that Cripps was off somewhere working as a mercenary or bodyguard when he heard the incoherent grunt of a man woken from a very deep sleep.

'Morning, Cripps . . . it's Carver.'

'Unnhh, morning, boss . . . fuck, me head hurts, and me guts.'

'Bad night, huh?'

'You heard about Schultz? Fuckin' terrible news . . .'

'Yeah, I know.'

'Me and some lads went out, give him a proper

send-off . . . It was unreal, you know. I only spoke to him yesterday – he said he was having a drink with you, as it happens. S'pose that never happened, right?'

'No, it did. I saw him . . .'

Carver said nothing, waiting for the penny to drop through the thick alcoholic fog filling Cripps's head.

'Oh fuck,' Cripps groaned. 'Was you there, with him . . .?'

'Yeah, that's why I was calling.'

'What happened? I mean, I heard all the bollocks on the news. But what's the truth?'

'We were under siege in that supermarket and we did what we had to do to survive.'

''Course you did . . . so what happened to Schultz?'

'He ran out of bullets. There were too many of them and he only had one working arm.'

'But he went down fighting, yeah?'

'What do you think?'

'Right . . . and then you got stuck into the fucking bastards.'

'Yeah.'

'Good for you, boss. They killed your mate. You killed them. So . . . what can I do for you?'

'Do you still have that old Mazda?'

Cripps laughed. 'Yeah, just about, but it's well knackered. I mean, it goes all right, but it's not exactly a luxury ride.'

'Doesn't matter. I'll give you ten grand for it.'

'That's a lot more than it's worth.'

'The money's not just for the car. There's something else I need you to do for me.'

'What's that, then?'

'Shit, shower, shave and put on a proper suit. Then go to Victoria Station and take a train to Shoreham-by-Sea. I need you there by half nine.'

'What the hell's in Shoreham-by-Sea?'

It took Carver another ten minutes to tell Cripps what he'd find that was so important in a sleepy little suburb of Brighton, down on the Sussex coast. He talked through the way the financial transaction would work, and what little extras Cripps had to take care of.

Before they hung up, Cripps asked. 'So where do you want the Mazda?'

'Anywhere near Victoria will do. Text me the location. Leave the keys in the exhaust and if there's a ticket to pay, just put that in the glove compartment.'

'Got it,' said Cripps. 'Right then, I'd better get going.'

When the call was over Carver swapped his black body warmer for an old windcheater someone had left on a hook by the front door. It was as miserable and unappealing as everything else in the place: a pallid sky-blue fabric, with a coating of grime that added a depressing grey top note: in short, just the kind of garment a man who looked the way Carver now did would wear. He transferred his wallet, phone and the head cam into its pockets, then screwed up a Tesco shopping bag and shoved that in, too.

He didn't want to be weighted down by the satchel and its contents, so he reset the iPad to its factory settings, deleting everything on it, wiped it clean of fingerprints and stuck it in a drawer in the kitchen. Satisfied that he had done everything his plans for the day required, he went into the bedroom and, still fully dressed, with the Glock beside him on the bedside table, lay down for an hour's sleep, his first in almost twenty-four hours. It was a long way from a proper night's kip, but it would have to do.

Novak was woken at half past six and told to get ready. Carver had been located. His current location would be virtually impossible to penetrate. But plans were under way to force him to move. He would be driven towards her, just as dogs drive game towards the hunters' waiting guns. It would not be long now.

69

Shortly after seven o'clock Robbie Bell, who had already been up for over an hour, received a call from Hartley Crewson: 'I presume you've seen the police pictures of the Second Man suspect.'

'Of course,' Bell replied. 'And so will everybody who was in that restaurant last night. I can't believe the police don't know that he was sitting at dinner with Mark Adams.'

'Well, we've had one stroke of luck. None of the blogs have picked up on it. There's not even a grainy photo on Twitter.'

'Then we need to make the first move. We have to be proactive, contact the police ourselves and then go public as soon as possible.'

'Agreed. Get on to Adams immediately. Explain the situation. Tell him what has to be done, and then do it fast. You have to call the police before they call you.'

'What's your view on Sam himself? It sounds like you want him caught.'

'Absolutely. I was thinking about it overnight. The fact is, we didn't have any connection with him, and it was pure bad luck he turned up at your dinner table. The sooner he's in a police cell, the sooner the facts can be independently verified.'

'So you're not planning anything more, ah . . . drastic, then?'

'Good Lord, no!' Crewson exclaimed. 'What kind of man do you think I am? The last thing we want is for the public to discover that the prime suspect for the Second Man had dinner with Adams, only for him to turn up dead somewhere. Everyone would immediately blame us. Hell, no . . . I don't want to harm a hair on that man's head.'

Bell gave himself two minutes to fix a cappuccino before he called Adams. But before the milk had even stopped frothing, Adams was on the line to him.

'What are we going to do?' he asked.

Bell did not need to be told what his boss was referring to. 'Go to the police immediately. Nip any hint of a conspiracy theory in the bud. Just think what it will look like: you having dinner with the Second Man, cracking open bottles of vintage Bordeaux . . . Well, it looks like a celebration, doesn't it?'

Adams sounded perturbed. 'I hear what you're saying, Robbie, but there are just a couple of problems. For one thing, we don't know for sure that Sam really was the Second Man. He might just bear an unfortunate resemblance to the real one. And then there's the whole issue of me, an ex-Para, grassing up another old soldier. All those white working-class males you keep telling me we need to get voting for us won't take kindly to that at all. From what I can see, there are plenty of people who think he was a hero for standing up to the rioters. If a load of them got killed, too bad; they were asking for it. That's quite a common view, and I have to say I have some sympathy for it.'

'Fine, then say so at the appropriate time. But right now we can't afford to be standing up for him. "Let the courts decide" – that has to be our motto.'

'I tell you what, though,' mused Adams, conceding defeat. 'That Alexandra Vermulen was a stunner. I'll miss the chance of working with her, I must say.'

'Maybe you can bring her in when you're the next Prime Minister . . . which you won't be unless I make the call. So, are we agreed?'

'Yes, I can see you're right. Make the call.'

Walcott was filling Keane in on the developments of the past few hours while she stood opposite him, chewing on a piece of toast. Once she was up to speed, he could head home for a very badly needed rest, but he'd saved the big news till last. 'We got a tip-off, a waiter who works at—'

'Hold on . . .' Keane held up a hand. The phone had started ringing halfway through Walcott's last sentence. She answered it and was astounded to hear Robbie Bell, Mark Adams's campaign manager, telling her that his boss had been joined at dinner last night by a man introduced to him as 'Sam' who had looked exactly like the Second Man picture released by the police.

'What was he doing at Mr Adams's table?' Keane asked.

'He was invited as the partner of a political consultant from America, with whom Mr Adams was discussing the possibility of raising his profile as an internationally respected statesman on that side of the Atlantic.'

'So who was this "political consultant", then?'

'Her name is Alexandra Vermulen, and she's currently staying at the Hyde Park Palace Hotel. To the best of my knowledge, the man you want is there with her.'

'That was Mark Adams's campaign manager,' Keane told Walcott a few seconds later. 'Apparently he had dinner with our suspect last night.'

To her surprise, Walcott did not seem fazed by that extraordinary information. 'I know. There was a witness. But how come Adams is coming straight to us before we've even tried to contact him? Suggests he didn't have anything to do with the riot.'

'Or he knows we're going to find out about the dinner anyway, but this'll make him look good.'

There was a forced, fake cough from behind Keane's left ear. She turned to find a uniformed WPC holding out a piece of A4 paper on which a grainy photograph had been printed.

'What's that?' Keane asked.

'It came in a few minutes ago with a covering note that said this was a picture of the Second Man, taken shortly before four a.m.' The WPC handed the piece of paper to Keane and went on: 'As you can see, he's entering a building. And you're not going to believe it, ma'am, but it's less than half a mile from here.'

'Do we know who sent it?'

'No, it was an email attachment from a Hotmail account. The sender's name was just a jumble of numbers and names.'

'Get the tech people to trace who it belongs to and where it was sent from. Tell them it's their top priority.'

'Yes, ma'am.'

Keane got straight on to her boss, Commander Stamford, to discuss the best way to handle the situation. There was absolutely no time to waste. Both leads had to be followed up as soon as possible. The suspect was presumed to be carrying the weapon taken from the armed officer at St Thomas' Hospital. Since there was a possibility that he could be at either the hotel or the apartment block, both operations would require support from SCO19, the Met's Specialist Firearms Command, the London equivalent to an American SWAT unit.

Still, they had to exercise extreme caution. As Stamford pointed out, 'Wherever he is, there are going to be people about. So we can't just go charging after him, guns blazing. We don't want another slaughter on our hands.'

Keane was landed with the task of organizing a mission that was fast, heavily armed and, if necessary, violent, whilst making sure that the full requirements of health and safety, in terms of both the public and police personnel, were fully observed. And she still hadn't managed to finish her toast.

Celina Novak didn't give a damn about anybody's safety apart from her own. If the completion of a mission involved collateral damage, so be it. As she set herself in the optimum position to take the shot when the moment came, she did not care how many bullets hit the wrong people, just so long as one of them took out Samuel Carver.

And when he was dealt with she would turn her attention to her dear friend and former comrade, Alexandra.

Robbie Bell hammered out a press release. It was headlined, 'Mark Adams MP, Leader of the United People's Party, Leads Police to Second Man Suspect.'

Beneath that the text read,

At approximately 7.30 a.m. this morning, a member of Mark Adams's staff contacted the Metropolitan Police on his behalf to provide information as to the possible identity and whereabouts of the so-called Second Man suspect in the Lion Market Massacre.

Mr Adams believes that he encountered the suspect shortly after his triumphant and mould-breaking speech at the O2 Arena last night.

He will be giving a press conference at 10.00 a.m. at the headquarters of the United People's Party, Shepherd's Bush Road, London W6. Accredited media only.

He emailed the release to his entire address book, tweeted it, made it the morning's status update on the party's Facebook page and his own, and blogged it on the party's official website.

Ten minutes later he was frantically calling every staff member who wasn't already in work to get their arses into the office immediately, or the next thing they'd get from him would be their P45. The party office had a conference room with a lectern and UPP backdrop at one end that was perfectly adequate for most media briefings. But this was different.

'I think we may have to find somewhere bigger for your press call,' Bell told Mark Adams. 'Like the Hammersmith Apollo.'

70

Alix had flown in from Washington DC barely forty-eight hours earlier. Her body was still on American East Coast time, the suite's bedroom curtains were heavy and the double-glazing kept out all the street noise. What with one thing and another it was past eight by the time she woke up.

It took her a second to register that Carver wasn't lying beside her in the bed, and another to remember why. He had gone. She might not see him again for months, if she ever saw him at all. And meanwhile she was feeling wretched with morning sickness.

She turned on her phone and listened to Carver's message. He was talking about Plan B but she didn't get it at first. Her mind was so overwhelmed by what was happening to her body that she couldn't quite focus on the world at large. Then she remembered what Carver had told her last night. She switched on the TV and flicked through the news channels. Every single one of them was covering what they were calling the Lion Market Massacre. Until then she hadn't grasped the reality of what Carver had been talking about: she'd seen it all in terms of his pain and confusion. She'd had no concept of the scale or horror of it all. And then she saw the picture of him come up on the screen and knew that she couldn't afford to be a helpless pregnant woman for a single second.

If the police knew about Carver, then they would surely know where he was staying. How long would it be before they arrived? Not long, surely.

She needed to get out. But she couldn't just run, thoughtlessly. First she had to get dressed: practical clothes that would allow her to move fast and if necessary defend herself. Then she needed her passport, wallet and laptop: there were too many leads to Carver on that to let it anywhere near the police.

The night she'd met Carver he'd given her precisely sixty seconds to change, grab her possessions and get out of an apartment in Paris before the whole place blew up. She made allowances for the passing years and gave herself ninety seconds this time. She was already dressed and piling her possessions into her tote bag when the phone rang.

Keane's car was no more than a minute from the hotel, siren blaring and lights flashing, driving other traffic before it as it raced towards its destination. She was talking to the hotel security manager.

'We have key-card confirmation that Mrs Vermulen's

companion exited the hotel at one twenty this morning. We have not seen any sign of him since, nor has his key been used to re-enter the hotel, so we must assume that he has not returned. Mrs Vermulen has not left the room since she returned to it shortly before midnight.'

Keane thanked him for the information and passed it on to the SCO19 officer who would be leading the active phase of the operation. It looked as though they would, once again, fail to capture their prey. But her frustration was mixed with a certain relief: a standoff between armed police and a dangerous man in a crowded hotel was a potential recipe for disaster.

'We have no reason to believe that Mrs Vermulen is armed or likely to pose any threat,' she said. 'So we need to show restraint. She's a US citizen with influential contacts in Washington – that's why Adams wanted to hire her. We don't want a diplomatic incident on our hands.'

'I still have to go in hard,' the officer said. 'If there's any chance at all that chummy's there, I can't afford not to.'

'Fine . . . but I don't want that woman to get so much as a torn fingernail if he isn't.'

The officer didn't reply. He was too busy ordering his men out of their vehicles.

'We've got the green light. Go, go, go!'

71

Carver was still asleep when a police driver in a hurry, blocked by drivers who refused to clear a path for him, turned on the siren he had hitherto kept silent. It was only a short blast – five seconds, maybe: ten at most – and the driver killed it the moment that the first fractional gap appeared in the traffic in front of him, but it was all the alarm clock Carver needed. As he woke he was already processing the subconscious awareness that the noise had been getting closer. Seconds later he learned something else: the reason that the driver had turned on his siren was that he'd been left behind by his mates.

The MI6 flat was located on the top floor – the third – of a low-rise, redbrick development, a mix of flats and small terraced houses arranged in a rectangle around a central courtyard. The only way in by car was through an arched entrance. The bedroom was directly above the arch.

Carver heard the sound of an engine passing beneath him through the arch and stopping in the courtyard. Blue lights flashing thirty-five feet below danced across the bedroom ceiling. He could hear men piling out on to the tarmac, the sound of pounding on the outside door and a voice shouting, 'Police! Open up!' Lights were being turned on in windows all around the courtyard.

Downstairs the police crashed an Enforcer battering ram, otherwise known as a 'big key' into the outside door. When they smashed through that, they would have six short flights of stairs and the door to the apartment itself to deal with.

Now they were on the stairs.

Carver didn't rush. He picked up his gun, walked out of the bedroom, turned right and went into the open-plan kitchen and living area where he'd been working earlier. There were windows either side of the room, facing towards the courtyard on one side and the slip road down to the entrance on the other. The courtyard was filled with police vehicles. Carver opened the window on the slip-road side and looked out. God bless the Plod, they'd not left anyone to keep watch from the road. He looked up: no helicopter. Not yet.

There was a crash from the door to the apartment. It had a steel frame and Banham locks top and bottom as well as the regular Yale. It wasn't going to be broken down without a fight. Whatever the flat lacked in aesthetic appeal it gained in security. It was a safe house, after all.

Which begged the question . . . No, no time to think about that now. Concentrate on the job in hand.

Carver opened the window and climbed out on to the window ledge. A steady drizzle was falling, leaving a slick of water on the glossy white-painted ledge. There were two steel handholds, one above the other, hammered into the brickwork immediately above the window frame. Carver grabbed the cold, wet metal with one hand and used the other to close the window behind him. He pulled himself up: one handhold, then the other. He grabbed hold of the gutter above his head and it twisted a little in his hand, sending a splash of cold rainwater on to his head and down the back of his neck. Carver swung his legs up, scrambled for purchase on the gutter and pulled himself up on to the roof.

Perching low on the slate tiles Carver watched more police vehicles racing down the road towards the apartment block. In a few seconds they would be close enough to see him, even if the first arrivals had not. He made his way across the roof in a crouching, simian lope, turned the corner on to one of the short sides of the rectangle and stopped by the junction between the guttering and a downpipe. Another quick look around. The street below him was empty. Anyone living in the apartment block would have rushed to their windows on the other side of the building, overlooking the courtyard.

The far side of the street, directly opposite him, was dark and lifeless: a new development of luxury townhouses, abandoned half-built when the builders had gone bankrupt. There wasn't much of a demand for luxury these days. Survival was the best anyone could hope for.

Carver climbed down the drainpipe and crossed the

road. The development where he'd been staying had its own basement garage. The only cars left out on the streets were rusting, burned-out wrecks, little different to the ones in Netherton Street, relics of an earlier, long-forgotten civil disturbance.

A chain-link fence surrounded the abandoned construction site, but great holes had been punched in it. Several of the poles had been knocked down. Carver walked unimpeded into the site and then picked up speed, wanting to clear the area as soon as possible. He jogged between the hollow shells of the unfinished buildings, sticking to the shadows, staying alert to any signs of pursuit. The rain eased up a little, the clouds began to part. As he ran, Carver kept turning his head to look behind him, making sure that there was no one on his trail.

The site was littered with unused concrete building blocks. Carver wasn't watching where he was going. He tripped on one of the blocks, catching his shin painfully on the edge. He uttered a sharp, quickly stifled gasp of pain, lost his balance for a second, half-fell on to the stony ground, stuck a hand out to support himself, and for a second found himself perched like a sprinter rising from the starting blocks. His head was up, his eyes looking down the path ahead of him, and at that moment a shaft of sunlight shone through a keyhole of clear sky and glinted off something bright and metallic up ahead.

Carver did not need to be told what that was. Even before the first shot had been fired he was flinging himself to his right, splashing in a puddle as he landed, and rolling towards the gaping empty doorway to one of the

unfinished buildings while the gun made the character-
istic hammer-tapping-on-metal sound of a suppressed .22
pistol, and bullets ricocheted around him. Somehow he
survived unscathed for long enough to reach the shelter
of the bare brick walls. He crouched beside a hole where
a window should have been and looked out across the
site. At first he could see nothing, but then a sudden
movement caught the corner of his eye and he turned
quickly enough to see the slender black flicker of a
female silhouette darting between two buildings, topped
by a streaming red mane of red hair.

Novak!

He'd had no idea she was still alive. Alix had told him
about her fight with Novak at the Goldsmiths' Hall, the
night that Malachi Zorn had died, but he'd simply
assumed that Novak had ended up as one of the un-
identifiable bodies lying pulverized in the rubble. More
fool him.

Carver scampered to the back of the building, looking
for a way out. He was spoiled for choice: there were
spaces for French windows and a back door. He got to the
doorway, pressed his back against the brick beside it,
moved his head fractionally into the opening to give himself a view of the surrounding area and then jerked it
back again as the whipcrack of a passing bullet skimmed
past his newly shaved scalp.

He couldn't fire back. His Glock had no suppressor
and the sound of it would bring the police racing over
from Grantham's flat with far more firepower than he
could muster. He couldn't get out of the building. Now
what? Looking around he saw a rectangular hole in the

ceiling, a little closer to the front door: the opening for an unbuilt staircase. If he could get some height he would at least be able to look down on the site and have a better chance of tracking Novak's movements.

Carver sprinted across the bare concrete floor, jumped with his hands above his head and grabbed a bare joist intended to support the unlaid first floor.

For a moment he was suspended, full length, with his back to the kitchen door and French windows. If Novak came through them now, he'd be a sitting duck.

72

Alix had gone over to the window to check what was happening outside. She saw the flashing blue light behind the radiator grille of an unmarked police car screaming down Sloane Street, coming straight towards the hotel. She looked from the car to the front of the building and saw a faceless black figure slip like a wraith beneath the portico over the front entrance.

They were here already.

Alix didn't panic. She slung her bag over her shoulder, left the room and hurried down the corridor. As she passed the bank of lifts she saw that one of them was on the way up. It was passing the third floor: five more to go. There would be police officers on it and more coming up the stairs. But there was an external fire escape, too: the old-fashioned metal kind running up the side of the building. The way out to it was at the far end of the corridor, a good thirty metres away. She broke into a sprint.

There was a chambermaid's trolley up ahead, parked by the right-hand wall of the corridor, just beyond an open bedroom door. Alix heard a familiar sound, an echo of her childhood. It was a hotel maid, about her height, humming the old Russian folk song 'Semyonovna' as she walked out of the door in her hotel uniform, with a small cotton headscarf tied over her hair. The maid was lost in the cheerful tune as she approached the trolley and turned her back to put something in the trash bag at the rear of it.

Forget the fire escape. Alix had a better way out of here.

She did not break stride. She picked up her bag in both arms, holding it in front of her as she lowered her shoulder and barged into the maid, catching her completely by surprise and sending her sprawling back through the door into the room. Then she grabbed the handle at the back of the trolley and pulled it with her as she followed the maid, who was now sitting on her backside in the middle of the bedroom floor, winded and gasping for breath as she tried to get back to her feet. Alix shut the door.

Across the room, by the window looking out on to Knightsbridge, a room-service trolley had been set up for a guest's breakfast. Someone had ordered steak and eggs and a steak-knife, crusted in dried yolk, was lying on a dirty plate. Alix walked towards the trolley. The maid was in her way, now upright, but hunched over, desperately trying to gather enough breath to scream for help. Alix slapped her hard on the side of the face as she went by, stunning her. She grabbed the knife, came back to the maid and grabbed her from behind, putting one hand over her mouth, pulling her head back to expose her throat to the touch of the sharp serrated blade.

Outside in the corridor came the sound of heavy, running footsteps and a man's voice, several rooms away, shouting, 'Open up! Police!'

The girl was crying. She was badly hurt and extremely frightened. She couldn't have been much more than twenty, if that, and she had a soft, placid passivity to her. The capacity to fight back against a sudden physical assault just wasn't in her nature. It shamed Alix to bully her like this, but she had no other choice.

'Listen to me very carefully,' she said, in Russian, as the policeman shouted again. 'If you do exactly what I say, you will come to no harm. If you do not, then the edge of this knife is the last thing you will ever feel. Nod if you understand.'

The girl gave a series of frantic little nods that made her whole upper body quiver.

'Good,' said Alix. 'I need your uniform. Take it off. Now. Your shoes, too.'

She let go of the maid who did as she was told, stripping down to her underwear and tights.

There were three loud hammering noises from down the corridor as the police battered at the door to Alix and Carver's suite, followed by the crash as it finally gave way.

'And your scarf, please,' Alix told her.

The maid pulled it from her head and handed it over. 'That was a Christmas present . . . from my mother,' she said, looking utterly miserable.

Alix took off her earrings. She could hardly pretend to be a chambermaid with diamond studs in her ears.

'These are a present from me,' she said. The girl's eyes widened in amazement at this unexpected bounty, and she hurried to obey as Alix said, 'Get in the wardrobe. Keep quiet. And stay there.'

Alix heard more shouts – the sound of angry, frustrated, disappointed men – as she shoved one of the two heavy, silk-upholstered armchairs in the room up tight against the wardrobe door. It had taken all her strength to shift it. She didn't see the maid being able to open the doors too quickly.

She put on the uniform, which was a little large for her, and the shoes, which were at least a size too small; close enough. She put her own clothes, shoes and bag in the trash bag at the back of the trolley. She checked herself in the mirror, saw that her make-up was much too good for her newly reduced status, and spent twenty seconds in the bathroom splashing soapy water on her face, rinsing it off and towelling herself down.

When she got back to the room she saw that the maid was pushing hard against the wardrobe doors and had even managed to open them a fraction.

Alix put all her weight against the chair and slammed the door shut again.

'Don't move,' she snarled. 'Or I'll use the knife . . . and I'll take back the earrings.'

The latter threat was the one that did the trick. Alix heard a thud as the maid sat down on the floor of the wardrobe.

'Sensible girl,' she said. Then she took the trolley and

pushed it out of the room and into the corridor, going back the way she'd originally come, towards the service elevator, whistling 'Semyonovna' as she went.

A police officer wearing black battle-dress and a bullet-proof vest and clutching a sub-machine gun emerged from her suite. 'Stop!' he commanded her. 'Have you seen anyone come out of this room?' he asked.

Alix screwed up her face in incomprehension. 'Don't understand,' she said. 'English not good.'

The policeman rolled his eyes and muttered, 'Fucking immigrants,' under his breath. Then he repeated, with exaggerated slowness and clarity, 'Have you seen a man . . . or a woman . . . coming from this room?'

Alix thought hard and then said, 'No. Have not seen nothing.'

The policeman stood there, glowering at her.

'Must go now . . . for work,' she said.

'Piss off then,' he snarled at her, and disappeared back into the suite.

73

Celina Novak was furious with herself. She'd had the chance to kill Carver without the slightest risk to herself. She'd known it had to be him from the moment she'd seen him step through the gap in the chain-link fence. Who else could it possibly be? The police had arrived, exactly as she'd been told they would, and then Carver had taken the obvious escape route. She'd recognized his walk, too.

Like all former Eastern Bloc intelligence personnel, Novak had been taught the three-point identification method, developed by the East German Stasi. Using academics from a range of fields, from anthropologists to zoologists, they'd identified hundreds of markers that define an individual: the shape of their eyes, their stride-patterns, their posture and so on. Agents were trained to take three of these markers, apply them to someone they were trailing and then consider those three markers – and nothing else – when they were looking for that individual. A person could change their clothes, their haircut, add a false beard or wear spectacles, but as long as one or more of those markers remained consistent, they could never escape observation.

Novak had observed Carver at the closest possible range when they had been together, back in Greece. She had automatically filed away the markers she would use to identify him. The shabby, balding, mousey-haired man hurrying towards her across the building site had still retained the essential characteristics of Samuel Carver. And yet she had somehow been unsure. She had hesitated; only for a second, but that had been long enough.

Now she would have to hunt him through this god-forsaken warren, which reeked of failure and broken dreams almost as much as it did of the methylated spirits and rancid urine of the drunken tramps who'd spent the night there and were now lying dead in the bare basement beneath an unfinished townhouse. She hadn't wanted any witnesses, even ones with addled brains.

Novak put a fresh magazine into her long-barrelled Ruger MK II pistol, and walked towards the house where she'd last seen Carver, the gun held in front of her in both hands as she peered into the relative darkness of the interior. She was only about ten feet from the entrance, walking at a slow, steady pace, alert to any movement. And then she heard the sound of footsteps above and ahead of her and looked up to see Carver leaping from a gap in the ragged brickwork of the house's unfinished upper storey and flying through the air towards her.

She raised her gun to shoot him. But at the very

moment she fired Carver crashed into her, flinging her backwards and sending the shot harmlessly wide. She hit the ground back first and was winded as Carver gripped her right wrist and slammed her hand against the rough, concrete-studded surface, forcing her to let go of the Ruger. She was still gasping for breath as he rolled off her and scampered after the gun.

Carver grabbed it, got to his feet and spun round to face her. Now she was lying on the ground and Carver was standing over her, the gun-barrel aimed right between her eyes.

'Morning, Ginger,' he said.

74

Alix reached the hotel basement and entered the warren of kitchen, laundry, housekeeping, security and management facilities that acted as the frantically paddling legs that kept the graceful five-star swan up above moving forwards. She played dumb. She was the new girl at work, not sure of her way around, needing directions back to the staff changing rooms. She got back into her regular clothes, but kept the scarf on and put on dark glasses the moment she got outdoors, going through the service entrance and across the road into Hyde Park as quickly as she could, away from prying eyes and security cameras.

The park wasn't quite the urban oasis it had once been. Clumps of litter blew like plastic tumbleweed across the unkempt grass, and when she got to the glass-fronted restaurant that looked out over the waters of the Serpentine, two of the great panes had been replaced by temporary boarding and there was graffiti all over the brickwork. But the place was open, and Alix was able to order a cup of coffee and a stale, flaccid croissant, although in truth she didn't feel like consuming either of them. In the adrenalin rush of escaping from the hotel she had forgotten how lousy she felt, but now the fatigue and nausea seemed to have gripped her again.

She scrolled through her phone's address book, trying to find someone in London she could call on for shelter. She needed them to be reliable, discreet, and not have a family: she didn't want anyone's kids getting caught up in this. The first man she tried was a banker. He lived in a high-security residential block on Canary Wharf that had round-the-clock armed guards. His office said he was away on a trip to Singapore. She tried a female friend – a high-level political PR – but the way she said, 'I'd love to help, darling, but . . .' told Alix all she needed to know. She hung up before the woman had got halfway through her phoney excuse.

Her third choice was a forty-eight-year-old diplomat called Trent Peck the Third, or TP3 to his friends. He was handsome, rich, educated at Harvard before taking his Masters as a Rhodes Scholar at Oxford, and only recently emerged from a really savage divorce. Alix had lunched with him two or three times when he had been working at the State Department and she had been seeking favours for this or that foreign client. She and Carver had also met Peck and his ex-wife at social events in Washington. Peck was the kind of man who never let minor details such as the presence of spouses and partners prevent him trying his luck. Alix had spent more than one evening trying to fend him off, and Carver had noticed enough to put a cold, narrow-eyed look on his face that made Alix genuinely concerned about what he might do next.

In the end she'd managed to calm Carver down. 'I know . . . you're right,' he'd said, admitting that a swift, brutal act of violence wasn't the answer to this particular problem. 'The man's a wanker, though. You do know that, don't you?'

Alix had agreed then, and she still felt the same way now. But she was a beggar who couldn't afford to be choosy, so she made the call.

Answering his cell phone, Peck came on strong, right from the word go: 'Alix! How great to hear from you!' He exuded an automatic, artificial charm. 'I can't believe it! A call from the most beautiful woman in Washington DC! To what do I owe the pleasure?'

'I need a place to stay,' she replied.

'Really? Don't you have a reservation at a fancy hotel? I can't believe they're all booked up – not in this economy. But, hey, maybe it's just me that you're after . . .'

'No, Trent, this is serious . . . I'm in trouble. I really need your help. I can explain everything. But please . . .' Alix suddenly felt pathetically desperate and tearful – no stronger than that poor little hotel chambermaid. Her emotions were all over the place this morning, swung this way and that by her hormones. Life was so unfair some-times. Why didn't men have to put up with this?

At least there were some advantages to the whole feeble-female routine: it gave men a warm glow of strength and protectiveness.

'Hey, Alix, it's OK,' Peck was saying. 'I'm sure I can help, but first things first: where are you?'

'Hyde Park,' she said, with a sniff. 'At the Knightsbridge end of the Serpentine.'

'Great. That's not too far from me. Listen, I have an apartment in St John's Wood. That's no distance. So what I want you to do is walk down towards Hyde Park Corner. You'll come out by the Queen Mother's Gates . . .'

'Yes, I know where you mean.'

'OK, so you know where the Hilton and the Metropolitan hotels are? There's kind of a drop-off area, like a turning circle, right off of Park Lane. I'll meet you there in fifteen minutes. I drive a black Range Rover.'

'I'm on my way,' Alix said.

'Outstanding,' Peck replied. 'See you in fifteen.'

75

'Get up!' Carver commanded Novak.

'Or what?' Novak replied, propping herself up on her elbows and looking directly up at him.

'Or I'll . . .' The words died in Carver's mouth as he saw her face full-on for the first time. His first reaction was shock, followed by something close to pity – and a personal sense of his own loss as he thought of the times he'd looked down on her during those few days and nights they'd spent together. She'd been lovely then. Her face had glowed with life, personality and humour. It was all put on, of course: everything she did was calculated, every single smile or laugh an act of manipulation. Yet even so she'd been captivating. He thought of the way the freckles had dusted her cheeks, the softness of her lips and the barely perceptible little groove at the very tip of her nose. And now all that had vanished.

It wasn't so much that her face was now grotesque that

made it so disturbing, for her features were where they should be and in the correct proportions. It was that all the life and movement had somehow been drained from her expression. She looked blank, immobile, waxen; like her own death mask. It struck him that this chilly, soulless facsimile of a beautiful woman was actually a much truer reflection of the inner Celina Novak than the deceitful animation of her old face had been.

'Go ahead, stare,' she said. 'But just answer me this. Did your little bitch-whore Petrova ever tell you what she did to make me this way?'

'What do you mean? How could she possibly—'

'By smashing my nose against the edge of a counter top. By putting a flame to my face and burning off half my skin.'

'You're lying!'

'You should be proud of her,' Novak said, ignoring him. Her expression had not changed at all while they'd been talking. She could open and close her eyes but she could not frown. She could open her mouth to talk, but she could not smile. 'It was the night Zorn died . . . She took me by surprise. She kicked me in the knee and had me down before I even knew what was happening. And she did it all for you. She thought you were in danger. She thought I could help her save you.'

'I wasn't even there,' Carver said, as though that would somehow disprove what Novak was saying.

'Well, isn't that ironic? All of this for nothing . . . You know, I spent months wrapped in bandages. I had so many operations, so many nerves cut that if my skin is touched I cannot feel it. If I try to smile, it is so twisted, so ugly that I told my surgeon: "Fill me with Botox, that way I can't even try."

'Now I only have one expression, but like they say about a stopped clock, it has to be right at least a couple of times a day ... Oh, come on, Carver, wasn't that funny? Give me a smile. No one's put Botox in you.'

Carver couldn't say anything. He was filled with a sense of the world unravelling. First the massacre in the supermarket; now this zombified ghost of a real woman rising up out of the past; and all around the evidence of an entire society falling apart. For the first time in his life, he was in a combat situation and he couldn't make the next move. Not when the next move meant shooting her in cold blood.

Novak knew it. Her expression was as blank as a show-room dummy, but she could still put a sneer in her voice: 'At least I still have some fight left in me. You've not got the balls for this any more. It's obvious. If you let me live, I'll kill you, and the Petrova bitch too. You have to kill me now. But you can't ... can you?'

Carver said nothing. He couldn't let her walk away. But it was as though Novak had somehow hypnotized him. She was actually getting to her feet, and he was just letting her do it. He forced himself to drive all the memories of last night from his mind. He couldn't afford to be handicapped by them now. He had to be as callous as the enemy in front of him. He had to ... for Alix's sake.

Now he had a justification. If he didn't kill Novak, she would surely take advantage of her reprieve and she would do it at Alix's expense. His eyes narrowed with a newfound resolution. His finger tightened on the trigger.

And then he felt the cold kiss of metal on the back of his neck and a man's voice with a slight Russian accent said, 'Drop the gun . . . And take the other one out of your pants. Hold it in your fingertips . . . Now drop that, too.'

Carver saw the Glock join the Ruger on the ground in front of him and then his head exploded in pain as the gun-barrel that had been pressed against his skin was lashed across his skull, just behind his right ear.

He fell to his knees, and stayed kneeling for a second or two as he fought to shake off the pain, the tight, sick feeling in his throat and the white noise filling his brain. Then his body slumped forward, face down on the cold, hard, wet ground.

Carver was only unconscious for a minute or two, but when he awoke Novak was gone. He was alone. He was unarmed. And he'd just been betrayed by the one man on earth he'd been stupid enough to trust.

76

Mara Keane was in the hotel suite, consoling an extremely frustrated group of SCO19 personnel, and organizing the collection and forensic analysis of the belongings left in the room by its two former occupants, when a man in a hotel staff uniform appeared in the doorway and called out, 'Excuse me!' And then again, when no one paid any attention to him, 'Excuse me, please!'

'Yes?' said Keane.

'There's a noise coming from room 827, down the corridor. It sounds as though there's someone in there, and I think they might be trapped.'

Four of the SCO19 men were dispatched to investigate. They returned a couple of minutes later with a terrified, tearful half-naked chambermaid, wrapped in a blanket. Between her sobs she managed to tell Keane what had happened to her.

'I thought you said Mrs Vermulen didn't pose any

threat,' said the SCO19 commander when the chamber-maid had finished.

'Evidently I was misinformed,' Keane replied.

Just then her phone rang. It was Commander Stamford. 'I need you back at Kennington,' she said. 'Go through all the evidence we've collected in the past few hours and tell me what we've got. There's a situation developing and we need to sort it out.'

Walcott was on the ragged edge of exhaustion. He'd accompanied the team who'd been dispatched to the flat where the Second Man had been. They'd arrived a fraction too late. It had been a matter of seconds, but the suspect had got out and vanished into the maze of side streets that surrounded the flat. If they'd had dogs there might have been a chance of tracking him, but half the police dog units had been disbanded as a cost-saving measure, and the remaining handlers were on strike, protesting against new regulations that required them to buy their animals' food. He had officers out patrolling the area, but the chances of spotting, let alone apprehending, the suspect were minimal. Still there had been some news, which he was passing on to Keane.

'He didn't have time to cover his tracks before he got out,' Walcott told her. 'We found an empty packet of hair dye and there were dark hairs in the plughole of the bathroom basin. So we need to update the photofit to make the hair shorter and more blond. Also he left a black quilted waistcoat behind, so either he's very cold now, without that and his coat, or he's found something else to wear. And one other thing . . . I got one of the lads at the station to run a Land Registry check to find out who owned this place. And it belongs to the Foreign Office.'

'Is it the kind of place where they'd put up visiting dignitaries?'

Walcott laughed. 'Not unless they wanted a diplomatic incident. This place is a dump. No, it's where you put someone you want to hide away.'

'So it's a safe house?'

'Looks like it.'

'And if it's owned by the Foreign Office, then it belongs to MI6.'

'So why are they keeping this guy safe?'

'I don't know,' said Keane. 'And I'm not sure I really want to know, either.'

Carver was making his way through the streets of Lambeth on foot, trying to work out why he was still alive and what the Russians were doing sticking their noses into all this. At least some of his questions had been answered, though. He knew now exactly who had ordered the riot and why, and he was determined to find a way to prove it in the hours before he could put his escape-plan into effect. During that time he had to keep himself and Alix alive and deal with Novak. Things were going to get messy, and he needed the weapons to cope with any situation. His gun might have been taken from him, but that wasn't the end of the world. Just as Carver could make bombs out of pizza flour, so he could create his own personal arsenal just by going to the nearest shops. And he had Novak to thank for one thing, at least.

She'd shown him very clearly that the traumatic events in the Lion Market had taught him the wrong lesson. There was nothing to be gained by refusing to take life when that was the only sensible option. The next time he got her in his sights, he wouldn't be afraid to fire.

'Why didn't you let me kill him?' Novak fumed. 'He was helpless. He should be dead by now.'

'Our orders were only to observe and if necessary protect you,' replied FSB Major Oleg Kutchinski, who was sitting next to her in the car driving them back across the Thames and into Central London. 'I am in constant contact with Director Gusev himself. He specifically instructed me to extract you from the construction site, but not to assist you to kill Carver. In the first place, that would place us much too close to the killing. And in the second, Director Gusev judged that it was not the correct time for Carver to die. It is his view that events can be managed so as to do far greater harm to the British government. Rest assured, you will be allowed to carry out your mission. And we will be of great use to you. But for now, you will obey Director Gusev's commands.'

'Why? He is not my director. I do not belong to the FSB any more.'

'Oh come now, Novak, you know that is not true. You may say that you have left the FSB. But you, like all of us, belong to it for life.'

77

Alix sent Carver a text as she walked across the park: 'Plan Z (no other option): "3rd-rate" wanker from DC. St J's Wood. Ax'. There wasn't anything very cryptic about that location, but it would have to do. There were a lot of flats in St John's Wood. It would be impossible for anyone to find her unless they knew which particular wanker she was referring to. And speak of the devil . . . less than a minute after Alix got to the rendezvous point, the black Range Rover swung off Park Lane. She recognized Peck looking impossibly preppy and all-American behind the wheel. He pulled in by the side of the road and she ran across to the car. A door swung open as she approached.

'Get in,' Peck said. There was no trace at all of his playboy persona in the brusque, impersonal way he greeted her. This was a very different, much more businesslike Trent Peck. He gave Alix a moment to put on her seatbelt. He checked the road was clear, pulled away, eased into the rush-hour traffic, then swung round in a U-turn at the bottom of Park Lane and headed up the other lane, going north. Peck suddenly floored the accelerator as a gap opened up in the traffic ahead of him and raced ahead, moving from lane to lane as he dodged in and out of the traffic. There was a flash of light behind them from the speed camera opposite the Grosvenor House Hotel.

'Don't worry,' Peck said. 'They can't get me ... Diplomatic plates.'

The car slowed as the traffic thickened again and Peck looked across at Alix. 'Suppose you tell me what the hell this is all about. And do me a favour. Make it real.'

Alix sighed. 'There's someone in my life – someone I care about very much – and he's in trouble. I need to get out of the way ... for his sake.'

'You mean the guy I met that time in DC ... what was he called? Sam Carver, wasn't it?'

She nodded.

'So what kind of trouble is he in? Has he done anything criminal? This is serious, Alix. I'm a US Foreign Service officer. I can't afford to get mixed up in any kind of illegal activity.'

'Well, the police are after him ... but I don't know that what he did was really illegal. And I'm certain it wasn't wrong.'

'Why don't you just tell me the facts?'

'I can't ... I just ... I can't ...'

'Well, maybe then you could tell me why we're being followed.'

'What do you mean?' Alix said.

'Grey VW Passat saloon. It's about three cars back of us right now. But when I hit the gas it stuck with me all the way.'

'I have no idea. I really don't. It can't be the police. I'm sure they didn't see me leave the hotel.'

Peck looked at her in a way that suggested he'd explore the implications of what she'd just said in more detail later. For now he just asked, 'Do you have a phone?'

'Of course . . .'

'Could you give it to me, please?'

'Why?'

'Just give it to me. Give it to me or I stop the car and kick you out right here.'

She looked at him for a moment and saw that he meant it.

Peck took the phone. Up ahead the traffic was moving again. Peck darted forward and manoeuvred the two-and-a-half-ton car as nimbly as a hot hatchback until he was positioned directly in front of a double-decker bus. Then he opened his window and dropped the phone out on to the road, where it was crushed beneath the bus's wheels.

'What did you do that for?' Alix cried, immediately fearful that Carver would be unable to contact her.

'Because that phone is one of the finest tracking devices ever invented. And if you're in as much trouble as you say you are, you sure as shit don't want the whole world knowing where you are.'

Alix glared at him furiously. Peck ignored her. 'So what was it Carver did?' he asked.

'He got mixed up in something . . . completely by accident. I mean, it was a million-to-one chance. He was having a quiet drink and a riot broke out and—'

'You have got to be friggin' kidding me . . . Your boyfriend is the Second Man?'

Alix nodded in admission as Peck gave a long, soft whistle. 'Jeez . . . Well, I can see why you're confused about the rights and wrongs. But as an officer of the Senior Foreign Service, then I have to point out to you that both you and I are obliged to respect the laws of this country and . . . excuse me a minute . . .'

They were just going round Marble Arch. Peck was still driving with a controlled, expert aggression, forcing his way through the traffic as he turned down Oxford Street, before cutting across the inside lane of traffic, provoking a furious barrage of horns, and turning left, back on to his previous northbound course. He looked in the mirror, clearly concerned that he was still being followed. Then he turned his attention back to Alix and carried on as if nothing had happened, 'I have to advise you that the best course of action for both you and me would be for me to accompany you to the nearest police station and stay with you to ensure that your legal rights are upheld while you give a formal statement to the Metropolitan Police.'

'No,' Alix said. 'I can't do that.'

'And suppose I say that for the sake of my career, and because it's my actual duty, I am going to be obliged to inform the police of our conversation over the past half hour?'

'Then I will say that, as you know, I have many good

friends in very high places who could cause even more damage to your career if you did not help me. And I will add something that you might not know. Sam is on President Lincoln Roberts's Christmas card list . . .'

'Him and about a hundred thousand other people.'

'No, he gets a personal card, signed by the President – the same one who invited us to Lusterleaf at the weekend.'

'You're kidding . . . how come?'

'Because he saved the President's life and Roberts has never forgotten it.'

'OK . . . I can see that this is going to require a little thought. Let me just ask you this, just to ease my nerves a little . . . Where were you last night, at the time of the riot?'

'At the O2 Arena. I had an appointment to meet Mark Adams. It was a business meeting. Mr Adams, his wife and many other people could testify that I was there, and that I went to dinner with the Adamses afterwards.'

'So, you had no knowledge of the riot as it was happening?'

'No.'

'And you first found out about it . . . when?'

'When Sam told me some time after midnight.'

'And why didn't you report that information?'

'Because I love him.'

'Maybe, but that's not what you tell the cops, when they ask. What you say is, you were frightened of him, scared shitless of what a man like that might do to you if you ever betrayed him.'

'That's a lie, and I'd be betraying him by telling it.'

'It's a lie that keeps you safe. Trust me, that's what he would want.'

Peck kept driving the same way, making apparently random turns, racing forward whenever possible, running red lights.

'OK,' he said eventually. 'As you can see, we're taking the scenic route. The irony is, if you're not trying to shake off a tail, it's pretty much straight up Park Lane and Edgware Road all the way to my place. I live on Abbey Road, by the way.'

'Like the Beatles record?' Alix asked, happy to keep the conversation light.

'Exactly. I can actually see the zebra crossing – the one on the cover – from the terrace of my apartment. It's ridiculous, I know, but that's pretty much the reason I rented the place.'

Alix smiled. 'Can I ask you a question?'

'Sure.'

'Have you had your picture taken walking across it?'

Peck laughed. 'Guilty as charged!'

'And can I ask another question?'

'Go ahead.'

'Where did you learn to drive like that?'

Peck looked at her with a knowing half-smile. 'Oh, I don't know ... pretty much the same kind of place, I guess, where you learned how to escape from that hotel.'

78

The United People's Party headquarters was packed to bursting with the world's media. The conference room made the Black Hole of Calcutta look spacious and underpopulated. Every other office, corridor and stair-well in the place was rammed with reporters. Screens and speakers had been set up so that they could all get a view of what was going on – the same view they would have got in much more comfort had they just stayed at home. Outside there were more news-crews sending reports back to their studios and interviewing passers-by. All the outside broadcast vans that had been in Netherton Street a few hours ago were here in the Shepherd's Bush Road now, creating a logjam that was backing up the rush-hour traffic across a great swathe of West London.

What none of the media knew, however, was that Robbie Bell had fought like a man possessed to prevent the whole damn thing being cancelled. He'd been involved in a series of heated conversations with the police in the form of Commander Mary Stamford.

'I must ask you not to go ahead with this event, Mr Bell,' Stamford had told him when civilized appeals to his better nature had failed.

'Ask, or order?' Bell had asked.

'You know I cannot order you not to communicate with the media.'

'Precisely. So that's what we're going to do.'

'But I can arrest you and Mr Adams for obstructing or even perverting the course of justice if anything you or he says in this press conference hinders our investigations or makes it harder to bring legal proceedings at a later date. I would also remind you that the man you have identified to us has not yet been apprehended, interviewed, arrested or charged, still less found guilty in a court of law. If you say anything that might damage his reputation, you will leave yourself open to civil proceedings at a later date.'

'I'm well aware of the laws of libel, Commander,' Bell hit back. 'But let me tell you a few laws of politics. I went public with this story because it would have leaked from your force if I hadn't.'

'Not if I'd had anything to do with it . . .'

'*You* might not have done it, but somebody would. Then it would have looked like we had something to hide, and there would have been even more blood on the carpet – Mark Adams's. Our campaign cannot afford to be anything less than totally transparent.'

'It can't afford to have you two carted off to Kennington nick to explain yourselves to our detective, either. Bear that in mind, Mr Bell.'

Bell put his phone away, thinking, Bollocks to that. A few hours ago, his campaign had been going down the crapper. Now he could put his man right back at the top of the news agenda and screw every other party up the arse while he did it. And if some copper thought she was going to stop him, she had another think coming.

Moments later he was striding into the conference with a confident spring in his step and taking his place behind the lectern to address the expectant crowd. 'Before we begin, I'll just explain what will happen. Mr Adams will read a brief statement. He will then answer questions. He will not, and cannot, however, give you any names, either of the suspect he has brought to the attention of the police or of anyone associated with that suspect. I'm sure you'll understand . . .' Bell gave a wry grin, pointed at a notoriously feisty TV newsman and got a laugh as he added, '. . . even you, Gerry, that this is a matter of police operational security. At this time of crisis, it is the duty of all of us to assist the police in any way we can, and we are doing everything in our power to help, rather than hinder, their inquiries. And now, without further ado, let me introduce the leader of the United People's Party, the Right Honourable Mark Adams, MP!'

Mary Stamford did not appreciate being messed around by a jumped-up PR man. First Bell had made a nuisance of himself outside the event last night: now this. She called DI Keane, who was now back at Kennington. 'Mara,' she asked, 'how far have we got with all that Berwick Street evidence?'

She listened thoughtfully to what Keane had to say,

then asked, 'Anything useful come out of the hotel room yet?'

'I see,' she replied after Keane had answered her. 'Well, I think it's time we brought the public up to date with our investigation.'

'Does that have anything to do with wanting to get your own back for this Adams press conference?'

Stamford laughed. 'Well, just a little bit, maybe.'

'Then I'll get on to it right away, ma'am. Do you want me to run this through Public Affairs first?'

'No, I'll take care of all that. Just stick to the facts . . . and don't be too obvious.'

'Of course not,' said Keane. 'I quite understand.'

79

Carver had gone shopping. In a Boots Opticians he bought a pair of spectacles with clear glass, choosing the frames specifically to complement his existing appearance, by making him even more pathetic-looking than he was already. When the chatty salesgirl asked him why he wanted clear glasses he explained that he had an important job interview coming up, 'And I want to look more intelligent.' He'd almost got to the door of the shop before she could no longer contain herself and burst out in helpless giggles.

Now he just needed to purchase the following:

- A powerful, cordless nail gun. In a country that bans the sale of firearms, this was the next best thing.
- A short-handled axe with a high carbon steel head, that would chop through flesh and bones with its

razor-sharp edge, or, when reversed, act as an effective sledgehammer.

- A Genghis 'Ultimate Fear' 10cm ground mine – the loudest firework available in the UK, and as close as commercially available products come to the 'flash-bangs' used by special forces to stun and disorientate opponents. The Genghis website had a video clip showing the Ultimate Fear going off, and Carver had checked it out. The firework sent up a spectacular show of sparks before its main detonation. He timed the length of that show: twenty-three seconds.

The final entries on his shopping list were:

- A length of strong nylon rope.
- A pair of scissors.
- A plastic bottle of mineral water.
- A backpack – as bland and unappealing as possible, to match his new persona.
- A packet of windproof camping matches.

Once he'd got them all he would have a scaled-down civilian equivalent to the gear he'd once taken into battle as an officer in the SBS. The only thing missing would be the opportunity to use it. But Carver had little doubt that he would not have long to wait before that arose.

80

Mark Adams walked up to the lectern holding a piece of paper which he carefully smoothed out in front of him as he looked around the room. He cleared his throat and began to read. 'Last night, following a very successful political meeting, I went out to dinner with my wife, Nicki, my campaign manager, Robbie Bell, and a political consultant of impeccable personal and professional reputation, with whom I was discussing various aspects of my campaign strategy. The consultant, who is female, had mentioned to me that her partner had served in the British armed forces. As a former military man myself, I said that he was welcome to join us for dinner. She called him and he met us at the restaurant.

'The gentleman arrived wearing a long brown suede jacket, a black quilted waistcoat and dark-blue jeans.'

Those words sent a palpable surge of energy through the room. Everyone knew immediately that this wasn't just a publicity stunt by an unscrupulous politician. It could be a genuine, major story.

Adams felt the change in the air as he went on, 'My guest was about six feet tall, slim build, with short dark hair. As you will gather, this precisely matches the police description of the so-called Second Man. During the meal, he and I had a conversation, in the course of which he mentioned that he had been having a drink earlier that evening with a former comrade who had been in the Royal Marines. I must stress that I had no knowledge at that time of the events now known as the Lion Market Massacre. As I am sure you will understand, my attention had been entirely devoted to the speech I was giving. So I did not then understand the significance of what I am now telling you.

'As the meal wore on Mr Bell noticed small dark marks or stains on my guest's jacket. Again, he had no reason to think that there was any significance to them. But early this morning, Mr Bell and I both saw the pictures released by the police of the man they were looking for. We immediately realized that the safety of the public and the obligation on all of us as citizens to assist the ongoing investigation both demanded that we should inform the police of our suspicions, which we then did.'

Adams folded his script up again and said, 'I will take a few questions now.' A forest of hands went up and he pointed at one reporter: 'Mary . . .' he said.

'Can you give us some idea of what kind of a man your dinner guest was?' asked Mary Wainright, a political commentator on the *Telegraph*. 'Did he act in any way like a man capable of cold-bloodedly killing around forty of his fellow human beings?'

'Not in any obvious way,' Adam replied. 'To be honest, he seemed like a perfectly decent bloke . . .'

There was another flurry of action as the phrase, 'he seemed like a perfectly decent bloke' was tweeted, texted and emailed around the world.

'He was intelligent, articulate and had a decent sense of humour. He certainly knew about military matters. I remember we discussed the assassination attempt on me last night, and how he had known – as I had done – that the gun was firing blanks. Now I come to think of it, he actually raised the subject of the riot and its aftermath, but there was nothing at all in his manner to suggest that he was connected to it or to arouse our suspicions. Next question . . . the gentleman at the back there.'

'Frank Preston, CNN . . . I'm finding it hard to believe that a man can kill forty people and then just go out to dinner. Was your guest some kind of psychopath, do you think? Or are we talking about a case of mistaken identity?'

'I'm not a psychiatrist, Mr Preston, so I can't give you a diagnosis. But I have been to war as a soldier. So let's suppose, for the sake of argument, that this really was the Second Man. Within the previous hour or so, he had been involved in an extremely stressful combat situation. A close friend had been killed, and he had used extreme methods to save his own life and those of the other people with him. Well, I'm sure you've all seen old war films about pilots coming back to base after a mission. They've seen their mates getting shot down, but they don't sit around moping. That's not what fighting men do. They go to the pub, have a drink, dance with a pretty girl, sing rowdy songs. They live, Mr Preston. They try to be as alive as possible because they have been surrounded by death . . . John.'

John Murphy, an ITN reporter, asked, 'The Prime Minister's office today issued a statement saying that there was no place for vigilante behaviour in British society. They have described the bombing of the Lion Market as, quote, "a cowardly act that is no better than terrorism". How do you respond to that?'

'I say that if there was an act of terrorism, it was carried out by the rioters. They were the ones who planned to take people's lives, wreck their businesses and disrupt an entire community. From everything that I have heard, what happened in the Lion Market was a spontaneous, unplanned reaction to the threat the people there were facing—'

'I'm sorry, Mr Adams,' Murphy interrupted, 'but how could anyone make a "spontaneous" or "unplanned" bomb?'

'Well, I could have done it,' said Adams, provoking an audible gasp from the audience. 'Any soldier who has served in the special forces or another elite unit could do it, though I'm not going into details in public.

'As for the Prime Minister, he has a nerve accusing men who've fought for this country of cowardice. He may go off to country estates with all his posh pals and blast away at defenceless pheasants. But he's never had to stand up to anyone who's shot back. He's a spoiled, pampered toff, and he's using these accusations in a blatant attempt to cover up the truth, which is that a terrible event like this would never have happened if the government had given the police the means to crack down hard on the very first riots. But they didn't. Just like they didn't deal with the underlying causes of these riots: the broken communities, the racial tension, the deadly effects of alien cultures being introduced into this county . . . all the things that ordinary people can see all around them every day. And the result is more than fifty people dead in a street in South London.'

Adams had managed to turn the press conference into a miniature version of his rally, getting across the arguments that the riot had silenced last night. Now he just had to drop a final quotable bombshell and go. He gave one of his slow, meaningful scans of the audience and said, 'I have a message for the Prime Minister, and it is this: the blood of those dead people is not on the hands of the so-called Second Man. It is on your hands. And I will hold you to account.'

Then he leaned a little closer to the microphone, said, 'Thank you very much,' and strode briskly from the stage.

81

Carver was standing in front of a display of nail guns. He'd concluded that the best use of the cash he'd drawn out earlier that morning was a Paslode IM90i Framing Gas Nailer. It was capable of firing thirty-seven 90mm nails deep into the timber frame, joists, roofing and floor-boards of a house at the rate of three a second. It wouldn't have any problem blasting into human flesh and bone.

The phone rang: Kevin Cripps.

'Victoria's a bloody bastard for parking,' he said. 'Anyway, I went on one of them websites where you can park at someone's gaff, and got a garage in this mews by the Vauxhall Bridge Road. I'll send you the address by text, yeah?'

'Is the garage locked?'

'Nah, just pull up the door.'

'So where are you now?'

'Just past Haywards Heath on the train to Shoreham-by-Sea.'

'Then give me your bank details as well as that address, and I'll stick the ten grand in your account.'

'Quality!'

'When you get there, make sure the bloody thing works. Get him to show you, all right? If he needs encouraging, call me and I'll put a ten per cent deposit down, so he knows the money's real.'

'What do I say if he asks why I want it?'

'You say that your client is a very wealthy man with a very spoiled son. Roll your eyes. You're just a normal bloke working for a rich prat. He'll understand.'

'So you're a rich prat, yeah?'

'No . . . but my life would be a lot easier if I was. Call me when you've got everything.'

There was a brief pause on the other end of the line and then Cripps asked, 'You all right, boss?'

'Don't worry,' said Carver. 'I'll manage.'

82

Trent Peck the Third hurried around his penthouse apartment, clearing the empty packets of last night's Chinese takeaway from the table in front of the leather sofa where he'd been sprawled eating dim sum and watching a box-set of the first season of *Prison Break* (ten years old but still a classic) on his 55-inch Loewe TV. He checked that his built-in espresso maker was stocked with beans and water, then cast an eye around the open-plan living area that stretched right across the front of the apartment. Once he'd thrown the surface trash in the bin, the rest of the place wasn't too bad.

All the while he was giving Alix the kind of detailed examination that hadn't been possible while he'd been driving through London like a lunatic, trying to shake off that damn VW. She had to be forty, at least, he figured, but she'd taken a lot of effort to keep her looks, succeeded and knew it. Peck admired women like that.

They were grown-ups. They knew their value in the marketplace, and they weren't coy about what they wanted in the sack, but they'd also been around long enough to be realistic in their expectations.

Trent gave her the benefit of his most charming smile. 'Can I get you a cup of coffee? Reckon I make the best in London.'

'Sure, that would be great. This is just so, so sweet of you, taking me in like this. Your place is amazing, by the way.'

He fixed a cappuccino with low-fat milk, no sugar, for Alix, and a double espresso for himself. Then he led them across to the big leather sofa, offered Alix one end, took the other, waited till they'd both had time for a sip or two of coffee and then said, 'So, what on earth are we going to do now? Seriously, we need to figure out your next move. Mine, too, come to that. I can't just keep you here, you know. I need to talk this through with some-one.'

Her eyes widened in alarm. 'No you can't! No one must know I'm here – absolutely no one!'

'Trust me, the guy I'm thinking of is totally reliable. He's not going to tell anyone anything. But I really value his advice.'

'So who is he?'

'Someone at the embassy . . . a mentor, I guess you could call him.'

'Promise me you're not going to hand me over to the police.'

'I promise . . . on one condition: everything you've told me has to be true. If I find out you've been bullshitting, or there are things you've not been telling me – like illegal activity on your part, or involvement in any of Carver's alleged illegal actions – well, then all bets are off. Is that fair?'

She nodded.

'Great,' Peck said. 'Then we've got a deal. Now, I've gotta get to work, and I'd better not take my automobile. Don't want to be followed again.'

Trent Peck stood on the pavement outside his building for half a minute till a cab came by. He hailed it and told the cabbie, 'US Embassy, fast as you can.'

Two men in a parked C-Class Mercedes saloon watched the taxi disappear down the road. They'd arrived less than a quarter of an hour earlier, having taken over from the men in the VW Passat who'd first picked up Petrova's trail when she'd left the hotel. They had pictures of her arriving at the apartment building with a male, whose car had diplomatic plates. They had pictures of him leaving. Now the driver of the Mercedes called Oleg Kutchinski, who was sitting in an office in the white stucco mansion on Kensington Palace Gardens that houses the Russian Embassy.

'Petrova is now alone in the apartment,' said the driver.

'Good. Stay where you are. Maintain observation of the apartment. Wait there until you receive further orders.'

'What if she leaves the apartment?'

'Then inform me and follow her. Wherever that woman goes, I want to know about it.'

83

Carver went to a diving store, where he bought a light-weight triathlon wetsuit, a wetsuit balaclava to cover his head, a pair of short 'zip-fins' designed for building up fitness over long swims, a face mask and a snorkel.

He removed the nail gun and its accessories from the box, disposed of all the packaging, loaded the gun and placed it inside the Tesco bag. The axe, firework, rope, scissors, matches and water went into the rucksack, along with the wetsuit balaclava, the fins, the mask and the snorkel.

Having given the matter considerable thought, he concluded that he had no option but to wear the wetsuit under his clothing. Even though he had specifically chosen the lightest, most flexible possible suit, it would still get as hot and sweaty as hell over the next few hours, but he couldn't see a practical alternative.

'It's a personal thing,' he said to the male shop assistant who'd taken his order.

'What a perv,' the man had muttered, under his breath, but loud enough that Carver could hear.

It was just as well that the assistant hadn't known what his customer actually had in mind for the rest of the day. The harmless predilections of a rubber fetishist would seem charmingly innocent in comparison.

At Kennington police station, the resident computer wizard had been set to work to compile two new photofit images of the Second Man: one with a floppy bush-hat over his face, the other with much shorter, lighter hair. Neither looked exactly like the newly disguised Sam Carver. They did not, for example, show him wearing glasses. But they were closer to the present truth than the original portrait had been. And once Inspector Keane had passed them on to the press office for immediate distribution, it was only a matter of time before somebody out there made the connection.

She knew it would not happen at once; that would be too much to ask for. But if Sam, or whoever the Second Man really was, did something either bold or public enough to attract anyone's attention, then spottings of him would soon be reported to the police. Keane was absolutely confident of that.

84

London had been a crucial base for American intelligence for more than seventy years. In 1942, the newly created Office of Strategic Services, the forerunner of the Central Intelligence Agency, set up an office of its Secret Intelligence Branch, or SI, in London, from which more than a hundred agents were sent into Nazi-occupied Europe. For decades afterwards, the extraordinarily close, if sometimes fractious, relationship between British and US intelligence led to almost constant communication between the two nations' agencies.

Many CIA personnel, based among the diplomats at the US Embassy in London, were entirely open – within the profession at least – about their jobs. They were well-known to their British counterparts – or 'cousins' as the two nations' spies referred to one another, with heavy, knowing irony. Others, however, were undercover, for one of the dirty little truths about espionage is that one spies on one's allies quite as much as one's enemies.

One of these undercover CIA agents was Trent Peck the Third.

When he got to the US Embassy he slipped into the office of the CIA Head of Station, John D. Giammetti, for a quiet conversation. As he recounted the story of Alexandra Vermulen's call to him, her plea for help and her arrival in his apartment, Giammetti was searching through the files on his desktop computer.

'Well, I gotta say, Trent, you can pick 'em,' he said, when Peck had come to the end of his story.

'Yeah, she's pretty hot,' Peck said, assuming Giammetti was referring to a photograph of Vermulen.

'I wasn't talking about her looks. You know she's Russian, right, by birth? Ex-KGB, in fact.'

'Jesus! That explains how she got out of that hotel without being caught by Scotland Yard's finest. But how did she ever get citizenship?'

'Marrying a retired US Army general, I guess. Don't worry, she's been checked out. Far as anyone can see, she had a brief career as a young woman, doing all the things that hot young women in the KGB used to do, you get my drift. Looks like she quit the trade once the Soviet era ended.'

'Ha!' Peck exclaimed. 'There's no such thing as ex-KGB.'

'That's not what the file says,' Giammetti insisted. 'She's been clean for a long, long time. The Bureau kept a watch on that lobbying business she runs for a while, but they couldn't find too much to worry about.'

'Well, that may change. She's dating some Limey called Samuel Carver. And get this: he's the Second Man.'

'What? From the Lion Market Massacre?' said Giammetti, incredulously.

'One and the same. He's got every cop in London after him. And from the way the Prime Minister's been talking, they're treating him like the second coming of Osama bin Laden.'

'Yeah, well, that tells you what's wrong with this friggin' country. Guy risks his life to save two helpless women and some Asian shopkeepers, blows a bunch of douchebag rioters to pieces, and they think he's a criminal. Back home he'd already have his first movie deal and an invitation to lunch from the mayor.'

'She said this guy is some kind of personal buddy of the President's, though. Is that for real?'

'Let me have a look,' said Giammetti, consulting his screen. He gave a low whistle. 'OK . . . So, this Carver dude is ex-British special forces. Did some work for the Secret Service a few years back. They hired him to test the security precautions at Roberts's private compound down in Carolina. Carver staged some kind of phoney attack.'

'Why did they get a Brit to do it? Why not use the SEALs or Delta Force?'

'Dunno, it just says he was hired on account of his "specialist professional expertise".'

'Does that mean he's some kind of hitman? Makes sense of the way he behaved last night.'

Giammetti scratched the back of his head. 'You know

what? I think you did a smart thing coming to talk to me. And I'm going to do another smart thing and cover all our asses. Time to talk to our cousins.'

Giammetti pressed a speed-dial number on his desk phone. 'Hi, honey,' he said when the call was answered. 'Your boss available? Oh, OK ... well, when he gets out of the meeting tell him John Giammetti needs to talk to him. And yeah, I would say it is kinda urgent.'

'So who did you call?' Peck asked.

'Grantham,' Giammetti said. 'You wanna get something done, it's best to go straight to the top. Now, do me a favour: head back to your apartment and make sure your house guest is being a good little girl.'

Alix's presence in Trent Peck's apartment was also attracting considerable interest in Moscow. The FSB were, of course, well aware of Peck's status as an undercover CIA operative. The fact that he was now sheltering the former agent Petrova provided even greater potential for causing massive embarrassment to both the British and American governments than anyone had anticipated. Novak had been parked in an FSB property in North Kensington and told to wait for her next orders. It was not yet time for her to proceed against both Petrova and Peck. But that time was not far away.

'Tell her to make her way to Peck's property,' said Gusev. 'She should coordinate with our people on the ground there, but she must not do anything beyond that. There are still further characters to arrive on the scene.

But there is no need to be impatient. It will not be too long before they make their entrance.'

It took almost an hour for Grantham to reply to Giammetti's call. His morning schedule had been blown to pieces by the need to cope with the fallout from the police's arrival at the flat where Carver had spent the early hours of the morning. He'd expected them to put two and two together, of course, but not quite this quickly. Not before Carver could be safely got out of the way.

Faced with the combined forces of Scotland Yard and the Home Office, not to mention MI5, hanging around the affair like hyenas waiting for some nice, dead prey to feast on, Grantham had been hard-pressed to keep them all at bay. He'd been forced to resort to a blank, outright denial of any Secret Intelligence Service involvement, pleading total ignorance of how the suspect had managed to find his way into the safe house. But that line wasn't going to hold for long.

Then he called Giammetti and an already lousy day took another turn for the worse.

'Let me make sure I've got this straight,' Grantham replied after the CIA man had said his piece. 'The woman Vermulen – she's run for shelter to one of your guys. Now, she's a US citizen, and Adams has already vouched for her presence at the O2 and subsequently at dinner with him for the entire evening. So unless Adams was behind the whole riot, which I dare say is possible, and she was involved in that in some way, I don't see that she has anything to worry about. It's not an offence to be a murderer's girlfriend. And it's equally acceptable for a citizen of a foreign country to seek help from one of their own nation's diplomats.'

'Well, I'm glad you see it that way.'

'On the other hand, your president may soon be exposed as being best buddies with a man who killed forty civilians in a London supermarket. If you ask me, John, that's where your problem lies.'

Grantham put the phone down, feeling certain that he'd taken care of Giammetti. He'd be fully occupied getting on to his bosses at Langley and warning them of the massive embarrassment that could be coming the President's way. But that still left Grantham with a world of troubles of his own to solve.

He did not regret his decision to have Carver killed. The logic of the situation demanded it. Either he would be caught by the police, in which case there was always a chance that embarrassing, not to say career-ending, information might emerge. Or, far more likely, Carver would escape capture and dedicate himself to uncovering, tracking down and killing whoever was responsible for the riot. Since Grantham did not want to die at Carver's hands, he had to get to him first. And in a situation of such extreme urgency, he'd been left with little option but to reach for an operative he knew would be keen to take the job. He'd acted in haste, and had been repenting it ever since.

There were worrying signs that Novak had gone rogue, or – even worse – was playing a double game, working for someone else too. He'd tipped the police off to Carver's whereabouts and given Novak an ideal killing zone in which to take him out. He was virtually certain that she had gone as planned to the abandoned building site. According to the Met's latest information, three vagrants had been found dead in a basement there, and one of the unfinished houses was peppered with .22 rounds. But there was no indication that anyone had been hit. Carver's body certainly wasn't there. Nor was Novak's, come to that. It was barely believable, but somehow two of the planet's most dangerous inhabitants had fought one another without either suffering any damage. And that made Grantham suspect that there had been a third party in the mix somewhere.

He'd been a bloody idiot to call Zhukovskaya. They'd worked together in the past, but that didn't mean she wouldn't sell him out in a heartbeat. And he knew exactly who she'd call. The Russians were getting in on the act somehow, and anything Giammetti knew, they'd know too. Alix might as well have sent out change-of-address cards. If Novak was getting help to track her down, she'd go straight to Peck's place, and suddenly there'd be US diplomats with CIA connections and women who were personal friends of the President getting blown away on Grantham's patch. Not good.

He tried to get to Novak and tell her to forget Alix and concentrate on Carver, but she'd gone off-grid. Probably just as well. He had to assume that any calls to her, Peck or Alix were being monitored. If he got back to Giammetti, he'd only be giving the whole game away. He'd have to sort this out the old-fashioned way: go there in person and get Peck and Alix out of the flat while he still had the chance.

Grantham buzzed his secretary. 'Something's come up. I've got to leave the office. So cancel the rest of my appointments for the day. I could be gone some time.'

85

Carver couldn't help wanting to be near Alix. Part of it was a natural feeling of protectiveness. And then there was the nagging fear that no matter how hard she tried to hide herself away, Novak would somehow manage to find her. If or when that happened, he had to be able to do something about it.

He'd tried to call Alix, but her phone was unavailable. All he knew was that she was at Trent Peck's flat, somewhere in St John's Wood, so he headed to Regent's Park, which was pretty much next door. It was also a large, open area with very few CCTV cameras and plenty of space for a man to get lost in. Carver navigated a path through the wilderness of unmown grass, stinging nettles, broken bottles and used condoms and found himself a relatively intact park bench. Then he started thinking.

Peck was a US diplomat, so his phone and address

wouldn't be listed. But he was also a rich bachelor at a loose end in the big city, and it struck Carver that he might just be daft or egotistical enough to stick himself all over a social network or two. In point of fact, it had nothing to do with ego. Peck was in the business of creating an image for himself, a smokescreen behind which he could hide his true purpose, and the self-indulgent playboy has been a pose for spies as long as secrets have been hidden and uncovered.

Either way, it took a minute or two on Carver's smartphone to uncover Peck's Facebook account. Though his Wall was restricted to Friends, most of his photos were not. So Carver sifted through countless shots of TP3 living large at poolsides, parties and polo tournaments. And then he hit pay dirt: an album modestly titled, 'John, Paul, George, Ringo . . . and Trent'.

There was Peck, posing with his kids as they strode across the zebra crossing in Beatle-esque poses with the caption, 'Can't believe I live about fifty yards from here!'

In the next shot, there he was again, standing on a roof terrace, pointing back down at the road, with the famous white stripes just visible in the background and another caption. 'Told ya so!'

So he lived on Abbey Road. Carver logged on to Google Earth, opened up the Streetview shots of the area and soon found Peck's flat. The jammy little sod had a fifth-floor penthouse on top of a modern, glass-fronted building just down the road from the legendary Abbey Road Studios. It was actually more like eighty yards from the crossing, but that was just being picky. More importantly from Carver's point of view, the satellite photo showed that Peck's building, which was named The Glasshouse, butted right up against the block next door. Both buildings were of very similar heights and had flat roofs. This neighbouring block was right beside Peck's penthouse, which occupied half the top floor. It had two large glass lanterns in its roof, bringing natural daylight into the rooms below.

Carver kept Googling, and found countless property ads for apartments in The Glasshouse, including an old one for Peck's apartment which not only gave him pictures of the open-plan living area, the kitchen and one of the bedrooms, but also provided a plan, which he promptly downloaded to his phone. The images of the interior layout were tiny, but he could make out the key features nonetheless.

He knew exactly where Alix was now. He could picture the rooms where she was sitting. Was she making polite conversation with Peck? Was she having to give him more to ensure his cooperation? Carver knew she loved him, but he also knew she had been trained to use her body to bend a man to her will.

It took every ounce of self-control to stop himself going there now, standing guard outside the door, or simply charging in and beating the crap out of Trent Peck the bloody Third. But he knew the reality of the situation. He could not compromise Alix's security by leading anyone else to her. He was a mile and a half from her now, and that was as close as it was going to get.

Still, now that he'd found one of the women in his life, what about the other? Ginger's number was still in his address book. He sent her a message: 'Ginger, darling, enjoyed our chat this a.m. v much. Care for a walk in the park? Sam Cx'

It was the first feeler sent out from one opponent to another. Carver was certain it wouldn't be long now before contact was made. He could sense it in his bones.

Novak got the message. She would have grinned with delight if she'd been capable of such a thing. Instead, she called Kutchinski: 'Carver's made contact. He wants to meet. Do I have clearance to act on his invitation?'

'No,' she was told. 'We have other plans.'

'What if this is my only opportunity? He could be captured by the police. He could leave the country. Anything could happen.'

'Be patient. Just bide your time and you will have him. You will have it all.'

86

Grantham had a personal driver, but this wasn't a journey he wanted recorded on any official log. Instead he walked to Vauxhall underground station and took the Victoria Line to Green Park and then the Jubilee to St John's Wood. As he scurried down Grove End Road, past the Hospital of St John and St Elizabeth en route to Abbey Road, Grantham prayed he wasn't too late. He might have affected a blasé attitude to Giammetti, but he knew how much danger Alix and Peck were really in. If harm should befall them in a flat owned by an American diplomat, well, it would just be one more rusty nail in the coffin of the not-so-special relationship. And if Giammetti should then choose to reveal the contents of their conversation, then life could get very nasty for J. Grantham too.

Now he'd reached the corner of Abbey Road. He wanted to get to the other side of the road, and there was a zebra crossing right in front of him, but a group of people were standing on it in stupid poses taking pictures of one another, so it was much more difficult to get across it than it should have been. Grantham had never taken the slightest interest in music. He neither knew nor cared what the appeal of this particular crossing might be. He looked at the numbers on the buildings beside him. Not far to go now.

Celina Novak had been given the go signal. She was standing in the shadow of a tree that stood in the fore-court of a Baptist church, just across the road from the glass-fronted building, wondering what the best way was to get access to Trent Peck's apartment, when she saw the nondescript figure in the dark-blue overcoat walking up Abbey Road. It took her a second to realize that this was Jack Grantham, and she guessed at once that he was coming to warn Petrova of the threat that she was facing. Well, the two of them would soon discover just how great that threat was. As Grantham turned left off the pavement and walked between two rows of ornamental trees towards the front door, Novak slipped out from under the tree and started walking towards that same door.

Grantham pressed the buzzer of the apartment building. It was answered by a man. The sound was muffled and crackly but when the voice said, 'Hello?' Grantham thought he detected an American accent.

'Is that Peck?' Grantham said.

'This is he,' the voice replied, with the grammatical formality that was now far more commonly found among well-educated Americans than the English of any class. 'To whom am I speaking?'

'Hello, my name's Grantham. Your boss just called me.'

'Jack Grantham?' Peck said, incredulously.

'Yes.'

'You're kidding me, right?'

'Trust me, I'm not. I'm here because of Mrs Vermulen. She's in very serious danger.'

For a few moments there was nothing but interference coming through the speaker. Then Grantham heard the American again: 'I guess you'd better come up.'

The door buzzed. Grantham pushed it open and stepped through. And as he did he felt something hard in the small of his back, smelled a delicious waft of a woman's scent and heard a female voice in his ear say, 'Good afternoon, Mr Grantham. My name is Celina Novak.'

He stopped dead in his tracks, but immediately felt a sharp pain in his kidneys as his back was jabbed again and Novak said, 'That's a gun. And I will not hesitate to use it unless you do exactly as I say.'

They proceeded down the hall towards the lift. Novak remained behind Grantham. 'The deal's off,' he said. 'I no longer require your services. But don't worry, I'll pay you in full.'

Novak laughed. 'What you do or do not require is no longer relevant. I have new orders. Now, I believe we're going up.'

The lift arrived. The doors opened. Grantham got another shove in the back to remind him to walk in.

'Fourth floor,' she said. He pressed the button, the doors closed, and it was only then that the pressure in his back eased and he felt able to turn around and look at the woman who now had him in her power.

She certainly was a remarkable sight. And almost all of it was spectacular to behold. Grantham could hardly fail to notice the length and shapeliness of her legs in her spray-on jeans; or the slimness of her waist; or the fullness of the breasts that were tantalizingly displayed behind her semi-unzipped jacket. He was not blind to the tumble of her hair, the gloss of her lips or the cool inscrutability of her dark glasses. But then he saw past all those things to the waxwork artificiality of her face, and suddenly everything about Celina Novak seemed somehow terribly wrong.

'She really fucked you up, didn't she?' Grantham said. 'Losing to her must have been bad enough. But losing your looks as well . . .'

He was trying to make her lose her temper and with it her self-control. If he did that, maybe she'd start making mistakes. But Novak had no intention of giving him that satisfaction. She pressed the 'pause' button on the lift and they stopped, halfway between the second and third floors.

'You will press the doorbell,' she said. 'You will introduce yourself. You will not do or say anything at all to suggest that there is anything wrong. When the door is opened, you will go inside. If you do not do these things exactly as I say, you will die. Do I make myself clear?'

'Yes.'

Novak pressed the 'start' button again and they

continued upwards. When they reached the top, the doors opened and Grantham stepped into a small hallway. There were just two penthouse flats on the top floor, with one door on either side of the hall. He went up to Peck's and pressed the bell.

The door had a small peephole. Novak stood with her back pressed against the wall, just next to Grantham, where she could not be seen. Her gun was still pointed directly at him.

There was a pause while Peck looked through the peephole, examined Grantham and satisfied himself that he really was who he claimed to be. Then the door opened.

Grantham stepped into the flat and walked past Peck, who was still standing right by the door. He seemed to whisper something to Peck as he walked by. Peck turned to catch what he was saying. He caught the words, '. . . a trap', and tried to respond, but it was too late. Peck still had his back to the door as Celina Novak stepped through it with her gun in her hand and blew his brains out.

87

Trent Peck the Third slid down the wall beside his front door, leaving half the contents of his skull smeared across the creamy paintwork as he went.

Novak did not stop to look. She stepped straight over the corpse towards Jack Grantham, who had turned round to see what was happening.

Grantham was a desk officer, not a field agent. He had no way of defending himself when she flicked out her right arm, with all the speed and accuracy of a striking cobra, and punched the hot tip of her pistol's suppressor straight into his Adam's apple. He bent double, clutching at his throat as he desperately gasped for air, and was completely defenceless as she kicked him very hard in the balls with her carbon-fibre-tipped ankle boots. Grantham fell to the floor beside Peck's body.

He would be out of action for several minutes, but it never hurt to make sure, so she kicked him hard in the side of the head, and while he was still dazed patted down his jacket till she found his phone, took it out and slipped it in the small bag she had slung diagonally across her body. There was a zip-up inside pocket in the bag. It contained a number of plastic cuffs that were really just oversized cable ties, twisted into a figure of eight that could be pulled tight around a pair of wrists or ankles. Two of the cuffs left Grantham's arms and legs immobilized. There might come a time when he would have to die, but he was still too useful a negotiating tool to dispose of just yet.

Now for the main attraction.

'Alexandra ... my darling ... where are you?' she called out. 'Please won't you come out to play?'

Her words faded away into absolute silence. There was nothing at all to hear except the distant sound of traffic from the road and a radio playing in a downstairs flat.

'Very well, then,' Novak said. 'If you won't come out, I'll just have to come and find you.'

Alix was sure that Novak would hear the fearful pounding of her heart. She was crouched behind the kitchen island that stood at one corner of the huge living area. In her hand she was clutching the longest, most vicious-looking knife she'd been able to find in the butcher's block beside the cooker. Peck was the kind of man who almost never cooked, but still equipped himself like a Michelin-starred chef. His knives were Henckels Professionals: perfectly balanced, razor-sharp and capable of filleting a live human being just as easily as a joint of meat.

The island was set at right angles to the double-door that led from the hall into the living area. Alix was planning to let Novak come far enough into the room so her back was exposed, and then try to get to her before she could turn to defend herself. It was a long shot. But it was the only chance she had.

She heard the sound of doors being opened as Novak methodically worked her way through the three bedrooms, each with its own en suite bathroom, and the large built-in cupboards on either side of the hall. Now she was coming closer.

The drumming of her pulse in Alix's ears felt almost deafening as Novak opened the doors into the living area. Alix dared not lift her head above the island to look where Novak was going, so she had to judge by the sound of the other woman's footsteps on the parquet floor as she came into the room and seemed to turn right, away from the kitchen, across the lounge where Peck's armchairs and sofas were arranged. There was a door on to an open terrace at the far end of the lounge. Perhaps that was where Novak was heading. She probably thought Alix was hiding out there, or had even tried to make her escape across the roof.

Alix closed her eyes and took a deep breath, summoning all her strength and courage. Then she got on to all fours, pushed with every ounce of strength in her legs and hurled herself across the floor towards the glossy black bullseye of Celina Novak's back.

Novak had been caught out once before. It wasn't going to happen again. She spun round at the first scuffing sound of Petrova's feet on the hardwood floor. There was actually time for her to have raised her gun, aimed and fired, but that would have been too easy and much too fast. Novak wasn't interested in killing Petrova. She wanted to make her suffer, pay her back with interest for the pain she had caused. So she threw her gun to one side, freeing up both her hands as Petrova raced towards her, crouching low to present the smallest possible target, and only straightening up as Petrova came within a couple of paces and drove her knife upwards in an underhand stab aimed straight at Novak's guts.

Novak met the oncoming blade in the classic cross-block defence that she and Petrova had both been taught when they were still little more than teenage girls. She crossed her forearms over one another and then pushed downwards, away from her body to trap Petrova's knife-hand in the 'V' of her crossed arms, catching it at the wrist. It took every ounce of Novak's strength to hold Petrova there, but she succeeded in stopping the thrust, and the knife came to a sudden halt just millimetres away from the shiny fabric that covered Novak's stomach.

Alix had anticipated the cross-block, and allowed for its obvious shortcoming: both Novak's arms were now occupied. She couldn't afford to let either of them even relax, still less move, or Alix would be able to complete her thrust and stab the knife deep into Novak's guts. But Alix still had one hand free.

She swung her left arm round, grabbed hold of a fistful of Novak's hair and pulled hard.

Novak shrieked as her head was yanked sideways. Her arms gave way a little and Alix let her shoulders swing round, so that the pull of her left hand was matched by the punch of her right as it drove the needle point of the knife right up against Novak's jacket.

Another fraction of a second and Alix would have completed the thrust and finished the job she'd started back at the Goldsmiths' Hall.

But then Novak's scream turned to an exultant yell of delight. Her head snapped back to the vertical and Alix found herself with nothing in her hand but a glossy bunch of extensions that had been pulled from their moorings amidst Novak's natural hair.

Alix was taken totally by surprise. She was distracted as her mind tried to come to terms with what had happened. Her muscles relaxed. Her guard was down. Novak felt the change in her opponent and in that instant she attacked again.

Novak grabbed Petrova's knife-hand with both of hers, gripping it as tight as possible and jabbing her nails deep into her skin.

She pushed the trapped hand towards Petrova's wrist, so that the back of her hand was at right angles to her arm. The pressure and pain of that unnatural angle made Petrova's arm give way and her elbow retreat.

Novak kept moving, forcing Petrova to bend and turn her body so that suddenly the hand clutching the knife was being forced up behind her back, her shoulder was screaming in agony and it was her turn to cry out in protest.

The fingernails pressing into the flesh of Alix's hand and wrist were like little daggers stabbing her, and the pain was so intense that she was hardly conscious of her fingers losing their grip on the knife. It clattered to the floor, and as it hit the ground Novak stamped her boot down into the back of Alix's knee, and then as her body crumpled, hit her with a karate blow to the back of her neck.

Alix didn't feel a thing as she hit the floor. She was lost in the deep, dark void of unconsciousness.

Novak took a few moments to enjoy the sight of her most bitter enemy lying beaten at her feet. Then she walked across the floor to pick up her gun and put it in her bag.

On her search of the apartment, Novak had noticed that Trent Peck the Third had installed a large brass bed in his room, the kind whose frame is absolutely perfect for tying up or cuffing a sex-partner, just to add a little spice to lovers' games. Novak picked up Petrova's unconscious body and began dragging it across the floor, thanking the late Mr Peck as she went for choosing such a nice, slippery surface. She continued down the hall, past Peck and the unconscious Jack Grantham and into the master bedroom. That was covered with soft, thick carpet, which made it considerably harder to shift Petrova. The blonde bitch had obviously become fat and lazy in the contentment of her relationship with Carver, because she seemed to weigh as much as a baby elephant.

Novak was breathing heavily and her back was aching

as she finally hefted Petrova on to the bed; the top half of her, at any rate. She was just able to stretch one of Petrova's arms far enough to secure it to one of the brass rails at the back of the bed frame with another one of the plastic cuffs. Then she shifted a bit more of Petrova's flabby backside on to the mattress, and that was enough to enable the other arm to be tied nice and tight. From there it was a relatively simple business to heave her legs up on to the bed. Novak was about to tie them too when a thought occurred to her.

She walked back to the kitchen and rummaged through the drawers until she found a heavy pair of kitchen scissors. Then she returned to the bedroom and used the scissors to cut right up the front of Petrova's top, from hem to collar, so that it opened up, exposing her torso and bra beneath.

Novak kept cutting. She went across the shoulders and down each sleeve so that Petrova's shoulders and arms were visible. Then she grabbed the top in both her hands and tugged until the whole thing slid out from under Petrova. Next she cut off her bra. Then she pulled down her trousers and knickers.

Only when Petrova was completely naked did Novak finally tie her ankles to the foot of the bed. She cast an appreciative eye over the helpless body spread out before her. There was one last touch. She needed a means of closing Petrova's mouth, one that would leave most of her face still accessible, and in a man's apartment – particularly an American's – she knew just what that would be.

There was a cupboard in the hall filled with cleaning

equipment, tools and general domestic hardware. Novak had opened it just a few minutes earlier while searching for Petrova. She returned there and, sure enough, soon found what she was looking for: a roll of duct tape. She took it into the kitchen, took a pair of cook's scissors from a drawer and cut a strip about 15cm long. Then she went back to the bedroom and stuck it over Petrova's limp, unconscious lips. And, as she did, Celina Novak pondered on exactly how she would send sweet, adorable, innocent little Alix Petrova silently screaming to her grave.

88

Carver was still on his park bench. He had just wired more than sixty thousand pounds from the account of one of the Panamanian-registered shell companies he used to hide the very large amounts of money he had earned from killing bad men – and the much smaller amounts obtained by keeping good ones safe. He had made the deal that would secure his escape. But where was Novak? Why hadn't she replied?

Celina Novak gave considerable thought to the tools she would need for the job she had in mind. She selected a knife: the very knife, in fact, with which Petrova had just so feebly attacked her. To that she added a pair of secateurs, found in the same cupboard as the duct tape. There were large ceramic flower pots arrayed on the terrace outside. Perhaps the American had liked to fill them with plants in the spring and summer and tend them himself. Perhaps he'd fancied that he had – what was the English saying? – green fingers. How apt.

Novak found the sharpening steel that the American had used to sharpen his precious knives. She turned on the gas hob to full flame and laid the steel on top of it. She was just wondering what to do next when she heard a groan from the hall. Grantham was waking up.

Novak walked back to him and kicked him in the head again, but that wasn't exactly a long-term solution. So she got down on her haunches and took off Grantham's shoes. Underneath were two sweaty, stretchy black woollen knee socks. Perfect.

Grimacing slightly at the smell, she took the socks off, too. Then she rolled one into a ball, pulled the end back over the ball to hold it in place, forced open Grantham's mouth and shoved the sock in. Before Grantham could spit it out, Novak pulled the other sock across his face, and, stretching it to the utmost, knotted it tight round the back of his head. The tied sock pulled hard against Grantham's mouth, shoving the rolled-up one deeper down into his throat, making him retch, and pulling his lips back in a grotesque parody of a smile.

She went back to the kitchen and turned the sharpening steel so that both sides would be heated equally. It was almost time to begin, but if she wanted her party to go with a swing, she needed a full complement of guests. Carver wouldn't be far away, she was sure of it: no more than five minutes, ten at the most.

She called the men in the car outside.

'Carver will be coming here soon,' she said. 'He will be in a hurry and therefore more likely to be careless.

Remain alert and let me know the second you first see him.'

The only issue now was time. There was a lot to do, and only a few minutes in which to do it. She hurried to the cleaning cupboard, took the most powerfully caustic drain-cleaning fluid she could find, and brought it through to the bedroom. Then she went to get the rest of her tools, except for the sharpening steel. That would stay on the gas hob gathering heat until the very moment that it was needed.

Before she began she wrote a quick text: 'Hello, Sam. I have your bitch. Just about to leave my mark on her. Gingerxxx'

Novak sent the message. Then she took the top off the drain cleaner and placed the plastic bottle right under Petrova's nose so that she could not escape its powerful, ammoniac vapours. Immediately Petrova started coughing and gasping for breath, only to find that the duct tape across her mouth was making it impossible for her to do so. That jolted her into consciousness. Unfortunately it also put her in danger of suffocation, and Novak was obliged to loosen the tape for a few seconds until Petrova could calm her breathing again. Before she had recovered enough to scream for help, Novak stuck the tape back down again.

Then she smiled and said, 'Hello, Alexandra. I'm so glad you're awake. I think we'll have so much more fun together if you know exactly what I've got planned . . .'

89

Carver ran. He raced across the great open grassland at the heart of the park, heedless of any attention he might draw or stares that he provoked. It was too late for discretion or concealment now. He had only gone a couple of hundred yards before the drawback of wearing a wetsuit became apparent. It was hot and, by definition, completely air and watertight. Less than a minute after he had set off he was already sweating like a pig.

His lungs and legs were betraying him, too. Carver kept himself fit, but only to the standards of the prosperous civilian he'd been for the past two years. He didn't have the muscular endurance or heart-lung capacity that he'd once taken for granted. He told himself the pain was an illusion, a mirage generated by a frightened brain to prevent the body from over-exerting itself. And he kept running.

He was two-thirds of the way across the grass when he

received another text. It just said, 'I am alone with her. Just imagine what I am doing. Gx'

He told himself that this had to be some kind of sick joke – a taunt to bring him on all the faster, to make him so mad with rage and fear that he would cease to act like a trained professional and blunder in like an amateur.

Carver kept running, darting in and out of people on the path. A couple of young guys, aged maybe seventeen or eighteen, were coming towards him in the opposite direction, kidding with each other, not paying much attention to what was around them. Carver tried to get around them, but then one of the guys moved into the space he was aiming for. They banged shoulders, and the impact sent the kid Carver had hit spinning into his friend. They shouted angrily after him and then one of them said to the other: 'Do you know who that was?'

'Yeah, your dad.'

'Nah, seriously . . . look . . .' He got out his phone and went on to Twitter, quickly finding #secondman where a dozen or more recent tweets had links to the latest police photofits.

''Kin 'ell, you're right. That's him . . . that's the Second Man.'

'Well, call the police, bro. Maybe there's a reward, like thousands of pounds or something.'

'Ah, that would be well mint.'

'Well, get a picture of him, quick! Before he gets too far!'

When they called the hotline thirty seconds later, theirs was the first report of Carver's mad dash across the park and up into St John's Wood. But it would not be by any means the last.

Carver was shattered. His body was liquid inside its neoprene sweat box. His legs were screaming from the build-up of lactic acid, and his lungs were wheezing like broken bellows. But still he ran. And still the taunting messages from Novak continued.

'She's aching to see you – but where are you? Gx'

'Having a great time – wish you were here!! Gx'

'Would you love her – even if she was VERY ugly?? Gx'

He'd run past the Lord's cricket ground, down smart, leafy streets that seemed untouched by the anarchy, round the corner into Abbey Road. Then, finally, he forced himself to slow. He had to get his pulse-rate down, gather his wits and prepare himself for what he had to do next. Carver assumed that Novak, or someone working with her, was watching the approaches to Peck's flat. He had to cover the ground towards it as unobtrusively as possible, but now he had a stroke of luck. A double-decker bus was making its way down the road in a line of slow-moving traffic. Carver jogged along next to it, using it as cover, past the white, two-storey studio. As the bus passed the red-brick block of flats that stood next to the building where Alix was being held he darted unseen up to the front door and reached into his bag. He got out a thin strip of clear plastic, cut from his empty water bottle while he'd been sitting on the park bench, and slipped it between the lock and the door jamb, carefully manipulating it until the bolt slid back and the lock clicked open. Carver dashed to the lift, waited for fifteen agonizing seconds till it arrived – telling himself that it would still be quicker and less draining than taking the stairs – then pushed his way in before the doors had fully opened and hammered the palm of his hand against the button for the top floor.

In Trent Peck's bedroom, Novak had finally fetched the sharpening steel from the kitchen and was standing by the foot of the bed, looking at the splayed cruciform of Petrova's writhing, defenceless, cruelly exposed body. Petrova was staring at the glowing red-hot metal with the wide, frantic eyes of a trapped animal, and the silver tape around her mouth was rippling with the desperate motions of the lips beneath. It took Novak a second to realize that these were not just the muffled screams or cries for help that she had become used to over the past few minutes. No, Petrova was trying to say something specific – something of huge importance that she desperately needed Novak to hear. And when Novak listened very closely to the garbled, strangulated utterances she thought she knew what it was. But she peeled back the tape, just a little, to make absolutely sure.

Yes! Novak was right. With the very last strength in her body, Petrova was begging for mercy. But it was not for herself. What she was saying was, 'Not the baby . . . please, not the baby.'

Novak closed the tape again. She thought she had been enjoying herself up to now. But this . . . well, it took her pleasure on to a whole new level.

90

Carver got out of the lift, ran up a short flight of stairs, crashed through a fire door and emerged on to a flat asphalt roof, surrounded by a low parapet. He dropped to a crouch and scuttled across it, keeping as low as possible. Then he raised his head just far enough above the parapet to be able to look across towards the building where Novak was holding Alix. The penthouse level was inset from the rest of the structure. From where Carver was perched there was a drop of about three metres to the terrace that ran right along the side of the penthouse. To his right, at the front of the building, were a set of French windows that led to the living room. Traversing to the left, Carver saw three windows: two bathrooms and a small bedroom, if he remembered the plans correctly. Then came the long blank wall of the master bedroom, whose windows faced towards the rear of the building.

Carver was on the same level as the roof directly

opposite him and could clearly see the two glass lanterns that lit the heart of the apartment. Those lanterns were his target.

The phone pinged: another text. It read, 'Bye-bye baby.'

What the hell did that mean? Was Alix already dead? Had he got there too late?

Then he got the answer. Another text: 'Did you know she was pregnant?'

The shock hit Carver like a stab to the guts. Alix was having a baby . . . their baby . . . his baby.

Move! He had to move, right now.

He scrambled left till he was opposite the blank wall, then vaulted over the parapet and landed with his knees bent on the roof next door. He sprang forward taking three long strides and then jumped up the wall of the penthouse, grabbing the top and pulling himself up on to its roof.

Novak had to have heard that. Now she knew he was coming. He sprinted across to the far side, above the other, smaller flat, expecting at any moment to hear the sound of gunshots being aimed up through the ceiling at him.

None came. Novak was smart. She was holding her fire, not wasting rounds on shots that had a minuscule chance of a hit. Carver took his pack off his back, removed the Ultimate Fear and lit the fuse. It flared up in a dazzling geyser of white-hot sparks. He crept much more carefully across to the rear lantern – the one above the hall – and put the blazing cardboard cylinder down on the roof next to it.

By now it had been burning for twelve seconds.

Carver took the axe from the pack, holding it with the blunt end down. That took another four seconds. He counted to three, then smashed the axe down using all his strength. As the glass shattered, he could see two male bodies lying on the floor below him. One of them belonged to Jack Grantham, and Carver was pleased to see that it was twitching. The other lay quite still with its head like an island in a lake of blood. Novak was coming out of the door of the master bedroom. Her eyes were raised towards him, but she was looking from a brightly lit room towards the dismal grey murk of a November afternoon.

Carver slung the open, half-empty pack over one shoulder, picked up the firework and held it away from his body, over the hole in the lantern.

Novak saw that all right. She brought her gun up towards the blazing light and fired just as Carver let go and ran like hell towards the side of the building.

Twenty-three seconds after it had first been lit, exactly on schedule, the Ultimate Fear produced an explosion of scorching glare and brutal noise that made everything that had come before look like a child's sparkler. The bang was so loud that it literally shook the building: Carver could feel the vibrations through the soles of his shoes as he ran, jumped back down on to the terrace and turned towards the French windows.

Carver needed to punch a hole big enough for him to get through. It required five hits with the axe this time: one in each corner to weaken the integrity of the glass, and the fifth smack bang in the middle to complete the job.

The window gave way with a smashing of fragments on to the living room's parquet floor. Carver charged through the shattered glass and raced towards the hall through the thick, acrid smoke created by the detonation of the Ultimate Fear. The effects of the blast would be significant – there was a good chance that Novak's sight and hearing would both be seriously impaired – but that would only be very short-term, and she was a tough, experienced operator. Carver had to get to her before she regained full possession of her senses, and every second counted.

They practically collided in the middle of the floor as he dashed over from the window and Novak stumbled in from the hall, her stride still unsteady and her eyes screwed up as she struggled to regain her vision and peer through the billowing grey fumes. She still had the gun, though, and she fired blind: three quick, wild shots that went nowhere near him. Then she stood there waving the gun helplessly, not knowing where to point it next. She was helpless, Carver realized. She had no way of defending herself.

Good.

He stepped right up to Novak and swung the axe with all his strength into the centre of her chest, between her breasts, right below the throat. It smashed through her sternum, and she didn't even have the power to scream. Amazingly, though, she was still alive. She staggered forward a couple of paces, with her hands feebly grasping the handle of the axe, trying to pull it from her body, and Carver had to step back to stop her crashing into him.

So he reached into his bag, pulled out the nail gun and

started firing. He put a dozen nails into her throat and head in under four seconds, keeping firing even as she fell to the ground. He had the gun set to maximum power, so many of the nails went straight through, punching their way like bullets out of the back of her neck and skull before embedding themselves in the walls and floor.

Now Celina Novak was categorically dead.

In the flat below, an Italian woman called Maria Donatelli was racked by indecision. Signor Peck was normally a very good, quiet neighbour. He liked to have a lot of lady friends over, but he was a man, so what else was one to expect? But this afternoon there had been strange sounds: scurrying feet, thuds on the floor and then a blast, like a bomb, so powerful it had made her whole apartment shake. Then more thumping on the floor that sounded almost like people fighting.

She felt she should call the police, but she did not want to get Signor Peck into any kind of trouble. On the other hand, what if his apartment had been raided by burglars, or worse, terrorists? He was an American. He could easily be a target. But then, if she called, she might put herself in danger, too.

What should she do?

Maria Donatelli wavered this way and that. But in the end, she decided to behave like a good citizen and she dialled 999.

Carver laid the nail gun on the floor, picked up Novak's Ruger and made his way through the flat, looking for Alix in the spare bedroom and its bathroom, even though he was certain she would not be there. He desperately wanted to discover her, and yet at the same time he dreaded what he would find so much that he was almost trying to delay the moment as long as he could.

Carver was in the hall now, right by the two bodies. The dead one had to be the owner, Peck. Grantham was lying next to him. He had been right by the firework when it went off and was looking around him with the wide, sightless eyes of the blind, trying to call out through the gag around his mouth.

From the moment he had seen Novak in that construction site, Carver had known that Grantham had been behind the riot. Who else could have tipped the police off to his presence in the MI6 flat? Who else knew enough about Celina Novak to choose her for the job of tidying up the loose ends?

He would deal with Grantham in due course, but now he kept going to the door of the master bedroom, the same door Novak had come through less than a minute before. He took a deep breath. He turned the handle. He walked in.

And he stepped into a charnel house.

91

Alix was lying splayed, naked and ruined in the midst of a crimson eruption of blood. The sheets around her were sodden with it. Blood was dripping from the brass bed frame, sprayed and smeared across the wall behind the bed, pooled on the floor beside it.

She had been abused.

She had been tortured.

She had been eviscerated.

An incision had been made from her pubis up across her stomach almost to her ribs. Novak must have reached inside and pulled out Alix's entrails, stringing them across the skin on either side of the cut.

It struck Carver that she might have been hunting for the baby, seeking out their embryonic child. It was somewhere in that glistening tangle of pink and crimson entrails, lying dead in its mother's violated womb. He thought of the text, 'Bye-bye baby', and he had to lift a hand to his mouth to stop himself from vomiting.

It had been barely fifteen hours since he had walked into the ruins of the Lion Market and seen the dead and dying lying there so thickly that there was barely room to step between them across the floor. He'd thought that he had never seen anything as bad as that before, and never would again. He'd been wrong.

As he stepped closer, Carver saw how specifically Novak had taken her revenge. She had told him how Alix had surprised her with a kick to the knee. In return, Novak had kneecapped Alix: putting a bullet through the soft tissue just above each knee. Then, repaying the hands that had done her such harm, Novak had cut off every one of Alix's fingers, one by one, leaving nothing more than two blood-drenched paws.

Finally he forced himself to look at the face of the woman he loved, the face that had always been able to make his heart sing. She had a smile that could light up the darkest corners of his soul. She had lips he could not go near without wanting, no, needing, to step close enough to kiss them. The vivacity in her eyes had given him life and hope at times when it had seemed both would be lost.

And now that was all gone.

Her mouth had been closed with a strip of silver duct tape. There were two blistering, disfiguring welts running in parallel down Alix's cheeks, and a third, horizontal one across her forehead, branding her for ever.

Her hair had all been hacked off, almost down to the scalp, and it lay in a golden fan on the mattress around her head.

And she had no nose.

Novak had hacked it off – a repayment, with interest, for her own shattered nose – leaving a gaping black hole in the middle of Alix's face.

The mutilation was terrible, and Carver tried to comprehend how much Alix must have suffered in the last minutes of her life. He had known real agony himself; far more than anyone should ever have to endure. But nothing that he had been through had remotely compared to this.

Just to see her there, spreadeagled, was more than he could bear. He was consumed with guilt at the thought that this was all his fault. If he had just had the guts to kill Novak when he'd had the chance, Alix would still be alive. Let her at least be given some comfort and dignity in death.

He was at the head of the bed now, and he took out the hunting knife and cut the ties that held her arms to the bed frame, gently taking her hands in his and laying them straight by her sides. He peeled the tape from her lovely mouth. He tried very hard not to look at the tools of Novak's butchery arrayed on the bedside table: the carving knife, the sharpening steel and the secateurs, all steadily glueing to the table-top as the blood that had dripped from them congealed and coagulated into a sticky, solid mass.

Carver turned his eyes back to Alix and as he looked down at her, his vision blurred and it was only then that he realized he was crying. He wiped his eyes and his nose like a little kid, sweeping his sleeve across his face. And that was when he noticed . . .

She was alive.

Her eyes were flickering. She was looking at him, tilting her head up just the smallest little bit, and her mouth was moving soundlessly.

'I'm here, my darling, my love,' he said and bent his head so that she could try to whisper into his ear.

'Please . . .' she said. 'Please . . . it hurts so much.'

'Oh darling, it's all right . . .' He was scrabbling for his phone. 'I'll call an ambulance. It's all going to be all right.'

She moved her head, a tiny, fractional shake. 'No . . .' she gasped. 'No ambulance . . . Please, Sam . . . please . . .'

And then he realized what she was asking him, and he said, 'No, baby, no . . . you'll get better . . . you'll see . . .'

'Begging you,' she said. 'I love you . . . Please . . .'

Then her eyes closed again, her head fell back and her chest rose and fell as she gasped for breath.

He thought to himself: They could put her back together. It's battlefield medicine. They could do incredible things these days. People could survive for years, decades in fact.

But how could he refuse her? She did not want to be that person, the disfigured recipient of other people's pity. She wanted to be put out of her misery, future as well as present. And if he loved her, his final gift to her had to be a quick, merciful release from her pain.

He got down on one knee on the floor beside her. As he stroked her head with his left hand he looked into her eyes and said, 'I love you so much . . .'

His right hand reached for the gun.

'I love you,' he repeated softly, and thought he saw the faintest flicker of a smile in her eyes.

He kept stroking her head as he raised the gun.

'I love you . . . I love you . . . I love you . . .'

He took his left hand away from her head and put the gun to her temple.

'I love you . . . I love you . . .' he murmured.

Then Carver pulled the trigger and killed the woman he loved.

92

At Kennington police station DI Keane's office door burst open and a young detective constable ran in.

'Ma'am, ma'am, they've found him!' he exclaimed.

'The Second Man?'

'What's happening?' called Commander Stamford down the line.

Keane switched to speakerphone just as the DC went on, 'There were a couple of reports of a man answering his description running hell for leather through Regent's Park. Then more of him on Wellington Road, and by the studio at Abbey Road.'

'So where is he now?'

'Well, that's the thing,' said the DC. 'He was spotted going into a building on Abbey Road, and then about a minute later someone called up saying a bomb had gone off.'

'Get over there at once, Inspector,' Stamford said.

'Take whoever you've got. I'll call SCO19 and get them on the move. This time we're damn well going to get him.'

The Metropolitan Police weren't the only ones on the move. When someone gets on the phone and reports a bomb going off, key-word programs at GCHQ in Cheltenham and the National Security Administration at Ford Meade, Maryland immediately signal an alert. When the address given by the caller is the same as that of a US diplomat, it becomes a red alert. Within less than a minute of the 999 call concluding a message was on its way to John D. Giammetti at the CIA in London. And within a further sixty seconds a team of armed field agents had already been scrambled and were running for the black, bullet- and bomb-proof Chevrolet Suburban people-carrier that would take them straight to Abbey Road.

93

Carver took one last look at Alix, then left the bedroom and closed the door.

A clearly defined sequence of events was forming in his mind, and it began with locating the duct tape that Novak had used on Alix. It was sitting on the kitchen island with a pair of scissors neatly placed across the top. Carver grabbed them both and retrieved the nail gun that was lying not far away. He went back to the hall and crouched down beside Grantham, just as Novak had done a few minutes earlier. He placed the tape and scissors on the floor. He took the head cam out of his jacket pocket, switched it on and held it in his left hand, pointing it at Grantham. With his right hand he placed the head of the nail gun against Grantham's crotch.

Grantham's eyes widened. Clearly his sight was returning. What about his hearing? Speaking very clearly, with his mouth not far from Grantham's ear, Carver said, 'Can you hear me?'

Grantham nodded.

'Good. Now here's what's going to happen. I'm going to remove your gag. If you try to call for help, I will fire the nail gun. I'm then going to ask you some questions. As you see, your answers will be on camera. I already know what happened, so don't try to lie to me, or pretend you don't know what I'm talking about, or my trigger finger will start itching. I've already tried this gun out on Novak, and it works pretty well. So unless you fancy life as a eunuch, I'd advise you to do precisely what I say. Nod if you understand.'

Grantham nodded.

Carver put the camera down for long enough to pull the gag from Grantham's face and the sock from his mouth.

'Right,' he said, picking up the camera again, 'let's get started.'

As Carver began his interview the CIA's black Suburban was rounding Marble Arch and taking the direct route to the flat, straight up Abbey Road. The driver was paying no attention whatever to speed limits, red lights or road safety. He tilted his head back and shouted out loud enough for all the men in the back to hear: 'Estimated time of arrival: four minutes!'

Metropolitan Police vehicles were also converging on the scene from several different directions. They were a little way behind, but they had the advantage of lights and sirens. Keane had the longest distance to travel. She radioed the officers in the leading car. 'How long till you get there?'

'Five minutes at the outside, ma'am.'

'That won't do,' she insisted. 'I need you there faster than that.'

'We're going to keep it very simple,' Carver said. 'Just answer yes or no. So, are you Jack Grantham, the Head of the Secret Intelligence Service, otherwise known as MI6?'

'Yes.'

'Did you order a man called Danny Cropper to organize a series of riots, including the one in Netherton Street last night?'

Grantham paused for a second. Carver pressed the nail gun into his balls. Grantham said, 'Yes, but—'

The nail gun fired. Carver had pulled his hand back a few inches. The nail blasted into the floor between Grantham's legs. The blood drained from Grantham's face and Carver said, 'Just stick to yes or no . . . You were going to say that it wasn't supposed to be violent, weren't you?'

'Yes.'

'Well, you know what field ops are like: anything that can go wrong will go wrong. Next question: were you planning to frame Mark Adams?'

'Yes.'

'You wanted everyone to think that he had set up the riots?'

'Yes.'

'Then his whole campaign would be totally discredited and he would face criminal charges?'

'Yes.'

'Were you working under orders?'

'Not exactly . . .'

'Tut-tut . . . that's not quite a yes or a no, is it? All right, then . . . your specific actions were deniable . . .'

'Yes.'

'But someone wanted you to go after Adams, even if they didn't want to know how you were doing it.'

'Yes.'

'Someone close to the Prime Minister?'

'Yes.'

'Let me guess: Cameron Young?'

'Yes.'

'Thank you. That's all I need.'

Carver turned the camera off and put it back in his jacket. Then he took the nail gun away from Grantham's crotch. Grantham's shoulders slumped as the tension left his body, but a second later his eyes were widening in protest again as Carver shoved the sock back in his mouth and replaced the gag. Carver said, 'I really don't want to have to look at you any more,' and wound the duct tape round and round Grantham's head until everything was covered and sealed tight except a small breathing-hole beneath his nose.

It was time to go.

There was a side-table beneath the mirror in the hall and on it a small, hand-carved wooden bowl in which Peck kept his house and car keys. Carver took them. He also discarded his windcheater and glasses and swapped them for a smart dark-brown leather bomber jacket hanging on a coat rack, a vivid purple baseball cap with a white letter 'H' on the front that was dangling from the next hook, and a pair of aviator shades that had been left on the side-table next to the bowl of keys. The effect on Carver's appearance was instantaneous. All trace of his previous, loser persona had entirely disappeared. As before, he transferred his phone and wallet into the new jacket. But he left the head cam in the old windcheater. He wanted it to be found.

Carver trod down hard on Grantham's feet to hold them still and pulled on his bound arms until he was virtually upright. Then Carver dipped his right shoulder and hoisted Grantham over it in a fireman's lift. 'Right,' he said. 'We're going for a drive.'

94

The Suburban's tyres squealed as it turned hard right across Maida Vale, ignoring the oncoming traffic, and hurtled down Hall Road. Abbey Road was less than a hundred and fifty metres up ahead. Turn left, drive to the end of the first block and they'd arrive at their destination.

The first of the police cars was racing north on the street that became Abbey Road. All it had to do was keep going: no need to turn at all.

'What the fuck do you think you're doing!' the police driver shouted as the black people-carrier pulled out in front of him at the crossroads, forcing him to slam on the brakes to avoid a collision. The Suburban pulled up, just ahead, and the two officers in the police car looked on as the doors all opened and half a dozen men in dark suits and ties, five carrying handguns, the sixth with a lock-busting shotgun, leaped out and ran towards The Glasshouse's front door.

* * *

Neither group of men even noticed the black Range Rover turning off Abbey Road not very far up ahead, as it made its way at a calm, legal speed towards the turn that would take it back down towards Victoria Station. It had always been one of Carver's guiding principles never to drive in any way that might attract the attention of the law. Once a cop pulled him over for speeding, who knew where it might end?

He had carried Grantham down in the lift, thanking his lucky stars that no other residents had chosen that particular moment to get in. When he'd got to the basement garage he'd pressed the key and been guided to the Range Rover – of which there were three parked among the Mercedes, Porsches, Audis and BMWs – by the flash of its lights. Grantham went in the boot. Carver got in the driver's seat. He drove straight at the metal gate covering the entire opening to the garage, trusting to the fact that properties in this building were so expensive there was no way their owners would expect to have to open the damn gate. Sure enough, it slid aside at the Range Rover's approach.

As he got to the street, Carver looked right and saw the blue police light flashing a few hundred metres away. He therefore turned left and then left again, catching a fractional, momentary glimpse of the Suburban in his rear-view mirror as he did so. Then he drove away with his eyes fixed firmly on the road ahead.

It had long since become a staple cause of tabloid outrage that health and safety regulations meant that officers could be severely disciplined for exposing themselves to even the slightest risk of personal injury, an idea that had come as a shock to members of the public naïve enough to believe that one of the functions of the police was precisely to risk danger on their behalf. But even the most curmudgeonly man-of-the-people columnist would concede that two unarmed officers had a right to be cautious when confronted by a number of gun-toting Americans smashing their way into a smart London apartment building. They called the incident in and then stayed in their car until armed and body-armoured reinforcements arrived.

It was at about this point that the car containing the two FSB operatives discreetly left the scene.

The CIA agents, having fired one breaching round into the front door of the building, put another through the lock of Trent Peck the Third's front door, thereby spraying Peck's body with fine particles of debris from the shattered lock. This was the first, but by no means the last, way in which the agents compromised the crime scene as they made their way in mounting horror through the flat, discovering their dead colleague, the horribly mutilated body of one female victim in the bedroom and another female with her chest smashed by an axe and her throat and face used as a pincushion for 90mm nails on the living-room floor.

The Metropolitan Police, meanwhile, were forced to treat this as a siege situation, evacuating the building while attempts were made to discover who was up in the penthouse and why. The Suburban led them very quickly to the US Embassy, but they were initially met with a solid wall of intransigence and denial. The police contacted their masters at the Home Office, who passed the message across Whitehall to the Foreign Office and on to MI6. The head of the agency had gone missing and so the responsibility bounced back from Vauxhall to King Charles Street and it was the Foreign Secretary herself who called up John D. Giammetti and told him, bluntly, 'Get your men out of that building. Now.'

Giammetti protested that one of his people was in that building, lying dead in a pool of blood, and they weren't leaving him behind.

'Please don't be over-dramatic,' the Foreign Secretary said. 'You're not Marines on Iwo Jima. You're foreign agents in the middle of London, and if someone has died that is the responsibility of the Metropolitan Police. When they have completed their inquiries we will of course inform you, and the body will be released. And, by the way, your men are carrying firearms. So if anyone in the building has died of gunshot wounds we'll need those weapons too.'

'You gotta be kidding me. Peck and the two women were already dead when my men got there.'

'Then there won't be any difficulty proving that your weapons weren't responsible. In the meantime, please just think of the Special Relationship and let our police do their job.'

'Special Relationship my ass,' said John D. Giammetti.

* * *

And so Carver had the CIA to thank for the fact that he had already driven to the discreet, private mews where Cripps had rented a garage for the day and, unobserved by any cameras, moved Grantham from the Range Rover to the old Mazda; taken the Mazda out of the garage; put the Range Rover in its place and then driven away in the Mazda before anyone even began to link the mysterious disappearance of Britain's top spy to the simultaneous vanishing act performed by the Second Man.

It took time to ascertain that Peck's car was missing; more time to establish that it was a Range Rover, and still more to get the registration number. Then the car's journey from Abbey Road to the mews had to be painstakingly pieced together from myriad traffic cameras. The minor residential road off which the mews ran was not fully covered by cameras, so it took time to ascertain that the Range Rover had turned into it but never come out, and then to confirm that it had not been parked on that street and so must have been concealed in the mews.

Even when that had been done, police were obliged to track down the owners of five garages, each of which was advertised on the internet as being available for daily rental. Two were at their properties, one was away on holiday in Miami, a fourth had gone racing at Sandown and the fifth was in hospital having an operation on his gall bladder. Four of them knew nothing about a black Range Rover: the fifth was under anaesthetic.

So then all the garages had to be opened and the Range Rover was found in the garage belonging to the man who'd gone to the races. He had enjoyed a liquid lunch, as plenty do on such occasions, and found it hard to recollect much about the customer who'd rented the garage, except that he'd paid cash for the whole day, up front, and he certainly hadn't been driving a Range Rover.

'What was he driving, then?' the garage owner was asked.

'I dunno. It was red, I remember that. And old, very old . . . an 02 reg, I think. It was one of those Japanese makes. A Honda, maybe . . . or a Toyota? Basically a bloody boring, old, red Japanese saloon.'

Images were examined from the traffic cameras covering the main roads surrounding the mews during the fifteen minutes after the Range Rover was lost from sight. A number of different cars were found that matched the age, colour and rough description provided by the garage owner. Each car was examined in detail and drivers who were not male, Caucasian and aged thirty-five to fifty-five were discarded. That left three possibles.

The owners of all three cars were contacted. Two were able to vouch for their movements throughout the day. The third was called Kevin Cripps. He was rung on both his home and mobile numbers without success. When the location of his mobile was tracked, however, it was shown to be somewhere in Shoreham-by-Sea. Further investigation revealed that Cripps's credit card had been used to purchase a railway ticket from Victoria to Shoreham shortly before nine that morning. So he could not possibly have been the driver.

And then an officer carrying out routine checks on all

the possible drivers noticed something interesting about Kevin Cripps.

He was a former lance corporal in the Royal Marines.

95

Through all this time Carver was driving south, first through South London, then the prosperous towns of north-east Surrey, and finally into the Sussex countryside. From time to time there would be a thump from the boot as Grantham tried to make his presence felt, but by and large he was undisturbed.

Carver's main priority was just holding himself together until he reached his destination. Images of Alix's mutilated body kept flashing, unbidden, into his mind. Great waves of emotion were rising up inside of him, tearing at his guts, ripping the breath from his lungs and filling his eyes with tears. The slightest thing could set him off: a pretty blonde on the street who just for a fraction of a second reminded him of Alix; a model on a billboard whose smile was a little like hers; a half-heard song from a passing car window. He needed to regain control of his thoughts and emotions, so he made a conscious effort to process the events that had brought him to this particular point. If he could look at the facts objectively, no matter how disturbing they were, perhaps he could come to terms with them.

In trying to save six people from violent attack, he had condemned far more people to death. By refusing to kill a helpless woman who was his enemy, he had condemned the woman he loved. Maybe this was karma: some kind of payback for all the violence and death he had doled out over the years.

Looking back, it seemed to Carver that, for as long as he could remember, he'd spent too much time doing things in which no man with any conscience could possibly take any pleasure. He'd done a lot of harm to an awful lot of people. Of course, it was satisfying to know that the vast majority of them had deserved it. He'd tried to make the world a marginally better or safer place, even if there was always someone else coming down the line determined to make it worse again. And it had been exciting sometimes. Carver was like anyone else who made their living doing something dangerous: he never felt more alive than when he was risking death.

He'd been lucky, too, he couldn't deny it. He'd put himself in harm's way time and again, yet somehow the Reaper had never come calling. He'd made a lot of money without ever having to work a regular week, spend all day in an office or grovel to a boss. On balance, as lives went, it hadn't been a total waste of time.

He wondered, too, about the future. What would happen when a police officer, searching through Trent Peck's flat, came across the discarded windcheater?

Carver was reasonably sure that they would find the head cam. But how long would it take for anyone to work out what it was, still less examine its contents? And then what? The material that first Random and then he had recorded would answer any questions anyone might have about how and why the riot had occurred and what had led to the supermarket massacre. But it would take police officers of extraordinarily strong, incorruptible character to act upon the information revealed in the interrogations of Bakunin and Grantham.

If they decided that the two confessions had been extracted under duress, then the whole thing could be buried and no one would ever know what had really happened. On the other hand, if they had the courage to do their jobs properly, investigate in full and make the findings of their investigations public, the government was doomed. Cameron Young would end up in jail and the Prime Minister would be lucky not to join him. He would, at the very least, suffer lifelong disgrace. But then, inevitably, Mark Adams would triumph at the next election, and Britain would discover, once and for all, whether he was their saviour or their tyrant.

What was for the best? Carver was grateful that it was not his decision to make. He had found out what he wanted to know. He had put the information out there. From now on, it was someone else's problem.

He passed a road sign that read, 'Shoreham 6'. Not long now.

At Kennington police station, Keane was trying to make sense of the information she had just been given. She went on her computer and called Shoreham-by-Sea up on a map. She looked at the screen for less than ten seconds.

And then the penny dropped and she realized precisely why the Second Man was meeting Kevin Cripps at that particular seaside town.

_____

96

The day had been reasonably fine up to now, but the rain started falling again as Carver turned off the dual carriageway, drove down a narrow, unmarked road, passed a series of warehouses used as office or industrial spaces, and pulled up in a small visitor's car park outside a building that was a fine example of 1930s Art Deco-inspired modernism. Its lines were sleek. It was painted in pure, simple white, albeit that the purity was somewhat marred by the rust stains, brought on by the salty sea air, that spread from the metal fittings attached to the building, like the railings around the top of the walls and the loudspeakers wired to either side.

This was the heart of a facility that was the oldest of its kind in the entire United Kingdom: Shoreham Airport.

Kevin Cripps was waiting to meet him.

'She's over there,' he said, pointing to the ranks of private aircraft lined up on the apron. 'Second row back, third from the end. I've got the key and, oh yeah, here's the other thing you asked for.'

He handed over a surprisingly insignificant starter key, and a blue object that looked like a car-seat cushion, with a strap at each corner. It was an emergency parachute, designed for aerobatics pilots who found themselves in trouble and needed to bail out, fast.

'Thanks,' said Carver. 'You got the money?'

'Every penny.' Cripps grinned. 'And I even got the car back, and all. Oh, while I remember . . . the way the wind is blowing, you'll want to use this runway, right here.' He pointed out across the field to a point just beyond the lines of planes. 'You'll be starting at this end, so you shouldn't have any trouble getting there. Then just turn the plane into the wind, slam on the power and you're off.'

'It's a bit more complicated than that, but thanks. The plane's ready to go, right?'

'Absolutely. Had her filled and pre-flight checked by the bloke who sold her. He even gave me a little test flight, just to prove she was in perfect working order, nice little spin round the airfield.'

'You'd better help me on with this,' Carver said, holding up the parachute.

Neither man was a qualified pilot, but both had their parachute wings, so Cripps was swift and efficient as he helped Carver into the harness.

The job had just been completed when Carver heard a sound with which he was becoming altogether too familiar: the sirens of approaching police cars.

'Looks like I'm going to need the car a little bit

longer,' Carver said. 'Thanks for everything.' He held out his hand.

Cripps grinned, held out his and was taken completely by surprise when Carver swung his right arm up and hit him hard the special forces way, with the heel of his hand, just to the side of his chin. Cripps reeled with the blow and Carver grabbed his shoulders.

'Listen to me,' he said. 'You bought the plane for me in all innocence. You had no idea why I wanted it. When I got here, I attacked you and overpowered you. Like this . . .'

He let go of Cripps's arms, swung his leg round and tripped him over. Cripps lay sprawled on the ground as Carver got into the car and drove straight at the low metal fence that separated the car park from the apron. The Mazda smashed through it and Carver drove straight towards the nine-year-old Cessna 172 that he had found online that morning and then asked Cripps to buy.

Shoreham is only a very minor airport and on a cold, grey afternoon in November, with the light failing as the rain sets in, traffic is almost non-existent. A single Shell petrol bowser was filling up one of the aircraft about fifty metres from Carver's craft, but that aside there were no signs of life anywhere.

Apart, that is, from the police cars that could be seen coming through a gate on the very far side of the airfield, racing in Carver's direction.

He got out of the car, opened the boot and slung Grantham over his shoulder, noticing only too late the damp, acrid wet patch at the front of Grantham's trousers that was now pressing against the shoulder of Trent

Peck's fancy leather flying jacket. Carver opened the door of the plane and hefted Grantham on to the passenger seat, where he lay, wriggling feebly, until Carver sat him up and strapped him in.

Then he took his place in the pilot's seat.

Carver had never in his life flown an aircraft. But as the 9/11 bombers had demonstrated, it was possible to do a great deal with an aircraft without qualifying as a pilot. And he didn't need to do much beyond getting this thing up in the air and pointing it in the right direction.

One of the tasks he had been undertaking as he'd sat in front of his iPad, eating his porridge and chocolate bars, was to look at some of the very many clips on YouTube showing the pre-flight and take-off routines for a Cessna 172, which has been built in greater numbers than any other aircraft on earth. He had also downloaded and worked on a flight simulator. He was pleasantly surprised to discover how similar the imitation had been to the real thing. The instrument panel in front of him was entirely familiar, as was the routine.

He pulled the big red fuel-mixture knob fully out. He pulled the throttle out a little less than a centimeter. He turned the battery and the fuel pump on, let it run for a while, and turned it off again.

Then he turned the key, the engine caught at the first attempt, and the propellor started whirling round in front of him.

Carver pushed the fuel-mixture knob back in, made sure the flaps were up, and moments later the plane was taxiing towards the runway.

Up ahead Carver could see the lights of the police cars

cutting across the grass outfield. He presumed they were aiming for the middle of the runway, trying to head him off. They'd probably be trying to radio him, too, telling him to turn off his engine. But the radio wasn't on, and anyway he didn't have a headset, so the hell with that.

He had to admit that his steering could do with a little refinement. The plane slewed around the apron like a Saturday-night drunk, but it was only a matter of seconds before he found himself at the start of the runway, pointing directly at the lights of the oncoming cars, and maxing the throttle.

And then he noticed that he didn't just have cars to worry about. A police helicopter, stationed at the airfield, was rising into the air from an apron to the left of the runway. It hovered for a second, maybe twenty metres above the ground, and then darted to its right.

Now Carver was picking up speed.

The police cars were coming straight at him.

The helicopter was cutting across his path.

Aircraft speed is measured the same way as the speed of ships: in knots. Carver had memorized the take-off speed of a Cessna 172, which was sixty-four knots, or a little less than seventy-five miles per hour. From what he could gather from his research this morning, it took between ten and fifteen seconds for a plane like his to get up to that speed.

He had been heading down the runway for eight seconds. The cars were coming towards him at least as fast as he was heading towards them. Call it an impact speed of a hundred and fifty miles per hour; enough to write off anyone involved in the collision.

If the helicopter were to crash into him in mid-air, everyone in both crafts would certainly be killed, as might anyone caught beneath the falling debris.

The oncoming cars were now so close he was dazzled by their headlights.

The helicopter was buzzing around so insistently its engine was audible over the racket of his own.

Someone had to back down within the next second or they'd all be dead.

And Carver kept going. He didn't slow down. He didn't veer off course in any way. Because he knew he had a single decisive tactical advantage over everyone else on or over the airfield.

He really didn't give a damn if he crashed.

They did. They wanted to go home for their tea that night. That was why the stream of cars divided to the left and right of the Cessna. The helicopter veered away. Carver pulled on the joystick and the plane rose up into the air and headed straight ahead, over the airfield and the town and out across the English Channel beyond.

97

The airspace over southern England is managed by the London Area Control Centre, at Swanwick, Hants. It handles something in the region of 5,500 flights every single day of the year. Any international flight can only take place after a detailed flight plan has been filed and approved. Any flight without such a plan immediately attracts the attention of the authorities, even if it is, for the time being, heading away from the English mainland. If the pilot does not respond to attempts to make radio contact, then the control centre contacts the RAF base at Coningsby, Lincolnshire, and declares a 'QRA situation'.

The acronym stands for Quick Reaction Alert and its immediate effect is to scramble a flight of three Typhoon jets belonging to RAF 3 (Fighter) Squadron. A Typhoon can travel at a top speed of 1,400 miles per hour. The distance between Coningsby and

Shoreham-by-Sea, as the crow flies, is a little over two hundred miles. A fighter travelling through congested airspace cannot travel quite as directly as a crow. But even so, it can catch up with a Cessna 172 heading slowly south-west on a bearing straight down the Channel towards the Atlantic Ocean very quickly indeed.

Its problem is knowing what to do when it gets there.

The Cessna 172's standard cruise speed is around a hundred and twenty knots, but Carver had throttled back to less than seventy-five. This had given the RAF pilots a problem. They couldn't just shoot him down, because he had the Head of the Secret Intelligence Service on board. On the other hand they couldn't fly alongside him because they simply couldn't go that slowly without stalling their planes. They were therefore having to loop around him in figures of eight, which was far from ideal when flying in close formation through weather conditions that combined low cloud, high wind, driving rain and appalling visibility.

The rain was beating so hard against the glass the wipers weren't getting rid of it, just moving it around. Carver's personal 'Learn to fly in a day' campaign hadn't got as far as finding the heater controls – even if there were any – so he was seriously bloody cold. There was absolutely no way he was ever going to bring the plane in to land. But for all that, the funny thing was, Carver was in pretty good shape.

He felt as though he was, to some degree at least, in control of his own destiny. And in the end, that was probably the best you could hope for.

Of course, in the long run we all die. Carver wasn't the kind of man who dealt much in metaphors, but it struck him that Jack Grantham's situation was an appropriate metaphor for the human condition. He was blind, dumb and utterly helpless to change anything at all about his fundamental circumstances. Whether he liked it or not, there would soon come a time when the fuel tanks ran dry, the engine cut out, the plane tumbled down into the ocean and his lights went out for good.

Carver, on the other hand, still had some ability to act. Soon he would, of his own free will, make the choice to throw himself from the plane. He reckoned that the plane would soon be passing the tip of the Cherbourg peninsula. The French coast would then be about fifteen kilometres away. By any reasonable calculation, the chances of him making it were slim to non-existent. Even if his chute opened, parachuting into high seas was an insanely risky procedure. Plenty of experienced special forces men had died because they hit the water too fast, or too heavily loaded, and kept going right on down to the bottom. There was an obvious danger of becoming tangled in one's lines or the canopy itself. If by some miracle he was able to splash down successfully, there was then the minor issue of staying alive in cold, stormy seas, finding the proper bearings, and swimming long enough and far enough to bump into a passing boat or the coast itself.

When you started considering all the different variables, all the things that had to go perfectly in order for him to make it, the odds entered the realm of a lottery win, or a jackpot on a Vegas slot machine.

But at least he was giving it a go. And maybe it would all work out. Maybe he could get to France. If he did, it really wouldn't be much of a problem for him to get anywhere in the world from there. Carver imagined himself somewhere warm, by the sea: the Atlantic coast of Brazil, maybe. He'd run a boat: nothing fancy, just a good, solid, working boat he could use to go fishing or for travelling up and down the coast. Maybe he could even get a little plane, just like this one, but with floats so he could fly to distant islands and land in crystal-clear lagoons. He'd not want for money and there'd be a woman somewhere that he could get along with, even if he couldn't imagine loving anyone else just yet. He'd spend most of his time outdoors, doing simple, satisfying work. He'd always been better at blowing things up than building them in the first place, but maybe he could pick up the basics of carpentry and bricklaying and build his own home, with a vegetable garden out back to feed him.

But what would any of it mean if Alix wasn't there?

She was the reason he wasn't scared of dying. Carver didn't believe in God or an afterlife. He wasn't opposed to religion, and he'd always respected the work that military padres did, comforting the dying or the relatives of men who'd been killed in action. He just couldn't find any faith within himself. It was an absence of sensation, like being colour-blind or tone-deaf. The life he'd led hadn't helped. He'd seen too much evil, too much pointless suffering and pain to imagine that there was any point to it all. But he could imagine being at peace. And if he and Alix had both gone into that endless night, then they would in some way be together again. Or at least he wouldn't feel the desperate sense of separation he did now, as if they were divided by an infinitely high, impenetrable wall.

Whatever happened, when he jumped out of the plane, he'd accept it. He'd made his choice. He'd chosen his departure. He was fine about that.

He looked up at the rear-view mirror and adjusted it so that he could see Grantham behind him. Grantham had become progressively more agitated as the flight had gone on, and was now writhing in his seat as his mummified silver-taped head darted up and down and from side to side, as if he could actually look for some means of escape. It was impossible to hear anything over the sound of the engine, but Carver presumed that there would be muffled squeals and grunts coming from that gagged mouth.

The plane was constantly being shaken by the wind and rain, like a rattle in the hands of a giant baby. Suddenly there was an even more pronounced buffeting, and a roar loud enough to overwhelm every other noise in Carver's ears, as the Typhoons blasted past at point-blank range. The message was obvious: we can't shoot you down and we can't force you to land, but we can make your life bloody uncomfortable.

Oh no, they couldn't.

As the jets sped away to the far end of their turning circle, Carver took the fins, mask and snorkel from his pack. He put them on and then undid his seatbelt and opened the door. Or rather, he tried to open it. Taken together, the speed of the plane and the storm-force headwind amounted to a hurricane, and it took every ounce of Carver's strength to shift the door, inch by inch, degree by degree, until he could twist his knees round and use them to keep it from slamming back in his face.

He was looking out under the wing now, trying to judge the move he would have to make to get out, step on to the wheel-guard and then jump as far away from the plane as possible. He didn't mind taking his chance with the sea, but it would be just a little bit tragic if he had his brains knocked out by a stabilizer before he'd even pulled the ripcord.

A thought came unbidden to his mind, the memory of a time he'd thrown himself from another doomed plane. Alix had been with him that time. They'd only had one parachute between them . . . and that had been attached to an armed atomic bomb set to detonate the moment it dropped below an altitude of fifteen hundred metres. Next to that moment of rampant insanity, this jump was a Sunday-school outing.

A great grin crossed Carver's face as he thought of Alix and all the times they'd had together.

Somewhere off in the distance he saw the lights of the Typhoons as they turned and came in for another run.

Carver gave them the finger. 'Fuck you,' he muttered. Then he inched his legs out of the cabin and down until his fins were resting on the wheel-guard. He gripped his left hand against the door frame to hold himself, and then shifted his bodyweight out of the plane, with his back pressing against the inside of the open door.

Now he was perched on the side of the plane. He thought of his captive writhing and twitching inside the cabin. He thought of the jets turning round for another approach. He thought of the house he would build by the sea in Brazil.

Above all, he thought of the woman he loved.

Then Sam Carver shouted, 'Ali-i-i-i-i-x!' and he jumped off the plane, into the storm-tossed skies and down towards the chilly, grey-black embrace of the sea.

The Accident Man

Tom Cain

12.19am
A Mercedes leaves the Ritz hotel.

12.25am
A car loses control in a Paris underpass.

3.57am
Three people are pronounced dead.

3.58am
Samuel Carver realizes he's been set up . . .

Samuel Carver makes bad things happen to bad people. He was once a Royal Marine, now he's freelance, the frontline weapon of a group so secretive even he does not know the true identities of the people who command him.

Now Carver wants to quit. He's had enough of death. There's just one last hit, planned at extremely short notice. The target, they say, is a high-ranking terrorist. It will take place in a Paris underpass.

But the whole job is a set-up.

When Carver discovers his victim's true identity, he becomes the next target. He knows too much. Unless he can track down the men who planned his murderous mission, his life is over . . .

'Audacious, authentic, full of tension and tradecraft . . . maybe it's true and maybe it isn't, but either way it's a great thriller read'
LEE CHILD

'This is the best first thriller I have read since *The Day of the Jackal* . . . With one mighty bound Tom Cain has vaulted over Archer and Grisham and stands close on Freddy Forsyth's tail'
WILBUR SMITH

The Survivor

Tom Cain

Sam Carver is a hard man to kill.

But he's been beaten, tortured and left to die. He wakes up in a Swiss sanatorium to discover that the woman he loves has vanished.

Can he summon the strength to track her down? And can he complete his mission when one of his targets has escaped and is plotting a monstrous revenge?

He's good at his job, but nobody's perfect . . .

Carver's hunt will take him across Europe, deep into the heart of a conspiracy in which the lives of millions are at stake. But his hardest challenge of all may be the agonizing choice between his duty and his heart . . .

'Another stunner . . . compulsive and vastly entertaining reading'
WILBUR SMITH

Assassin

Tom Cain

'Like the Bourne movies meets Frederick Forsyth'   *GUARDIAN*

The Assassin

A gangster is poisoned. A crooked financier dies in a car crash. A bomb explodes in a crowded hotel. And all the evidence points to Samuel Carver.

The Target

The newly-elected US President promises to end global slavery. Now the world's most powerful people-traffickers want him dead. And it looks like Carver's taken the contract.

An Innocent Man

But Carver swears he's out of the game. These days he works to protect people, not kill them. So who is setting him up? What hidden enemy wants so badly to destroy him?

A Race Against Time

Alone and on the run, hunted by MI6 and the US Secret Service, Carver must fight to clear his name. And the only way he can do it is to confront an assassin even deadlier than himself . . . and stop a fatal shot that will be heard around the world.

Dictator
Tom Cain

Africa has had more than its share of dictators, but Henderson Gushungo may be the worst. Millions starve and opponents are flung in jail, while Gushungo and his cronies get rich on the country's rich natural resources.

A powerful consortium of political and business interests offer Samuel Carver the job of enforcing regime change. Can the taking of one life save millions of others? And can Carver trust the men who hired him?

As the action hurtles from the plains of southern Africa to the teeming streets of Hong Kong, and an old enemy rises from the grave to haunt him once more, Carver becomes both the hunter and the hunted in a deadly game where the survival of a nation is at stake.

'Like the Bourne movies meets Frederick Forsyth'
GUARDIAN

'A byword for intelligent, topical, articulate action . . .
Carver is a reliable treat'
DAILY TELEGRAPH

'Tom Cain goes from strength to strength. If you
have yet to sample his books, start soon. It's like
James Bond, but even better!'
crimesquad.com